DESIRING A WITCH
EMERALD WITCHES BOOK 3

HEATHER McCORKLE

FOR THOSE WITH SECRETS TO HIDE.

DESIRING A WITCH

Desiring a Witch
An Emerald Witches Novel

Copyright 2023 Heather McCorkle

All rights reserved. No part of this book may be used or reproduced by any means, graphic, electronic, taping, or by any information storage retrieval system without the written permission of the publisher except in the case of quotations embodied in articles and reviews.

If you received this from anyone other than the author or publisher for free, it is a pirated, therefore illegal, copy. Pirating harms authors and their ability to continue publishing books. Please report all incidents of book piracy. To receive an author's books for free, sign up for their review/ARC team, sign up for the publisher's review/ARC team, and watch the author and/or publisher's social media sites for giveaways.

Ebook ISBN: 978-1-939469-32-8
Paperback ISBN: 978-1-939469-33-5
Hardback ISBN: 978-1-939469-34-2

Cover images from Deposit Photos. Cover design by McCorkle Creations. No part of this cover, or this book were created using AI.

Compass Press release date: October 2023

THE NINE WORLDS SERIES BY HEATHER McCORKLE:

EMERALD WITCHES SERIES:
Honoring a Witch's Heart
Escorting a Witch
Desiring a Witch

CHILDREN OF FENRIR SERIES:
Clawed & Cornered (novella)
Bitten & Beholden
Tempered & Turned
Bared & Betrayed

SHIFTER SEEKER SERIES:
Holiday Hunting (novella)
Raven Rousting (novella)
Coyote Calling
Tiger Tracking
Bear Baiting (Coming 2024)

NIFLHEIM SERIES:
The Dragon Empire (Coming Soon)
The First Dragon Ambassador (Coming Soon)

OTHER BOOKS BY HEATHER McCORKLE:

CHANNELER SERIES (YOUNG ADULT):
Born of Fire (Short Story)
Fire With Fire (Novella)
The Secret of Spruce Knoll
Channeler's Choice
Rise of a Rector

CHANNELER NOVEL STAND ALONE:
To Ride a Púca

AUTHOR'S NOTE:

This novel began its life as another novel in another genre as Deirdre's True Desire, a historical romance. My intention was for it to be a historical fantasy about fae descended Irish women making their way in America during and after the Civil War. It was intended to be a story not just of tragedy and hardship, but also filled with the magic and wonder of Irish folklore. However, when I got the idea for it, I talked to my agent about it. They convinced me there wasn't much of a market for historical fantasy. It was too much of a mashup of genres, they said, and they wouldn't be able to sell it to a publisher.

They convinced me I should write it as a historical with no fantasy elements. After extensive, exhaustive research on all things American Civil War related, I did so, and they helped me sign it with a publisher. I hold no ill will whatsoever to that agent. They had good intentions and advised me as they thought best based on the selling genres of the time. But, it did crush something in me to compromise on what I wanted for the story.

After several years of mediocre sales, I got my rights back, and now I've rewritten not just this book, but the entire series as it was originally intended to be. Here's hoping the industry was wrong, or at least has changed enough, and you love this book of my heart just as much as I do.

CONTENT WARNINGS:

These content warnings contain **spoilers**, some of them are quite substantial, but I will separate those out in case you want to skip them. My hopes are that if you read through them all, they won't detract from the enjoyment of the novel for those who would like to check them before proceeding.

The characters are fae, and they practice a type of druidism, worshipping the gods of the Irish Celts. This novel is about a widow whose husband judged her for her mixed blood and became cold and distant after finding out. There is a love triangle, but it is not a 'why choose' novel. Sexism toward women and racism toward African Americans, Mexicans, and Irish is occurs, but not to a violent degree. Religious oppression and terrorizing of witches is mentioned and threats are made to women believed to be witches. The expectation of unwilling sexual favors by an employee is briefly mentioned but not shown. A character is pregnant throughout the book. There is a Mabon ceremony, and a handfasting ceremony.

Large Spoilers: The main character is attacked by a man but overcomes him. She is struck over the head and is knocked out. Other characters are attacked and overcome their attackers. A few men are killed, one by the main character.

Large spoiler: There is also a character who is Mayan and worships their ancient gods.

Large Spoiler: Homes are lost in a fire set by people.

Large Spoilers: A second character is revealed to be pregnant at the end of the book.

Triggers are a very personal thing and are not the same for

everyone. As such, there is a chance I may have inadvertently missed calling attention to something that may trigger some readers. I hope this isn't the case, as it is not my intention to overlook any potentially triggering things.

1

Deirdre

1866, August, Nevada

The plants sang their exuberant song of late summer to Dierdre, drawing her deeper into the juniper forest. All around her rich, deep reds, oranges, and gold hues decorated the land. Bone tired not from traveling, but from the tedious company of their escorts, she walked deeper into the trees. The moments she could steal for herself were precious few. Thinking her off answering nature's call, the men hired to escort and protect her and Sadie from Omaha to California wouldn't come looking for her for at least another few moments. Most of the aloof brutes were likely catching a nap anyway. In this bloody heat it was almost impossible not to given the slightest opportunity.

The very thought made her tug at her cotton dress where it clung to her sweaty thighs. What she wouldn't do for a hoop to keep the blasted material away from her. Or better yet, a brisk ride on her horse to get the wind moving through her hair. But, due to the dangers of the trail, her escorts were adamant about not letting her stray far from sight. As if she were a dog that needed to be kept at heel. Her jaw clenched. If only they knew what she truly was they would understand how little she needed their help. But their knowing would put her in far more danger. So her secrets remained hers. Well, hers and Sadie's.

Another week and they'd reach their destination in California. That kept her going when she wanted to strangle their escorts. She knew it was wrong to think ill of these men. They were friends of Sean MacBranain's, her good friend's husband, men he had fought alongside in the war, men he trusted not only with his own life, but her life and Sadie's as well. And they had proved true and good in every aspect. Maybe if any of them were interesting enough to be attracted to, she would warm to them more. But the lot of them were too stoic, boring, or repressive toward women for her tastes. Despite the fact they weren't her kind, she had tried to get to know them and weigh their characters for something more than a passing acquaintance. The time when her parents got to choose her husband were past her. And unlike them, she had no intention of choosing based off pedigree or a good match financially. The one thing her late husband had given her was financial stability.

Now, she was ready for a romance that would sweep her off her feet—a love match filled with passion. Clearly, it would not be with one of their escorts.

The day's heat lost some of its bite as she stepped into the shade of a large juniper tree. Letting out a long breath, she leaned against the twisted trunk. The rough bark scraped at her back, snagging her dress, but she didn't care. The life energy thrumming through the tree soothed her, causing a sigh to slip from her lips. It surrounded her, touching her energy, recognizing what she was through it.

What she wouldn't give for a river. Even a stream would

do. Water wasn't exactly plentiful in Nevada. Regret pulsed from the tree.

No water nearby, Steward. My roots are deep and still barely touch what lies ten times my height into the ground. The communication from the tree didn't exactly come to her as thoughts, but her mind translated it that way. It came more like feelings, impressions, but she understood. The plants tended to think of her as a steward, a protector, which she endeavored to be.

The snap of a branch yanked her from her musings with a start. She slid around the tree trunk away from the noise. As much as she wanted this trip over with, she wasn't ready to crawl back into a stifling wagon just yet. Bluish juniper needles brushed against her hair, catching in the long, dark locks. She grabbed the branch before it could snap back and make any noise—or worse, harm the tree.

Oddly, no one called out to her. If it were one of the men, or even Sadie, surely they would have called out. A grunt filled with pain sounded close by, too close by. Deirdre froze. She broke through the paralysis to reach for the knife she kept nestled in her deep cleavage.

"Is someone there?" came a man's raspy voice.

Her fingers closed around the small handle of the knife.

"Please, I mean you no harm. I need help."

She remained silent and hidden. Something about the man's voice made the skin on the back of her neck tighten. But did she dare judge a man on an undertone? It could merely be pain. Leaning around the trunk, she peered through the branches. A lone man in torn and bloodied clothes stood amidst the sage brush. He leaned heavily on a makeshift cane. Bandages that looked like they might have once been the sleeves of his shirt were wrapped poorly around his right calf. In a holster resting on a belt nestled a large pistol. Both the remains of his tattered shirt and his breeches hung on him as if he'd recently lost weight, or the clothes weren't his. The pockmarked skin of his face ran a shade just north of death. Dark circles surrounded his squinty eyes.

The sight of him only confirmed what she had heard in his voice; he wasn't to be trusted. Her little knife felt woefully inadequate. But if she needed them, the trees and sage brush would answer her call.

"I know you're there. I can see you through the tree. Please, help me," he said.

Her conscience wouldn't allow her to just leave the man. "Put the pistol on the ground, step away from it, and I'll come help you."

Using the branch he had fashioned into a cane, he limped a few steps closer. "Oh thank you so much. You're a Godsend. I—"

"Stop right there and put the pistol on the ground," she commanded.

Gaze skittering about, she considered calling to her escorts. The energy of the tree pulsed in response to her anxiety.

Help steward, it thought/felt. Its branches swayed as if in a breeze, though one did not exist.

No. I'm fine. But thank you. I will ask if I need help, she thought to it. A few deep breathes helped her calm herself. It would not do to upset the tree and make it think she was in danger. When plants thought she was in danger, things tended to happen that made it difficult to hide what she was. And when she couldn't hide what she was, bad things followed.

The man stopped, free hand going up to show he meant no harm. "Sorry, I got so excited. I haven't seen another soul for a week is all. Thought I was going to die out here alone," he practically whispered.

It occurred to her that each time he spoke he had whispered, even when he'd grown excited. The skin on the back of her neck became even tighter. Suppressing her anxiety became difficult. What she wouldn't have done for a bow at that moment. What good was being a champion archer if she didn't have a bow at a time like this? But like most of her belongings, it was packed away in a wagon.

The man finally did as she commanded and lay his pistol at his feet.

"Now take a step back," she said.

She could call for help. Maybe she should. But she knew if he did mean her ill, he could be on her before anyone from the wagon train could reach her. Or worse yet, Sadie would be the one to reach her, then she'd be in danger, too. Her friend was still weak from heat exhaustion. No. It was better to take care of him herself. He took two small steps back. Emboldened by his obedience, she stepped out from behind the tree.

The man's beady eyes opened wide. "You're even prettier than you sound," he said, voice too eager for her liking.

"That is hardly a proper thing to say to me considering the nature of our meeting," she said.

His eyes traveled over her, feeling like the cool, slick hide of a snake against her skin. As she feared they would, they caught on her cleavage. "Name's Cofield, in case you want to call it out later," he said through a sneer full of broken and crooked teeth.

He lunged for his pistol. Several small roots of the tree she'd been leaning against shot out of the ground and wrapped around his hand, pinning it against the dirt. They held him fast. Teeth bared, she strode to him and placed a boot on his hand. His bones ground beneath her heel. He cried out. The second he looked up, she asked the tree to send a root beneath his chin, applying just enough pressure to make sure he knew it was there. It did so in the fraction of a heartbeat. Gasping, his eyes shot open wide.

"Your first mistake was being a blaggard who would attack a woman. Your second was taking me for a daft fool. I'm not going to give you a chance to make a third," she warned him in a voice that was as steady as her iron control.

"What is this witchery? You're hurting me," he whined. "Please, I've been attacked by bandits and wolves. I was just afraid."

"Of a woman?"

"It was a woman who did this to me." He pointed to a scabbed-over gash on the side of his head.

"A woman bandit?" she asked, raising her voice loud enough that she hoped the men from the wagon train would hear.

"Yes," he insisted.

Shifting her foot, she ground her heel harder against the butt of the pistol. "Let go."

"You have my hand trapped."

"Then pull it out. That or I'll crush it, your choice."

As he pulled, she asked the tree to let him go. The roots retreated into the ground. His eyes grew wide as he watched them go. Despite his shock, she felt him try to take the pistol with him as he pulled, but he couldn't get it out from under her foot. Once his hand was free, she covered as much of the pistol with her foot as she could.

"Crawl away from me, slowly."

He shuffled backward on his hands and knees faster than she was comfortable with, but she let him go regardless.

"You're like her, a witch," he hissed.

Gaze locked on him, she bent and picked up the pistol. When her hand closed around the grips, he dove for her. She brought it up, but he blocked the arm holding it and bore her to the ground. While his hand wrapped around her one wrist, she slammed the butt of the pistol into the side of his head. As he fell, she twisted so he went face-first down into the sage and dirt. She scrabbled away and to her feet.

A brand new wound on the opposite side of his head from the other one bled freely. The fluttering eyelid that she could see soon disappeared in a wash of red. Though it was a lot, to be sure, she didn't think it was a fatal amount of blood. Having grown up with a brother, she knew just because a head wound bled a lot didn't mean it was that bad. The fact that the man seemed only half-conscious was another matter.

Steward needs more help? the tree asked.

No. Others are coming. They would see. I am safe. Thank you, she told it.

Footsteps pounded through the scrubby forest toward her. Pistol held at the ready, she took a step back from Cofield—just in case—and turned in the direction of the steps. A tall Negro woman with skin that shone like brown porcelain plunged through the trees. She stumbled to a halt, barely remaining on her feet. Her gaze moved between Cofield and Deirdre. With a shake of her many braids, she shrugged off her shock and half-jogged, half-stumbled toward Deirdre.

Deirdre met her part way, grabbing hold of her arm to steady her. "I'm all right, Sadie."

"I had a dream you were in trouble and knew something was wrong. What happened? Who is that?" Sadie asked, only the barest hint of an accent in her voice.

Deirdre's eyes narrowed at the man. "A fool who did not know whom he was tangling with. He called himself Cofield."

Holding tight to Deirdre's arm, Sadie leaned in the man's direction. "Did you kill him?"

"Not sure."

Sadie covered her face with one hand. "A fool indeed." The exhaustion weighing each of her words struck a vein of concern in Deirdre.

"You shouldn't be out here. You haven't yet recovered from being in the heat too long yesterday," Deirdre said.

Two more sets of steps pounded their way. "That's precisely what I told her, but she insisted she weren't in danger— oh. Oh my, are you all right?" came a man's voice.

A man old enough to be her father flanked by a tall, skinny man came through the sparse trees. The older man, Jack, approached the two of them. The skinny one, Sam, went to Cofield.

"I'm a fair spot better off than he is," Deirdre said.

Jack held his hand out for the pistol and Deirdre gladly gave it to him. She hadn't the first clue how to use the damnable thing. But it did seem to work rather well as a blunt weapon.

"He's alive, though knocked well and good out," Sam called from where he crouched by Cofield. "What should we do with him?"

"Bollocks," Deirdre murmured under her breath.

Sadie slapped her arm. "Deirdre," she reprimanded.

Eyes opening wide, Deirdre asked, "What? He's dangerous."

"I only meant to mind your language."

The half-smile on Sadie's full lips helped sooth Deirdre's nerves.

Jack ran a hand through his thinning, dark hair. He looked to Deirdre as he so often had during their journey west. While he was officially in charge of their wagon train, he had quickly learned that no one was in charge of Deirdre Quinn.

She shrugged. "Leave him here for all I care. He clearly meant me ill."

Sam's brow pulled down into a scowl that nearly made his eyes disappear. "He attacked you. He's dangerous and should be handed over to a lawman for punishment."

Eyes going wide, Sadie's grip on Deirdre's arm tightened. "Won't it be dangerous to take him with us?"

Breathing out sharply through his nose, Jack flicked his wrist, popping open the cylinder of the pistol that held the bullets. He spun it, mouth moving in a silent count of each bullet within, flicked it back closed, and pointed it at Cofield. "We've less than seven days to go. We'll keep him bound. Go fetch some rope, Sam."

With a nod, Sam rose and took off at a jog. A groan issued from Cofield. Not wanting to leave Jack alone with the man, Deirdre waited for Sam to return. He did so in a few moments, rope in hand.

She nodded to Jack. "You seem to have this well in hand. I'm going to get Sadie back to the wagons."

Jack nodded to her. "Of course."

One arm going around Sadie's back, Deirdre turned her in the direction of the wagons. The way her friend sagged against her proved the outing had been too much. She hated that the woman's prescience had drawn her out of the comfort and shade of the wagon. On the other hand, the bit of excitement had gotten her own blood flowing, and that was a welcome change. Deplorable though Cofield clearly seemed, at least he brought intrigue to their day. Regardless, she wasn't about to let her guard down around him for one moment.

It was going to be a long week.

2

Deirdre

Late August, California

The wait was killing her.

Or her patience, at least, which was a delicate thing prone to a quick death on the best of days.

The light of the stars gave way more each moment to the brightening dawn. She missed them as they left, for they had faithfully guided her here and were a symbol of the wonders that awaited in this new land. Warm sunlight filtered through the leaves of the sheltering oak stretching overhead. It felt good on her shoulders, but only served to remind her of how the morning began to wane. Beneath her feet, its welcoming energy thrummed, inviting her to stay a while and hear its stories.

Oh how I would love to, Great One! she thought as she pressed a hand to its expansive trunk.

But exciting things awaited.

The hilltop provided a tantalizing view of the town below as the sun's rays crept across it. Fields turned gold by the chilly nights of late August surrounded a grouping of log and brick homes and buildings. Civilization. How she longed for it after so many months on the California Trail! But this little town was more than just that. It would be their new home. It was where her and Sadie's dear friend Catriona O'Brian and was. And she couldn't wait a moment longer to get there.

She stroked the bark of the tree. *You slumber, Old One. I'll be back to hear your stories*, she promised it. And she meant it. This would be a wonderful place to get away from it all and think.

Excellent! I have one about a squirrel…

That elicited a grin so huge as to be considered unladylike. *I'm sure you have many about squirrels, and I look forward to hearing them all soon*, she teased.

Red leaves crunched under her heel as she spun and marched back to the wagons. The four armed men lounging in the shadows of one of the three wagons nodded in acknowledgment as she approached. The two working on the broken wagon wheel didn't look up.

"How much longer do you expect it will be?" she asked.

The four idle men rose like the good soldiers they had once been and the gentlemen they still were and removed their hats. One of the men working on the wheel grunted. The other answered without looking up. "At least another hour, Mrs. Quinn." He went on to say something more about the axle, but it was all gibberish to her.

Grunting in frustration, she gathered up her deep blue skirts and strode to the largest of the three wagons. The smooth satin mocked her fingertips. She had worn the fine dress with the intention of making a good impression as they arrived in town. At this rate, they wouldn't make it there today. She flung open the canvas flap covering the back and began to dig in one of the boxes. On the makeshift bed of quilts deeper in the wagon, a figure stirred.

"No need to rouse yourself, Sadie. 'Tis only I," Deirdre said.

A head of countless, tiny black braids poked out from under the blankets. Long lashes blinked several times before chestnut eyes peered out of a lovely, dark-skinned face. "Have we arrived?" she asked with only the slightest hint of the African accent she had picked up from her mother. To Deirdre's ears it only made her sound more lovely.

An age ago, upon seeing a young, pregnant girl fresh off the slave ship from Africa, Deirdre's parents had purchased Sadie's mother and granted her and her unborn child freedom. At that time, such acts of humanity had been taking root in the eastern United States and growing in popularity. Loyal to the bone, Sadie's mother still worked in the household of Deirdre's parents. Remembering the kind woman usually made Deirdre a touch homesick, but not today.

"Sadly, no. They're still working on the wheel. I'm sorry to have woken you."

Her fingers closed around the leather browband of the bridle she was searching for. She pulled it out and draped it over her shoulder.

"'S all right. You are going to ride there on your own. I dreamt it," Sadie said in a voice still slurred with sleep.

Before answering, Deirdre put the lid back on the box and opened another. She didn't dare give her friend more time to respond than necessary. From the top of the box, she grabbed her bow and quiver of arrows. The residual life energy of the tree she had formed the bow from hummed in her hand. That was part of the beauty of wood. It was never truly dead, which was part of why it held warmth. Next she took up her sidesaddle. The bow and quiver she slung over her shoulder, the saddle she propped on her hip. "Aye, I am. The town is only a short ride from here. I'm taking Ciaren the remainder of the way."

Deirdre grabbed a saddle pad, stepped back, and closed the wagon flap. She all but jogged to where the half dozen riding horses were tethered to a line strung between two trees. Just because Sadie had 'seen' in one of her prophetic dreams that she would strike out on her own didn't mean she wouldn't protest.

A pitch-black equine nose lifted from the grass at her approach. The mare whinnied and tossed her head, sending her long, black mane into the air. She started to paw at the ground. Approaching the big thoroughbred mare, Deirdre smiled. The horse was one of the famed McCaffery bloodlines. They were some of the finest horses once raised in Ireland and now in New York since Catriona's grandparents immigrated and brought their best breeding stock along.

"I know, lass. Me too," she said as she patted the horse's muscular neck.

She placed the pad on Ciaren's back and hefted the saddle up next.

"Deirdre, you could at least let one of the men escort you," came Sadie's voice from the wagon.

She didn't bother to answer. There was no point. Fingers moving with a speed born of familiarity, she cinched up the saddle and had the bridle halfway on Ciaren's head before she heard the creak of the wagon as Sadie climbed from it. The woman's usually mahogany skin had a sickly hue to it, closer to that of sun-kissed topaz. As she took a few unsteady steps away from the wagon, she grew even paler. Holding tight to the horse's reins, Deirdre jogged back to her friend's side. She grabbed hold of her elbow to steady her.

"Don't worry yourself about me. I've got my bow should I come across trouble." She leaned in close and whispered, "And there is plenty of fauna here to assist me should I need it." After patting her arm, she stepped back. "You shouldn't be up."

Sadie waved her hand and swayed as if it threw off her balance. Deirdre gripped her arm tighter. "Nonsense, I need the fresh air. You and that bow! Listen, I know you're a good shot, but an arrow isn't adequate against a pistol," Sadie insisted in a weak voice. "And I know as well as you do that you can't risk using your fae power and exposing yourself," she whispered, which, considering her exhausted voice, could scarcely be heard.

Her dear friend wasn't wrong. For generations Deirdre's family—along with Catriona's and several others—had managed to hide their true race in New York. According to her parents, Ireland had been another story, one without a happy ending. Keeping their secret was tantamount to their success and safety here in California. This new country believed her kind to be the stuff of myths and legends. Instead they would label them witches, which could be worse.

Eyes widening, Deirdre leaned closer. "Did your dream show me coming across someone with a pistol?

"Well no, but you know they aren't always accurate," she said. "Maybe I should go with you."

"Nonsense. You're still recovering from the heat. You need to rest."

Heavy footsteps approached from around the side of the wagon. Beneath the shadows of a gray-and-black plaid cap, a bearded young man fixed a disapproving gaze on Deirdre. Jack.

Bloody hell, of the lot of them, it had to be him.

The youngest of them all, he had tried to woo Deirdre, but she'd found the poor lad dull as a plank.

His furrowed brow relaxed into a gentler expression as his gaze shifted to Sadie. "She's right about that, Miss Sadie. You ought to be resting. We'll be done and on our way soon enough," he said, shooting Deirdre a glare at the last part.

Snorting, Deirdre looked skyward.

"Perhaps Mrs. Quinn will be a good lass and help me get you back to the wagon where we can tuck the pair of you in to be nice and safe for the remainder of the trip," he continued.

Deirdre relinquished Sadie's arm to the man and promptly draped the reins over her horse's neck. "Nonsense. You're a strapping young lad, quite capable of assisting Sadie all on your own."

She strode over to the back of the wagon, leading Ciaren along beside her. Gathering her skirts in one hand and a clump of Ciaren's mane in the other, she started to climb up the wagon, using it as a make-shift ladder. Jack gasped while Sadie only sighed in resignation. Neither had a chance to move before she made it onto the sidesaddle. As she guided Ciaren away, she smoothed her blue dress over her knees.

"Where do you think you're going, Mrs. Quinn?" Jack demanded.

"To town."

Sadie crossed her arms beneath her breasts. "It isn't safe. Don't forget Cat's stories about Ainsworth and how he hired men to stop her and Rick from getting here. That man lives somewhere near this town and I don't think he'll take kindly to our arrival," she said, her tone already sounding defeated.

Circling back around to her friend, Deirdre leaned down as close to her as she could get and pointed. "Look there, that's the town. On Ciaren, I can reach it in less than an hour." She patted her bow. "And no need to worry. For one, Ainsworth failed the moment Cat and Mr. Fergusson made it here. For two, you know how good of a shot I am." And how quick the trees would react to her in need—but of course she dared not say that part out loud.

Sadie shook her head. The motion caused her to sway. Jack gripped her arm with both hands. "Easy there," he warned. She tried to shrug him off and step toward Deirdre, but her movements were too slow and weak to be effective.

"Surely we'll be there by nightfall," Sadie tried to reason with her.

Though he looked to the side first, Jack nodded. "'Tis likely. That, or by morning at the latest if this wheel gives us too much trouble."

Sadie's shoulders sagged in defeat as she watched Deirdre pick up the reins. The smile Deirdre gave her turned up the corners of Sadie's mouth ever so slightly. "And I shall greet you there with open arms and a glass of wine," Deirdre said.

Anticipating her desire by the shift of her weight, Ciaren arched her neck and began to prance in place.

"I know. Do be careful," Sadie beseeched. The confidence with which she said it meant she had 'seen' it. Excitement replaced Deirdre's tension.

Her grin grew wider. "Come now, Sadie, you know me."

"That's precisely the problem."

Deirdre laughed. "Fair enough. But I *shall* steer clear of trouble, you have my word."

The laugh Sadie gave in return was short and filled with

disbelief. "My dear friend, that's impossible, seeing how it follows you."

At a tap on his arm from her, Jack helped Sadie sit on the back of the wagon before letting go of her and looking to Deirdre. "Give me just a moment to saddle my horse and I'll escort you," he said, a touch of demand in his tone.

Deirdre only turned her grin on him in answer. Nodding, he strode off toward the horses.

"I wouldn't bother if I were you," Sadie called after him.

"Nonsense. We'll be fine," he protested.

Sadie shook her head. "That's not what I meant."

The moment the man disappeared around the side of the wagon, Deirdre winked at Sadie and blew her a kiss. She took a heartbeat to reach out as far as she could and connect to the grass, flowers, and bushes that covered the valley. Their energy mapped out the path before her, showing no holes or hazards to a horse's hooves as far as she could feel—which was several dozen yards. A press of her foot launched the big thoroughbred into a canter that no other horse present would be able to match.

"*That's* what I meant," she heard Sadie proclaim behind her.

Wind whipped at her hair, threatening to pull her raven locks from the thick braid that bounced against her back. Ciaren flew through the stalled wagon train. Other horses called out at their passing, a few pulled at their lead ropes, but none tried to bolt after her. They were all too docile to get overly riled up. Which meant even if any of the men could get saddled up straight away, they'd never catch her. Ciaren's bloodlines were unmatched when it came to speed.

The cooler air of California was a welcome blessing after

the heat of Nevada. It danced across her skin as she leaned into it, and flowed down her bodice between her breasts. As soon as she dropped over the hill and out of sight of the wagons, she lifted her skirts and threw her right leg over Ciaren.

"Let's go girl!" she said as she squeezed with her legs.

The mare launched into a canter. Deirdre let out the reins and leaned forward. Ciaren rewarded her with a burst of speed. Her heart pounded in time to the horse's rhythm. Straddling a horse like a man allowed her to ride faster and harder. But that wasn't the only reason she loved it. It made her feel wicked and free, two things she treasured.

The short grass of the hillside gave way to tall, golden stalks when they plunged into the valley below. For Ciaren's safety, Deirdre was forced to rein the mare in some. Without remaining connected with the plants of the area, it was impossible to tell what type of terrain lay beneath the tall grass once they passed the area she'd scanned. And at this speed, she had no time to reach out again. She allowed Ciaren to maintain a slow canter for another mile or so before slowing her to a trot. No hoofbeats sounded behind her, but she glanced back just in case. A single rider on a brown horse picked its way slowly down the hill. Already she was too far away to discern who it might be. Long legs stretching out into an animated trot, her mare arched her neck and held her head high.

Deirdre grinned. She couldn't blame her for enjoying herself. They'd been plodding along behind that wagon train for four and a half months.

To the southwest, she spotted a dirt road winding its way through the valley toward town. Upon reaching the road, she let the reins out. Ciaren launched into a canter that ate up the soft dirt. In only moments, she put the hill that the wagon train had stopped on far behind her. Once her pursuer was no longer even a spot in the distance, she slowed back down to a trot. Over an hour later, the first of the outlying houses came into sight. She reined Ciaren to a walk as she passed the first two.

They dotted the landscape, surrounded by several acres of farmland or gardens that had mostly been harvested. Big orange pumpkins adorned the dark green vines that covered several acres of a field to her right. Cornstalks grew along the roadside. Tall trees of different varieties hovered over many of the homes like shade-giving guardians. With all the plant life, the place literally buzzed with fertility. The leaves of all the deciduous trees had begun to turn shades of yellow, orange, red, and gold. Their colors made the landscape look like the canvas of a color-loving artist.

"What will winter be like here?" she wondered aloud.

After the harsh heat of Nevada and monotonous browns and faded greens, the colors and weather of this place were refreshing. Even the sky shone a lovely robin's-egg blue, as opposed to the washed-out, sun-bleached hue of the desert. To be fair to Nevada, her guides had assured her such intense heat wasn't typical this late in the year, but nor was it unheard of.

Here, the scent of salt filled the moisture-laden air.

Oh, how I missed the ocean! She could hardly wait to see it again.

The fields soon gave way to more homes, and the road split off in three directions. While the forks before her and to the left looked more traveled, she chose the one to the right, which had grass growing ankle-deep down the middle. The enormous home at the end of the road had a man outside it doing something in a flatbed wagon. Going deeper into town might only slow her down. If she could get directions from this man, she might be able to bypass town altogether and save time. From Cat's description of the property, she knew it was on the outskirts. Exploring town could wait for another day.

To either side of the road stretched fields of grass shorn to the ground and picked up for harvest. The energy of the fauna slumbered, its job for the year nearly complete. Still, this land felt vibrant and alive. The fact that it felt this way even in the early fall made Deirdre feel instantly at home.

The large house at the end of the drive was the sole one on the road. A barn—large enough by most standards, but dwarfed by the massive house—sat slightly behind and to the left. A few paces down the road a finely carved wooden sign proclaimed, "O'Leary Inn."

That explained the size of the place.

It took some time before she grew close enough to get a better look at the inn. At least a dozen windows adorned the two-story structure constructed mostly of logs. A covered porch big enough to host a proper ball wrapped around the first story. The rugged look of the house had a pleasing quality that surprised her. Even more pleasing was the shirtless man loading large bales of hay onto the back of a wagon. He whistled a lively tune as he worked, lifting his burdens seemingly with ease, but levering them against the wagon to slide them when possible. Only a few more remained on the ground. Corded muscles in his arms and back moved beneath skin kissed to a lovely tan by the sun.

Such bales indicated the property owner either owned a hay press, or had borrowed one. To find such a rare device had made its way this far west surprised her. That surprise swiftly became eclipsed by desire upon seeing the sweaty, muscular body up close. His tan was so dark as to be considered unseemly, working class, by those in high society. Deirdre disagreed. She thought the nearly brown skin made him look like a man who wasn't afraid to work hard. And it went nicely with the shoulder-length black hair tied back at the nape of his neck. Wiping sweat from his brow with a forearm, the man turned in her direction. A sculpted chest, strong brow, and high cheekbones void of any hair didn't disappoint, either. Something about him looked decidedly exotic.

Heat rushed to Deirdre's core in a deeply visceral reaction that took her completely by surprise. She hadn't felt this depth of instant attraction since…well, ever. Too late, she remembered to drape her leg back over and sit properly on her sidesaddle. She focused hard on rearranging her skirts, keeping her head down to hide the furious blush that burned her cheeks. Most of the men where she came from would consider a woman riding astride to be quite inappropriate, bordering on scandalous. It wasn't the first impression she wanted to make. She recovered quickly and met the man's gaze.

"Begging your pardon for the interruption, sir, but I'm hoping you might be able to help me locate my friend," she said, careful to keep the Irish brogue from her voice like her etiquette teachers had drilled into her. Months on the trail had allowed it to slip back in, but now that she'd reached civilization, the old oppression returned on instinct.

The corners of his lips started to turn up as he stared at the bow poking up beyond her shoulder. It turned to a smirk that reached his eyes, lighting them up and bringing to mind the tiger's eye gemstones Deirdre had seen Sadie wear on occasion.

The sight took her breath away. He grabbed a beige shirt off the wagon and put it on. The meticulous way his fingers worked their way up the buttons—slowly hiding that darkly tanned chest—ensnared Deirdre's attention. It seemed such a terrible shame to cover up such a work of art. She had to suppress a sigh.

"I fear I'm the one who needs to beg your pardon, dear lady, for the state of my undress. Despite the mild weather, these heavy bales are quick to make a man sweat," he said. He had a low, handsome voice that flowed like a singer's. The barest hint of an accent touched his words, but she couldn't for the life of her place it.

As he finished buttoning the shirt, she finally tore her gaze from his body and forced herself to meet his eyes. No longer caring about the blood that heated her cheeks, she let her smile break through. "You are certainly pardoned, since 'tis I who am at fault, arriving unannounced."

The man shrugged. "Such is to be expected at an inn. You mentioned a friend you wanted to locate." His gaze never left her as he took a long drink from a canteen.

Watching him lick the moisture from his lips nearly made her forget he had prompted her to speak. "Hmm, yes. Catriona O'Brian."

Eyes widening, a smile tugged at his wet lips. "You must be one of the friends she's been expecting from New York."

"I am."

Looking down the road, his brows pinched together. "But where are your escorts, your wagons?" The genuine worry in his tone caused a warm flush to spread through her chest.

"Not long behind. I grew weary of waiting and decided to forge on ahead since our destination seemed so close," she admitted.

Something flashed in his eyes. Was it mirth, amusement? She couldn't tell. A raise of his eyebrows and a half-hidden smile made her think maybe it was. She liked that his reaction was mirth instead of anger at such unladylike behavior. How very unconventional and unique.

"I can't say that I blame you. Wagon trains are frightfully slow things." His tone didn't sound at all mocking, and his expression looked quite sincere. Another pleasant surprise.

She waited for him to mention the dangers of a woman traveling alone or some such thing, but he fell silent. After a long moment, she realized they were both grinning like daft fools at one another.

Finally, he went on. "The widows' property lies just over that hill, bordering this one. You'll know when you've reached it by the rock wall that runs partway between them. Most days Miss Catriona and Rick can be found working the southwest corner near the river." One dark eyebrow rose in a bold display of interest that made her skin tingle. "Would you be one of the widows?"

She loved how he asked without even the slightest attempt to disguise the question. For a stablehand, he was quite well spoken and perfectly mannered. But that had its drawbacks. Part of her wished he'd been ill-mannered enough to at least leave his shirt off. "I am, in fact."

His smile parted with intent, but a loud crash from within the inn drew his attention. "Ah no, I'd better see to that. I have a feeling you're quite capable of making it on your own." His gaze flicked to her bow again, and he smiled. "Nevertheless, it would be my pleasure to escort you, should you desire, if you can wait but a moment," he said.

A thrill ignited her blood. Never had a man spoken to her with such respect for her capabilities. She took in the way his biceps bulged beneath the sleeves of his shirt, how the material stretched taut over his chest. She desired all right... *Oh how I desire!*

Inclining her head and feigning a composure she did not feel, she told him, "Thank you, but I wouldn't want to pull you away from your work any more than I already have. You've been most kind. I shall endeavor to repay that kindness at another time. A very good day to you, sir."

He tipped an imaginary hat and gave her a slight bow as he started to walk backward toward the inn. "A very good day to you as well, dear lady. I shall see you again soon." He boldly maintained eye contact as he continued to walk backward.

The thrills that warmed her blood threatened to make it boil over. Holding his gaze to see how long he would keep at the game, she squeezed Ciaren into a walk. The man's open-mouthed grin grew. Did his boldness never end? And to assume they would see one another again, she rather liked that. A large part of her wanted quite badly to linger and discover the limits to his boldness. But she couldn't, not with her dear friend so close. After four and a half months on the trail, she had no idea how Catriona fared, or how her own trip across the states and territories had gone. The strong concern kept her hands loose on the reins. But this alluring man kept her gaze and thoughts on him. Just before reaching the porch steps, he waved and turned his back to her.

With a harder squeeze, she urged Ciaren into a brisk trot before she lost her will. It didn't occur to her until over half a mile through the field that she hadn't gotten his name.

3

Kinan

Fingers working through his freshly washed locks, Kinan slowly tamed them back into the confines of a silk ribbon as coal black as they were. As usual, he bound his hair up and around itself in an attempt to hide how long it truly was. The ribbon helped conceal the knot, but just barely. People in this small town frowned on deviations from popular fashion—which was short hair for an American man—so he did his best to conceal it most days. But he couldn't cut it. He wouldn't cut it. To do so would be to disrespect his grandmother's beliefs and culture. *Gods embrace her soul.* How much less was the disrespect of hiding it rather than cutting it, was hard to say.

Guilt nagged at him as he walked from the inn to the stables. The true reason he hid it today was in hopes of making a good second impression on the captivating Mrs. Quinn. Catriona would no doubt be bringing her back to the inn tonight. She had open reservations for her widow friends whom she expected to be arriving any day. Despite their lack of a proper introduction, Kinan knew from Catriona's description that the black-haired beauty he'd met today had to be Deirdre Quinn. Wouldn't Cat be surprised when Deirdre rode up on her own? He most certainly had been, but in the most refreshing way.

He couldn't get the image of her out of his mind: full lips always on the verge of a smile, bosom heaving from a mixture of exertion and excitement, and eyes like dark sapphires. *Oh, Itzamná, those eyes!* Fiery spirit emanated from that woman. Such a spirit, the likes of which he had never seen. Just thinking of it now pulled at him on a deep level that reached into his very soul. He had wanted to ride out after her, but he had a feeling not doing so would impress her more. The lovely blue dress she wore indicated she was out of mourning. Whether she was interested in the pursuits of a man again remained to be seen. But he planned on finding out.

Soft nickers in multiple equine voices welcomed him as he slid the barn door open. Two brown draft horse heads popped over stall walls as he approached. He patted their noses as he passed. He strode down the long aisle of empty stalls that awaited the upcoming guests, drawing in the scent of fresh straw and oats. Each stall was perfect, just as he had prepared them, but he double-checked just in case. It had been a long time since the inn had seen the number of visitors they were expecting. Everything needed to be just right.

The empty stalls served as a stark reminder that all the other business had been driven off. A white equine face emerged from the last stall at the end of the barn, ears pricking forward at his approach. Kinan spoke soft words to him in his mother's native tongue, and the stallion's ears moved as if trying to capture and hold the sound. He nickered softly in response. Kinan scratched beneath a forelock so long it nearly hid the horse's eyes. There was a lot to scratch. His head was nearly as big as that of a draft horses', thanks to his Spanish Lusitano sire.

Longing drew Kinan's gaze out to the pink-splashed

horizon. Normally, he and the stallion enjoyed an evening ride around this time. But Miss Catriona would be arriving with her guests any time now, and he did not want to miss Deirdre Quinn's return.

"Sorry, Balder. Tomorrow, I promise."

The stallion tossed his head as if he were greatly offended by the change in his routine. His white coat twitched. White tail flying up into the air, he spun and took off out into the attached paddock. Spirited though he was, such a reaction was far from normal. Something had to be amiss. He peered outside and it became clear.

A single rider on a brown horse made its way up the south road toward the inn. It couldn't be one of Miss Catriona's people. They had passed by in their wagons just a short while ago. When they returned, it would be via the northeastern road that skirted out around the fence to the widows' property. Both the defeated way the horse hung its head and the outline of the silhouette on its back revealed their identity despite the shadows of sunset that shrouded them.

Balder hopped about his large paddock, bucking and kicking. The rider's horse shied away from the fence that his paddock butted up against.

"Enough, Balder. It's not the poor horse's fault that his rider is a *culo*," Kinan said.

The stallion ceased bucking and kicking but continued to prance along the fence line. He couldn't blame the horse for his reaction. Animals knew when something evil was about.

Resisting the urge to pick up a pitchfork on his way out, Kinan left the barn and walked toward the road. The wooden fence lining the road and the closed gate at the inn's entrance would slow the rider down. Kinan lengthened his stride to reach the gate before the rider. He came around the edge of the barn and found the man's slowly plodding gelding still several horse lengths away. In two more strides Kinan reached the gate and leaned on it, making his intentions clear without a word.

Everyone knew a closed gate meant the inn was full. But this man wasn't coming for a room. The golden light of early dusk surrounded the lanky man sitting tall in the saddle. Brown hair was slicked back from a high forehead to reveal a hawkish nose and slits from which beady eyes peered. An officer's-issue six-shooter hung on his right hip. Kinan's teeth ground together. He knew for a fact this man hadn't been an officer in the war. Carrying a pistol was a new level of threatening for him, one Kinan didn't like the implications of one bit. Maybe he should have grabbed that pitchfork after all. If only he could use the weapons natural to him. But to do such a thing would be to expose himself to a very dangerous enemy. And he'd already come too close for comfort to doing that in the past.

"Did the cattle run you out of your big, empty house up on the hill, Ainsworth?" Kinan asked.

The man made a dry, hacking sound that passed for a chuckle. "Better a big house I can afford to keep empty than one I have to fill with strangers just to get by," he said in his raspy voice.

Though Kinan didn't smell an ounce of fear on him, he saw the caution in his eyes and stance, and in the way he held his horse's reins at the ready.

"Strangers only stay strange if you don't let them in."

Ainsworth's dark, bushy brows humped together like fornicating caterpillars. "You're an odd duck, O'Leary."

"Well, if you're looking for a room, I can't say I'm sorry that we're full up," Kinan said.

The man leaned to the side and hawked a spit-engrossed chunk of chewing tobacco onto the ground. "I wouldn't stay in the house of a half-breed if it were the only shelter in a blizzard."

"Can't say I'd mourn you freezing to death in that case, or any case, really," Kinan said.

Those beady eyes narrowed further. "I wouldn't expect a half-savage would."

Teeth grinding, Kinan refrained from replying. The man knew better than most that the half of him that wasn't Irish wasn't Native American either. Despite what they said, those filled with such inexplicable hate always knew exactly what it was they were hating, they just didn't know why.

"What do you want, Ainsworth? You aren't welcome here if you've come to harass Miss Catriona again," Kinan warned.

Mirth flashed in the slits that served as his eyes. "And if I've come for another reason, would I be welcome?"

"No." It came out sounding tired, instead of menacing like he'd intended.

"That's a shame, because I've come to offer you a business proposition."

"My Irish father taught me never to deal with the equivalent of a devil, as you well know."

Dropping his reins, Ainsworth held his hands up in a placating gesture. "All rankling aside, I mean it true. I'm offering to rent out your entire inn for the new crew I'm hiring to watch my cattle this winter."

"The inn is full."

Ainsworth leaned down a bit. "We both know that ain't

true, and soon as those widows get a bee in their bonnets they'll be off to stay somewhere else. I'll pay a third more than what you're charging them, per room, and that's guaranteed through the winter and into spring. Of course, we'd need the entire inn."

Such a steady income through winter certainly held a powerful attraction. Times had been hard. But they'd been hard because Ainsworth drove a lot of his business away in an attempt to get him to evict Catriona O'Brian.

"As I said, the inn is full and will be for some time. If you would like to check back when all the hells in all the worlds freeze over, you're welcome to do so. But as you said, you wouldn't stay here if it were the only shelter in a blizzard, so I fail to see why you'd have your men stay somewhere you would not."

The chuckle that slid from Ainsworth actually held mirth. "You're crafty, man. I like that. We don't need to be enemies."

To that, Kinan dipped his head. "I agree, we do not. However, it's clear we stand on opposing sides of the matter of the widows' land, and my stance on that won't be changing."

Ainsworth shook his head. "I don't get it. Why do you care whether I own the land or the widows do?"

Fury built inside him. Both his ancestors on his father's and mother's sides had been dealing with people with this exact attitude for centuries. Kinan's answer came through gritted teeth. "Because they own it and you intend to take it from them."

Waving a hand, Ainsworth sat back in the saddle. "The strong take from the weak. It's the nature of things. Women can't work land. It's going to remain unimproved and revert back to the county, then it will be mine." He took up his reins and turned his horse around. "You need to face reality and get on the right side of this. Things tend to end badly for those on the wrong side of a matter."

Hands gripping the wooden fence so tight a splinter began to poke at his palm, Kinan fought the urge to jump it. "Threatening me is a very bad idea. You do not want to be doing that."

A grin pulled up Ainsworth's lips as he turned his head back in Kinan's direction. "Oh but I do."

He kicked his horse with the massive spurs that jangled from his boots, launching the poor animal into a gallop. Curses spewed from Kinan's lips. Halfway up the fence before he realized it, he had to hold himself back from giving chase. For the man's treatment of his horse alone, he deserved to be pummeled. For the rest, he deserved much worse. In the paddock along the fence, Balder bucked and kicked as if in agreement. But chasing the man down and giving him the confrontation he so desired would do neither Kinan nor the widows any good. Of that he was certain. No, better to outwit the man and beat him at his own game. And the fool had no idea how good at games Kinan was. Dangerous games were a tradition his ancestors had perfected.

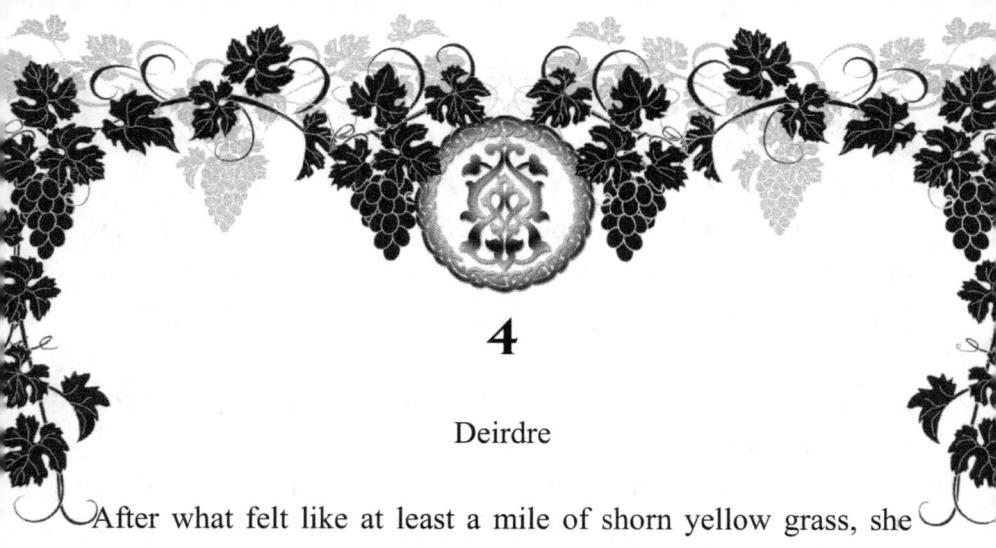

4

Deirdre

After what felt like at least a mile of shorn yellow grass, she finally saw what appeared to be a short rock wall in the distance. Throwing her leg over Ciaren to ride like a man, she let the reins out. All it took was a tightening of her thighs and a slight forward lean for Ciaren to launch into a canter. With only one stirrup on the sidesaddle, she couldn't rise up as was proper form for a jump. Instead, she gripped tight with her thighs and leaned forward a little more.

Easily synchronizing her rhythm to that of the horse, she relaxed and let Ciaren do what she did best. The rock wall came closer with each hoofbeat. Only four feet or so high, it presented very little challenge. Still, her heart pounded and she held her breath as the mare's haunches bunched in preparation. They launched from the ground. Less than a heartbeat later they soared over the wall with ease. The moment of weightlessness shot an explosion of sheer joy through Deirdre. Even as they floated through the air, she eyed the ground, anticipating their landing. Unlike the shorn field they had just come through, tall grass gone to seed covered this side. Her muscles tensed as she prepared for the worst and hoped for the best.

Risky as it was, she wouldn't have it any other way.

Ciaren landed solid and true-footed. The next beat propelled them into the new field. Caught up in the moment and emboldened by the thrumming energy of the fauna, Deirdre let the mare have her head and choose their speed. The wind soon drew tears from her eyes. Vision blurred, she picked up the reins to slow Ciaren down. Before she could even begin to pull back, the mare's muscles bunched for another jump. A curse in Gaelic slipped from Deirdre's lips. She did her best to shift her weight and ready herself the second before Ciaren became airborne again.

Beneath them the wild flower-dotted field opened up into a deep cleft. Water glinted, along with something else. A half-naked man stood waist deep in a creek, a squirming black calf draped over his shoulders. Surely that last bit had been her imagination. She hoped so, for her horse's hooves came dangerously close to the man's head. The moment they came down on the other side, she brought Ciaren in a circle that helped slow her momentum and allowed Deirdre to pull her to a halt.

At the bottom of the cleft, a creek maybe ten feet wide cut through the land. A few late-blooming orange and red poppies grew along both beds. Their energy all but sang to her. Crystal-clear water tumbled over smooth pebbles, filling the air with a refreshing scent. After the endless Nevada high desert, she had nearly forgotten how good fresh water smelled. Sure enough, a man stood in the creek, a calf over his shoulders. Blond hair framed eyes wide with surprise. Thankfully, no blood marred that lovely hair. Despite the comical look on his face, he was quite handsome, with a squarish jaw speckled by a few days of stubble. Muscles in his chest and arms flexed to perfection beneath the weight of the calf.

Two handsome, shirtless men in one day. She loved California already.

"My most sincere apologies. I didn't know either the creek, or you, were here. I hope you're unharmed," she called down.

Shock slowly drained from his face, his features transforming into a smile as he looked her over. "I'm not sure. I did just see a fae fly through the sky and now she speaks to me." His confident tone lent well to his easy humor. "You're all right yourself, I hope. It appears your horse got away from you a bit there."

Laughing, partly to cover her nerves over being called fae, Deirdre patted Ciaren's big neck. The man was only jesting. He didn't truly know her nature. She could see it in his eyes. Normal humans were either oblivious or in denial of her kind. "She can't be blamed. I got as carried away as she did."

Balancing the calf as if it weighed next to nothing, the man stepped from the creek and made his way up the embankment. Once he reached the top, he hefted the calf from his shoulders and set it on its feet. Bawling, it dashed off to join a small herd of cows not far away. Ciaren tossed her head at the thing and pawed at the ground. Hand tight on the reins, Deirdre held the mare in place. As soon as the calf reached the small herd, Ciaren calmed.

"That's quite the spirited horse you've got," the man said.

Deirdre searched his face but found no judgment hiding there. "Aye, she has to be to keep up with me."

His handsome grin grew. Bending, he began to search along the embankment. Much to her dismay, his hands withdrew a faded blue tunic from the tall grass. In response to that dismay, a nearby blackberry bramble snaked around the material at the last moment. Thankfully, the man's gaze was on her and he didn't notice. One of the thorns tore a sizable gouge in the material.

"Apologies for me state. Rescuing calves can be a messy endeavor," he said.

Breeches turned a dark brown by the water clung to his legs and groin. He pulled his shirt on over his head, slowly lowering it down. A tear across the chest exposed one defined pectoral muscle. She dipped her head to hide her smirk behind loose strands of her hair. The sight of the saddle between her legs quickly reminded she was straddling Ciaren in an improper manner for a lady in the presence of a man, yet again. To move now would only draw attention to the fact, though, so she held her position.

"Huh. Blasted brambles. Guess I'll have to get this mended. The name's Dylan O'Toole. And does me fae have a name?" he asked.

"I'm Deirdre Quinn."

His eyebrows rose. "Ah, one of the widows."

"Does everyone know of us?"

He shrugged one shoulder. "'Tis a small town."

"That's going to be an adjustment," she said, mostly to herself.

"Indeed. California is a far cry from New York."

Deirdre's brows rose, pushing at the strands of hair that had come loose from her braid. "I most sincerely hope so. Am I on the widows' property now?"

"Aye. You'll find Miss Catriona and Mr. Fergusson about a mile up the river working on the ranch. I'm headed that way meself if you'd like a traveling companion."

She was about to refuse when she realized he had no horse.

In good conscience, she couldn't very well let him walk when she was headed in the same direction. The warmth of the sun high above also served as a reminder that the day was advancing fast. If she got turned around in the wrong direction, she may not find Cat before dark.

"That would be most kind, but as I'm in a bit of a hurry, I hope you don't mind riding with me." It really wouldn't be proper, but that bothered her less than the possibility of the inn's stablehand seeing them. Hopefully he wasn't riding after her even now, as gentlemanly code dictated. She had to hurry this up just in case.

Dylan approached. "Don't mind at all. I appreciate the kindness, as it seems me horse has wandered off while I was down in the creek."

More to get better leverage than for propriety's sake, Deirdre threw her leg back over and clamped her thighs onto the sidesaddle bars. She reached a hand back over the right side of the horse, offering it to Dylan. Blond brows rose in a look of doubt that made Deirdre grin at the challenge. His hand gripped hers. Like a good rider, he kicked his leg up and out, using the direction and momentum to vault up. Deirdre's grip held true and the strength of her arm helped Dylan leverage himself. He landed securely on Ciaren's dark haunches.

"Don't know many women who could do that," he said, sounding impressed.

"Rather, I think you probably don't know any women who would do so in mixed company. But we are quite capable, I assure you," she said.

He kept his distance, just barely allowing his left leg to touch her thigh. While it would be more proper should anyone see them, her horse wouldn't take kindly to someone sitting on her rear end. "You'd best scoot up, less you aggravate Ciaren and she gets a mind to toss us both," she warned.

Ciaren was too well trained for such shenanigans, but it would be a bumpy ride. If he fell off, it would only slow them down more and increase the possibility of the stablehand seeing them—should he be riding after her, that was. Why she cared, she didn't know. On the other hand, it would be nice to have a handsome man touching her thighs.

She pointed Ciaren north and started walking her along the river. The only protest the mare made in regards to the second rider was a swishing of her tail. Deirdre found herself both regretting the bow and quiver that kept his chest from touching her back, and glad for it. Attractive as Mr. O'Toole was, she couldn't stop thinking about the other man's gemstone-like eyes and chestnut skin.

"Are you from Goldenvale, Mr. O'Toole?" Deirdre asked.

"Of recent, aye. Though I hail from Boston originally, having immigrated there as a lad with me parents." His warm breath reached her neck, causing bumps to rise along her skin.

The sensation traveled all the way to her breasts. Her eyes fluttered closed to better allow her imagination to conjure up more than his breath touching her. It had been so very long since her husband had gone off to war and not returned, leaving her bed and body cold. Not that he had been much of a lover. Fae blood did not a good lover make. She had her own devices that she put to good use, but still, there was nothing quite like the real thing. Thinking about such things while in close proximity to a handsome man made her insides flutter. That didn't mean she was going to refrain from such indulgent thoughts, quite the contrary.

"What about you?" Dylan asked.

His voice so close to her ear elicited all kinds of new fantasies, but she managed to keep her mind on track enough to answer. "I was born and raised in New York, though my grandparents were from North Carolina."

"Cotton country," Dylan commented in a tone that was neither judging nor telling.

Not one to hold her tongue, Deirdre nodded and went on. "My family owned a cotton plantation down there, or at least, they did before the war. They also grew grapes for wine. Since he disagreed with his brothers over the matter of slavery, my grandfather left the plantation to them and moved his new wife to New York to open a tailor's shop."

"From cotton and grapes to a tailor's shop. That is quite the change in professions."

At that she shrugged. "The world was changing, and for the better. My grandfather was committed to changing with it. We had a nice piece of property in the hills outside of town, and we still grew grapes and made wine."

"Had?" he asked.

So forward. Caution flared within. As a fae, she was used to hiding much about herself, her very identity, from anyone who wasn't other. "When I was matched with my late husband, I moved into the city."

"Is the city truly as grand as they say?" Dylan asked.

She brought her head to her right shoulder in a half-shrug. "As far as cities go."

The city had long ago lost its luster for her. It had fewer plants, less fresh air, and far too many people.

"I'd love to hear about it!"

His excited questions soon had her going on about everything from the architecture to the shops and factories. Despite her disenchantment with the city and its ever-busy citizens, his enthusiasm was infectious.

Soon, Dylan he drew away from her. Trained to respond to subtle shifts in weight, Ciaren slowed, ears flicking back to Deirdre. A slight shift of her own weight stopped the mare.

"Thank you kindly for the ride, but I best get down lest Mr. Fergusson sees us and thinks me taking advantage of you," Dylan said.

"Yes, I suppose that is best," Deirdre agreed with a touch of reluctance.

The warmth of his body disappeared as he leaped from Ciaren's back. The distant *thunk* of a hammer drew her attention. Not more than half a mile away stood a skeletal structure of logs that had to be the beginnings of the barn that would house the horses and winery. Deirdre had imagined it would be much further along by now. Still, the sight of it nearly brought tears to her eyes. It was all she could do not to spur Ciaren into a gallop. But she couldn't be rude, not if she hoped to see this man again. Which she found she did.

"How do you know Mr. Fergusson?" she asked.

"He's me boss, and a right good one at that. We've nearly reached the spot."

"This is it? This is truly my friend's land?" Deirdre asked. She spun the horse in a slow circle, taking in the rolling hills of thick grass dotted here and there with oak trees and aspen. Each tree, bush, and blade of grass glowed with an energy and life visible only to her fae eyes. It was the most beautiful sight she'd ever seen.

"Aye, from the rock wall to the south, and between the creek and those hills there." He gestured to pine-covered hills on the horizon.

"So much land," she murmured. The three parcels combined to equal close to a hundred acres, from what the deed said. She had read it enough times before leaving New York to have memorized it word for word. The legal description had seemed like a foreign language at first, but she'd made it her mission to understand it. Looking out over the land now, it all made sense, the degrees, the quarters, the measurements out from the river that ran through it all. It thrummed with a wildness that sang to her soul.

"Oh look, that's me horse!" Sticking his thumb and forefinger in his mouth, he whistled loud and shrill.

The thunder of hooves drew her gaze out across the golden fields. A tall, brown horse with legs designed for running put them to good use. Tail up in the air, neck arched, he galloped toward them at an impressive speed. Ciaren threw her head and pranced in such an animated manner that Deirdre was forced to shorten the reins and command the mare's attention. Skill derived from years of riding kept her on the saddle and in control.

Dylan's horse slowed to a trot when he grew closer, and eventually to a walk. On his back perched one of the Spanish-style saddles with the large skirting along the back and a horn on the front for tying a rope to. Rather than run straight to Dylan, the horse sauntered over and sniffed Ciaren's nose. Ciaren let out a squeal and stomped her foot, but that was the extent of her misbehavior. Beneath Deirdre, the horse felt like a simmering teapot ready to blow. A closer look at Dylan's horse revealed him to be an intact stallion. That explained Ciaren's response. The stallion shook his head and arched his neck. Before he could do anything more, Dylan snatched the reins and led him away.

Puzzlement filled his eyes as he cast a sheepish smile Deirdre's way. "Me apologies. He's usually much better behaved. I think he fancies that gorgeous mare of yours." The inviting look that accompanied his words made it clear he wasn't merely talking about horses.

Such forward—yet sly—advances forced her to fight back a grin. "Thank you kindly, both for the escort and the compliment. If you'll excuse me, I see my friend and can't bear another moment of waiting to greet her. It was a pleasure meeting you, Mr. O'Toole. Until we meet again."

His ruggedly handsome visage transformed into a smile that seemed to employ every muscle in his face. Such a youthful, carefree expression coming from a grown man warmed her.

"If that's your wish, I'll consider it me command," he said.

Grinning, she shook her head, pointed Ciaren in Cat's direction and tapped her heel against the mare's side. Wind whipped the ribbon from her hair, pulling long, black locks out behind her. But she didn't care. The joy of reaching California and finding it everything she had hoped for and more, carried her to her beloved friend.

5

Deirdre

The moment Ciaren came to a stop, Deirdre all but flung herself from the sidesaddle. She flew into her friend's arms, nearly knocking them both to the ground. "Oh, Cat, I've missed you so much!"

After a few moments of squeezing her tight as she could, she drew back and held Cat at arm's length. Cat's wavy red hair nearly reached her waist now—a waist that had filled out some. It helped her look less like a malnourished widow wasting away to nothing. But that wasn't the best part. Happiness filled her green eyes, along with a confidence Deirdre had always hoped for, but never expected to see in her again.

"You look absolutely wonderful!" Deirdre proclaimed.

Pink tinged Cat's cheeks, making her look far younger than her twenty-something years. Cat cupped Deirdre's cheek in her hand. "You're a sight for sore eyes as well. A bit skinny, but you seem hale enough," Cat said, with the hint of an Irish accent coloring her words.

Hearing it stole Deirdre's ability to respond for a moment. Cat had always worked diligently to keep her accent from her voice. The woman's oppressive mother had insisted on it, claiming it helped those of high society respect her more if they couldn't hear the Irish in her. Deirdre had always detested that woman.

"Well, four months on the trail tends to tighten one's belt. Something is quite different about you, my friend, and I mean that in the very best way," Deirdre said.

Green eyes widening, Cat cast a look over her shoulder at the man approaching from the framework of the barn just up the hill. Deirdre recognized him immediately as the one who had escorted Cat to California. Corporal Patrick Fergusson. He had shaved and lost the haunted look in his eyes. The pulse of a wild and free energy emitted from him, an energy not entirely human. She had most certainly not felt this about him back in New York. *Interesting.* She and Cat had much to talk about it seemed.

Patrick's expression filled with deep tenderness as his gaze caught Cat's. Deirdre could feel the vibrations between the two of them. The adoring look he gave Cat as he came to stand beside her made Deirdre clap and emit a wordless cry of joy. The blush that colored Cat's cheeks spread down her neck. That look told Deirdre that the two had shared more than just conversation on their trip here. And human or other, she cared not if he made Cat happy.

Clearing her throat and standing up tall enough to make her finishing teacher proud for once, Deirdre became the image of propriety. "Mr. Fergusson, 'tis good to see you again. Cat, I see we have much to discuss." She was quite proud that only the hint of a smile slid through.

Patrick laughed long and hard. The lighthearted, joyful sound did Deirdre almost as much good as the smile it brought to her friend's lips. Whatever lay between the two of them, clearly it was good for Cat. "Ah, Mrs. Quinn, you are just as I remember you. We're quite glad you made it, and that you're in such good health and spirits. I'm off to work again while you lassies get reacquainted. I'll take your horse for you if you like, get her something to eat and drink. We've got a paddock over this way," Patrick said.

"That would be much appreciated. Thank you so much," she said as she handed him Ciaren's reins.

He bowed deeply to her before taking Cat's right hand and placing a long kiss on the back of it. Her gloveless hand! The very implications nearly made Deirdre cry out with excitement. She restrained the impulse, but only barely. Cheeks flushing impossibly pinker, Cat hid behind her hair as Patrick took his leave. But it was Deirdre she hid from, not the ruggedly handsome man. When he was a few paces away, Cat extended her elbow to Deirdre. Working hard at suppressing her grin, Deirdre accepted and allowed Cat to lead her along the creek.

"'Tis so good to see you, but what of Sadie and your escorts?" Cat asked.

One hand waved away her friend's worries while the other clutched her tighter. "Sadie is good, a bit weary from spending too much time in the Nevada dry heat, but otherwise hale and excited to be nearly here. They're atop that ridge fixing a wagon wheel and hopefully should be along before nightfall." She paused to point in the direction she'd come from. "I simply couldn't wait a moment longer. But I wasn't alone for the entire way. A gentleman named Dylan escorted me a ways. He said he was an employee of Mr. Fergusson's, so he seemed safe enough."

Pale green eyes widening, Cat turned to stare hard at Deirdre. "Deirdre Quinn! 'Tis dangerous in these parts, as you well know from your travels. Less so for you, I suppose, with an arsenal of plant life at your disposal."

At that they laughed and touched their foreheads together in the very spot their magic concentrated. Such a touch was their equivalent of a warm embrace, and so much more. When they used their magic, the very spot glowed with the evidence of it. Only others—the supernatural—and those sensitive to magic could see it. But not all those able to see it were accepting of it. To allow another to touch the spot was to admit a closeness to them unlike any other.

Cat sighed. "Dylan is a good man. Thank Danu 'twas him you came across and not someone else," she said, smiling at the last. "I do hope your trip was uneventful."

Eyes rolling to the sky, Deirdre sighed dramatically. "Dreadfully so. Clearly far less eventful than your own. I want to hear all the details about you and Mr. Fergusson. Don't you dare hold a thing back! I can feel the otherness about him."

A schoolgirl joy filled Cat as she delved into a story about natives, wildlife, and greedy cattle barons sending assassins after them. It all sounded so fantastical, like something out of a penny-dreadful novel, but her friend never lied. Finally, she told her how she and Rick—as she called him, *so familiar!*—fell in love. Each detail and twist in the story made Deirdre's heart pound faster and eyes grow wider, but none so much as the story of her friend's romance.

"Oh Cat, how incredibly romantic! I'm so happy for you," she said.

Cat giggled and shook her head. "Did you not hear the part about the bison, the natives, and Ainsworth wanting our land?" she said.

"Yes, and I'm dreadfully jealous that your trip was so much more eventful than mine. But I'm glad you're all right." She shot her a big smile. "So, out with it. What is he?"

The wonder that lifted her friend's brows and joy that dimpled her cheeks filled Deirdre to bursting with anticipation. Sensing it, Cat delayed, slowly leaning close, then finally whispering. "*Faolach*."

"No! Truly?" Deirdre gasped in shock.

Both a man and a wolf, able to shift between one form and the other at will, *faolach* had one foot in the human world and one in the animal world. Werewolf, this new country called them. She couldn't imagine a better match for Cat whose magic was tied to animals. Rick was the first of his kind she'd ever come across.

"But I didn't feel his otherness back in New York," Deirdre mused aloud.

"He is quite adept at hiding his power. I didn't know it until toward the end of the trip. He didn't want to frighten me." The euphoric tone of her voice made Deirdre smile all the wider.

It made her wonder. "Have you lain with him yet? I bet he's a beast between the thighs!"

Cat turned nearly the shade of her hair. Emitting a squeal, Deirdre gripped her arm all the tighter. "You did! Tell me all about it! Was he a thoughtful lover? He better have been! Did you try any of the positions from the Kama Sutra book?"

An exclamation in Gaelic erupted from Cat, halting Deirdre's questions and fueling her excitement. Her friend had always been afraid to speak their native tongue. Her willingness to do so now seemed a very good sign. Both women fell into a fit of giggles.

"He's wonderful, in every way. I'll tell you all about it tonight, I promise. Oh Deirdre, he has proposed, and I've accepted! O' course, he wired my father to ask permission, but I would have said yes even if he had denied Rick," Cat said.

The dreamy look in her eyes made Deirdre want to swoon. She hadn't seen Cat this happy since she and her first husband had started courting. And that had been different. Then she had possessed the timid look of a girl with a crush—one that would lead her down a dangerous road of pain and heartache. This time she glowed with the strength and happiness of true love.

"That is the most wonderful news! We must celebrate!"

The look of joy started to fade from Cat's eyes. She patted the back of Deirdre's hand. "We will, most certainly. But first, I must tell you about Ainsworth." She gestured to the land on the other side of the creek. "That land belongs to Rick. His father found gold in this creek, enough to make his family very wealthy."

With a cry, Deirdre slapped gently at Cat's arm. "Your rugged guide turned out to be wealthy, and with gold of all things! And a *faolach*! This just gets better and better."

Cat laughed and shook her head. "Aye, but it gets worse as well. Ainsworth wants either Rick's land or ours so he can pan that creek for gold." She gestured to the skeletal beginnings of the barn that would be the stables and winery. "When he couldn't kill either Rick or I, he made sure no one would sell us materials to build."

Brows pulling together, Deirdre eyed the meager materials stacked next to where Rick worked on a partially built wall. "Surely the entire town doesn't support Ainsworth," she said.

"None of them support him, but most of them fear him.

What you see there is from those who are willing to defy him. We don't have enough to build the barn, let alone our homes. Worse yet…" she paused to swallow. The pain that etched deep lines on her face flared anger to life in Deirdre. "Ainsworth has convinced the county to cut our time short. If we don't have dwellings built on all three parcels of land by spring, we lose it."

Though anger broiled within her, Deirdre smiled and patted Cat's hand. "No worries, dear, we'll find a way around this. You know how I get when I set my mind to something," she said.

A smile swept away some of Cat's concern. "Aye, I do at that."

Three large shapes emerged from the other side of the hill to their right, wagons. "Ah look, there's Sadie now," Deirdre pointed out.

After much exclaiming and a bit of jumping up and down like a lass, Cat called to Rick to bring their horses.

"We'll go meet them, then I'll take you ladies to the inn," Cat told her.

"The inn?"

Cat nodded. "Aye. No more sleeping under the stars. Warm baths and a fine feather bed await you both at the O'Leary Inn. It would be unseemly to the townsfolk if we stayed out among the wolves and bears, and it wouldn't be appropriate for us to stay at Rick's, though he says we're welcome there any time."

"Aw, Cat, you didn't have to arrange that," she protested weakly. Part of her would miss the open sky above her and the fresh air, but the parts that ached from a long journey thrilled at the mention of a feather bed. Then her mind caught on the name. "O'Leary Inn, is that the one I passed on the way here, just on the other side of the rock wall?"

"Aye, 'tis."

Warmth flushed through her, and not just to her cheeks. "I met the most handsome stablehand there."

Cat laughed. "O' course you did. What was his name? I know most of the staff there."

A frown tugged Deirdre's lips down. "I didn't catch it."

"Cheer up, dear, you'll have plenty of chances to catch far more than just his name," Cat said through a smirk.

They fell into a fit of laughter as Deirdre smacked her friend's arm. All smiles, Rick approached and handed them the reins to their horses. He helped Cat climb onto a gorgeous, tall, painted horse of brown, white, and black. His hand lingered a moment on her leg before he stepped away. Grinning at her friend, Deirdre shook her head as Rick came to help her onto her own horse who seemed quite refreshed. Exchanging looks, she and Cat picked up their reins at the same time. Without a word, they both urged their horses into a canter off toward the wagon train. Laughter trailed behind them in the wind.

6

Dylan

The dark, quiet house absorbed Dylan's call. No scents of stew or porridge filled the air. The fireplace lay cold and empty with no pot hanging within. An empty bedroom with a smooth, perfectly tucked patchwork quilt made it clear no one had been in there since this morning. Where could she have gotten off to? Worry started to push away the exhaustion of a hard day's work, giving him a boost of energy.

"Victoria? Where have you gotten off to?" he called out, louder this time.

Still, the empty house did not answer.

Guilt chewed on him for taking so long with the beautiful Quinn woman. He should have been home an hour ago. It took only moments to search the other rooms of the small house. Chest heaving with deep breaths that only invited panic into his heart faster, he plunged back outside. An empty garden awaited around the back of the house. He dashed back out to the run-in shed where his horse stood munching on the hay he'd thrown it.

"Sorry, lad," he said as he slid the horse's bridle back on.

His mind going over all the places she could have gone, he vaulted onto the horse's back. Aside from the house or garden, there was only one place he could think of she would go. He pointed his horse toward the hill and squeezed him into a gallop. Rocky ground made the going hard. The steep hill soon slowed them to a lope that couldn't exactly be called a canter. He should slow the poor creature to a trot, at least, but fear wouldn't allow him to. Victoria could have easily slipped on the rocks, twisted an ankle, hit her head, or even taken a tumble. She could be lying somewhere hurt and alone, waiting for help.

His gaze scanned the hillside as they ascended it. Only rocks, tufts of grass, and the occasional wildflower covered the land. Finally, the slick rocks forced his horse to walk. He patted the creature's neck and murmured words of thanks and encouragement. They crested the top and he prepared to launch his horse into a gallop again. But there was no need. A woman sat on the ground not ten feet away, her navy-blue cotton dress bunched up around her crossed legs. One hand stroked the granite headstone poking up out of the grass before her, while the other clutched a bouquet of yellow and white wildflowers to her chest. Wisps of long, white hair that had escaped the bun at the nape of her neck blew about her wrinkled face, half-obscuring it from him.

"Victoria!" Dylan exclaimed as he slid from the saddle.

He dropped his horse's reins and gave him the command to stay. Confident in the animal's obedience, he jogged to Victoria's side. The horse wouldn't go anywhere without him unless he told it to, he was well trained. A fact that had recently helped ensure his meeting with a beautiful young widow. Kneeling down beside Victoria, he draped an arm around her thin shoulders. The skin of her arm felt chilly beneath his hand.

"I'm all right. No need to fret o'er me. I just wanted to come up and see me lad a'fore dinner. I didn't realize I'd gotten such a late start. I'm sorry to worry ya," Victoria said.

Dylan took his coat off and draped it around her shoulders. "Ah, Victoria, you should have waited. I'd have brought you up here. You're as chilly as a winter's breeze."

She chuckled but gripped the coat tight around her. "'Tis not so bad as all that."

The redness of her hands worried him. "If you've had a fair chance to chat with him a bit, we should get you back home and get dinner on. Something warm in your belly would do you a lot of good."

She patted his hand as he helped her rise. "And yours, no doubt, lad, as you've been working so hard. Me apologies for neglecting to think of that. Today was just a bit of a melancholy day is all."

Guilt stabbed icy fingers deep into his chest as he glanced at the headstone. It had been a year this month. While he wasn't sure of the exact day, as things had been so chaotic back then, he was certain of the month. Victoria probably had it down to the day. He hugged her a little tighter against his side. "Don't you worry none about that. I shouldn't have been late."

"Nonsense. You're a good lad, as much me son as Thomas was in many ways. You take good care of me and I'm right grateful to you for doing so. But you should be off charming lasses in your evenings, not doting over an old lady."

His mind filled with the image of a black-haired beauty sailing her horse over his head. "I did actually meet a lass today," he admitted.

"Did you now? Tell me all about her!" Victoria said with a clap of her hands.

As he helped her onto his horse, he recounted the tale of how he'd met the widow Quinn, leaving out the bits about the improper ride together—and, of course, his even more improper thoughts.

"Oh, she sounds lovely! And out of mourning, did you say?"

He took up his horse's reins and started to lead him down the hill. "She is," he said through a grin that he couldn't hold back had he wanted to.

Victoria squealed like a schoolgirl and clapped her hands again. The horse popped his head up, but otherwise behaved. "'Tis wonderful news! Are you going to see her again?"

The distant rolling hills of gold where the widows' land lay drew his gaze. "Not officially. But their land borders me boss's so I'm certain to run into her while I'm at work."

Eyes narrowing, Victoria thrust a finger at him. "You make a point of it. A lass likes to know when she's caught a man's attention, and she's clearly caught yours." One hand covered her heart and she fluttered her eyes in a dramatic gesture that nearly made him chuckle. "Besides, it would do me old heart good to see you find someone. I won't be on this earth forever, and I don't want you alone when I leave it."

A grin broke across his face. "Yes, ma'am," he said, purposefully not making it clear to which part he was being obedient. He wanted to make Victoria happy, more than anything. But the situation with Deirdre Quinn was complicated in ways he couldn't share with Victoria. Getting close to Deirdre would make Ainsworth look too hard at him. That was something he had to avoid at all costs. At least until he got what he needed from the man. Not to mention, he wasn't entirely sure Deirdre was interested in him. The unusualness of that alone made her fascinating.

To distract Victoria from the subject, he asked her about her day. As they descended the hill, she went on and on about the various birds she had seen outside her window and catalogued, and the state of her squash growing in her garden. Slowly, the last lingering bits of melancholy drained from her voice. His guilt didn't go with it, though. He should have been here for her, to take her up to her son's grave. Hell, to go himself. It had been months since he'd stepped foot up there. Perhaps tomorrow he'd take a bit of that good Irish whiskey he had left and share a shot with his old friend.

The distant shape of a lone rider coming up the road began to take form below them. Though the person was too far away to make out, the sight sent a chill through Dylan. Few people came down this road. The only place it led to was Victoria's small farm. All Victoria's friends were too old to travel out this far from town and all of his were either dead or in another state. But he didn't need to play the guessing game to figure out who it was. The icy pit of his gut told him.

"Looks like our evening visitor is early," Victoria said.

Dread spread up to his chest. "You're expecting a visitor?"

"Aye. Mr. Ainsworth came calling after you earlier today, said he'd be back to catch you this evening." Her cheery tone sounded genuine enough. Still, he worried.

"He didn't vex you in any way, or harass you about the rent, did he? He gave us an extra week and he knows Mr. Fergusson pays me on Friday."

Victoria waved her hand as if what he'd said was the most absurd thing she'd heard all day. "O' course not. He was polite as could be, a gentleman. He even stayed to have tea with me."

The palm of Dylan's right hand itched for the grip of a pistol he had long ago put away. Wrinkles pulling up into a smile filled with a naïve innocence, she beamed down at him. It was the look of a woman who believed in the goodness of others, who trusted them too much. The look of a woman who believed the lie that her son had died fighting in the Civil War.

Dylan swallowed hard. "Still, he shouldn't be calling on a lady alone. Ain't proper."

"I know. But I get so few visitors, and he is the landlord, after all." A touch of melancholy had worked its way back into her voice.

They reached the bottom of the hill and started toward the barn. The rider was less than a quarter of a mile down the road now, and Dylan could easily tell it was Ainsworth. He walked a little faster. He wanted to get Victoria inside before the man arrived.

"Do you know what he wanted, if not to talk about the rent?" he asked.

"Aye!" Victoria's excited words made the horse lift his head abruptly. "He wants to speak to you about a job. Says it'll pay enough that we won't have to worry about the rent for an entire year!"

He didn't want to ruin her excitement, but he didn't want her encouraging Ainsworth either—or worse yet, having him over for tea again. "A job like that's bound to be dangerous," he mused.

Her smile wilted. "Oh. Well, don't you be taking on a dangerous job just to pay me rent. 'T'aint worth it."

"Our rent. We're in this together, remember? And no

worries, I have a job, don't need another," he assured her.

When he reached up to help her down she patted his hand and smiled. "That's a good lad, such a good lad."

Setting her gently on the flagstone path, he gave her a lopsided grin. "Not at all, but I like it when you say so."

She giggled at their old game and patted his cheek. Little did she know how much he meant the words. Holding tight to his false smile, he walked her to the house and opened the door for her. "You get out of this cold now. I'll see to Mr. Ainsworth," he said.

Eyes widened, she stood straighter. "I'll get dinner on. I've got a nice apple pie waiting for after, so don't you be long."

His smile held until the door closed behind her. Shoulders squaring and spine straightening as much as it could under so much strain, Dylan turned from the house. He didn't bother to put the smile back on. Ainsworth would know it was fake, and the man wasn't worth the effort anyway. The best Dylan could hope for was to get this encounter over with as quickly as possible.

7

Deirdre

Butterflies erupted in Deirdre's stomach and tried to force her heart up her throat. Dusk painted the sign of the O'Leary Inn a lovely golden color. "I do wish I'd caught that stablehand's name," she breathed as she fussed with her hair.

Cat made a snorting sound. "I've no doubt you'll catch that and more soon."

From the back of the draft horse to Deirdre's right came an exasperated sound. "Oh, Deirdre, a stablehand? Must you pursue this silly idea of yours?" Sadie asked.

She swayed in the saddle as she rubbed her brow. Just in case, Deirdre steered her horse a little closer. Despite still being weak from heat exhaustion, her friend had insisted on riding with them. At least the borrowed wagon horse had a nice broad back that helped Sadie balance.

"Easy there. Don't fret on my account. You need only worry about building your strength back up."

Full, bright red lips turning upward, Sadie gripped the horse's dun mane tighter. "A good meal and a soft bed and I'll be right as rain, don't you worry none," she said.

"And a nice glass of wine," Cat piped in.

"Or a bottle," Deirdre said.

Her friends fixed her with wide-eyed looks.

"What? There's three of us, and two with Irish constitutions," she said.

"And fae at that," Sadie whispered with a wink.

They fell into fits of laughter that lasted until they rounded a bend in the road and the inn came into full view. Grin full of mischief, Cat flung the end of her long reins at Deirdre, tapping her legs with them to get her attention. "Out with it, then. What's this silly idea of yours?" she asked.

Tucking an escaped curl behind her ear, Deirdre fixed her friend with a serious look. "'Tis a sound deduction, not silliness in the least."

A snorting noise came from Sadie, but she held her tongue. For now. Deirdre knew if she didn't tell Cat, Sadie would.

"Seriously! As young women, we are molded and prepared to marry for station and wealth. We go through years of classes on how to be a good wife and please a man of means. I did my duty to my family, I married a boring, older, wealthy man of fae blood." Her gaze dashed to Cat. "A good man in many ways, but boring and judgmental nonetheless. Now 'tis time for me. I want to fall hopelessly in love with a man who cares more about me than he does his bank account or social standing."

"Here it comes," Sadie broke in.

Deirdre stuck her tongue out at her, causing Sadie to gasp, then giggle like a young lass.

"I want a selfless man who loves life, is adventurous, a bit wild in and out of the bedroom—"

"Deirdre!" Sadie cut in, her laughter taking all the admonishment out of her tone.

"Well, I do." Deirdre didn't miss a beat. "And I don't care

one lick if he's fae. And furthermore, I believe 'tis impossible to find all that in a man of wealth, least none that I've ever met. This time I don't have to marry for money, so I'm not going to," she finished with a firm nod.

Cat steered her big paint horse closer and leaned over. "I found a thoughtful, magnificent lover who turned out to be wealthy. Don't limit yourself," she said.

Sadie gasped and Deirdre exclaimed in Gaelic. "You must tell us all about him! And we want every sordid detail!" Deirdre demanded.

Every intention she had of teasing Cat slipped away as they rounded a bend and the property came into sight. Fields stretched to both sides of the road, cut by a finely built fence with a wrought iron gate across the road. Just beyond it lay a barn and a manor house past it. But that wasn't what drew Deirdre's attention, not at first, at least. Inside the fence and to the left, a giant sequoia stood in a field of bright yellow sunflowers. It had to be over two hundred feet tall with a trunk so wide it would take over a dozen people linking hands to reach around it. Even from this distance she could feel its energy. She'd seen several on the last leg of their journey, but to find one here felt...important somehow.

Then she saw him.

The shadows that cloaked the tall figure standing at the gate couldn't conceal his identity. That muscular frame and knot of hair at the base of his neck were as unmistakable as the confident way in which he held himself. Offering them a deep bow, he opened the gate as they approached. His gaze caught Deirdre's and didn't let go. A slight breeze tugged at shorter bits of his hair, sending raven locks flying across his eyes, and still he didn't break eye contact. Burgundy linen hugged his bulging arms while a black vest tailored to perfection framed his upper body. Only in the finest stables had she seen such a well-dressed stablehand.

"Miss Catriona, Mrs. Quinn, and guests, welcome to the O'Leary Inn," he said as he opened the gate wide. He nodded to the man driving the first wagon behind them. "You're welcome to pull straight into the barn. There's room at the back to park all three wagons side by side."

Deirdre smiled and nodded to him as she rode past.

"Ladies, the stalls on the right are ready for your horses. Take your pick."

"Thank you, Kinan. 'Tis most kind of you to receive us personally at such a late hour," Cat said.

He led the way into the barn, pausing to take a lantern off the wall and light it. "No trouble at all," he said.

Tingles worked through Deirdre. He had such a wonderful, deep voice.

Movement drew her attention to Cat who didn't hesitate to ride her horse straight into the stall. Many horses would balk at such a thing, particularly if their rider was even the slightest bit hesitant. But not Cat. Being able to talk to animals, she'd always been more comfortable around them than people.

Reining Ciaren in before the next stall, Deirdre marveled at her friend's newfound fearlessness. The way she'd spoken to Kinan with such ease and assuredness was a new thing. The Catriona that had left New York had closed up at the very sight of a man. Speaking to one was something she avoided at all costs. This was more like the old Cat, the woman she'd been before she'd married her late husband. It was a beautiful thing to behold.

Cat began to dismount on her own before Kinan got one step into her stall to assist. Polite words of refusal had him inclining his head and retreating.

Surprise welled up in Deirdre. Most men would insist on helping and refuse to leave, considering it their gentlemanly duty to take care of a woman. Perhaps she was imagining virtues merely to augment that handsome face and body, but she didn't think so. Even his most subtle characteristics held a depth and uniqueness that captivated her. Conveniently enough, her thoughts kept her distracted long enough that she remained in the saddle until Kinan stepped to her own stall door.

Unlike Cat, she didn't refuse him when he offered to help her down. She removed her leg from the sidesaddle bars, ensured her skirts were free, then placed her hands on Kinan's shoulders. As she slid down, he grasped her waist and eased her descent. The warmth of his big hands seeped right through her dress and corset. Guilt probably should have reared within her over enjoying the touch of a handsome man who wasn't courting her, but it didn't. She and guilt weren't often companions.

"I'm glad to see you found your friends, and glad you've made your way back," he said, leaning closer and nearly whispering the last. His breath brushed the side of her face like a caress.

She doubted he could see her blush in the dim light, which disappointed her some. She wanted him to know how he affected her. Looking up at him from beneath her long lashes, she said, "So, 'tis Kinan, then? My apologies for being in such a rush and not taking the time for proper introductions earlier. I regretted not catching your name." She allowed the breathlessness his nearness caused to reflect in her voice.

With him standing so close, she had to crane her neck back to meet his gaze. At nearly a head taller than her, he was a rarity in her experience. The warmth of his hands continued to scorch through her layers of clothing. She fervently wished the cloth would burn away so his skin could touch hers. If only...

"Apologies are not necessary. Reuniting with one's friends is far more important," he said, the last no less breathy than her own voice had been as he leaned closer.

Wonderful chills coursed through her, making her shiver. He leaned closer still. Teeth pulling a corner of her bottom lip into her mouth, she suppressed a sigh. Gaze fixed on that lip, he reached above her. She released the lip and started to close her eyes a touch. Danu help her, but if he tried to kiss her right here, right now, she'd let him. Not even knowing that her friends were in the next stalls over bothered her. The allure of this man was too strong. The closer he came, the harder her heart beat. All the while, he held her gaze. *Such boldness!*

His other arm rose above her as well. Was he going to press her right up against her horse? She wasn't sure what shocked her more, the fact that he might, or the fact that she would welcome it. Even her boldness—legendary among the widows—had never carried her to such a place. The thrill the encounter caused made her wonder why not.

Kinan's arms descended around her. As close as he was, she felt something restrained inside him, almost as if he hid it behind a wall. This only served to intrigue her more. Instead of drawing her close, he tucked something around her shoulders. She reached up and touched the edge of her shawl. Damn. She had forgotten it was draped over her saddle. Fingers trailing down her arms, Kinan stepped back.

"You looked as though you might be catching a chill," he said through a crooked smile.

She dipped her head. "That's very kind of you."

Not to be outdone, she stepped close, far closer than was acceptable, close enough that she could smell the lingering scent of soap and a wonderful, wild musk on his skin. His eyes widened as she reached up past his head. Deft fingers worked at buckles, and with a slip and tug, she came away with Ciaren's bridle. The surprised, and somewhat disappointed, look on Kinan's face made her laugh aloud.

"I think I shall enjoy getting to know you better, Kinan," she said softly enough for his ears only.

He stepped past her slowly, leaning down to whisper in her ear on his way. "And I you."

Air rushed out of the stall with him, leaving her well and truly chilled. Bumps rose all over her skin, traveling up to center around her breasts and turn her nipples so hard she gasped.

Wagons rolled by outside the stall as Deirdre gathered her composure while removing Ciaren's saddle. The moment she hung it over the stall door, Kinan swept past and picked it up. After the last wagon went by, she stepped out to look for a brush for her horse. The dim light of only two lanterns in the large barn revealed the door they had entered on one end, and the open space where the wagons had parked on the other. A moment later, Kinan emerged from a dark doorway midway down the barn. She started in that direction, figuring it likely led to the tack room.

Before she could ask, Cat stepped out of the stall beside her and swayed on her feet. Deirdre rushed to her side, reaching her a moment after Sadie did. When Sadie draped an arm over her shoulders the two began to sway together.

"Oh bollocks!" Deirdre cried as she grabbed one of each of their arms. "Steady there, lasses, I can't catch you both." With gentle redirection she leaned them against the stall fronts.

Sadie patted Cat's hand where it rested on her arm. "I'm supposed to be the one swooning," she said.

Both she and Deirdre looked to Cat. Most of the blood had drained from her face, leaving her typically pale skin nearly the color of porcelain. Her eyelids kept rising and falling as if she couldn't quite focus.

Sadie gripped Cat's hand. "Oh dear, Cat, are you all right?"

A smile came slowly to Cat's lips and she seemed to struggle with the effort to keep it there. "Quite so, 'tis just..."

The soft patter of someone jogging up the dirt aisle cut off her words. A tall shadow came between them and the light from the lantern near the barn door. "Miss Catriona, are you and your companions all right?" came Kinan's rich voice from right over Deirdre's shoulder.

Cat's weak smile grew bigger. "Aye, we're just a bit weary from the day's excitement is all."

He ducked between the two of them and offered each an elbow. "In that case, I shall escort you to your rooms straight away. You just leave the horses and wagons to our staff, we'll take good care of them," he said.

Cat looped an arm through his. "Thank you, Kinan. That's most kind."

Smiling, Sadie dipped her head, but didn't accept his arm. "Thank you, but I'll manage," she said in a voice that shook.

"I insist," Kinan pressed gently.

Eyes filling with surprise, Sadie slowly accepted his arm.

Too shocked for words, Deirdre could only smile as he started toward the door with her friends on each arm. It was one thing to be polite, but to treat the two women as equals was something that wasn't done even in the north. This man was something special. And it didn't hurt that he had a very nice posterior, which she watched as she followed.

On the way out of the barn, she paused to bid their escorts a good evening and thanked them for doing such a good job of getting her and Sadie safely to California. Two of the younger ones blushed at her praise and the others thanked her for keeping a dull trip eventful. Laughing, she waved off their compliments and expressed her good wishes for each of them. Though they would stay the night as well, she knew many would leave come morning and she'd likely never see them again. A touch of nostalgia washed over her at that. Dull they may have been, but they were loyal, good men, and she would miss them. Kinan waited while she and Sadie said their farewells. To the men's credit, they were just as gracious to Sadie. That could have a bit to do with her mothering them the entire trip. Their exchanges made Deirdre's eyes mist over.

When they finally stepped out into the dark, she was grateful for its concealment. She didn't want Kinan to see her cry for fear he would think her a woman who couldn't control her emotions. And the way he watched her from the corner of his eye made her very aware of the sting in her eyes. Dim light from the many windows of the house lit their way well enough across the grassy area between the house and barn.

The door opened before they arrived. An older woman with a graying bun atop her head and a crisp white apron around her thick waist offered them smiles and bid them welcome as they entered. In a sweet voice, she offered to take their wraps and told them she'd bring dinner straight up to their rooms so they could relax. So taken was Deirdre by the house, that she could only nod or shake her head in answer. It was a charming, Victorian-style home with polished wooden floors and an enormous foyer framed by a huge staircase that split in two directions at the top. Lace curtains hung over the windows. Lovely, plush furniture filled the nooks and crannies; chairs and couches in a sitting room to the left, a china cabinet along the wall to the right, and a slab of solid wood peeking from a corner of the kitchen. Such a home could almost make her forget it perched in the middle of nowhere out west.

A tapestry of a tropical location at night with a dark blue sky full of bright stars overhead and exotic people with feathered headdresses and elaborate masks captivated her. She halted her steps halfway up the first staircase. It was the strangest, most beautiful thing she'd ever seen. She could only begin to guess how long such a work of art, involving so many colors of thread, must have taken to complete. Enormous stones made up a pyramid that rose out of the jungle amid a few other stone buildings with carved statues all over them. The men in the tapestry wore nothing more than loincloths and masks, while the women's breasts and apex were covered only by animal skins or furs. The exotic, wild feel of the people thrilled her. Her hand went to her bosom, partly out of shock, and partly out of excitement.

A figure came into her peripheral vision on the stairs above her. Kinan, alone. Had she really been standing there long enough for him to escort her friends to their rooms and return?

"I usually have that taken down for guests or events, but

Miss Catriona said you ladies wouldn't mind. But I can take it down if it offends you," he said, voice softening at the last.

That allowed her to tear her eyes away to look at him as she shook her head. "No. Please don't take it down. 'Tis a captivating work of art."

His gaze dropped, and the slow smile that came to his lips almost seemed shy. He came down two steps to stand right behind her. The warmth of his nearness burned at her back as he leaned over her shoulder and pointed to a remarkable depiction of a massive lizard sitting on a leaf.

"A wonderful and generous description of it. See this iguana here? The tapestry is bursting with little details like this," he said, voice now filled with wonder. And was that pride? Such a thing made her wonder who had made the tapestry. Someone Kinan knew, perhaps? And that word, bursting, it made her heart speed up.

"An iguana, how fascinating," she said, rolling the strange word around on her tongue. She leaned in to get a closer look— and to get closer to his arm. "I could look at this for hours."

Again she smelled the scents of soap and something a touch wild. It made her realize how she must smell after such a journey. "Perhaps after I bathe," she added.

The warmth of Kinan withdrew. "Of course, how thoughtless of me, monopolizing your time when you're no doubt exhausted from your travels. Come, I shall take you to your room," he said as he offered her his elbow.

With a smile and a nod, she looped her arm through his and basked in that warmth once again. "Not thoughtless at all. I'd gladly stand here for hours while you showed me the wonders of this tapestry, but perhaps a bath, dinner, and a wee bit of sleep might be best first," she said.

An easy laugh spilled from him. So used to the calculated, fake chuckles of high-society men, this sound delighted her. This close, she realized his hair wasn't just pulled back, but wrapped around itself to disguise its true length. It looked like black silk, making her wonder how it would feel in her fingers. She had to look away as her mind pictured what the rest of her body would be doing while her fingers buried themselves in his hair. They came to the landing and turned toward the right set of stairs all too soon.

At the top of the short flight of stairs she spied a sitting room with plush couches, chairs, and a roaring fireplace before which Cat and Sadie reclined. To either side of the room, closed doors concealed what were no doubt their private rooms.

"There is but one bathing room, but I've put tubs in each of your rooms for your convenience. We'll begin bringing up warm water as soon as you're ready," Kinan said.

Deirdre's mind went to a wonderful place involving him and warm water. "That would be...transcendent," she said through a sigh.

The sparkle in Kinan's eyes made her think he might have a clue as to her thoughts. Just in case he had any doubts, she let him see the blush that heated her cheeks. His brows rose, as did one corner of his lips. Not a smidge of judgment or admonishment darkened his eyes. This intrigued her. Proper men of high society, even the ones who seemed like they might be a bit of fun, always looked down upon such unladylike flirtation. Such lack of judgment caressed her like a refreshing breeze. He stopped atop the second landing, a few feet before the arched opening to the sitting room.

"In that case, we'll begin heating the water straight away," he said. He withdrew his arm from hers with a slowness that made his reluctance obvious.

Feeling her friends' gazes heavy upon her, she stepped away and curtsied. "Thank you most kindly, sir."

His head dipped in a bow. "I bid you a good evening, ladies," he said, voice rising so Cat and Sadie could hear in the room beyond.

They each returned the sentiment. After a long last look at her, Kinan turned and started down the stairs. Deirdre watched his nicely shaped behind until it had descended out of her sight. The moment she could no longer see him, she spun away and marched into the room. Both women gave her knowing smiles. Sadie handed her a glass of wine the moment she sat on the couch beside her. Firelight danced along the red surface of the liquid. She inhaled as she lifted the glass to her lips. The scents of oak, cherries, and a touch of honey drifted to her. Possibly a bit sweet for her tastes, but more wonderful than anything she had drank for months.

One of Sadie's brows rose. "Cat tells me we have a handfasting to plan."

Deirdre lifted her glass high. "We do indeed. To Cat's handfasting!"

Cat and Sadie echoed the toast as they lifted their glasses to knock lightly against hers. The radiant smile on Cat's face made Deirdre smile all the more. This moment and these wonderful ladies deserved her full attention. She decided to put the matter of her own heart aside for now. Once they all lowered their wineglasses, she fixed Cat with a pointed look. "So, are we planning for a spring handfasting?"

Eyes shooting to the left, Cat picked up a large piece of yellow cheese from the table before them and began nibbling on it. Her long, red hair fell forward, but not quite far enough to hide the fact that she was blushing furiously. "Not exactly. Rick and I were thinking of a winter handfasting," she said.

Gaze fixed on the different cheeses, Sadie didn't see their friend's reaction. "So far away? Why the wait?" she asked.

To hide her grin, Deirdre took another sip of the sweet wine. When Cat didn't answer, Deirdre tapped Sadie's arm to make her look up. "She doesn't mean next winter, she means this December," Deirdre said.

Her heart thrilled at the reason why Cat would want to get married so soon. She had already admitted that she and Rick had made love, so it wasn't impatience to lie with him. That only left one thing…

"Cat, are you pregnant?" Deirdre asked when her friend still didn't respond.

"Deirdre Quinn! She most certainly isn't…" Sadie's words faded away as she watched their friend's reaction.

Face turning a lovely shade of crimson that matched her hair, Cat looked up with a start, eyes going wide. Surprise melted slowly into joy.

"You are!" Sadie lunged forward and embraced Cat at the same time Deirdre did.

They all laughed, hugged, and even shed a few tears.

"Truly, you're happy for me? You don't think me a ruined woman?" Cat asked, glancing from one to the other of them.

"Of course we're happy for you. After what happened with your first pregnancy, this is a blessing," Sadie said as she stroked Cat's hair.

A dark cloud passed over Cat's eyes. Deirdre took her hand. "She's right, the child is a blessing. We're thrilled you're pregnant. And you're not ruined at all. A man can stick his cock anywhere he pleases and they merely call it sowing his wild oats. It should be no different for a woman," she said with a roll of her eyes.

"Deirdre! While I might agree, at least whisper such a notion if you must state it!" Sadie begged.

Cat giggled, something she normally couldn't do after the mention of her deceased husband. Not because of his death, but because of what he had been in life. They hadn't thought she'd be able to get pregnant again, not after what Michael had done to her and her first unborn baby. The fact that Cat could recover so quickly after his mention spoke volumes about how she had moved on and about how good Rick was for her. Deirdre liked the man more by the moment.

She hated to press, but she had to be sure. "But Cat, that's not the only reason he proposed, is it? You deserve to be happy and to have a man that cherishes you. The last thing we want is for you to end up with someone like Michael again."

Perhaps it was a bit harsh to say so right after the big news, but Deirdre had to make sure. No matter what, she wouldn't let Cat make this decision for the wrong reasons. Michael had been a rash decision based on a pregnancy, and he had nearly destroyed Cat.

Though she sniffled, Cat straightened her back and held her head high. "Thank you for looking out for me, but no, we didn't find out about the baby until a few months after he proposed."

Joy mingled with the look of strength about her. It was a very good look for her.

"Good, because we're quite protective of you," Deirdre said.

Cat gripped Deirdre's and Sadie's hands tightly. "I know. Thank you. I'm very lucky to have you both. But Rick's a good man, nothing at all like Michael. I look forward to you getting to know him so you can see for yourself."

"As do we," Sadie said in a warm tone. But Deirdre knew it for the warning it was. If Sadie didn't approve of the man, he wouldn't last long. They'd gone through too much to get Cat back on her feet and confident again after Michael to see her with anyone less than perfect for her. "And don't think I didn't notice what he is. I picked up on his wolf energy the moment I laid eyes on him."

Leaning forward, Deirdre whispered, "As did I. What does that mean for the baby?"

After swallowing several times, Cat lifted her chin and answered. "It means they'll be strong and healthy, and beyond that, we'll figure it out."

Both of her friends nodded and made sounds of agreement.

"All right, out with the details then. We want to hear all about him, and don't you dare think you're getting away with not telling us all the saucy details!" Deirdre said with a wink.

Sadie gasped and held a hand to her chest, which only made Deirdre grin wider and Cat laugh harder. While Sadie pressed for details about the man's character, Deirdre pressed for details about their lovemaking and romance. Sadie and Deirdre finished off the bottle of wine—which tasted better by the glass—and suggested colors for the handfasting and baby names. Though it lay heavy at the back of her mind, Deirdre didn't bring up Ainsworth. There would be time aplenty to mull over that problem.

When Deirdre began to press her about sexual positions and how many times Cat had been with Rick, her friend shook her head. "Enough about me already. Deirdre here has her sights set on two men, and she hasn't been in town for even a day yet! There's much to discuss there."

Sadie fell back into the cushions. "Two, already? Oh Deirdre, what are we to do with you?" Rather than admonishing, her voice held a tone of envy.

Warmth filled Deirdre at the mention of the two handsome men she'd met today. That warmth spread down between her legs when she thought about how one of them was under this very roof with her. "I met Kinan on my way past here, then Dylan, a cowhand in Mr. Fergusson's employ. California is shaping up to be very promising. I want to hear everything you know about them both," she said, eyes narrowing upon Cat at the last.

Sadie waved a tiny square of cheddar back and forth. "Wait, Kinan is the man you mentioned before, the stablehand?" Her big brown eyes turned to Cat. "He doesn't look like any stablehand I've ever seen."

The grin dimpling Cat's cheeks drained away some of Deirdre's excitement. She didn't like that smile. It worried her. "That's because he isn't a stablehand," Cat said.

How forward he was with her despite the difference in their classes, how he spoke about the tapestry, and offered to have things done *for* her... She hadn't seen the truth because she hadn't wanted her simple stablehand to be more than what she imagined him to be. But part of her had suspected, had feared. And the look on Cat's face confirmed it before she put it to words.

"Kinan O'Leary owns the inn."

8

Deirdre

With a bit of spying and sneaking about, Deirdre managed to avoid Kinan all morning. Not that she didn't want to see him. She very much wanted to. To the point where she often caught herself fantasizing about what he might be wearing—or not wearing. But she couldn't. She didn't dare. If she let herself go down that path, it would end in oppression and boredom. No matter how handsome, high-society men couldn't help themselves. To remain high-society men, they had to be slaves to their fortunes and standing. While his status as an innkeeper alone didn't necessarily make him high society, from what Cat told her, the man came from a considerable amount of wealth on both sides of his family. And Deirdre had more than her fill of such things.

The wealth she'd inherited from not only her father, but her deceased husband—*Danu embrace their souls*—was enough for her to live out her days comfortably without having to worry about what high society thought of her. And more importantly, what they didn't know about her. Not marrying a fae man wasn't an issue. But marrying a man who was worried about his social standing meant she might have to hide what she was from him, and that was no way to live.

The fact that she had worn her finest blue dress with a silk and lace bodice only made her need to avoid Kinan all the more. She couldn't have him thinking she had worn it for him. A misunderstanding of that level would be difficult to remedy. *Misunderstanding, right.* She couldn't even convince herself of that. One glance at the desire in her eyes she couldn't hide, and he'd know she had worn it for him in a moment of weakness. But she wasn't feeling weak anymore.

Such was the thinking that had her bustling Sadie and Cat out of the house nearly at the crack of dawn with only half their breakfast eaten.

"But Deirdre, 'tis near to freezing out here still. Wouldn't you rather wait for afternoon to venture out?" Cat asked as she pulled her wrap tighter around her shoulders.

Rock crunched under the heels of their fine boots as they made their way across the circular path between the inn and the barn. Dawn dusted the horizon pink and made the dew on the grass and bushes sparkle. The fresh smell of damp earth warming in the sun invigorated Deirdre. She wished she had thought to go for a hack this morning through the fields with Ciaren. That would have got her out of the house quicker.

"I'm eager to get the word out about your engagement party. We haven't a moment to waste. And I'm also dying to see this new town of ours," Deirdre said.

"Are you warm enough, Cat?" Sadie asked, shooting Deirdre a reproachful look.

Cat took hold of Sadie's gloved hand. "Quite, no worries about me. I'm only trying to figure out Deirdre's plot."

Eyes widening, Deirdre blinked several times. "There's no plot. I'm merely eager to see our new town with my favorite witches, let them know we have arrived," she said, rolling the last word almost into a growl. They all giggled at the nickname they'd adopted in New York. The women of society had muttered it behind their hands and fans, thinking to shame and scare them. Instead, they'd leaned into it, embraced it. Perhaps a bit too much with the way some started to treat them. But they cared not.

One brow rising, Cat grabbed hold of one of Deirdre's hands. Even through the layers of knit cotton that hugged her own hand, and Cat's, she felt the woman's strong grip.

"Oh aye, I believe that. But I know you too well to believe there isn't more than that going on under all that black hair of yours," Cat said.

Free hand halfway raised to wave off the comment, Deirdre froze. Through the open door of the barn she spied Kinan bent over, a hoof of one of the dun-colored draft horses that was hitched to the wagon in his big hand. Though she could only see his backside, she knew it was him. The round shape of his buttocks in those brown breeches and the knot of hair at the base of his neck were unmistakable.

"Um hum, more indeed," Sadie said beneath her breath.

Steel rang as Kinan tapped a small hammer against the horse's shoe. He looked up, gaze gravitating to Deirdre, and smiled. Unable to stop herself, she smiled back. She forced herself to look away before she could encourage him any further.

"I hope you ladies are having a good morning," he said.

Deirdre couldn't focus well enough to form a sentence. Once again wearing a simple tunic and breeches, Kinan looked divine. Such clothes didn't layer and hide the enticing contours of his body like the fashions of high society did. Much about him seemed unconventional.

Perhaps... No. The pain of the last judgment she'd faced from a high-society man she thought had loved her still stung too much. Such men had circles of people to impress, business associates with expectations. The women in their lives came last, particularly when those women had earth-shattering secrets.

"We are, thank you. A good morning to you as well, Kinan. Is everything all right with the horses?" Cat asked, rescuing Deirdre from the silence.

Kinan's gaze broke from Deirdre's, allowing her to breathe once more. "Aye, well enough. While hitching them up my stablehand noticed this one's gait was a bit off. He has a loose shoe is all. I've fixed it up and it should hold well enough until the farrier comes tomorrow. Though I wouldn't recommend loping him," he said.

"Thank you for fixing him up. That's most kind of you," Cat said.

Walking around the front of the horses, Kinan watched the gelding with a scrutinizing eye. "You're welcome to use my team for the day if you'd like. We can get them switched out quickly enough," he offered.

The way Cat pursed her lips and cocked her head made Deirdre fear she was considering it. Any longer in this barn with Kinan would be bad for her resolve. Already, she couldn't stop thinking about how close he had stood to her in Ciaren's stall yesterday, and how she thought he'd been about to press up against her.

"That's quite all right. 'Tis best if we don't drive a strange team," Deirdre cut in quickly.

Hope filled Kinan's eyes as he looked to her again. "I understand. If you're able to wait until this afternoon, I'd be happy to take you ladies myself."

Oh, Dagda, I couldn't have botched that up worse if I'd tried. Invoking the God of the Earth wasn't going to help her now though. Her wide-eyed gaze shot to Cat. A slow blink of those green eyes communicated to Deirdre that she understood but didn't necessarily agree and certainly wasn't going to help. If she didn't get help, she didn't know how she was going to resist her attraction to this man.

"Thank you, Kinan, but I'm most eager to show my friends the town. Besides, we wouldn't want to pull you away from harvesting. I will keep a close eye on Patches here," Cat said.

For that Deirdre would most certainly hug her later.

Inclining his head to Cat, Kinan walked to the side of the wagon where Sadie stood and offered her his hand. The barest hint of a smile tugged at her lips as she accepted his help into the wagon.

"Thank you, Mr. O'Leary, that's quite kind of you," she said.

"You're most welcome, Mrs. MacMurphy," he said, holding her gaze and offering her a smile as he would an equal.

Hard as she tried not to be charmed by this man, Deirdre couldn't help but be impressed with his interactions with Sadie. Due to Sadie being of African descent, many men didn't notice her because she was too far out of their class to bother with. Or worse, they disagreed that the slaves should have been freed. Even up north some held such terrible beliefs, though they were few and far between. But Kinan appeared to not even notice

Sadie's skin was nearly as dark as his own hair.

Raw emotion burned across her face as Kinan turned to Deirdre too quickly for her to hide it. Someone treating her friends with respect meant the world to her. Yet it could be a ploy. Men had tried it in the past, though most were far more obvious about it. *Yes, that could be it.* They were out in the country with no one to witness Kinan's kindness. These justifications for his behavior helped Deirdre get her emotions under control. She fixed a stoic expression onto her face as she accepted his hand.

The rough skin of his fingers snagged at the yarn of her knit gloves. Most high-society men didn't have rough hands. A crack began to form in her resolve, only to be widened by the warmth that seeped from his skin into her glove. It could merely be from a hobby, not hard work. But she had seen him moving hay...

Bollocks!

Drawing her hand back as if his were afire, she mumbled a curt thank-you. His gaze sucked her in. The wagon felt insubstantial beneath her feet, so much so that she sat swiftly down on the bench next to Cat. Kinan held her gaze long after he stepped back. Curiosity, questions, and a bit of the pain of rejection swirled in that gaze. Unable to take its weight any longer, Deirdre used the excuse of getting a blanket out of the back to look away.

Focusing hard on the red-and-green plaid, she spread it over Cat and Sadie. "A Scottish quilt. Wherever did you get such a thing, Cat, and why?" Deirdre asked, happy to have a reason for further distraction from Kinan.

She took up the reins, gave a slight nod to Kinan, and started the team of horses forward with a click of her tongue.

"From Rick. He's half Scottish, didn't I tell you?" Cat asked in a poor attempt at an innocent tone.

"You most certainly did not!" Deirdre exclaimed in a voice loud enough to put extra energy into the horses' steps.

"Oh, Cat, a wild Scot? Are you sure that's wise?" Sadie asked.

Deirdre waved a hand. "Wisdom is overrated in matters of the heart. This is so exciting! We want to hear more about this wild Scot of yours."

As they pulled out of the barn she caught sight of Kinan grinning as if her comment pleased or amused him in some way. *Odd.* She shook the thought off, or tried, rather. The man clung to her mind.

"And you shall, I promise. But first, we need to talk about the eyes Kinan is making at you—and the fact you've been avoiding him all morning," Cat said.

Fearful he might have heard, Deirdre leaned out and peered around the side of the wagon. She might faint dead away if he had. Arms crossed over his chest, Kinan leaned against the open barn door, watching them pull away. How the man could make such a casual pose look so enticing was completely unfair. Even the way he rested one foot on the barn door was rakishly attractive. The casual air and relaxed manner that belied all proper behavior intoxicated her. Her cheeks grew hot as her gaze traveled up to his face to find him grinning. She was supposed to be acting uninterested. *Damn it all!* For that matter, she wasn't supposed to *be* interested. Someone grabbed ahold of her shoulder and pulled her back into her seat.

Sadie's judging stare pinned her to the back of the buckboard.

Eyes wide in an attempt to look innocent, Deirdre said, "I was making sure we were clear of the barn before turning the wagon." She promptly turned the team to support her words.

"Um hum. And you had to lean out so far you nearly fell from the wagon to do it?"

"Well, I couldn't see."

"Um hum. Like the flowers growing alongside it couldn't have told you."

Cat bumped Deirdre's shoulder. "Clearly, you're interested in the man, and he in you. You never know if he could be the true love you've been hoping for all your life, so why not encourage him and find out? He is handsome."

The road ahead captivated her, or so she made herself believe so she wouldn't look back at Kinan again. The packed dirt framed by wood fencing and shorn fields on both sides stretched toward the horizon, beckoning as if pulling her to the future. But all she wanted to do was go back to Kinan. Therein lay the problem: it would be going backward. *Wouldn't it?*

"Because he isn't right for me. Men of means care too much about societal expectations and appearances. And as you know, I have"—Deirdre paused, looking around, despite the fact that they were alone on the road—"a secret that high society would never accept if they knew."

Sadie laid a hand on hers. "Woman, you are a fool if you spurn the advances of that man. He's tall, handsome, fit as a fiddle, and kind to boot. And you don't know if he'll judge you like your husband did until you reveal all to him. I'm not saying tell him now, but if you explore a courtship with him and he seems to be the one, you could always tell him before an offer of marriage." Being fae wasn't the only secret she held close to her chest. And if one didn't send him running, the other most assuredly would.

When Deirdre remained silent for a long time, Sadie let out a snort. "And, child, the courtship alone could be worth it."

Mouth dropping open, Deirdre turned wide eyes to her friend. "Did you just snort at me?"

All three women erupted into a fit of giggles. The occasional snort from Sadie made the horses toss their heads and trot along on a tight rein, which only made the women laugh harder. The sound of that laughter melted Deirdre's troubles away. She had missed the sound, the feeling, more than she had admitted to herself. They could pester her about men all they wanted. It was worth it to be all together again.

When the laughter passed and they snuggled beneath the blanket sharing one another's warmth, Deirdre's mind turned to serious matters. The chill in the air served as a reminder that the year was swiftly getting away from them. The remnants of poppies withered along the roadside, their seeds dropped to the ground and wind. Fall would arrive shortly. At least that's what that meant in New York. Here, Deirdre wasn't so sure. The oak and ash trees had already begun to slumber, their consciousness just at the edge of her mind, almost out of reach.

"When does the first snow come here?" she asked, not wanting to wake the trees to ask.

Sadie pulled the blanket up a bit higher, as if the very question made the air chillier.

"Rick says it doesn't usually snow down here so close to the coast, but the hills and mountains start to turn white by November," Cat said.

"'Tis somewhat of a shame. I think I shall miss it a bit after the winters of New York," Deirdre said.

Sadie shook her bonnet-encased head—fur lined, at that. "Not me, not one iota," she said.

"But, in essence, that means we could build all the way through until the deadline," Cat said.

The news didn't encourage Deirdre. "Only if we can get the materials we need. Cat, you said Ainsworth has most people too scared to sell to us. Which means we need to get our materials by other methods," she mused aloud.

Lips pursed, Sadie nodded. "Is there anyone with timber on their land they might sell to us?" she asked.

Cat shook her head. "Sadly, no. Rick and I tried that. The only one is a gentleman up north, but the trees are juniper and his farm is two days away."

"Are juniper trees not adequate?" Sadie asked.

"No. While some are straight enough, the trunks are almost always twisted. They dull a saw in no time at all, and become even harder to cut once they're dead," Cat explained.

The mention of sawing trees made Deirdre cringe. It would be no easy thing for her, but she was practical enough to understand it had to be done. She remembered the short, twisted trees from Nevada. "And they're generally quite short, aren't they? Nothing tall enough for wall supports and trusses."

"Aye," Cat confirmed.

"What about any other nearby towns?" Sadie asked.

Again, Cat shook her head. "The closest one is two days' travel away, and they're on the coast with hardly a tree tall enough to speak of."

"Were it spring I could grow us tree houses," Deirdre said.

Sadie gasped. "And get us burned at the stake for such an

unexplainable peculiarity? No ma'am."

Discouraged, Deirdre let the conversation fall to a description of the shops in Goldenvale and the people who ran them. By the time they rolled into town, the warmth of the sun had begun to dry up the dew. The speed with which it had warmed up reminded her of the high desert of Nevada. On the other hand, the welcome moisture made it quite different. Fluffy gray clouds fleeing toward the brightening horizon suggested a beautiful, dry day was on the way. White clouds of smoke curled up from most of the chimneys, filling the air with the pleasant scent of hearth fires.

Many of the homes were grand Victorian-style architecture with long, fence-lined roads leading up to them. Still, the town managed to feel quaint in comparison to New York. Deirdre liked that. At the first crossroad, smaller homes gave way to merchant buildings proclaiming they sold all types of goods from crockery to candles. Many luxuries were available as well as necessities. Such a mixture meant there was plenty of money in the town.

"Where do the prominent ladies take their morning tea? We're going to need to get to know the locals to see who to invite to your engagement party," Deirdre asked.

The strangled look on Cat's face made Deirdre worry for a moment that her friend may have swallowed her tongue. "I don't think that's a good idea, Deirdre. People in this town are far too cautious of Ainsworth to associate with us. I'm perfectly happy with a small party of Rick's friends and family and my own. I don't need a big, fancy society wedding, just a proper handfasting," Cat said after a moment.

Pulling the reins to slow the horses, Deirdre fixed her with a look. "I understand, o' course, but people will expect a wedding, so 'tis best to hold one to keep the curious tongues from wagging."

Cat sighed. "I suppose you're right."

"And worry not, I only want to chat about our plans over the best tea in town. I have no intention of soliciting anyone to attend," she said.

"All right," Cat said, tone filled with suspicion. "Take the upcoming left, then the second right. Fran's Teahouse will be the third shop on the right. There's room for the carriage across the street."

Deirdre lifted her chin. "Oh, that's an unfortunate name."

"Deirdre!" Sadie exclaimed.

"What? I can't help but think of Fran the shrew from the Widows of the 69th, and how she used to heckle us all the time."

Groaning, Cat shivered. "Aye, she was terrible jealous of me marrying Michael, the fool."

"Fran is a fine name, and this Fran may be a nice, upstanding lady," Sadie argued.

Cat cast a thoughtful look at the road before them. "No, this one's a mean shrew, too."

She and Deirdre exchanged a knowing look and a nod. Maroon mittens going up in the air, Sadie groaned. "Danu help me now that we got the old Cat back. You two are going to run me ragged." She hugged Cat tight. "And it will be worth every moment."

An arm going around Cat, Deirdre hugged her from the other side. "I couldn't agree more."

"On which part?" Sadie asked through a smirk.

Laughter bubbled from Deirdre. "All of it!"

The clap of other hooves filled the street they turned down. Buildings of wood and occasionally brick rose up on both sides of the street. Many were two stories, with a balcony wrapped around the second story. Wagons and horses alike came and went on the street, their wheels and hooves stirring up the barest hint of dust. The damp left over from the dew helped, but it was clear in a few hours the sun would dry it. Already, the rays fell warm and heavy on Deirdre's face and shoulders. It wasn't enough to shrug off the blanket, but it would be soon. The morning chill lost more of its battle with each shadow the sun banished.

Without a single cue, the horses made their own way to a large lot and maneuvered the carriage into a spot amidst twelve other wagons. Well, without *traditional* cues. Power pulsed around Cat and a knotwork symbol of magic glowed on her forehead—her mark of power, visible only to her kind and those rare few humans sensitive to magic.

Deirdre quirked an eyebrow at her. "Someone's been honing their abilities," she said.

Glancing about furtively, Sadie stiffened. "Cat are sure there are no sensitives in these parts?"

An eyebrow raise was her only answer.

Sadie leaned close and whispered harshly, "What about this Ainsworth?"

Blowing air out between pursed lips, Cat waved a hand. "He doesn't come to this part of town. The man isn't exactly well liked."

A snort drew Deirdre's attention to the other carriages in the lot. Some had teams of fine thoroughbred carriage horses of brown, black, or white, while even more had half-drafts, Suffolks, and even a team of Clydesdales. All stood half asleep in their harnesses, scarcely lifting their heads as the women's wagon passed by. The half-draft team pulling Deirdre's wagon looked like lumbering chestnut-hued giants compared to the few thoroughbreds. Back in New York they'd be frowned upon, seen as working-class horses not fit to pull a lady's carriage. Yet the mixture of horses here made it clear this town held no such beliefs. Unless, of course, not all of these carriages belonged to ladies at the teahouse.

The social risk was unavoidable. Carriage horses would have been extra mouths to feed on the journey. Practicality had won out over fashion, and frankly, Deirdre didn't mind. She had grown fond of the half-draft team and wouldn't trade them in because of fashion. They settled in happily once she attached their grain bags to their halters, not giving her an ounce of trouble like her spirited team of thoroughbreds back in New York liked to do. But that could have been due to Cat's presence.

Adjusting her cloak, Deirdre offered an elbow to both Cat and Sadie. "Shall we, ladies?"

Cat smiled wide as she wrapped her arm through Deirdre's. "We shall."

At the road, they paused to wait for a cart to pass. The driver tipped his hat to them. His passenger—a strapping young boy in overalls—leaned out to watch them as the wagon passed. A gaze filled with appreciation traveled across Deirdre first, eventually making its way over to her friends. After a long moment, he seemed to remember his manners and tipped his hat. Cheeks reddening, he turned quickly back around.

Dry dirt ground beneath her boot heels as they started across the street.

"Does Ainsworth's influence truly reach everyone in this

town?" Deirdre asked, as they stepped onto the wooden sidewalk stretching along the front of the buildings.

A long, tired sigh eased from Cat. "Unfortunately, it does. I am afraid you will see by the end of the day."

Deirdre let the slightest smirk break through. "Well then, we shall just have to break that influence."

"That will be no easy task," Cat said.

"If it were easy, it would only be half as fun."

They remained arm in arm walking down the sidewalk, a united force to be reckoned with. Or at least that's how Deirdre like to think the passersby would see them. Few people traveled the sidewalk and only a few more rode through the streets. Each one of them looked their way, guarded gazes filled with curiosity. A few sneered in contempt when they looked Sadie's way, but only a few. Deirdre met each of their gazes with a smile and a nod, save for the latter. Those she pinned with a ferocious glare that had them looking anywhere but at her. Hostile or not, each person looked swiftly away, as if fearful of being noticed. Two of the men on the street only looked at her out of their peripheral vision while a third blushed and nodded to her in turn.

The last gave her hope. While it meant the odds certainly weren't in their favor, it was encouraging. In only a few feet, they came to an oak door with a bright blue sign hanging above it proclaiming it "Fran's Teahouse" in white. To each side of the door stood raised flower beds filled with coreopsis and chrysanthemum flowers. Some of the bright yellow blooms spread out wider than Deirdre's hand. The flowers leaned toward her as they approached, looking as if they swayed in a fall breeze. Sending them a touch of energy that would nourish them, she swallowed hard. That had been too close. She pulled her power in and locked it down. The excitement had gotten to her, and she'd slipped. It wouldn't happen again.

Deirdre released Cat's arm and opened the door wide for her and Sadie. She followed the women in and closed the door behind them. Tables topped with pristine white cloths set with lace doilies and crowned with dainty blue candles filled the room.

Out of at least two dozen tables, only three were unoccupied. Women of every age huddled around them chatting or sipping tea. Strong perfume of dozens of varieties tainted the delicious scent of tea that filled the air. Dresses of every color and fabric drew Deirdre's gaze here and there. Several of the latest styles were present, speaking of an interest in fashion despite the town's isolation. Over-teased hair and fine hats abounded.

Yes, this will be perfect.

One head turned their direction, then another, and another. Chin rising, Deirdre put on her best smile and looped her arm through Cat's again. She met the gazes that were bold enough to move across her. Each of them flitted away like skittish birds. These didn't appear to be mean, vindictive women. They were frightened.

A man young enough to still have a soft, babyish face breezed up to them from amid the tables. In his right hand he held a teapot, pinkie finger stuck out from the handle in a most delicate manner. His pressed black suit seemed to support a rigid posture most ladies worked years to achieve. It almost made Deirdre wonder if he hid a corset beneath those fine clothes. The thought brought a grin to her lips that the man readily returned. Unlike most, his eyes didn't stray to her bosom. His wasn't a look of flirtatious interest, but rather one of polite surprise—as if he hadn't expected her to smile honestly at him. From his vest pocket poked the top of a mother-of-pearl pocket watch.

"Good morning, ladies. Welcome to Fran's Teahouse. I am Francis, no relation to Fran, I'm afraid. Will it only be the three of you this morning?" he asked with a grin. He had the slightest French accent and a soft tone to his voice—one that got many a young man into a scuffle with those thinking lads shouldn't be so gentle.

Deirdre, on the other hand, believed the world could do with quite a bit more gentleness. "Thank you kindly, sir, just the three of us," Cat answered.

With the hand not carrying the teapot, he motioned to the table in the center of the room. "Right this way, if you please."

Cat's eyes went to the table in the corner and her mouth opened. Before she could say the inevitable, Deirdre patted the back of her hand. "That will be perfect," she said quickly.

Eyes narrowing beneath a pinched brow, Cat stiffened, but didn't resist as Deirdre led them through the tables. Thankfully, she didn't say anything, either.

In a show of impressive skill, Francis pulled each of their chairs out one-handed and scooted them in behind them without knocking the backs of their knees. The weight of every gaze in the room came to rest on them. Much of the chatter turned to whispers behind raised hands. Though Cat and Sadie squirmed and fidgeted, Deirdre grinned all the wider. This was exactly what they needed. Curiosity would always override fear. It was human nature. She would use that to her advantage.

"Thank you," she told Francis as he pushed her chair in. "My, that is an exquisite watch you have there."

He blushed ever so slightly and pulled it out for her to see. The colors shifted from pink to white as he moved it. "It was my mamma's. Not the most appropriate watch for a man to carry, I know, but she was ever so dear to me."

Oohing and aahing, Deirdre leaned closer. "'Tis absolutely lovely and the sentiment makes it that much more stunning."

Moisture shone in his eyes. He blinked it away. "Thank you ever so much."

He took a blue handkerchief from his pocket and dabbed at the corners of his eyes. After a long breath, his smile returned even bigger and brighter. As he turned over three of the china teacups on the table and filled them, he chatted about the cookies, biscuits, and pastries they had available. He had a friendly, open manner that Deirdre found refreshing. She remarked upon the familiarity of his accent and found out his family had emigrated from Paris when he was a baby. He took their orders and whisked away with a promise to return quickly.

The shocked look Cat gave her made her chuckle. "What?" she asked.

"You are such a charmer. I don't know how you do it."

Acutely aware of the eyes and ears on them, she let her voice rise a touch louder than table conversation—but only a touch. "Curiosity. People fascinate me. I love meeting new people and learning about them," she said.

"Aye, but you're better at it than anyone I've ever met," Cat said.

"That's our Deirdre," Sadie said.

Both Sadie's soft tone and the way she kept her eyes on her teacup, as if something in it fascinated her, bothered Deirdre. The subdued mannerisms and rigid posture told her volumes about her friend's discomfort. Sadly, it was a reaction she had seen all too often in Sadie due to the scrutiny of high society in regards to her and Cat keeping company with her. Though she had not seen it for some time. It had taken her and Cat years to get the ladies of New York to begrudgingly accept her among their numbers. To see her go through anything remotely like that again, after all that time and struggle, lit the flames of fury in her.

Acutely aware of the weight of nearly all the eyes in the room, Deirdre all but announced, "So, Catriona, have you thought about the colors for your wedding? We will need to know for the upcoming engagement party."

Several heads turned in their direction just enough to hear better, but Deirdre pretended not to notice.

A grin broke across Cat's face. "Since 'tis so close to the holiday, I was thinking of emerald and white. Sadly, I don't know of anyone in town able to take on such a task on such short notice."

Taking the bait she knew her friend was laying, Deirdre piped up. "That is quite all right, I have just the person in mind."

One of Cat's brows pulled down. "You've only just arrived. Who could you possibly have in mind already?" Her tone of surprise was badly faked, but Deirdre didn't think the teahouse women leaning in close to hear would care even if they did notice.

Though Deirdre leaned forward, she kept her voice loud enough for other tables to hear easily. "Only the most sought-after designer in all of New York, Mrs. Sadie MacMurphy." Deirdre indicated Sadie with a sweep of her hand.

It was difficult to tell if Sadie blushed under her dark skin, but her wide eyes suggested she did. "Oh well…um…I'd be honored, of course, but I do not know that—"

Deirdre laid a hand on her arm. "Do not be modest now, dear. 'Tis true after all. Cat deserves the very best. We need none other than a master dressmaker like yourself working on this project. All of New York will be watching, and Constance is eagerly awaiting the wire all about it so she can print the story in the Times." Deirdre held her hands up and spread them out wide. "'Head of the Widows of the 69th Weds California Gold Miner.' They will be talking about it for years!"

Cat put a hand atop Sadie's and gave her a genuine smile, free of any theatrics. "O' course, you must make my dress. I'd trust it to none other. Your work is truly exquisite."

Tears brightened Sadie's eyes. "I would be honored."

Deirdre clapped her hands then placed an arm around each woman's back. "Perfect. It will be sensational. You must do the bridesmaid dresses as well, please!" she said.

"I will, of course," Sadie said through a large smile.

Their host returned as they began discussing necklines and bodice materials. His eyes widened with interest and he leaned closer when he set their biscuits and pastries before them. "You're planning a party, how wonderful! What's the occasion?" he asked.

A euphoric look came over Cat and Deirdre knew she would be too choked up to answer the young man. Indicating Cat with a flourish of her hand, Deirdre answered for her. "Catriona O'Brian and Patrick Fergusson's much-belated engagement party, and subsequent wedding a few months thereafter."

The man gasped. "Congratulations! I'm honored to serve the woman who was able to tame Mr. Fergusson's wild heart. When is the big day?" The way he said Rick's last name spoke of his admiration for the man.

Knowing she had found her first ally, Deirdre grinned. Cat, on the other hand, blushed hot enough to set kindling aflame.

Thank mother Danu that isn't her power!

She cleared her throat and her features pinched together in that badly affected casual look that meant she was about to lie. "Well, we've actually been engaged for several months, so we're planning a mid-December wedding."

"How wonderful!" Francis exclaimed. "And when will the engagement party be?"

Put on the spot, Deirdre had to think fast. Though inside she wanted to swallow her tongue, she retained an outer air of confidence. Tomorrow was the first of September, which left only a little over three months plan a wedding and far less to plan the engagement party. "Mid-October," she said.

They'd have to work on building their homes during that time as well. But that could work to their advantage. If this Ainsworth believed they were focused on only the engagement party and wedding, he might not put so many obstacles in their way. She'd have to be sneaky about it, but that had never been a problem for her before.

"How wonderful! That will put the engagement party around La Toussaint—Samhain!" their host said, whispering the last part.

"Yes," Deirdre said. "We're still putting together the guest list, of course, but I have to wire it to New York by the middle of September, as they'll want it for the newspaper article," Deirdre said, voice hushed just enough to make the ladies at the far tables lean closer to hear. Every one of them did so. Whispers went up throughout the room.

Their server's eyes widened. "Well, what of Mr. Ainsworth? He's one of the most prominent men in town and he'll certainly be wanting an invite," he said, rolling his eyes at the last.

Deirdre found she liked this young man quite a bit. "Absolutely. I'm most eager to meet him, and the engagement party wouldn't be complete without him," she said.

A cacophony of wood scraping against wood filled the room as women pushed their chairs back and rose. All of a sudden, they surrounded the table, a flurry of busybodies offering congratulations and vying for either Cat's or Deirdre's attention. Calling cards began to pile up on the table. They all but ignored Sadie, no doubt thinking her little more than a servant. None were rude, exactly, at least not by societal standards. The very fact they thought of one of her closest friends as no more than hired help due to the hue of her skin rankled Deirdre to no end. Would this world never advance beyond the Dark Age? They had just fought and won a war in an attempt to change such things.

At every opening, Deirdre seized the opportunity to introduce Sadie—as did Cat—making it clear to the women she was their friend, not their servant. Most of the women took it in stride. The few who brushed off the introduction became ingrained in Deirdre's memory. Each time it happened, she and Cat exchanged a hard look. If those women were lucky enough to receive invitations, they'd be seated in a dark corner or near a drafty door.

Questions poured in, which either she or Cat answered.

"A holiday wedding, how wonderful!"

"My sister's shop has the most exquisite fabric."

"The Widows of the 69th, oh, we've heard so much about your organization!"

"I know just the place to get your lace."

"How did you meet?"

By the time the women all found their way back to their own tables, they had offers for services of nearly every type they needed. Everything party-related, that was. Not one person had referred them to anyone who would sell them anything remotely close to building materials. But it was a start. The smile on Cat's face as she gathered up the cards made it all worth it. The only problem was, now they had to invite Ainsworth.

9

Deirdre

Early September

Wrapped in her warmest shawl, Deirdre gazed out across the frosty field as she sipped her morning tea. The sun's rays made the tree-covered hills in the distance sparkle. Fir trees huddled on the horizon, their feathery boughs connecting to make them look like an impenetrable sea of green. What they needed to build their homes and winery wouldn't even make a dent. But every single tree was untouchable because they grew on Ainsworth's land.

Part of her was glad for it. The very thought of cutting down trees made her ill. The act would cause her physical pain because she could feel what they felt. Homesteading wasn't for the faint of heart, and that was for those without such a deep connection to plants. Yet she begrudgingly understood it had to be done. While she could convince the trees to grow into a suitable dwelling and feed them the energy to do so in only a matter of months, it would do more than lift a lot of eyebrows. It would raise suspicion that she and her friends were not as they seemed. Though they embraced the title of witches, they did so secretly, only among those they trusted with their lives. They didn't want fearful townsfolk thinking of them in that manner. That would complicate matters even further.

So they would have to do build their homes the 'normal' way. She would of course work to restore the balance and then some by planting at least one tree for every one they used to build their structures. Sometimes civilized society seemed anything but.

She shifted on the porch bench, pulling her shawl closed against the chill. The locals kept going on and on about how unusual the cold was for these parts. To her, it only felt familiar. New York winters started like this, chilly and then striking with a vengeance. If any chance existed of a winter even remotely like that here, they had less time than she hoped. Their good fortune at the teahouse the other day had not continued in their search for merchants. Each shop they visited refused to sell them anything close to building materials. They couldn't purchase so much as a bag of nails. The cold moving in more each day only deepened Deirdre's sense of urgency. It was as though the very weather itself conspired with Ainsworth.

The last sip of her lukewarm tea slid down her throat with a velvety heat that turned her thoughts toward Kinan. Every now and then she caught a glimpse of him as he moved about the barn. Over the last few days, she had learned he insisted on caring for his own livestock, despite possessing the financial means to hire someone to do it. He also worked in his own fields and garden. It perplexed her. Never had she seen a wealthy man muck out stalls or get his hands in the dirt. The sight was something to behold.

The sleeves of his fine blue linen shirt strained against his flexing arms. He had rolled the material up above his elbows, which showed a generous amount of his tanned skin. Each time he bent over, his breeches hugged his nicely shaped posterior so closely she didn't think he had drawers on underneath. Or rather, she hoped he didn't. No, she couldn't allow her thoughts to turn that way. The man was all wrong for her.

Movement on the road caught her attention. A plain brown horse she didn't recognize approached the gate. The rider was wrapped in a long, heavy coat with a fur cap pulled tight over their head. Kinan looked up from cleaning the outdoor paddock that bordered the road. Grinning and waving, he strode to the gate.

Deirdre rose from the bench and walked over to the railing. She set her teacup on the table beside the bench. Leaning against the railing, she strained to hear what Kinan and the person were saying. The honeysuckle vine twitched beside her elbow.

No, no. Sleep, dear one, Deirdre soothed.

One more twitch and it went still.

She desperately needed to take some time to ground and center. This new land had her power charged up like never before.

The USPS stitching on the rider's saddlebags doused her curiosity. The man handed Kinan an envelope, then trotted his horse briskly away. With a harsh exclamation she couldn't make out, Kinan thrust the pitchfork he held into the half-frozen ground as if it were butter. The show of strength thrilled her more than the anger concerned her. From what she had seen of him, Kinan was not a man prone to anger, so he likely had good reason. Renewed curiosity carried her to the steps as he approached the porch.

Thick lashes brushed his cheeks as he blinked long and slow. He blew out a breath, unlocking the muscles of his tense jaw. Even irritated, the man made her breath catch. "My apologies if you overheard any of that. Such talk is ungentlemanly."

She loved that he didn't say it wasn't suited for a lady's ears, but instead reprimanded himself for the conduct. The man made it exceedingly difficult to stay uninterested in him, even when he was so clearly out of sorts—or perhaps because he was out of sorts. His constant proper behavior was part of what made her cautious of him. Through his dark tan it was impossible to tell, but it appeared his face was so flushed it would be hot to the touch. Such thoughts drove away the morning chill in a dizzying rush. She looked down, head dipping to feign a demure demeanor she did not feel.

"There is no need to apologize," she said.

Chest giving one last heave, he ascended the final step and straightened, facing her. Deirdre's gaze traveled up slowly from his dirty boots to the gaping neck of his half-opened shirt, enjoying every inch of the journey. The barest hint of his defined chest was visible. Her stomach fluttered.

"It is with the deepest regret—and aggravation—that I be the bearer of this offense," he said as he handed her the envelope.

It took a few blinks before she could shift her focus from his chest to the envelope. She had completely forgotten about it. In the upper left-hand corner of the simple white parchment, an elaborate "A" had been scrawled. Anger started a slow burn deep in her chest. She tore into it with complete disregard for the preservation of the envelope. Inside nestled a single item: her calling card.

Two days ago, she had sent it to Ainsworth in the hopes of gaining an audience with him and discussing matters like adults. To return one's card in such a manner was a refusal to allow them to call upon you that bordered on offensive.

A wordless cry of frustration forced its way through her clenched teeth.

Kinan glared at the remnants of the envelope on the porch floor. "He is deplorable and uncouth to treat you this way, Mrs. Quinn," he said in a clipped tone.

Baring her teeth, Deirdre balled her hand into a fist, crumpling the letter within. "Deplorable indeed. To not even speak to me like a civilized person makes me believe perhaps he does not possess a civilized bone in his body," she huffed.

Kinan confirmed, "He does not."

She pressed her lips tight against the expletives that tried to fly from her mouth. Kinan being the gentleman that he was, she had to be smart about this. He seemed the type to go so far as to challenge the man to a boxing match to defend her honor. Romantic as that notion was, it was equally foolish. Men clinging to such ways often tended to be foolish, she reminded herself. Worse than even that was how the wilting daisies growing along the edge of the deck perked up and leaned her direction. A long breath helped calm the spike of anxiety over seeing the flowers move and tamp down her anger.

"Thank you for delivering the message, Mr. O'Leary, but I fear I need to be alone with my thoughts for a moment," she said with a gentle smile that she hoped hid the depth of her anger.

Eyes going soft with understanding, Kinan nodded. "Of course." He took a step toward the door. "If you need anything, anything at all, please do not hesitate to call on me." The sincere words and concern in his tone warmed her, but not as much as her anger. She nodded slowly and kept her gaze cast to the porch. If she looked up into those lovely brown eyes of his, she would lose her resolve.

Soft footsteps retreated. The door latch clicked open as he turned the knob. Not until the door closed behind him with a soft thud did she finally look up. A quick glance around confirmed she was alone on the porch. Before Kinan had a chance to tell anyone about the letter, she gathered up her skirts and dashed down the stairs. Not that he would, but she wasn't about to take the chance and give anyone the opportunity to stop her. Ground softened by the morning's heavy dew squelched beneath her boots, tugging at them just enough to suggest the beginnings of mud. Overhead, a cloudy sky threatened to make matters worse. But she wouldn't let that stop her either. Lifting her skirts higher, she strode to the barn at a brisk pace.

At the first clop of her boot on the dry, hard-packed barn floor, a whinny greeted her.

"Hope you're done with your breakfast, lass," she said when Ciaren poked her big, black head over the wall of her stall.

The mare bobbed her nose up and down as if in answer, but Deirdre knew it for the eager energy it truly was. Not wasting a moment with niceties, she marched right past and fetched her saddle and bridle from the tack room. Forgoing even the usual brushing, she tossed the saddle pad and saddle on and cinched it into place. She led the horse into the aisle to a mounting block that stood to one side and climbed onto the saddle. Tying her shawl closed, she prayed the wind wouldn't be too cold. If she went back for a cloak or gloves, someone would catch her and either try to stop her, or go with her. She wasn't going to risk that.

She let out the reins and tapped Ciaren's side with her heel. The mare leaped into an animated trot that forced Deirdre to post or else bounce like a sprite in a wind storm. Posting sidesaddle was no easy task, but like any repressed woman of the times, she was quite good at it. As they trotted across the drive, she glanced around the grounds. No one stirred save for the horses in the paddocks and pasture. Their whinnies as they bid Ciaren farewell were the only sounds to break the still morning. One stallion in particular, a big white creature with an arched neck and long hair about his hooves, loped up and down the fence line in an animated manner, his knees coming up high. For a moment, his beauty stunned her. She had only ever seen his like in books. A Spanish breed, if she wasn't mistaken.

To ensure the stallion didn't try to leap the fence and follow, Deirdre kept Ciaren at a slow trot. With a little trickle of her energy, the dormant grass in his paddock sprouted, sending up bright green shoots. The stallion's nostrils flared. He stopped and turned back to the fresh grass. Thankfully, she made it past the paddock and the house before anyone came out. If Kinan went to wake Cat or Sadie, it would be some time before they could get presentable enough to chase her. Poor Cat was likely hanging over a chamber pot, at the mercy of morning sickness, and Sadie had been sleeping in late to recover from their long trip.

Around the back of the house, Deirdre came across a freshly plowed field. The moment she let out the reins, Ciaren leaped into a canter. Her horse couldn't resist the smoothness of a plowed field any more than she could. Despite the cold, she smiled and leaned into the breeze. Soon, the inn faded away into the distance. She breathed easier. For the sake of endurance, she reined Ciaren back into a slow lope.

From speaking with the townsfolk, she had discovered the location of Ainsworth's home. A few discreet questions had given her a good idea of how to reach it. Unfortunately, it lay nearly half a day's travel away. The chill in the air worried her some, but it was morning. As the sun rose higher, it would warm up. This was California, not New York. Everyone's warnings about the climate of Northern California being a world different from that of Southern California reared in her memory, trying to warn her. But she brushed such negative thoughts away. California cold had nothing on New York's. She would be fine. Just for good measure, she slowed Ciaren to a trot that stirred up less of a breeze.

She rode along the rock wall that separated Kinan's property from the widows'. In places, the moss-covered rocks stood only a foot high, but for the most part they had been stacked to four feet or higher. The sight reminded Deirdre of her grandfather's stories about Ireland's rocky soil. Though the memory made her smile, it also brought a pang of loss. The years had not diminished the pain.

Her grandfather had given up their plantation in North Carolina for love. When Deirdre married, her husband promptly sold her grandfather's new home in Cold Spring and moved her to the city. He claimed their kind needed to get with the times and be where the action was happening, or risk being left behind in the old world to fade away to nothing more than legends and myths. Never mind that they already were because their race was a carefully guarded secret. His ambitions had led him into war not for the nobility of the cause, but for the honor and acclaim it would bring him. Ironically, he had only found his death there.

The widows' land would be her new family legacy, one that she wouldn't let anyone take from her or her friends. While they could purchase another plot of land, it was about more than that. Cat deserved this. Not another piece of land, but this one. The one that blaggard deserter of a husband of hers had planned to escape to with his southern mistress.

The widows would make this place theirs. Deirdre wouldn't allow anyone to stand in their way.

After a while the wind developed a bite to it that left her cheeks and hands stinging. It didn't worry her overmuch, at least not for the first hour. The soft plod of Ciaren's hooves had turned to a solid clip-clop, indicating at least partially frozen ground. Overhead, a thick, gray sky prevented the sun's rays from breaking through. Looking back, Deirdre realized they'd been going uphill, probably for at least the last half hour, considering how far they'd come. The inn was nowhere in sight. She also realized she had stopped shivering, not because it had grown any warmer, but because she had grown numb.

A bad sign, but she didn't want to turn back now. She looked over her shoulder. Far below, the valley stretched out in a patchwork of plowed and cut fields, some fenced, some enclosed by low rock walls, others only hedged in by a different type of field. Toward the horizon, a sliver of dark blue met the gray, cloud-choked sky. *The ocean!* She had no idea she'd ridden far enough up to see it. It was little wonder the temperature had dropped so much.

Numb fingers struggled to close her shawl tighter around her neck. Leaving without so much as a pair of gloves—what would her mother have thought? The square-neck dress she wore sat low enough to expose just a touch of her cleavage, which allowed cold air to flow straight down between her breasts.

Pine trees blanketed the hill less than a hundred feet ahead. A dirt road wound its way into them, disappearing into the shadows they cast. The feathery boughs of green wore a heavy layer of frost, and that was in the full light of day. Down in that darkness it would be much colder. But she had little choice. According to the information she had gleaned, Ainsworth's home was up that very road. She was over halfway there. Another hour and a half was nothing compared to crossing America. She could do this.

Hunkering down into her shawl, she guided Ciaren into the trees. The mare's hide twitched at the touch of the shadows. Or was it something else? Her mother would say brownies danced along her back with their sharp, little boots. But Deirdre hadn't seen a brownie since she left her parents' home years ago back in New York. Ears flicking back and forth at every sound, Ciaren dropped to a reluctant walk. The press of Deirdre's boot heels was barely enough to keep the mare moving forward. In the interest of allowing both of their eyes to adjust to the dimmer light, she allowed her to keep a slow pace. The tweet of a bird made Ciaren drop a few inches into a crouch that prepared her to launch into a run should she deem the situation dangerous. She whipped her head in the direction of the sound.

"Easy, lass, easy," she soothed, petting the mare's neck as she spoke.

Fear tried to rise, but she squashed it. Ciaren was a bit of a flighty, high-spirited thing, that was all. Likely nothing more nefarious than a few winter birds lay in wait. A twig cracked off to their right. Ciaren reared up—only a little, but it was enough.

The reins slipped through Deirdre's numb fingers. With nothing to hold on to, she started to fall backward. Legs clenching even tighter, she managed to stay on, but Ciaren lunged to the side and Deirdre began to tumble from the saddle. The pine needle–strewn ground rushed toward her.

Rather than end up in the forest duff, though, she collided with a warm body. Arms wrapped around her back and beneath her legs, cradling her in a catch that was almost perfect. The breath was knocked out of her so abruptly she didn't even have time to cry out. Pale blue eyes gazed down at her fondly from behind a fringe of hair the color of wheat. She recognized those eyes, and the handsome face they gazed out of. A smile came slowly, almost languidly, to the man's lips.

When she could finally draw breath into her lungs again, she asked, "Dylan O'Toole?"

"Aye, in the flesh."

The chiseled chest pressed to her side felt real enough. But he didn't put her down, and that seemed like a dream. The beginnings of a rather naughty one, the kind she wouldn't want to wake up from, but a dream nonetheless.

"But what are you doing way out here?"

"Hunting a cougar, which is why you shouldn't be out here."

After a long enough moment that it began to feel awkward, he set her on her feet. His words finally sank in. One hand flew over her pounding heart and she spun away. Ciaren's dark tail arced into the air in the distance as the mare cantered off the way they had come.

"Ciaren!" she called, though she knew it would be useless until the mare calmed. Some days she wished with all her heart for Cat's power to speak to animals.

Cold swept around her in the absence of Dylan's arms. She reached up for her shawl, but it was gone. Movement behind her made her turn back around. Visions of jungle cats with huge teeth gleaming in their gaping jaws filled her imagination. But it was only Dylan bending to pick up her shawl. He shook it off, then started to pluck pine needles out of the tightly knitted lavender-hued material. Pleasant as Dylan was to look at in his snug breeches and wool jacket, she couldn't stop her gaze from darting about in search of a cougar. She smiled to hide the fear that choked her.

The life energy of the towering trees stirred.

No, no. Sleep. 'Tis all right, she soothed them. If they woke in this cold, they could harm themselves. She wouldn't risk their lives for hers. Besides, she had a strapping young man at her disposal.

With a lift of his chin, Dylan indicated the brown stallion standing not far behind him. "We'll fetch her together," he said.

Glancing around the shadowy forest, wondering what might lurk behind each tree, she really didn't want to be alone. Something had made Ciaren run off, after all. What if it hadn't been just Dylan's approach? If it had been the cougar, her horse was in danger.

"Thank you. I would appreciate that."

Dylan gave her shawl a final shake, then stepped in front of her. All thoughts of cougars and fangs faded as he leaned close enough for her to feel the heat of his body. Until that moment, she hadn't realized how cold she was. Heat radiated out from his arms when he lifted them up to either side of her. He wrapped her shawl tight around her, gloved hands coming to rest on her arms.

His eyes widened. "Mrs. Quinn, you are so chilled I can feel it clean through the layers between us." Phrased in such a manner, the words sounded wonderfully intimate, but not nearly as intimate or wonderful as the heat of his hands.

"Why on earth would you leave the house in such weather without your gloves and cape?" he asked, voice thick with concern. Was that a hint of judgment? She wasn't sure. Irritation reared within her.

He began to rub her arms vigorously. The impropriety nearly made her protest, but the warmth it caused made her abandon such misgivings. "I am from New York, Mr. O'Toole. I had not imagined a California winter could begin to compare, particularly one without snow." As her body began to warm up, she started to shiver.

"Well, we're having unseasonably cold weather already, and this is Northern California, not the warm Southern California they tell you all about in the papers. It gets quite cold here, quite fast."

Through chattering teeth, she said, "Aye, I'm starting to realize that." She didn't have the energy or ability to enunciate and speak the Queen's proper English. Hopefully her da—Danu embrace his soul—would forgive her. The amount of coin he put into finishing school so she may be welcomed by proper society had been extravagant. But her face was so cold it was hard to get even those few words out.

Putting an arm around her, Dylan pulled her in close against his side. How he could be so warm in such frigid weather, she could not fathom, but she was ever so grateful for it. She snuggled in against him with a sigh. He led her to his horse, allowing her to lean on him so much he nearly carried her.

"We'd best get you back to the inn before the weather gets any worse."

Good as that sounded, she stopped walking. The pressure of his arm tried to urge her forward, but she resisted. "No. I have to get to Mr. Ainsworth's ranch."

Dylan drew away just enough to look her in the eyes. "Why on earth would you want to do that?"

She lifted her chin. "To try and talk some sense into the man."

A grunt issued from Dylan. "'Tis impossible, I'm afraid."

"That may be, but I must try."

After a long, hard stare at her, he nodded. "All right, then. I'm not one to deny a lass something she has set her mind to. But shall we find your horse first? She's a mighty fine mare and I'd hate to have her come across that cougar."

Her throat became tight and her heart thudded harder. She stepped to Dylan's horse and grabbed the saddle horn. "Aye, please." The possibility of something happening to Ciaren after the mare had made the long trek from New York was unacceptable. Particularly if it were due to her own stubbornness.

Rather than offer her his hands, as she expected, Dylan gripped her by the waist and lifted her up. She swept her dress beneath her and straddled the horse like a man. Even with the dress all bundled between her legs, it was much more comfortable and secure.

He led the stallion over to a fallen log and used it to help him climb up behind her. The flare of the back of the saddle kept him far enough away that none of his body touched hers, not even his legs. She longed not for his touch, but his body heat.

Thankfully, enough radiated from him that she felt it against her back. When he reached his arms around her and took up the reins, she leaned into him with a sigh.

"Forgive me, but you're so warm," she said.

Dylan chuckled. "I was about to ask your forgiveness for being so forward as to wrap me arms around you."

He didn't draw back, and for that she was grateful. "I think in this situation we can both forgive such forwardness."

"I'm glad you agree, because you're absolutely freezing. Ainsworth isn't worth freezing to death over, that's for sure," he said as he spurred his horse forward.

Rather than hold on, she trusted Dylan, and tucked her freezing hands into her armpits. "You've no love for Ainsworth, then?" she asked.

"O' course not. He's a bloody bastard who terrorizes this town."

"And yet you're hunting down a cougar for him?"

Dylan's body remained relaxed. "'Tis wise to keep one's friends close, and one's enemies closer. Besides, a cougar's territory covers hundreds of miles. One that threatens Ainsworth's cattle will soon threaten Fergusson's."

From what she'd read of cougars, his words rang true. Guilt stabbed her over having doubted his motives. But her nature was ever cautious and she couldn't help that, nor did she want to. It was hard enough for a widowed woman to survive in this man's world, let alone one of fae blood. She had to look out for herself and her friends. "True enough, I apologize for asking. I did not mean to offend."

"No apology necessary. I just get…passionate about the English terrorizing our kind."

While his brows rose and his eyes suggested things at the use of the word "passionate," he sounded distracted. "You sound like a man who has suffered directly at the hands of the English."

He stiffened behind her. "Aye, as have all Irishmen. Irish American's included," he said in a tone as cold as her numb cheeks.

"Sadly, quite true," she agreed, happy to have derailed him, but a bit guilty over how much it had clearly upset him.

She wanted to ask him more, but his clipped tone made her fear he wouldn't tell her. No sense in pushing things and upsetting the man. He snuggled closer, his arms tightening around her. The warmth of his body seeping into hers kept her from pulling away. They rode in silence for a while, speaking only to discuss direction now and then. Though the chill in the shade of the forest deepened, Deirdre stayed warm enough cozied up to Dylan's hard body.

After a while, Dylan asked, "Have you considered offering to sell Ainsworth your land instead of risk him forcing you off it?"

"No," Deirdre snapped, the idea angering her too much to say more.

"Now, I'm not saying sell it all to him. Maybe just a small bit along the river would get him off your back."

Her jaw clenched so tight she couldn't have answered if she wanted to. She leaned forward, not caring about the chilly air that worked its way between them.

"I just don't want to see you get hurt. I worry about the lengths that blaggard would go to." The sincerity in his voice cooled some of her anger.

"I appreciate your concern, Dylan, I truly do, but I will not kowtow to a bully," she said.

"I respect that. But he's a ruthless and dangerous man who's not above murder. You must be careful."

She knew that. Cat had told her all about the hired killers the man had sent after her and Rick. In Deirdre's fury over the returned calling card, she had allowed herself to forget such things. Foolish and reckless, yes, but such was the burden of pride and righteous anger.

"I know. I suppose coming here was a rash decision. I'm a daft fool."

"Nonsense."

Dylan leaned forward, head nearly coming to rest on her shoulder, his warm breath caressing her cheek. "You're a determined lass, I like that. Besides, we got to see each other again, that makes it worth it, in my opinion."

To her surprise, his arm slid around her waist. The layers of her shawl, dress, and his coat between them didn't diminish the intimate feel. Part of his arm brushed the swell of her breasts where they perched above her corset. Only a part, but it was enough to make her jerk upright and set his horse to dancing a nervous jig.

Undeterred by her startled reaction, he whispered, "I find it quite thrilling."

While the possibility of a tryst in the wild with a handsome man thrilled her, she didn't know him well enough for that yet. Sure, she had needs and an itch that hadn't been scratched in a long time. But she wasn't looking for a meaningless fling that would have the entire town talking if word got out. She wanted a love match. And her mother had taught her that many men only wanted one thing, and if they got it, they'd cut and run. Though she'd never been foolish enough to test that theory herself, she'd seen it happen to far too many women. Now if she knew Dylan better and thought he might be the one, that would be an entirely different matter.

Something moved in the trees and yanked her from her musings. Rather than speak, she pointed. Going tense, Dylan reined his horse in that direction. The stallion hopped quickly around. His neck arched. Horse hair slapped her leg as he swished his tail from side to side. The reaction told her what she suspected.

"Ciaren!"

The shape emerged from the trees. Equine ears shot forward and the mare went rigid.

"Ciaren, come!" Deirdre commanded, knowing what that look meant she was contemplating.

Letting out a squeal, Ciaren reared up just enough to get her front hooves off the ground, then took off running.

"Bloody hell," Deirdre cursed.

It had to be the stallion. Rarely was she this full of vinegar.

Dylan's arm tightened around Deirdre's waist. "Hang on tight," he said.

She let out a surprised squeal of her own as they took off after the mare. Wrapped in a handsome man's arm, galloping through the forest, moved Ainsworth to the back of her mind for the moment. The thrill of the chase was too much not to enjoy.

IO

Kinan

The white stallion pranced along at an animated trot, his shod hooves ringing against the frosty ground. Kinan knew to maintain the pace much longer would risk impact damage to the horse's tendons. Too long at it and the poor creature would end up lame for days. Balder was too loyal to drop out of the pace if it started to hurt. Kinan couldn't risk him getting injured, he wouldn't. Yet, looking above the frosty hills to the sun moving ever closer to the horizon, he couldn't stop, either. The cold of night would pose just as much danger to Deirdre as Ainsworth. He had to find her, soon. The thought of anything happening to her made him ill.

The very fact she had the tenacity to run off on her own to confront the man impressed Kinan. True, it was foolish and reckless, but it was also bold and daring. Perhaps that was part of why it thrilled him so. But then, considering she felt a little like something more than human, something beautiful, reckless, and wild, it came as no surprise.

If only he could figure out why she'd been avoiding him lately. When they had first met, he thought for certain the spark he'd felt had been mutual. She had certainly flirted with him enough to support the feeling. In his eagerness, he wondered if he had given her the wrong impression. If she thought he had unscrupulous intentions, he wanted to clear the matter up straight away. Not that he didn't think about touching, kissing, or even pleasuring her until she screamed, nearly every waking moment. But he was determined to be a civilized man who possessed the control dictated by propriety. Being from New York, he feared she may have heard the stories about the Wild West and put far more stock in the penny-dreadfuls than they deserved. The damnable things made all men in the West out to be rogues and outlaws.

Or worse, maybe the otherness in her sensed the otherness in him and didn't like it. Balder let out a great snort and shook his head and neck. Whether it was in disagreement or because Kinan had allowed his anxiety to break down the walls he kept meticulously erected around his otherness and the horse felt it was difficult to say. Taking a few deep breaths, he concentrated and walled off that part of him. He hadn't allowed himself to slip like that in a long time. Not since the incident.

A rhythm differing from that of his own horse's hooves drew his gaze to the northwest. From the distant tree line a horse without a rider approached. The shadows of late afternoon made it impossible to be sure, but he thought the horse might be black. Wild horses weren't uncommon in this area. The idea did not placate his hammering heart, not when he knew Deirdre's mare was coal black. He slowed Balder to a trot and made to steer him in that direction, but had no need to do so. The horse came straight for them. Kinan held tight to the reins. A wild stallion would charge them if it felt they threatened his territory. But Kinan's pounding heart was still not convinced it was a wild horse. Before he even saw the sidesaddle and loosely flapping reins, he knew it was Deirdre's mare.

"Bloody hell," he uttered one of his papa's favorite sayings. Such an expletive didn't often pass his lips, but he felt this warranted it.

Balder started to prance about and it was all Kinan could do to keep him under control. Reins so taut he feared the leather might snap was all that kept the stallion from bounding up to meet the mare.

"Manners, Balder, manners! We don't want to scare her off," Kinan warned.

The stallion calmed. Balder's ululating whinny pierced the air, drowning out the sound of the mare's approaching hoofbeats. The excited tone and cadence of the call revealed the stallion's amorous intentions. An equally excited call from the mare answered. Tail in the air, neck arched, she pranced right up to them and promptly placed her behind under Balder's nose. Cursing, Kinan wrenched the stallion away and spurred him alongside the mare. Before she could present to him again, he grabbed hold of the reins that dangled over her neck. Balder pranced and whinnied. The two horses sniffed noses, resulting in an excited squeal from the mare.

"Easy, there. You keep it sheathed now. You may have the mare's consent, but you don't have her owner's," he warned.

The stallion snorted and stomped, but otherwise behaved. Kinan praised him, though his heart wasn't in it. His gaze scanned the open field and distant trees, dreading what he might see. But no ominous shapes lay on the ground. Still, his heart increased its frantic rhythm. He had no doubt this big, fine mare was Deirdre's. Whether she had fallen somewhere in the woods, or was at the mercy of Ainsworth, the outcome could be equally as dangerous.

Balder settled and started acting like a gentleman. It soothed Kinan a touch as well. His anxiety wasn't born merely of guilt or a sense of responsibility. That feisty, intriguing woman had survived the long trip from New York. She deserved a chance at a life here. If Ainsworth had harmed her in any way, Kinan would gut the man and read the future in his entrails. Guilt and shame shot little barbs deep into him. While he would never actually do such a thing, merely thinking it gave credence to the rumors about him.

The mare tried to pull away, but he held fast. He turned them in the direction she'd come from and squeezed Balder into a trot. The hard ground hid any sign of the mare's passage, but he continued in that general direction. It was the best he could do. It took them in the exact direction he hoped it wouldn't— along the path leading into the trees to Ainsworth's property. As the cool shadow of the hillside covered him, a mounted figure rode out of the trees at an easy lope. The clop of hooves mingled with the voice of a woman. Not just any woman—Deirdre. He couldn't forget that scintillating sound.

The big brown stallion loping toward him could be none other than Dylan O'Toole's. Kinan's fists clenched tight around the reins when he realized Dylan rode behind Deirdre, one arm about her waist. For a split second, he thought about drawing the .40-caliber Smith & Wesson holstered at his hip. The fingers of his right hand twitched, almost letting go of the rein. But no, rogue that Dylan was, Kinan knew he'd never force himself on a woman. As much as he'd like to believe otherwise, he knew Deirdre was riding with him of her own free will.

The mare whinnied and pawed at the ground. Before she could get worked up, Kinan moved his stallion between her and Dylan's horse. Kinan's eyes bore into the man as he reined his brown stallion to a stop a few paces away. The bastard's smug smile made Kinan's fingers twitch all the more. The man had an arm around Deirdre's midsection, holding her tight against him. The urge to break that arm grew until Kinan knew his fury had to be showing on his face. But, thankfully, Deirdre only had eyes for her mare. Before Dylan's horse even came to a stop, she swept her skirts to the side and leaped to the ground. In a show of dexterity no pampered woman who did only needlepoint and tea socials could pull off, she hit the ground running.

Wide-eyed and shocked speechless, Kinan watched as she dashed to her prancing horse and hugged her tight around the neck.

By Itzamná, she is one hell of a woman.

At her touch, the mare's head dropped low to allow Deirdre to reach her better. She ceased stomping and her tail relaxed against her rump. The transformation impressed Kinan almost as much as Deirdre's leap from Dylan's horse. The last thought pulled his gaze to the man. Disappointment mingled with surprise in Dylan's eyes. Kinan had a feeling it was disappointment over Deirdre's departure rather than her lack of ladylike manners.

"Oh Ciaren! I'm so glad you're all right! I feared the cougar had gotten you," Deirdre told the horse.

Kinan raised a brow at Dylan, who only gave him a crooked smile. Ignoring the man, Kinan swung down from his horse. He untied the bundle from his saddle, tucked it under his arm, and approached Deirdre at a brisk walk. With a shake of the heavy blue wool, he unfurled the cloak and held it up at Deirdre's shoulder level.

"Mrs. Quinn, I'm so relieved to find you unharmed. Here, you must be frightfully cold."

Relief filled her eyes as she turned and stepped back into the cloak. Her red-tipped fingers fumbled with the clasp, unable to work it. Moving in closer, he hooked the clasp and drew the heavy material around her. Eyes closing, she let out a sigh that he felt all the way to his toes.

Long, dark lashes swept up and her sapphire gaze locked onto him. "Thank you ever so much, Kinan. Both for finding Ciaren, and for the cloak," she said.

Kinan fetched the gloves from the pocket of his breeches and helped her work her chilled fingers into them. Even though it was through layers of material, touching her in such a familiar manner both thrilled him and made him feel unjustly possessive. Once he got the gloves on her, she clutched his hands tight. Her eyes snagged him as surely as a fly in amber. Amid the gratitude in them, he saw a spark of interest, but it swiftly burned out as if she had snuffed it on purpose. She let go of his hands and took a step back.

"How did you find her?" she asked, turning to her horse. She stroked the mare's head, checked the buckles on the bridle, and then moved to check the saddle and cinch.

"Truly, she found me, or Balder, rather. I think she may fancy him," Kinan said.

Did he imagine it, or had Dylan's gaze narrowed at him and envy flashed through his eyes?

"O' course, she's always had an eye for the big, exotic lads," Deirdre said with a laugh, as she patted the mare's neck.

Heat surged in Kinan at the comment. *Does she know?* It was possible Dylan had told her Kinan's secret. One of them anyway. The mundane one. Thankfully, the rogue didn't know the other one. Still, the other was bad enough to ruin him in her eyes. But if so, surely she didn't mean what he hoped she meant by the comment. Considering the way she had been pulled tight against Dylan, it wasn't likely she still held any interest in Kinan. More likely, the comment was only a coincidence coupled with his fear that Dylan might have revealed one of his secrets. *But would Dylan stoop to such a level?* Kinan gave the man a long, hard look. Dylan continued to smile, though the expression began to look tight.

The cowhand cleared his throat. "'Tis a shame your stallion isn't a thoroughbred, in that case, Kinan. Wouldn't want to muddle such impeccable bloodlines." His narrowed gaze suggested the words were another dig to rattle Kinan's confidence. Though it sowed doubt to be sure, Kinan hid the fact by returning the cold stare.

Deirdre made a dismissive noise. "Oh, I'm not particular about such things, but I've no intentions to breed her just yet." She scratched both sides of the mare's face and stared her in the eye. "And she'd best not be getting the notion on her own," she warned the horse. A radiant smile came over her. To Kinan's dismay, she turned it on Dylan. "You have my deepest thanks for rescuing me from that fall, and for helping me find Ciaren. I am in your debt."

Dylan's blond brows wiggled in a most ungentlemanly manner. "You can repay me by allowing me to call on you sometime," he said.

Eyes going wide, Deirdre dropped her head and from

beneath her dark, curling locks, her gaze darted between the two men. She seemed to have trouble swallowing. Kinan wished he could believe it was interest in him that caused such a reaction, or at the very least a touch of indecision, but more likely it was due to Dylan's impropriety. Best not to get his hopes up.

"Mr. O'Toole, I must protest. To make the lady feel obligated to receive you for a service you should have given freely is most inappropriate," Kinan snapped, moving instinctively between Deirdre and Dylan's horse.

Dylan rolled his eyes like a spoiled lad. "Lighten up, O'Leary, I was only jesting." To Deirdre, he said, "But I would like to call on you."

Movement behind him made Kinan realize Deirdre was preparing to climb into the saddle on her own. Fingers weaving together, he spun around and offered her a hand up. She nodded, her expression guarded. Stepping into the basket of Kinan's hands, she grabbed Ciaren's mane. He boosted her, holding her weight with ease while she got a foot in the stirrup and wove her legs around the sidesaddle bars.

"Thank you," she said with enough formality to make his heart sink.

Had his handling of her been too lingering, too forward after Dylan's comment? *Dammit.*

Her lips turned upward slightly as she looked to Dylan. "Mr. O'Toole, I'm certain we'll see one another again soon at the home sites. Until then."

While cleverly put, it was still a refusal. For once, Kinan was glad of his tan complexion, for he knew it would hide the blush that scorched his face. The small flush of triumph that no doubt lit his face up was another thing altogether. But he didn't mind Dylan seeing that, not one bit.

Glare disappearing, Dylan tipped his ridiculously wide-brimmed hat to Deirdre, offering up a charming smile that was so big it almost looked predatory. "I look forward to it." He started to turn his horse, but stopped. "And I do hope you'll think about what I said."

The urgency to his tone made it clear he didn't mean his desire to call on her. Something else had transpired between them. Her smile tightened, but she nodded. The look both encouraged and worried Kinan.

Dylan nodded. "Good day to you, Deirdre." His eyes turned to slivers of blue ice as they flicked to Kinan. "O'Leary."

Swallowing his rage over Dylan being so familiar as to call Deirdre by her first name, he nodded in return. "O'Toole."

Kinan's shoulders didn't relax until the man's horse trotted toward the west. Turning, he smiled at Deirdre, only to have the expression wilt away when he found her staring after Dylan. Was that frustration or interest in her eyes? Weighed down by defeat, he returned to his horse and swung up into the saddle. Again, he wondered if Dylan had told her his secret. It wouldn't be the first time the man had ruined Kinan's chances with a woman by employing that tactic. But, if Deirdre was susceptible to such things, she really wasn't the type of woman Kinan wanted to be with. His head accepted the argument, but his heart was another matter.

He pointed Balder in the direction of home. Some small inkling of victory flashed when Deirdre's mare followed of her own accord. In only a few steps, he brought his stallion to a halt. Head cocking to the side in a manner both devilish and adorable, Deirdre gave him a curious look. A thrill shot through him that ended in his groin.

"I will escort you to Mr. Ainsworth's home if that is where you wish to go," he said.

Her brows rose and she stared at him for a long moment before responding. "You truly would?"

"Truly."

Another long moment passed while she looked him over, her curiosity turning to what he thought might be respect. "Thank you, but no. I would like to return to the inn and warm up."

"But of course, and I'll have a hot bath drawn for you the moment we arrive."

She blinked long and slow. "That sounds divine, thank you."

It was wrong to picture her in that bath, bubbles up to her floating breasts…but he did it anyway. The cold afternoon grew considerably warmer—or he did, at least. They urged their horses into a trot that carried them swiftly away from the shade of Ainsworth's hills. Their horses soon fell into a perfectly synchronized rhythm, side by side. Once or twice, Kinan thought he caught Deirdre glancing at him.

While he didn't want to sound like a jealous fool, he couldn't hold his tongue after a while. "I do hope Mr. O'Toole was a gentleman with you. Some say he can be a bit…uncivilized at times."

"Danu forbid a man be uncivilized," she murmured, or at least he thought that was what she said. The clop of horses' hooves nearly drowned out her low voice, so it was hard to tell. Had she truly said 'Danu', as in the mother goddess of the Celts? He knew the stories well from his da's tales. It gave him a tiny clue about the otherness he felt in her from time to time.

"I didn't mean to imply that anything untoward happened, or to besmirch your character in any way. My deepest apologies if it came across in that manner," he said quietly.

Deirdre shook her head sharply once to the left and to the right. "No apology is necessary." She sounded defeated, and disappointed. In what, he could only guess. Why, he could fathom even less. He had tried so hard to do and say everything right. He was terrible at this. A desperate need to recover came over him.

"You're a smart, capable woman, and I admire that about you. I didn't mean to imply otherwise," he said.

Her lips inched up into a smile. "Thank you," she said with genuine feeling. Chest expanding with a deep breath that made her breasts rise, her mouth opened as if she wanted to say more. But no words came. After a few strides, she closed it.

For a solid quarter of a mile he waited, hoping she might change her mind and speak her thoughts. As they rode, he stole glances at her. Several strands of her beautiful black hair had come free and bounced on her shoulders with each stride. Dim as the light was, it still managed to dance along the silky strands. Gods, she was beautiful, so beautiful and fierce it made him shiver. Or maybe that was the cold.

Now that he focused on it, he realized it had grown considerably colder. He looked up expecting to see a cloud moving over the sun, but instead saw a huge, dark gray mass of them moving in swiftly from the horizon. On the breeze came the heady, earthy scent of damp dirt and trees. Sheets of rain swept over the hills, all but obscuring them. From the amount of ground the front was eating up, he knew they wouldn't be able to outrun it. With Deirdre already so cold, the damp could make her sick. That left him only one option.

Pointing his horse toward the southwest, he told Deirdre, "Follow me, please."

A gentle squeeze of both legs propelled his stallion into a gallop. Deirdre caught up in only a few strides. Wind whipped at her long hair, having pulled it mostly free of the bun that bound it. Locks of it flew about her like smoke and shadows. "We can't outrun it. We should go back to the forest," she called to him.

"No time, and I have a better place," he said.

He more than half-expected an argument, but she only nodded and kept riding. The pace she kept was impressive, especially for one riding sidesaddle. He had to let the reins out and allow Balder to run at full speed to even keep alongside her. Smiling, he leaned into the moist wind. A fat drop of rain splashed onto the back of his right hand, soaking nearly half of it. Another plopped on his arm, darkening his maroon-colored cotton sleeve. They crested a slight hill and started to run down the other side. In a hollow halfway down, surrounded by four massive oak trees, lay their destination. Nestled beneath the arms of the oaks crouched a small dwelling most would consider a hovel, despite the fine condition Kinan kept it in.

Anxiety twisted him up inside. Never had he shown this place to anyone outside of his family, and he certainly didn't want Deirdre to see it before she got to know him better. But it was either take her here to wait out the storm and get her warmed up, or keep riding and risk her getting ill from being cold and wet. What she thought of him hardly mattered in comparison to her health. Rain began to pour down on them as if to solidify his fate. It fell so hard the bounce-back spray made it look like Deirdre and her horse rode through a thick mist.

Pointing toward the trees, Kinan slowed his horse to a trot. Balder slipped now and then on the wet grass, forcing Kinan to lean back in the saddle. After a few dozen yards, the steepness of the hill mellowed. By the time they reached the dwelling, his woolen cloak felt like it had tripled in weight. From the knees down he was soaked through, and a steady stream ran down the back of his neck. Cold seeped all the way down into his bones. He could only hope Deirdre's cloak had kept her drier.

The torrent of rain ceased to assault him as soon as they rode beneath the roof that extended off the side of the dwelling. He nosed Balder all the way up to the stack of firewood against the house. It was just deep enough to get the big stallion's rear out of the weather. The overhang was easily wide enough for both horses to fit in if they behaved themselves. It had originally been designed for firewood storage, but Kinan had since redesigned it to corral a horse as well. From the look of the dark skies, the horses wouldn't have much choice but to use it if they didn't want to get wet.

Not bothering with the stirrups, he kicked his feet free and leaped down. He wrapped Balder's reins around the hitching post in front of him. It would have to do for a moment. Two long strides carried him to Ciaren, where he reached up and grabbed Deirdre around the waist. Her eyes widened behind strands of wet hair, but she allowed him to lift her from the saddle and set her on her feet.

He let go the moment she appeared steady. "I do hope you will pardon me, but I feared you might fall from being so cold," he said.

Something flashed in her eyes. *Is it disappointment over me letting go?* It came and went too fast for him to be sure. *No, certainly not from such a refined New York lady.* Likely, he merely wanted her to be disappointed so much that he had imagined it.

A bow from the nearby pine tree brushed against his arm. Odd, he hadn't felt a breeze that could have stirred it, pushing it beneath the overhang. Yet it wove and bobbed as if caught in air currents. It brushed against Ciaren's rump, causing the horse to sidestep. Deirdre put a hand against the horse's wet shoulder to steady herself. Her wide-eyed gaze shot from the pine bough to him.

Is that fear in her eyes? With a gasp, she looked down quickly, then gazed up at him from beneath her long lashes. His cock stirred in his wet breeches.

"Thank you, Mr. O'Leary. I fear I would have indeed fallen."

Ah, so it had been embarrassment and gratitude, then. But of course it had. What had he been thinking? While he tied her horse for her, she studied the earthen walls rising up beyond the woodpile.

"What is this place?" she asked, voice full of wonder.

Surprise widened his eyes. His fear about bringing her here eased some. But he hadn't taken her inside yet. "It's my family's original homestead. My father and grandfather built it together. I keep it in good condition out of nostalgia," he said, feeling the need to explain before she saw the inside. Afraid she might still be unsteady, he offered her his arm. "We can wait out the storm inside. Once I get you settled, I will return and tend to the horses."

She had enough heat left in her to blush, though it barely showed on her lovely sun-kissed skin. If she held any reservations about going into a building with him without a proper escort, he couldn't be sure, because she accepted his arm.

"I shall be the utmost gentleman, you need not worry," he assured her.

She nodded, using the motion to hide her expression behind her hair. She hadn't struck him as the demure type, so the reaction surprised him. Could it be she hid her expression for another reason? Likely she was worried about her reputation, as any lady would be. His gaze followed the raindrops that trailed down into her wonderfully deep cleavage. The desire to lick that rain away pumped blood straight down to his groin. Turning his head, he forced himself to look at the heavy oak door they approached. Being a fine New York lady, surely she didn't harbor such lascivious thoughts as a less refined person such as himself. If he could not rein in his desire, he would surely lose any thread of a chance he might still have with her.

The weather-swollen door creaked as he opened it. He stepped aside and allowed Deirdre to enter first. With the window to the main room shuttered, the light from the open door was the only illumination. Undaunted, Deirdre strode into the dark room without hesitation. Such a show of bravery and trust thrilled him. Not a single woman in town would go into a dark room with him. But then, they had heard the stories. He still wasn't sure if Deirdre had. So, perhaps it wasn't trust after all.

Eyes widening, Deirdre did a slow turn to take in the large room. Her gaze snagged on the colorful tapestries that covered the earthen walls, some reaching all the way up to where the domed ceiling began to arch. Unlike the ones at the inn, these depicted subjects and acts too questionable for the judging eyes of society. One tapestry focused on a muscular warrior wearing only a loincloth and elaborate headdress of feathers and gold, arms spread wide as if beseeching the stars stretched above the pyramid he stood atop. Another depicted a sunrise through stone sculptures with a starry sky fading above, a third, scantily clad warriors playing a deadly game with a ball amid a stone city of idols and statues. Deirdre walked to the one with the man atop the pyramid.

Breath caught in his throat, Kinan waited for her response. He readied himself for her disgust, scandal, or even fear. Such art was not shown in proper society—which was part of why he kept it here. For that reason, and because he didn't want to offend her, he wanted to apologize. The words clung to the back of his tongue like turned milk.

She stroked the colorful threads of the tapestry with a gentle caress that seemed close to reverence. Her gaze perused every inch of the art. That particular tapestry depicted a Mayan stone observatory for the stars. A smile slowly spread across her lips. Kinan let out a breath and drew in another. Wonder filled her eyes as she turned to look at him.

"Kinan, these are stunning, so exotic, so…" Her voice trailed off as she moved to touch the next one. When she finally spoke again, it was barely above a whisper. "So stimulating."

Both the fact that she had called him by his first name, and her reaction, sent a shiver through him. As his cock jumped to attention, he found himself in need of a distraction that would allow him to turn away. "Thank you. I'm touched that you think so. These tapestries have deep meaning for me," he said. The last part had been a mistake. He wasn't ready for her to ask about that.

He walked to the open fireplace that took up a fair amount

of one wall and checked the woodbox beside it. Thankfully, it was empty, giving him the excuse he needed. "Please, make yourself comfortable." He gestured toward the leather couch sitting before the fireplace and the chair seated in a corner by the full bookshelf. "I'll only be a moment. I'm going to care for the horses and fetch some firewood."

With a nod, she moved on to the next tapestry.

He dashed from the cottage, closing the door behind him. Cool, moist air swirled around him, drawing the heat from his skin and helping him drive down his desire to a manageable level. By the time he had unsaddled the horses, given them enough grain to keep them occupied for a while, and secured the poles in place that enclosed the covered area, he had a firm grasp on his manners. As much as he wanted to profess his interest in Deirdre, he didn't dare do it now. Not only was he hesitant because of her distant manner of late, but here, alone, couldn't be a more inappropriate time and place. It might make her feel vulnerable, or worse, fearful. As a high-society lady, she would expect him to be a gentleman, and he would not let her down.

Gathering as much firewood as he could in one arm, he went back inside. Deirdre stood at the bookcase, her back to him. The scent of wet wool drew his gaze to where her damp cloak hung on a hook next to the door. But he couldn't look away from her for long, no matter how he tried. Wet strands of dark hair wove their way over her shoulder and down her back. Where the locks touched her lovely purple dress, the satin shone a hue almost as dark as her hair. Bumps from the damp and chilly air freckled across her exposed arms. Engrossed in the books as she was, she didn't seem to notice her body was trying to tell her it was cold.

The books, oh revered Itzamná, the books! What if she came across the one he kept hidden on the bottom shelf behind the vase?

Her fingers stroked the binding of one of the many on the shelf. Wooden whistles carved to look like a frog and a jaguar's head propped it up. The sight of them made his heart pound even harder. Surely, she would think them only trinkets.

She pulled the book out and opened it. Even from this distance he could see it and knew which book it was. Chills of dread splashed across him. It was not the book he had feared, but still one that might disturb her. The picture on the page she studied depicted a Mayan sun god, smiling, tongue thrust out. At the sound of his steps, Deirdre turned. The look of wonder on her face stopped him in his tracks. She smiled, the look transforming her into the most beautiful creature he had ever seen. Forcing himself to look away, he carried the firewood to the fireplace and began to pile it inside.

"This book, these images, they are gorgeous, Kinan," she said.

A flush of relief and pride went through him that banished the chill from outside. "You really think so?" he asked. It wasn't that he doubted the sincerity in her voice, just that most people thought such exotic images and books were savage and below the notice of polite society. Rather than look to her to see the response he so desperately wanted, he focused hard on piling the kindling just right.

"Aye, very much so. Wherever did you get them?" she asked.

This time fear took the edge off his pride. He didn't want to reveal too much of his history, his family, to her just yet. But he would not lie to her. "My mother gave them to me." On one hand, he wanted to say more to see how she would respond, on the other, he was terrified of her response.

"The subject matter, is it related to the tapestries?"

After a few good strikes of flint and steel, he had to blow on the sparks. She put the book back and continued to peruse the shelves, patient for his response. Once flames licked at the wood, he joined her at the shelves.

Standing as close to her as he dared, he said, "It is."

"Is this Mexican culture?" she asked.

"Close. It's Mayan, which is a culture that existed in Mexico centuries ago," he said.

"From the look of it, they were a culture of artists," she mused as her fingers brushed another book. "And these carvings. They are beautiful. What are they?"

It was all he could do to relax enough to be able to unlock his jaw and answer. "Whistles."

"How fascinating!" she exclaimed, tone filled with delight.

Standing close as he was, Kinan saw that she was shivering ever so slightly. He left her to her perusing and headed for the bedroom. If he tried to draw her attention away from the books and whistles, he risked raising her suspicion. Besides, she was looking at the top shelves, so he was safe.

On the way, he paused at the fireplace long enough to hang a teapot over it. From the small bedroom, he fetched a heavy quilt. Before leaving, he glanced around the room. With its four-poster log bed, small dresser of the same make, and petite window of thick, cloudy glass, it wasn't exactly luxurious. But it was immaculate, and he hoped if they had to stay the night, Deirdre would find it adequate. At least it would be out of the weather. Etiquette dictated he should close the door, for the sight of the bed was suggestive—but he didn't dare. The heat from the fireplace needed to be able to reach this room. He'd rather take the risk of her thinking him inappropriate than have the room be chilly if she needed it later.

Her chin lifted in his direction as his steps echoed on the wood floor, but she didn't look away from the shelf. No, it was not the shelf that held her attention any longer, he realized. Now she stroked the very wall itself. To let her know he approached, he made his steps a touch heavier. For a moment, he held the quilt behind her, waiting. Despite her shivering, she remained too engrossed in the wall to notice the blanket he offered. He held his breath and draped the quilt around her shoulders. She sighed and leaned back into it—and him. He knew he should step back, he tried to, but he couldn't.

Going after what he wanted—fighting for it—were strong drives in his nature, so strong they often tried to override the sense of propriety his parents had worked so hard to instill in him. Not that he would be so forward as to do anything Deirdre didn't want—no, never that. He wasn't that kind of man. But in his experience, a woman would change her mind about what she wanted when society deemed it inappropriate.

He had mustered the will to step back when she reached up and touched his hand where it still clutched the quilt. The skin-to-skin contact set him on fire. Touching a lady in such a manner was entirely unacceptable, unless one was courting her, or married to her, of course. While her palm was soft against the back of his hand, her fingers felt a touch rough, like they might have calluses. Curiosity got the better of him and he leaned over her shoulder to look. His groin inadvertently brushed her buttocks, sending that fire straight down. When she didn't pull away from the contact, he held his breath and dug deep for his will.

It was nowhere to be found. Closing his eyes, he froze. After a long moment in which his heart doubled its speed, she leaned back against him. Those firm buttocks pressed against his groin. His cock swelled, stretching the buttons of his breeches. Still she didn't move away or let go of his hand. She had to have felt it.

"You're an interesting man, Kinan, and quite fetching," she all but purred in a breathy voice. The familiarity with which she addressed him felt almost as intimate as her touch. Almost.

But her distant manner of late confused him. He had thought she'd lost interest in him.

Her head turned, tilting back to look up at him.

"And you're an intriguing woman who is as beautiful as a summer sunset on the San Francisco coast."

Her eyes fluttered and her full lips arched into a smile. Those lips looked so inviting that he started to lean down. Her eyes slid closed as she tilted her head back a little more, just enough to be at the right angle. Need began to override reason. From the moment he first saw her, he had wanted to kiss her. That desire had only grown stronger with each little thing he learned about her. He slid his arms around her waist, reveling in the feel of her satin dress against his rough fingers. No doubt her skin would be just as smooth, and he wanted to touch every inch of it. That brought him back to himself and stopped him when less than a breath remained between their lips.

That wild nature his father warned him about was trying to get the best of him. This was too close to what happened last time he'd been interested in a woman. Deirdre was different, the pull he felt toward her stronger than anything he'd ever felt. He couldn't lose her because of his failure to be a proper gentleman. He wouldn't.

Besides, his actions weren't fair to Deirdre. Even if she felt the same spark between them, she barely knew him. She deserved to know him better first. And if they were found out it would ruin her and merely add a feather in his cap in the eyes of society.

"My deepest apologies, Mrs. Quinn. I didn't mean to disrespect or dishonor you by acting inappropriately. Please rest assured, it won't happen again," he promised, hoping he sounded as sincere as he felt.

Jaw tense, Deirdre blinked long and slow. She straightened and pulled the blanket tighter around her as she let out a breath. Anger darkened her eyes, but whether it was anger over him taking advantage in the first place, or withdrawing, he wasn't sure. No, he couldn't let himself think that way, couldn't let himself hope for that. Her right brow twitched up and down. He found it adorable, and that only made him want to kiss her more.

"Socially inappropriate, aye," she said in a huff, eyes cast to the floor.

She drew in a deep breath—which made her breasts swell in a way that tried to lure him in—and met his gaze. Thankfully, he had looked up in time to avoid being caught leering.

"You have no need to apologize, Mr. O'Leary."

She removed a book from the shelf, walked over to the couch before the fire, and sat. Firelight lit her face in an orange, flickering glow as she opened the book and started to read. It was one of his many books on astronomy. The teapot over the fireplace began to whistle, saving him from the awkward silence, and giving him something to do with his pent-up energy. He took it to the small counter that served as the cottage's kitchen and fetched two ceramic cups from the single cupboard above it. The aromas of mint and rosehips wafted up to him as he opened the container holding the loose tea. He scooped a generous heap of the leafy mixture into a metal basket infuser shaped like an egg, and dropped it into his cup.

"How would you like your tea?" he asked.

Without looking up from the book, she answered, "Strong and sweet, if you have honey, that is." She sounded distracted.

He smiled. Strong and sweet, just like her. The way she interacted with her friends, treating them with such kindness, and holding Sadie as an equal, spoke of a very sweet, giving soul. If only he could stop mucking things up with her. She was a conundrum of contradictions that he just couldn't decipher. Teacups in hand, he returned to the couch and set her cup on the table by the arm of the sofa that she had curled up around. She was several pages deep into the book, her finger slowly trailing down the page. Rather than be so bold as to sit on the sofa beside her, he stood in front of the fireplace.

"Do you have an interest in astronomy?" he asked.

At last she looked up. The beautiful smirk on her face moved him on a level so deep that it stole his breath. "Very much so, despite my mother insisting that academic pursuit isn't at all ladylike. To think, there are not only other planets, but galaxies! 'Tis fascinating to know the universe is such a massive place, so much bigger than it seems."

Her enthusiasm sparked his own passion for the subject. They immediately engaged in deep conversation about the 1846 discovery of Neptune by astronomers Johann Gottfried Galle, Urbain Le Verrier, and John Couch Adams. Deirdre impressed him by arguing that Galileo Galilei had actually been the one to discover it inadvertently, while sketching its moons long before. Two cups of tea and half the book later found them seated together on the couch, bent over the pages head to head. They talked long into the night. Never had Kinan found a woman so knowledgeable, so interested in such things. It thrilled him to no end.

Only when Deirdre nodded off did they finally stop. Looking at her all curled up on the couch, Kinan couldn't very well leave her there. The poor thing would have a terrible kink in her neck when she awoke if he didn't move her.

"Mrs. Quinn," he called softly as he leaned closer. "Deirdre," he said a little louder.

Though she groaned, she didn't stir. Carefully, he lifted the book from her limp hands and put it back on the shelf. By the time he returned, she had nestled deeper into the couch. Slow breaths made her bosom rise and fall, pushing her cleavage together in a tantalizing manner. Her skirts had hiked up enough that he could see the frilly lace of her pantaloons above the creamy white skin of one ankle. Hot blood pumped through him. Closing his eyes, he shook his head, trying to rid it of lecherous thoughts.

Tonight had revealed many things about Deirdre Quinn to him. The foremost was that she was much more than just another beautiful woman. And temptation be damned, for he would treat her with the respect she deserved. As much as he wanted to kiss her and claim her as his own, he would not. He would do his best to win her heart without appealing to her mutual attraction for him.

He touched her arm, careful to do so where her sleeve covered her skin. "Deirdre, you would be more comfortable in the bed," he said.

"Hmm…the bed, yes…" she murmured through a smile. The sleepy, sultry tone of her voice made him think of all the more interesting things they could do in a bed. He forced such thoughts down as deep as he could, and imagined locking them away.

Left with few other options, he bent and scooped her into his arms. She stirred only enough to turn in against him and snuggle closer. Waves framed a flawless face smooth with the relaxation of sleep. Long lashes brushed cheeks several shades darker than was typical for an Irish lass. But then, she had just spent months out in the sun and weather traveling across America. Not that her olive-toned skin mattered to him. It was beautiful. He carried her into the bedroom and lay her on the bed. Her hands pulled slowly, almost reluctantly—or so he hoped—from his sleeve. Eyes fluttering beneath her lids, she sighed and nuzzled into the feather pillow.

To his relief, she had removed her boots while they'd been talking earlier in the evening. If he'd had to remove them, it might have put him out of his mind. The thought of removing any piece of clothing from her… He tucked the quilt around her and fetched a second from the trunk at the foot of the bed. At the door, he hesitated, unable to turn away. The sight of her on that bed, black waves splayed out across the pillow, inspired him in more ways than one. How a woman he had only known for a few days could have such a profound effect on him, he didn't know. What he did know, was that he would do his best to give Dylan

O'Toole a run for his coin for the chance to court her.

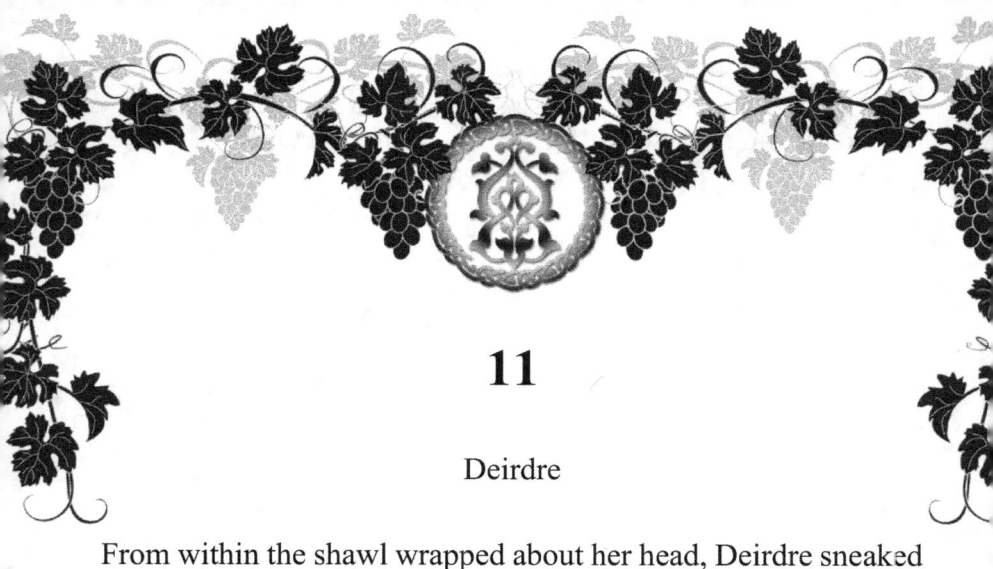

11

Deirdre

From within the shawl wrapped about her head, Deirdre sneaked glances at Kinan as they rode through the chilly morning air. The horses' hooves crunched through the dusting of white crystallized flakes that had covered the ground while they slept. Last night's interaction left her befuddled. Kinan's insistence on being proper deepened her fear of him being just another high-society man being boring and old-fashioned. But then he had been so damned interesting. Never had a man spoken to her so candidly, engaging her in deep conversation as if she were his equal in intellect. The more she got to know him, the harder it became to remain uninterested. If only he had kissed her…

"This little bit of snow probably looks quaint to a New Yorker like yourself," Kinan's deep voice resonated in the stillness.

She shrugged and finally allowed herself to look at him. Black hair brushed unshaven cheeks ruddy from the cold, giving him a rugged look that made the muscles between her legs tighten. Even packed in layers covered by a woolen cloak, the man's muscular frame enticed her, which was precisely why she'd been avoiding looking at him. She refused to become romantically interested in a man who she couldn't confirm she resonated with sexually. Life was too short to have dull carnal relations again. Besides, she theorized it was a sign of a man who would cling so tight to proper ways that he would repress her. But could a man with a voice that could make her wet and a mind that set her afire really be a bad lover?

Worse, possibly, he could condemn her for her secrets. Revealing such things would put her at the utmost vulnerability. The fear of him telling others, of him condemning her, made her chest tighten until she could barely breathe. She liked him far too much to face such rejection from him. *Dammit.* When had she let herself become so attached? But he was interested in other cultures. *Perhaps…*

Bloody hell, he had asked something! What had it been? New York…snow…yes! "A bit quaint, but unexpected," she said. The high clouds in the sky meant it was unlikely that any more would fall. That made her feel a bit nostalgic. "Is it silly that I wish for more?"

The smile he gave her warmed her much more than her cloak did. "Not at all, what with the holiday a mere three months away. You must be used to a snowy Christmas," he said.

Memories of horse-drawn sleighs plodding through snowy streets filled her mind, making her smile. "Oh, yes, most certainly. But my people celebrate it as Yule.

"Truly? My family celebrates something similar," he said with the barest hint of a smile tugging at his lips.

Was that hope in his eyes, delight? *Surely not.* She had to be imagining it because she wanted it so badly. More likely it was condemnation and shock. She shouldn't have said it. Why she'd let the words slip out, she had no idea.

"Something similar?" she prodded, trying not to allow the hope she felt slip into her voice.

"Yes, the winter solstice. We don't get snow often here, but up in the hills where we get our holiday tree, it is always snowy. Which reminds me; the inn usually gets its tree the first Sunday in December. Before we get it this year, however, I wanted to make sure it was a custom that you embraced," he said.

It took several breaths for her to recover from the shock of not being reprimanded for embracing traditions outside of those accepted. Not only had he not scoffed at her statement, but he'd also taken her feelings regarding traditions into consideration by asking. His openness and respect for other beliefs encouraged her. "O' course I do, Kinan. As my people are, shall we say…unconventional, we embrace other cultures and would never condemn their traditions so long as they don't harm us or others. But that is very sweet of you to ask."

"Are you sure? We tend to go all out, with a big tree in the foyer, garland and candles throughout the inn and such. But we don't have to if it conflicts with your decorations for the wedding," he said.

Deirdre sat up so straight and fast that Ciaren came to an abrupt halt. "The wedding? At the inn?"

He reined his horse to a stop a few steps later. Squeezing Ciaren's sides, Deirdre rode up until she stood beside the stallion.

"You weren't aware Rick and Cat asked to hold it there? I apologize. I believe Cat may have meant to tell you yesterday but didn't get the chance." While he didn't sound at all condescending, he didn't need to. It was her own fault Cat hadn't had the chance to tell her. "You are of course welcome to decorate any way you want for both the engagement party and the wedding. I and my staff will be at your disposal for anything you need," he finished. The slightly husky tone of his voice as he said the last almost made her hopeful he'd bend his proper notions about intimacy.

She forced her mind back to the task at hand. The more she thought about it, the more perfect she realized it would be. The inn was beautiful, with a huge foyer and large, Y-shaped staircase. And if Kinan's staff could help decorate, she could focus more on building their homes.

"Thank you, I do believe that will work out perfectly."

They began riding again. Soon they left the snow-dusted hills behind. Green trees, turning leaves, and brown earth gave her an idea. "I'll speak with Cat, but I think a holiday-themed wedding would be splendid. If she agrees, I would love to coordinate decorations with you, and help pick out the tree, if that isn't too much of an intrusion." Doing so would allow her to search out an area of the forest in need of thinning, thank the tree properly for its sacrifice, and obtain a seed from it that she could plant so it might be reborn.

The large, joyful smile Kinan gave her sent a rush of heat through her, so powerful that it felt as if she stood before a furnace. "It would not be an intrusion at all, it would be a pleasure. And if there's anything else I can do, you have only to let me know," he said.

She cleared her throat and did her best to sound businesslike. "There is, actually, but I don't want you to feel obligated in any way. If you can't do it, or don't want to, I won't think any less of you." She looked to the horizon. Ciaren's pace picked up a touch as they crested a hill and the inn came into sight.

"I'm intrigued. Do tell," Kinan prompted.

She decided to come completely clean with him, where her plan was concerned, at least. While she may not trust him with her deepest, darkest secrets yet, she knew she could trust him with her plans.

"I plan to use both the engagement party next month and the wedding two months later as covers. I want Ainsworth to believe we are so engrossed in planning the events that we're waiting until spring to build our homes." She let out a laugh. "Shouldn't be hard to convince him. Most men believe women are obsessed with parties."

Kinan's shoulder dropped, and he looked down at her. "In our defense, many women *are* obsessed by parties."

Huffing, Deirdre flung her hair over her shoulder, taking on an imperious air. "Perhaps, but only because most men block them from pursuits of business and the like."

His smile took her by surprise. "Touché," he said, in what was possibly the worst French accent she had ever heard.

It elicited a laugh from her. "First astronomy, and now he speaks French. Next I'll be discovering that you're a world traveler."

The serious look Kinan gave her said she wasn't far off base, which piqued her curiosity.

"Sadly, that is close to the extent of my French. As for being worldly, actually—"

A feminine voice calling from some distance away halted his words. Deirdre was about to prompt him to go on when she saw shapes in the distance. Three riders approached from the direction of the inn. The big painted horse was unmistakable.

"Deirdre!" came Cat's faint voice once again.

The horses started running toward them. It took almost no urging at all to launch Ciaren into a canter. Slowing her down once she reached the painted gelding was another matter. When Kinan reined his white stallion in beside her a few moments later, the mare settled and eventually stood still enough for Deirdre to dismount. A moment later, Cat leaped down and embraced Deirdre. Wild red curls tickled Deirdre's cheeks. All that brilliant red hair hung loose in a full mane about Cat's entire upper body. The fact that she had left it unfettered spoke of how desperate she had been to get out of the house this morning. Beautiful though it was, in Deirdre's opinion, Cat never left her hair completely down. Guilt gnawed at her over having worried her friend so much that she had abandoned her routine—let alone rode like a wild woman while pregnant.

"I am so sorry to have worried you, Cat."

Cat drew back and grabbed her by the shoulders. "What were you thinking, running off like that, Deirdre Quinn? I could shake you. I shall shake you!" She gave Deirdre's shoulders a few good shakes—which Deirdre endured with a smile.

"I deserved that. I wasn't thinking at all."

Cat drew back, but didn't let go. "Clearly not! Sadie told me about the man who attacked you on the way here, the one your escorts turned over to the sheriff. Deirdre, we need to talk."

All anger drained out of her, replaced by a hushed fear Deirdre found much worse. She wanted the anger back; it made Cat stronger. She couldn't blame her, though. The actions had been beyond reckless. But what they had to do with the man who had attacked her back when they first arrived in California, she had no idea. He was in the sheriff's custody and posed no further threat. Ainsworth, of course, was another story.

The clip-clop of trotting hooves announced the arrival of the other two riders. Rick approached on a big buckskin, and Sadie rode beside him on a brown mare. The somber look on Sadie's face struck dread deep into Deirdre. "Whatever could have you both so rattled? I'm quite all right, thanks to Kinan."

Sadie sagged in the saddle, shoulders rolling until it looked as though she drew in on herself. "Oh I know. I saw as much and tried to tell Cat. But it isn't that." She looked to Cat.

After a breath so deep it shook her chest, Cat said, "Cofield, the man who attacked you on the trail to California, is the same one who tried to kill Rick and I."

Gathered around the great-room fireplace at the O'Leary Inn with a hot cup of tea in her hands, Deirdre listened as Cat and Rick took turns recapping their tales of Cofield. Throughout it, Deirdre and Sadie exchanged knowing looks. Cat remained fearless as she told the story, her head held high, anger darkening her tone. To see her once-damaged friend so strong in the face of such adversity heartened Deirdre.

Tea tray in hand, biscuits and cookies in the other, Kinan entered the lavishly furnished room. Setting the plates on the low table the group had gathered around, he turned to leave. Deirdre touched his arm. He stopped.

"Please stay," she said softly.

He dipped his head in answer and took one of the empty chairs facing the glowing fireplace. An idea was forming, and she wanted him to be a part of it. He had offered to help her maintain the illusion of distraction, after all. Or, at least, that was the reason she convinced herself that she desired his presence. It wasn't because of the concern written in the lines of his tense body, or the way the firelight danced across his tanned skin and the highlights of his black hair. *No, it has nothing to do with that. Absolutely nothing.*

A deep intake of breath brought her attention back to Cat, who sat on the small couch between Sadie and Rick. "Well, he won't be of concern much longer. Rick checked with the sheriff, and Cofield is being moved to stand trial in a city to the south."

Kinan scratched at his stubbly chin. "That could be for the best. Our judge is paid off by Ainsworth."

Cat nodded. "We figured as much. As is the sheriff, Rick says. Which leads me to wonder, why is Ainsworth allowing his man to be transferred out where he will likely give testimony that could incriminate Ainsworth to save his own neck? All Ainsworth has to do is say the word and the sheriff won't transfer him."

Kinan's long lashes shot wide open. "Because the man could do the same here. This gives Ainsworth a chance to have him killed in transit and eliminate the risk."

Cat looked at Rick, then back to Kinan. "We fear as much as well."

With a gasp, Sadie clutched the obsidian moon pendant hanging around her neck. "What a monster!"

Nodding, Cat patted Sadie's arm, though from the look of worry knotting her brow, the gesture may have been just as much for her own comfort. Deirdre sipped her tea as she let her mind work over things. Cat went on about the morality of allowing such a thing to happen to a man who would have killed them all given the chance, but she scarcely heard. It wasn't whether the man lived or died that concerned her—he had made his bed—but rather, if there was a way they could use him. He was an opportunist, a survivor.

The room went quiet sometime during her contemplating. Cat and Sadie stared at her. "I don't like that look," Cat said in a voice tinged with alarm.

Sadie drummed her delicate fingers against her teacup. "Indeed not. That look means trouble."

One corner of Kinan's lips pulled up in a crooked grin. "I like that look," he said. The bold words sent a flush through Deirdre.

"You daft fool, you'll learn soon enough," Sadie warned.

Deirdre set her cup down and leaned over the table. "What if we could reach Cofield's transport wagon before Ainsworth's men?"

As if wanting to distance herself from the very suggestion, Cat sat back. "And do what with him?"

"Free him, o' course," Deirdre said.

Sadie whispered to Kinan, "You see, you just have to wait for the crazy bits. There it is."

The widening smile on Kinan's lips made her think maybe he didn't mind the idea of her being a little crazy. *No, that has to be merely wishful thinking on my part.*

"I know you haven't gone soft on us, so why on earth would you want to do that?" Cat asked.

From the way Kinan rubbed his hands together, Deirdre knew he had figured it out. More thrills shot through her over the fact that he was excited. "To use him," he said.

Sadie threw a hand in the air. "You've completely lost your ever-loving mind, woman! The man's a killer, dangerous, in case you missed Cat and Rick's story, and forgot about how he attacked you."

Deirdre gave her a steady look. "From what Cat and Rick have told us, the man is no professional. He simply did what Ainsworth commanded because he was afraid not to. To save his own skin, I believe he'll cooperate with us."

Head tilting to the side, Cat eyed her with curiosity. "What exactly is it you'd have him do for us?"

"Since he worked for Ainsworth, he'll know the layout of the man's land, which means he'll know how we can sneak through and avoid the road Ainsworth won't let us cross."

Sadie held up a hand. "Now, wait. Why would we need to get through Ainsworth's land?"

Schooling her expression so she didn't look overeager, Deirdre said, "To bring home the timber we're going to purchase from the northeast."

"Why would we purchase timber to the northeast?" Sadie asked.

A slow smile worked its way onto Cat's face. "Because, 'tis the one place his influence doesn't reach that has what we need. Mostly that's because he knows there's no way to it that doesn't go through his land." She looked at Deirdre. "But guide or no, what makes you think he won't catch us bringing it through his land?"

Deirdre's own smile tried to break through, but she held it back. "Because he'll be distracted."

"By what, pray tell?" Sadie asked.

Deirdre looked to Kinan, who watched her with a mixture of curiosity and interest that she found quite stimulating.

"By Sadie, Kinan, and I bringing in a wagon of party supplies big enough to make him suspect we're hiding timber in it."

Kinan's grin grew. "That's brilliant!"

Whether the flush of emotion came from his words or smile, Deirdre couldn't be sure, but she knew it would be trouble either way.

Sadie and Cat erupted into conversation, one arguing for it, the other against. After a prolonged discussion that lasted through another cup of tea, they agreed to try it. Deirdre leaned over and patted Sadie's hands. "Don't look so glum, we get to go shopping!"

Eyes softening, Sadie gave a small shrug. "At least there's that."

Grinning all the wider, Deirdre's gaze danced between Cat and Kinan as she said, "Now, we just have to figure out how to hijack a prisoner wagon."

12

Deirdre

September

"I still say this is the worst idea I have ever heard."

Dylan tried to grab the pistol off the tack box before Deirdre could reach it. He remained a foot away by the time it was in her hand. If she weren't so irritated at him, she might have thrilled at being alone in a tack room with him.

"I don't recall asking your opinion," she said.

Putting one booted foot up on the tack box, she started to hike up her skirts. Dylan's gaze didn't shift away until she started to strap on the small thigh holster Rick had given her.

"A lady shouldn't put herself in this kind of danger," Dylan protested.

That comment ruined her enjoyment of his eyes on her. She jammed the small pistol into the holster, put her foot down, and smoothed her skirts slowly and carefully.

"Do you even know how to use that?" he demanded.

Near to boiling over, she had to take a deep breath and let it out slowly. While doing so, she did her best to glare a hole clean through him. "Of course I do. I spent months traveling across the wilds of America. I can handle myself," she said. Of all people, she had thought Dylan would be all right with this. His reaction disappointed her to no end.

Dylan held his hands up. "I wasn't saying you couldn't. I'm just saying this might be something best left to us lads."

A sound that was half-grunt, half-scream tore from Deirdre's throat. Grabbing Ciaren's pad and saddle, she shoved past Dylan and marched out of the tack room. "That is *not* the plan," she snapped.

Feet pounded after her. "Then maybe we can change the plan. Surely Rick doesn't want you in danger—"

"Rick trusts that I can take care of myself. In fact, he didn't so much as raise a brow when Cat decided to go along," she interrupted, stopping herself before she could make a comment about Cat's condition.

"Aye, well, 'tis just…"

She ignored his bumbling and proceeded to saddle Ciaren. Just outside the open doors of the barn, she heard the creak of the carriage as Cat and Sadie situated themselves inside.

"At least ride in the carriage where it will be safer," he said.

She decided she liked it better when he couldn't get out a full sentence. Well-placed pressure on Ciaren's side made the mare step into him, forcing him out of the stall. When Deirdre moved to lead her out, Dylan blocked the way.

Her eyes narrowed. "You mean where I'll be trapped if things do not go according to plan."

He braced a hand on either side of the stall door. "Where you will have cover if bullets start to fly," he said in a hard tone. Dropping his arms, he took a step closer to her.

With less than two feet between them, she could smell the

soap he'd used on his freshly shaved face. This close, his eyes were so blue they made her think of the sky—vast, and endless enough to lose oneself in. Sadly, it wasn't a place she wanted to get lost. She took a step back just as he reached for her. He was faster and didn't seem to notice she was trying to move away.

Suddenly, she was in his arms, pressed to his chest, her heart beating so hard she knew he felt it. But the look of passion darkening his eyes made it clear he misunderstood her thundering heart. In the strength of his arms she felt a possessive urgency, yet his lips pressed soft enough against hers to melt into. But she didn't want to melt into them. She was too angry. Those supple lips started to part.

Hands on his chest, she shoved at the same time Ciaren bumped her hard in the back, pushing both of them out of the stall. They came apart when Dylan stumbled over the lip of the stall floor. He caught himself by grabbing a beam and swinging around it in a show of dexterity that was frustratingly stimulating.

"I can take care of myself, Dylan O'Toole, and I'll thank you not to overstep propriety again," she snapped.

Eyes soft with concern beseeched her. "Me apologies. I thought you desired me as much as I do you. I meant no disrespect, either with the kiss, or by what I said. I'm worried about you, is all," he said in a low whisper that felt scandalously intimate—almost as intimate as their kiss.

His hand covered hers where it rested on the stall door. She yanked hers out from under his, not caring about the rough wood that scraped at her palm. Attraction buzzed through her like a glass of fine wine. But Brigid damn her traitorous body, she didn't want to feel attracted to him just then. A shadow fell across the opened barn door right before rapid steps approached. When

Dylan looked in that direction, Deirdre took the opportunity to step away from him.

"Is everything all right, Deirdre?" came Kinan's voice. It may have been wrong of her to enjoy the edge of jealousy that sharpened his tone, but enjoy it she did.

She pushed past Dylan, trusting he would move out of the way of her horse, but not caring if he got stepped on if he didn't. Marching out into the aisle with Ciaren in tow, she smiled at Kinan. "I am now, thank you." The moment the words left her lips she knew she shouldn't have said them.

Kinan's eyes turned hard and dark as chips of brown jasper. "If he has bothered you in any way—"

She held up a hand. "No need to get worked up. I can handle myself."

He glared at Dylan a moment longer, but said nothing more. All that anger and resentment fell away when she reached his side.

"You can at that," he agreed as he offered her a hand up.

The hand she put in Kinan's shook a bit. She hadn't been afraid Dylan would press things any further. He didn't seem like that kind of man. It had nothing to do with the unwanted kiss. Her anger just got the better of her when a man didn't believe she could take care of herself. It brought up frustrating memories of her late husband. She settled onto the saddle—shifting her legs when the pistol pinched—and took up the reins.

"Thank you, Kinan."

He dipped his head low in a very gentlemanly bow. The chivalrous act combined with his respect for her capabilities calmed her wildly thudding heart and cooled her anger. With a press of her leg, she urged Ciaren out into the warm sunlight. The mare touched noses with Kinan's white stallion while Kinan swung up into the saddle.

"You are most welcome. Shall we go break out this outlaw of yours then?" he asked through a grin so large it was clear he was enjoying himself to no end. The sheer joy in his eyes made it impossible not to return his smile.

"We shall," she said as she rode with him up to the carriage.

The fast clip of a trotting horse came up behind them. "Careful, innkeeper. You could put the lady in more danger by making light of the situation," Dylan all but growled. The words made Deirdre bristle. In her experience, such a man responded poorly to the type of secrets she held. Perhaps she'd been wrong to allow interest in him to bloom.

She was about to give him a piece of her mind about the cool heads and capability of ladies when from around the side of the carriage came a stout buckskin that would have seemed big were it not for Kinan's tall stallion. On its back sat Rick, reins held loosely in one hand, the other resting on his thigh beside his pistol. Both the pistol belt and wide-brimmed hat made him look like a ruggedly handsome outlaw out of a penny-dreadful novel. The wolf that lay beneath shone in his eyes. A shot of envy for Cat having snared such a catch mingled pleasantly with pride in her friend. Rick tipped his hat to her before glaring at Dylan.

"Is there a problem, lads?" he asked.

Kinan waved a hand. "Not at all. Dylan here was just expressing his concern for the ladies' welfare."

As Kinan rode up alongside her, Deirdre realized he had a rifle holster rigged to his saddle. Her thighs clenched together, but not out of fear. She hadn't thought Kinan had it in him to be so bold, so daring as to partake in the potentially dangerous—

and illegal—part of this. It thrilled her in an entirely unexpected way to think of him as a fighter.

Rick laughed. "Clearly you don't know my Cat, or Deirdre, well enough. 'Tis the deputy's welfare you should concern yourself with," he said.

At that Deirdre smiled. She really liked this man. "Or Sadie. You should see the woman when it comes to someone messing with those she cares about. She is downright frightening," Deirdre said.

The carriage window slid open and Sadie's carefully tamed bun of hair popped out. "Did I hear my name? Deirdre, you're not riding with the men, are you?"

"Oh no, I'm merely riding alongside the carriage to entice the deputies to stop by showing a bit of ankle."

Cat's head came out next. "What's that Deirdre's up to?"

Sadie's bun bobbed. "Just scandalizing us all."

"But o' course," Cat said.

Deirdre rolled her eyes. "Oh, you two! Would you rather we let the men go in pistols blazing? You run the risk of sounding like Dylan."

Cat's gaze narrowed as it fixed on Dylan, who was climbing into the saddle of his brown stallion. "No. I will not have innocents harmed to free Cofield."

Dylan held his hands up in surrender. "Easy there, Miss Catriona. I only meant to warn Mrs. Quinn of the dangerous nature of our endeavor," he said.

A sharp laugh shot from Cat. "That was a mistake of epic proportions. Now she'll be downright impossible," she said.

Both women sat back in the carriage and began conversing in harsh whispers. The window panel slid shut and a loud rap on the roof sounded from within.

Rick grinned at the driver. "That's our cue. Let's go break out an outlaw."

13

Deirdre

Chains rattled from within the back of the prisoner transport wagon as it rolled to a stop. The moment the big bay draft horses halted, Deirdre gave Ciaren the cue. The mare reared up and pawed at the air—a neat little trick Deirdre had learned from Cat. Though her grip was strong and her seat secure, she cried out and wobbled with a dramatic flair. At a press of her heels, Ciaren backed away from the carriage Sadie and Cat sat within. Their driver looked up from where he was bent over a slightly askew wheel and feigned a cry of surprise.

Once again, Deirdre cued the mare to rear. Ciaren went up onto her hind legs and pawed the air like a wild thing, enjoying the game a little too much. A glance back showed Deirdre she was in the designated spot. Crying out in fake alarm—brilliantly, if she did say so herself—she pinwheeled her arms and tumbled from the saddle. Ferns reached for her, and along with them a bed of fallen leaves from years past and forest duff softened her landing. Brown and yellow leaves blown up by her impact floated back down to land around and on her. She lay still, feigning being stunned. As she lay there, she subtly rolled off the ferns and fed them energy. They sprang back up, no worse for the wear. Better even, now filled with her fae magic.

Ciaren's big nose soon blocked her view of the cloudy sky. The horse sniffed at her, big brown eyes filled with judgment. In that moment she didn't need Cat to tell her what the horse was thinking. Deirdre blew out a breath, trying to shoo her off. The whiskers around her mare's nose moved, but Ciaren did not.

"You're supposed to run," Deirdre whispered harshly. The nose came closer. "If you snort on me…"

The creak of someone stepping down from a wagon halted her words. Another creak followed and two sets of footsteps approached.

"Oh no, Mrs. Quinn!" came the voice of Henry, the elderly man who had been pretending to work on the carriage wheel. He groaned and wheezed as he tottered along at a rushed limp that wouldn't outrun a snail. The two deputies approaching from the wagon reached her long before he did. Ciaren's equine snout disappeared and a young man with a bushy beard took her place. From the chest of his blue, wool jacket shone a silver star.

"Are you all right, ma'am?" he asked.

She fluttered her eyes and groaned. Another face came into view, this one with mutton chops and a full beard, but not a speck of hair on his head. His fingers worried over a hat in his hands. The younger man knelt down and reached toward her.

"Wait now!" the bald deputy said. "Me uncle's a doc and he says you've got to be careful of moving a person when they've taken a fall. She could'a hit her head," he warned.

While they fussed over her and discussed what to do, she groaned and faked being on the edge of consciousness. Through her lashes, she saw Henry, Cat, and Sadie coming closer. After much discussion, and some pretty decent acting on her friends' parts, they decided to try and sit her up. Mostly to sneak a peek at the prisoner wagon, Deirdre opened her eyes. Behind the wagon she saw Kinan and Rick helping Cofield climb out. Thankfully, Cat and Sadie were making enough racket fussing over her to cover any sound the men might have made. Just for good measure, Deirdre groaned a little louder.

Rubbing the back of her head, she asked, "What happened?"

The deputies fumbled over each other trying to explain, and her friends continued to chat in excited tones about her welfare. She glimpsed at Henry, who gave her the sign to keep it up.

"Where am I?" she asked, batting her lashes at the deputies.

They devoured her flirtations, going so far as to let her stroke their badges and answering her every question about their exciting jobs. The older one finally offered to help Henry with their wheel. It was about bloody time. She had started to fear he'd never offer.

"That'd be splendid, thank you," Henry said.

The deputies each took an arm and stood with her until she stopped swaying, which she dragged out only as long as she dared. During that time, Henry gave her a slight nod, the all-clear sign they had agreed on. The deputies walked her to the carriage, with Cat, Sadie, and Henry in tow. Taking great care, they eased her down onto the step of the carriage.

"Thank you ever so much. You're both too kind," she said as she patted each of their hands in turn.

The younger deputy grinned, his cheeks turning bright pink. He became tongue-tied, so the elder answered for him. "You're quite welcome, miss." He looked to the younger man. "Go wait back at the wagon, I'll help the ladies here."

The young deputy straightened, pushing his chest out a bit. "Why don't you wait at the wagon," he mumbled.

The bald deputy shot him a glare that sent him marching back to the prisoner wagon, grumbling all the way. To keep the younger deputy's attention on her, Deirdre leaned forward to give him an eyeful of her cleavage, and shot him a disappointed look. Cheeks deepening to scarlet, his gaze descended to her breasts, which she heaved with a deep sigh. He climbed into the driver's seat of the prisoner wagon without taking his gaze off her once. Running her finger along the square neckline of her bodice, Deirdre chewed her bottom lip and watched him from beneath her lashes. He stared back.

The elder deputy soon finished helping them secure their wagon wheel, bid them farewell and rejoined the other deputy in the driver's seat of the prisoner wagon. Henry pulled their carriage around and got out of the way. The deputies waved as they drove past. Deirdre smiled in triumph. Keeping an eye on the retreating wagon, she rode alongside the carriage. The chilly morning air exposed each breath as puffs of white mist. She pulled the collar of her cloak up higher and ducked down into its warmth. Up ahead, a copse of trees surrounded the road, spindly white and black trunks choked so close together they were impossible to see through. More telltale puffs of white let her know their menfolk waited within. White branches adorned with yellow leaves beginning to turn brown stretched overhead in a mesmerizing web that served as a concealing canopy. Or at least, she hoped it would be concealing, should anyone be watching. Halfway through the trees, she reined Ciaren in. Henry stopped the carriage behind her.

The creaks and groans of the carriage eventually settled.

Deirdre's back went rigid as she waited for the men to emerge from the trees. She could no longer see their breath, or that of their horses. Not knowing what direction they'd come from made the skin on the back of her neck feel like a brownie tap danced across it. Her encounter with Cofield back on the trail to California ran through her mind. Such a ruthless, opportunistic man was capable of terrible things. What if he had overcome the men? No, that wasn't likely. Rick was a big half-Scot—not to mention faolach—and both Kinan and Dylan were quite strapping in their own rights. She recalled Cofield being thin and gangly. Surely he couldn't overcome them, could he?

The thought of Kinan or Dylan coming to harm because of her scheme made her feel ill. And Rick, of course. She didn't want Rick hurt. But knowing what he was, that hardly seemed a possibility. Her gaze darted about the trees as she contemplated drawing her pistol. Just as she started to lift her skirts, leaves crunched under several sets of hooves. Deirdre scooted the blue satin back over her legs just as three horses emerged to her right. Ciaren rumbled beneath her as she neighed to Kinan's white stallion. A smirk pulled up one corner of Kinan's lips, and he had a brow raised, gaze fixed on her legs. She smiled back and shrugged. Beside him, Dylan glared in annoyance, not at Kinan, but at her. Was it the look she had given Kinan that bothered him, or the fact that he guessed she'd been about to draw her pistol? Regardless, it only exacerbated her irritation toward Dylan.

Ropes knotted about Cofield's hands tethered him to Rick's buckskin horse. He stumbled along behind, his beady gaze darting every which way. Those eyes fixed on Deirdre and narrowed, but it wasn't anger that filled them, it was confusion and terror. Dylan positioned his horse slightly between her and

Cofield, while Kinan rode to her side. It was all she could do not to snap at Dylan for being so ridiculously overprotective. But, with Ciaren being taller than Dylan's horse, she could still see Cofield. That would do for now. She could lecture Dylan later. Right now, they needed to display a unified front.

Rick gave the rope holding Cofield a little jerk. Yanked forward by his bound hands, the man sprawled face-first into the dirt and leaves. Seeing him treated in such a manner stirred regret in Deirdre that she hadn't been the one to do it. Not only had he once taken her at knifepoint, intending to use her for leverage, but he had also tried multiple times to kill Cat and Rick. Despite the fact she had overcome the man, he had made her feel weak and afraid, and she hated that. It made her wonder if she really could work with him after all.

"All clear," Rick called.

The carriage door opened and out strode Cat, each step of her boots sharp. Long, red hair flew about her upper body like flames eager to devour any that got too close. Her fierce countenance and aggressive steps made both Rick's and Dylan's horses take steps back. Deirdre grinned. Eager to join Cat, she started to free her legs from the sidesaddle bars. Kinan appeared on the ground at her side before she could leap down. At first she thought him there to stop her, but then he reached his hands up to her. Eyes going wide, she nodded. Hands on her waist, he eased her to the ground. They shared a long look during which she tried to read what he was thinking. The man was too adept at hiding his emotions, though. But one thing was clear, he wouldn't stop her. She gave him a deep nod of gratitude before marching over to Cat's side. Out of the corner of her eye she noticed Dylan watching her, glowering.

Cofield let out a groan as he pushed himself upright. When his gaze traveled up their dresses to their faces, his eyes went wide, then his gaze darted to Rick. "Not like this. Killed while bound, on my knees, by witches. At least do me the courtesy of killing me yourself," he begged.

Rick's chin lifted. "You talk to them, not to me. If it were up to me, you would die a slow, dishonorable death."

Cofield looked to Kinan, who lifted his chin. "My sentiments are the same," Kinan said.

The man's desperate gaze turned to Dylan. "You'd be dead already if it were up to me," Dylan all but growled. The vehemence in his voice startled Deirdre and made her wonder. She realized she didn't know much about him. Had he served in the war like Rick and Kinan? Could some of his overprotective attitude be that of a soldier's nature to protect?

Cofield turned back to her and Cat. Knowing how much her friend needed this, Deirdre let Cat do the talking. "I rather like the idea of you dying by our hands, bound and on your knees," Cat said through a smile that bared teeth.

The sort of purring noise that came from Deirdre was in no way friendly. "As do I." In response to her anger, a spiky leafed aloe near his leg stretched over and poked him.

Wide eyes going from her to the plant, Cofield's bottom lip quivered. He scooted away from it. Teary eyes beseeched them. "Please don't. I…I can be useful to you."

A quick glance around told Deirdre no one had noticed the plant but Cofield, Cat, and Sadie. She turned her gaze to Cat. The two of them smiled. "Aye, you can," they said in unison.

Cofield's brow furrowed and confusion clouded his already muddy eyes. At first, he shook his head, then he began nodding as if the words had finally sunk in. "Yes, yes, I can, very useful!" He half rose, jerking to a startled halt when his rope went taut. The fear in his eyes disgusted Deirdre as he glanced back at Rick.

"'Tis going to be a long, cold winter, Cofield. I don't imagine you want to spend it on the run, do you?" Cat asked.

His mouth gaped, as if he weren't sure how to answer and was afraid to get it wrong. A touch of guilt pinched at Deirdre for enjoying the effect they had on him.

"Well, uh...no. But if that's what you want, I'll do it," Cofield said. Throat working, he swallowed hard. "As long as it isn't...evil." The last word was no more than a whisper.

"Ugh," Deirdre groaned and rolled her eyes.

Again, she and Cat exchanged a look, this time a long, thoughtful one, as if they hadn't figured out how he could be useful yet. Deirdre shrugged. "If he went south, Ainsworth would catch him and finish him off so there's no chance he'd testify against him," she said.

Cat cocked her head as if in thought. "Well, he can't go north or east, else he'll get caught in the Sierras and likely die chewing his own arm off, like that poor Donner party," she said.

Mention of that recent, frightful incident almost made Deirdre shiver, but she suppressed it. Around the dark of the campfire their guides had told it like a ghost story with a horrible lesson for any who wanted to take that shortcut. "Likely," Deirdre agreed.

Sweat started to drip down Cofield's brow despite the chill in the air. "Useful, I can be useful," he mumbled as his eyes cast to the ground and flitted across the leaves as if they held the answers.

"But he's Ainsworth's man. What use could he possibly be

to us?" Deirdre asked.

A dramatic sigh came from Cat that might have been overdoing it if Cofield wasn't so out of his mind with fear. "We can't have him ask Ainsworth to allow us to cross his land with the timber we're purchasing. The man would shoot him as soon as look at him."

Deirdre waved a hand. "Maybe we should just let him. I don't see what use he could be to us."

Cofield stood a little taller. "Timber, you need timber?" he latched on to the words.

Finally, Cat looked at him, but her expression was aloof, doubtful. "Aye, but Ainsworth has everyone south of town convinced not to sell to us, and he won't let us cross his land to get it from anyone else. You can't help us with that."

A wild desperation entered Cofield's eyes. He stood. "But I can. I can show you how to get through his land without him ever knowing. The man has two thousand acres and doesn't know his way around but a hundred of it."

Deirdre's gaze narrowed on him. "And you do?" She wanted to say more, to prod him along faster, but she didn't dare. It would work best if he thought this was his idea.

Cofield nodded so vigorously it looked like it hurt. "Yes! I could sneak an entire garrison through those woods and he'd never know it."

"Really?" Cat asked, disbelief evident in the lines on her face.

"Really, I can do it. I was a guide before Ainsworth made me do the things he did. And I was a good one."

Sadness worked at Deirdre, not for Cofield, but for all the lives Ainsworth had ruined in some way or another. She hadn't known it was possible to dislike someone so intensely that she'd never met.

"I don't know about this. Snow will be covering the hills in less than two months," Deirdre persisted.

Palms pressed together as if in prayer, Cofield held his hands up. "I'll take you through this very moment if you wish. Just to the northeast of Ainsworth's property, on the other side of the hill, is a rancher who I know would sell you timber. We could probably get three loads over the hills before the snow falls," he said, so fast his words tumbled over each other.

Cat pretended to exchange a doubtful look with Rick. Cofield looked up at him. "And I'll keep taking you so long as the weather allows." His gaze shot back to Cat and he put on a pitiful look. "I only need somewhere to hole up for the winter, somewhere Ainsworth won't find me."

Rick let out a long breath. "We like Ainsworth even less than we like you. I suppose we have a hatred of him in common. I have a small hunting cabin in the hills of me property. If you really can deliver, I guess we could hide you there for the winter," he said.

Peering through his scraggly hair at Rick, Cofield asked, "Is it secluded?"

"Aye, 'tis nestled deep in the birch and hemlock. No one knows 'tis there."

Head darting every which way to take them all in, a nervous grin split Cofield's face. "We have an agreement then. I will do this for you and you will hide me through the winter. I'll deliver, you won't be disappointed."

Fists clenched, Cat took a step closer to him. "I'd better not be, or we'll turn you out for either the wolves or Ainsworth to get—and this time, I'll be sure they finish the job. You know I'll do it," she said in a voice so chilly it made bumps rise on Deirdre's arms.

The man looked to Deirdre, and she gave him a grin filled with dark promise. Cofield's throat worked hard. "You won't be disappointed, I promise."

Leaves fluttered as Rick leaped down from his horse. The air around his hands shimmered. Long, sharp claws grew out from his fingernail beds. Breath coming in short gasps, the smaller man cowered. "We had better not be," Rick snapped.

In one fast slash, he cut the bonds from Cofield's wrists. The man's eyes closed for such a long moment, Deirdre thought he might faint. The claws drew back into Rick's hands, the tips of them smoothing into the half moons of human fingernails. He handed the reins of his buckskin horse to Cat. She nodded. He helped her into the saddle, hand lingering on her leg as he gave her a meaningful look. Face going hard once again, he turned to Cofield, who had finally opened his eyes. "You'll ride with me in the carriage. 'Tis best to keep you out of sight."

The man's wide eyes fixed on Rick's hands while they walked to the carriage. Twice, Cofield tripped and nearly fell, but he never took his eyes off him. Deirdre wished she could have been a fly on the wall of that carriage. Still, she couldn't help but fear they may have made a deal with a dullahan to try and outwit a devil.

14

Dylan

Mid-September

Dylan put on his most charming smile as he rapped on one of the massive double doors of Ainsworth's house. His scarred and calloused knuckles made a succession of loud booms that echoed through the quiet place. The patter of small, feminine feet soon sounded on the stone floor within. A moment later, the front door opened. In the open doorway stood a petite Hispanic woman wearing an apron. Her long, dark hair was swept up into a bun and pretty eyes made Dylan fear she likely was expected to do more than just clean Ainsworth's house.

"Can I help you?" she asked in impeccable English that held the barest hint of an accent. Of course, the bastard would have demanded no less from his help. Dylan struggled to hold his smile as his mind conjured up the horrors this woman likely had to endure at Ainsworth's hands.

Not having a hat to doff, he instead dipped his head in a deep bow to her. "Most certainly, lovely lass. I have news for Mr. Ainsworth. May I speak with him?"

Her cheeks twitched as if she wanted to smile but couldn't

quite recall how. He feared she wasn't used to compliments. Sad as it was, that would make this far easier.

"I'm afraid he is out with the cattle. You'll have to come back," she said, reaching for the door.

Of course, Dylan had known he was out with the cattle, along with all of his ranch hands. It was precisely why he had chosen this moment. Frowning, he put on a fear-filled look. "Oh, well, you see, he told me to come straight away with this news. He'll be angry as a badger if I don't get it to him the moment he returns."

A sympathetic look filled her eyes, and she nodded. "I understand. You can wait here on the porch."

Dylan's eyes widened and he swallowed hard. "I'm afraid that'd be a bad idea. You see, Mr. Ainsworth doesn't want anyone to see me delivering this news. Waiting in his study, so he is the first to see me, would be best."

Again she nodded, adding a sigh as if this didn't surprise her in the slightest. "Ah, that kind of news. In that case, right this way."

Taking note of each hallway and door in the open layout of the sprawling cabin, he followed the housekeeper to Ainsworth's study. Rugs woven in patterns favored by the Cherokee covered the polished wooden floor. It surprised Dylan to see them. On many occasions, he had heard Ainsworth express a dislike for any culture that wasn't English. But then, he supposed, just like the young woman hunched in on herself walking before him, Ainsworth appreciated things he felt he had dominated.

Down a long hall, the housekeeper opened the second door to the left. Finely crafted bookshelves lined three walls, while a large window took up the fourth. Sunlight poured through the glass to bathe a monstrosity of a desk that looked like it had been hewn from one solid piece of oak. A huge wingback chair with plush upholstery that resembled a throne sat on the far side of the desk, and a small, straight-backed chair sat on other. The housekeeper gestured to the small, uncomfortable-looking chair.

Still holding his smile in place, Dylan sat. "Thank you kindly, miss."

Gaze cast down, the woman began to back out of the room. "You are welcome. I will bring tea if he has not returned at the hour," she said.

"That would be wonderful, thank you."

His gaze flicked toward the clock mounted on the wall above the window. Twenty minutes until the top of the hour. That should be plenty of time. The moment the door clicked closed behind the housekeeper, Dylan was on his feet. Not so much as a paperweight cluttered the top of Ainsworth's desk. Keeping one eye on the pasture that sprawled outside the window, Dylan dashed behind the desk and pulled open the first drawer. Parchment, an ink pot, and two quill pens perfectly placed were all he found.

Mounted beneath the top drawer he felt a pistol. He took it out and checked it. Only half the chambers of the six-shooter were filled. He spun the cylinder so the bullets occupied the last three chambers. One never knew when one would need a head start. This was Ainsworth, after all. Nothing else of interest occupied the immaculately organized desk drawers. Dylan moved on to the bookshelves. He perused every single book carefully, even checking behind them to make sure nothing lay hidden.

A glance at the clock told him he had only ten minutes left

before the housekeeper returned.

On a whim, he returned to the desk. The hollow sound of the floorboards beneath his boots drew his attention. He pulled back the blue-and-red woven rug. A small but distinct groove had been cut into one of the boards. Breath held, he lifted it. Several boards came up as one, a door of sorts. Beneath lay another door, this one iron, and boasting a complicated-looking lock. Dylan grinned. It had to be in there.

Lucky for him, he had a knack for unlocking things. As he reached for the lock, he heard Ainsworth's voice raised in anger. A loud slap followed. Dylan leaped up, repositioned everything precisely as he had found it, and all but flew back to the chair on the other side of the desk. The chink of spurs accented the clip-clop of heavy bootheels coming down the hall. Heart pounding, he relaxed back into the chair, rested the ankle of his right leg on his left knee, and crossed his arms over his chest. He slouched a bit and let his head hang as if he'd been catching a nap.

The door to the office flew open hard enough to slam against the bookcase behind it. Ainsworth strode in, lips pulled back from his teeth like a snarling animal. Dylan sat upright with a start, feigning grogginess. Some of the ire drained from Ainsworth's eyes, only to be replaced by hunger. The man looked like a femorian—evil and greedy.

"You have information for me?" he asked as he closed the door.

"I do." He hadn't wanted to divulge anything, but he'd also come prepared.

Ainsworth strode over and sat on the edge of his desk. "Well, out with it."

"This Saturday, O'Leary is taking the Quinn and

MacMurphy women on a shopping trip," Dylan began.

Ainsworth's dark brows pinched together, but a sinister interest darkened his eyes. "And why should this interest me?" he asked in a tone that made it clear he knew there was more to it.

"Because of the size of the wagon they're taking."

A languid, serpentine smile worked its way across Ainsworth's lips. "One big enough to haul logs in."

"That's what it sounded like. They clammed up as soon as they knew I was within earshot."

The humorless laugh that burped from Ainsworth made Dylan's skin crawl. "Good work, Mick! Stay close, earn their trust. Find out all you can."

Dylan nodded and kept his gaze on the ground, allowing his blond locks to fall down and hide the anger scorching a crimson trail across his cheeks. The racial slur was almost more than he could take, especially coming from an Englishman. But this Englishman had something he desperately needed. Until he had it back in his hands, Dylan had to play along. Lives depended on him keeping a cool head.

"I will."

Laughing, Ainsworth turned to the shelf behind his desk that held a whiskey decanter. With the man's mood having turned so good, Dylan decided to press his luck just a bit.

"About Victoria's rent..." he trailed off.

Amber liquid sloshed into a glass so clear it had to cost a week's wages. Dylan remained silent while Ainsworth smelled the whiskey, took a long, slow drink, and lowered the glass. All the while he fantasized about strangling the man with his own belt. It helped to keep the anger at bay.

"Consider it paid for the month," Ainsworth finally said.

Relief pulled a long breath from Dylan, and he let Ainsworth hear it because he knew it would feed the man's ego. "Thank you," he answered simply, unable to debase himself any further than that.

Ainsworth peered at him over the top of his glass. "Keep the information flowing and the old bat will keep living rent-free."

Lips pulled tight in the best semblance of a smile he could manage, Dylan nodded. Taking another long drink, Ainsworth turned to gaze out the window, effectively dismissing him. Dylan strode from the room as fast as would be considered polite. He couldn't get away from the man quick enough. Ainsworth's dark presence followed him like the oily spray of a skunk.

15

Deirdre

The day spent shopping with Kinan and Sadie turned out to be far more pleasant than Deirdre imagined it would be. Kinan was insufferably proper and polite, as she feared he would be, but he was also gracious and thoughtful. In a surprising manner that went completely against her nature, Sadie took every opportunity to leave the two of them alone.

To Deirdre's disappointment, Kinan's gentlemanly manners remained flawless. Not even her scandalously low-cut bodice seemed to sway him. She had so been hoping it would. But his eyes never so much as strayed down to her cleavage. Though he took every opportunity to touch her hand or back while helping her in and out of the wagon, the gloves he wore made the touch far less intimate than she would have liked. And those touches never lingered longer than was proper.

Regardless, she had a good time. Their conversations on astronomy and exotic cultures stimulated and engaged her. Not only did he ask for her thoughts and opinions, but he leaned close when she answered, listening eagerly to her ideas. Throughout the day, he indulged their every whim, taking them to some shops they hadn't even thought to ask to stop at, and he carried all their packages without complaint, never once asking their driver to do it for him.

He couldn't have been more different from Deirdre's late husband. Unless, of course, he scoffed at her secrets and judged her for them. But that was a trestle over a gaping chasm she wasn't sure she was willing to cross yet.

They stacked the huge wagon from boards to arched canvas cover with all manner of things: bolts of fabric, ribbons, thread, glassware, furniture, and presents for both the upcoming holiday and the wedding. Not an ounce of space remained when they set out to return to Goldenvale.

Beside Deirdre, Sadie reclined amid a bundle of blankets that cocooned her sleeping form like a butterfly in the making. Though she pretended differently, it was no longer exhaustion that made Sadie sleep, but rather yet another attempt to leave Deirdre and Kinan as alone as possible. She faked it rather well, even throwing in a little ladylike snore, but Deirdre knew better. The way Sadie stretched out forced her and Kinan to sit so close their legs and shoulders touched. His body was hot as warming coals placed beneath the covers on a cold night. The thought made her wish he'd slide beneath the cover that spread over her lap.

He relaxed against her, leaning over every now and then as they conversed. Each time he did, her heart beat a little harder. Had his breathing sped up, or was her hopeful mind simply imagining it? As the first buildings of town rose up on either side of the road, he moved away.

"Some think the patterns of stars can affect things just as the moon affects the tides," Kinan said.

The concept fascinated Deirdre. "Do you believe such

things?" she asked.

He nodded. "I do indeed. I believe there is much we can learn from the stars."

Head tilting to the side as it did when something occurred to her, Deirdre said, "I think the people in your books and tapestries likely believed such things. They seemed enamored of the stars."

Eyes lighting up, his expression became impassioned. The look tugged at something deep inside her. "They were. They believed you could learn many things from the stars, even divine the future from them. I have a book on the subject you may find interesting."

She lay her hand atop his where it clutched the reins. His gaze darted to the houses set back on either side of the road as if afraid someone might see. The road remained empty save for them for at least another quarter mile, and the few people working out in their gardens weren't looking their way. At least not now, and Deirdre didn't care if they did. She didn't let go of his hand.

It was time to be more direct. "Are you so worried about what others think, about the proper rules of society and courtship?" she asked.

He stuttered and stumbled over his words for a moment before finally breaking into a large smile. "Actually, I just don't want to disrespect you. And I would like you to know all about me before we start anything serious. Which, I would very much like to start," he said, voice dropping an octave at the last part in a sultry way that resonated through her.

Could he possibly mean what she hoped he meant? "In that case, tell me all about yourself." If confiding in her was all that held him back from being more amorous, then she wanted it done and out of the way. She could imagine nothing short of him having worked in a French whorehouse or fighting for the south that would change how much she was drawn to him. And the likelihood of either was slim. That thought made her grin as she pictured him working in a French whorehouse.

"All right. Well, uh…I am…" His hesitant words halted.

At first, she thought him merely building the dramatic tension. The wide-eyed look of surprise on his face only made her think so more. She gave his arm a playful slap, hand lingering afterward. The swell of biceps under her fingers made them explore farther down his arm. But when he didn't go on, or look at her after a long moment, she followed his gaze.

Two men sat beneath the covered awning of the sheriff's building that their wagon had just started to pass. The man with a friar-like bald spot that shone even in the muted sunlight was easily recognizable by the glinting star pinned to the left breast of his coat. His arms crossed over his paunch, which spilled so substantially over his pistol belt that Deirdre didn't think he'd be able to draw the weapon. He chewed absently on a twig, which from the scent of it came from the apple tree stretching its limbs over the building.

It was the second man that held Kinan's fierce gaze. The intense look the other man gave them made her skin feel like bugs crawled across it. Long, spindly legs stretched out before the man as he lounged back in his chair, leather boots crossed. One hand held a cup to his lips, the other rested on the butt of a very large pistol. Calculating eyes stared at them from beneath the brim of a leather hat.

So intent was she on watching the second man, that the

wagon coming to a halt took her completely by surprise. She jerked forward on the bench, stopped only by Kinan's arm reaching across her. Thankfully, Sadie had been nestled into the bench so securely that it barely jostled her. Her head popped up from the bundle of blankets, eyes wide and fully aware.

Puddles splashed beneath the boots of the two deputies who now held the harnesses of Kinan's draft horses.

"Good day, deputies. What can we do for you?" Kinan asked in a tone dark with contempt.

Off to their right, the sheriff and the spindly man rose and approached. The spindly man unfolded more than rose, his long limbs extending like those of a spider. A flick of his wrist erupted dark liquid from his cup into the street. In a very ungentlemanly manner, he spat the applewood twig out, then set the cup on his chair without breaking eye contact with Deirdre.

Sadie leaned across Deirdre and whispered to Kinan, "Is that Ainsworth?"

Before he answered, Deirdre knew. She felt it in her bones.

"Yes," Kinan confirmed, his tone chilly.

"Mr. O'Leary, I trust you'll cooperate," the sheriff called out as he waddled up. "You see, Mr. Ainsworth here had some property stolen and we're checking wagons, just to be on the safe side."

Kinan thrust his hand down the street. "I suppose that doesn't include that wagon that just passed before us unmolested?"

The sheriff held his hands out, palms toward them. "No need to get riled, now. The items stolen were too large to fit in a wagon that small."

A clever enough ruse, she had to hand it to him. Ainsworth

walked up to Sadie's side of the wagon, stopping close enough he could have reached up and touched her if he wished. But Sadie may as well have been invisible, for his hard gaze never left Deirdre. The look in his dull, gray eyes held something akin to a predator. It tried to send a chill through her, but she suppressed it. She would not show an inkling of weakness to this man. Anger swiftly burned away the chill. The limbs of the apple tree casting the shadows over them danced as if caught in a breeze.

But there was no breeze.

Rest. I am well. Only temperamental, Deirdre assured the tree.

"Mrs. Deirdre Quinn, I presume," he said in the harsh voice of one who partook of too much tobacco and had for some time. Hidden in his voice, she detected a tone of admiration, slight though it was. The long look he took at her cleavage made it clear what he admired about her. His lips turned up into either a grimace or a smile—she wasn't sure which. "No one mentioned how lovely you are," he said, sounding irritated about the fact.

Lifting her chin, Deirdre gave him a steely gaze. "You would have discovered that if you had received me when I sent along my card."

He shrugged. "I regret that I've been unable to receive guests. The holiday is nearly upon us, as you know. The year is quickly waning." At the last part, his predatory smile grew wide enough she could practically see all his teeth.

One deputy remained at the head of their team while the other walked back around the wagon with the sheriff. Kinan leaped down from the wagon and stormed out of sight, boots thudding against the frozen ground.

Ainsworth dipped his head in a mockery of a bow and set

his hat back upon it. "If you'll excuse me, ladies," he said in a tone that sounded entirely too pleased.

As soon as he disappeared around the side of the wagon, Deirdre and Sadie exchanged a smile. They scrambled from the seat in a most unladylike manner and hurried to the back, where the men had gathered. Deirdre placed her hands on her hips and feigned indignation.

"You cannot possibly believe we would steal anything from you. My friends and I have adequate means of our own—and honor atop that. We would never do such a thing," she said.

Ainsworth's oily gaze slid to her. "I certainly hope not. But widows alone in a man's world can become quite desperate."

The calculation in those eyes, the weight of his gaze—they were traits of a dangerous man. She had encountered his like in New York, but she had never been the focus of such a man before. To be so now, on her own, without a husband to shield her, was disconcerting enough to make her queasy. But at the same time, it felt liberating. "And you've had a lot of experience harassing bereft widows, have you?" she asked before good sense could stop her.

The grin Ainsworth gave her remained humorless as his gaze crawled up her body. Something dark and horrible lay in that gaze, something that chilled her to the bone and made her heart nearly skip with fear. "Adequate experience with women, yes, I do have that. Harassing widows, certainly not." A dull pink tongue wetted his lips. "I wouldn't suspect such a…lovely, proper lady as yourself of wrongdoing. But, you see, you have taken up with an unsavory sort." A hard, dark edge entered his eyes as his gaze flicked to Kinan and back. "Though, as you are new in town, I suspect that isn't your fault."

The sheriff looked to Ainsworth, who nodded without so much as turning his head in the man's direction. Right hand on his pistol, eyes on Kinan, the sheriff flung the tarp covering the contents of their wagon aside. Both Ainsworth and the sheriff's smug grins melted away at the sight of the colorful bolts of fabric nestled amid furniture and wooden boxes. Ainsworth's jaw clenched.

"One would think you are moving into the inn, Mrs. Quinn. Perhaps there is an announcement I missed." At the last, he shot a sharp glare toward the sheriff. Eyes going wide with fear, the sheriff shook his head.

An unexpected pang of sympathy for the man pierced Deirdre's heart. No one should have to live in that much fear. She lifted her chin. "I am decorating it. And, in fact, you did miss an announcement when you failed to allow me an audience."

Ainsworth's thin smile grew wide, and disturbingly, thinner. "I am intrigued, do tell."

The deputy reached up to touch a bolt of lace only to have his hand promptly smacked by Sadie. Glaring, he turned to her. She stood tall, her fierce countenance a warning that things would not go well for him if he persisted. Alarm rattled through Deirdre. An old, rotten apple that had been clinging to the tree overhead suddenly fell, smacking the man on the shoulder. With a start, he looked up and took a step back. Deirdre looped an arm through Sadie's, effectively cutting off the deputy's access to the wagon.

With Sadie placated, and the young man safe from her wrath, Deirdre looked to Ainsworth. "We're decorating for Patrick Fergusson and Catriona O'Brian's engagement party, which is occurring next month," she said.

The skin around his eyes tightened briefly, but that was his only sign of displeasure. "Ah, my invitation must have been lost by the courier."

"Not at all. I feared sending it only to have it returned. But I do indeed have an invitation for you."

His brows pulled up. "You would like me to attend?" The question sounded like a challenge.

Deirdre put on her most sincere face. "Of course, I would. Mr. Ainsworth, you are a pillar of this community, and our neighbor. We have every reason to be cordial and cooperate with one another."

Ainsworth made a humming noise low in his throat that sounded as if he could be in agreement or disagreement.

Deirdre sighed, making it sound as dramatic as she dared. "I understand that we have conflicting interests, but that doesn't mean we can't be neighborly. There is a wedding afoot, not to mention the holidays. Surely, we can put our differences aside for that. At least until the spring when things with our property truly get under way."

Something flashed in his eyes that might have been triumph, before he swept his hat off and dipped his head to her in a gesture that almost looked genuinely gracious. "You are quite right. And who knows. By then, we may not be at such odds." Were it not for the flat look in his eyes, she might have thought he meant it.

"In that case, I do hope you'll be able to attend the engagement party. It won't be complete without you." Eyes wide, Deirdre looked to Sadie. "Do we have any invitations with us?"

Nodding, Sadie dug in a small satchel. She produced a fine

envelope with a green wax seal of Celtic knotwork upon it. Deirdre had to tug it from her fingers. Sadie's eyes pinched into slits, but Ainsworth ignored her as if he couldn't feel the glare. As much as Deirdre hated people ignoring Sadie, in this case, she didn't mind. Escaping this man's notice was a good thing. Besides, it meant he underestimated Sadie, and they could use that to their advantage.

Deirdre batted her lashes a bit, curtsied just enough to give him a good look down her cleavage, and handed the invitation to him. If he thought her the fool for using her feminine wiles, all the better. His brows rose with a look of interest as he took the envelope.

"I will attempt to make it," he said.

"Wonderful! I do hope you will. I shall save a dance for you," she said in her sweetest voice.

"I look forward to that," he said, sounding sincere for the first time in their conversation.

To hide her look of disgust, Deirdre dipped her head in a feigned demure move that spilled black waves of hair across her face.

Ainsworth took a step away and put his hat back on his head. "I shall let you get back to your event planning. Until Saturday, Mrs. Quinn."

"Until Saturday," she agreed with far more cheer than she felt.

The sheriff and his deputies left to join Ainsworth in the street. Deirdre held eye contact with Ainsworth only so long as would be considered proper, smiling all the while. She fought the instinct to give him a coy look, knowing it would do more harm than good. He was too intelligent for such blatant tactics to be used too frequently.

Kinan started for the front of the wagon. Deirdre took hold of Sadie's hand and followed at a clipped pace. She suddenly didn't want to be very far away from him. Even as Ainsworth's steps retreated toward the sheriff's building, she felt the weight of his gaze on her. It made the skin all across her back crawl and gave her a powerful urge to walk faster. Instead, she slowed her pace. Couldn't have Ainsworth thinking she feared him. It would ruin her plan.

With his long strides, Kinan easily beat them to the front of the wagon. The warmth of his hand beneath hers as he helped her in made her realize how terribly cold she had grown. While it was cold out, she feared the chill came from the encounter with Ainsworth. Only moments passed as Kinan helped Sadie into the wagon then climbed in himself, but it felt like an eternity. She couldn't get away from Ainsworth fast enough.

Fixing a smile in place, she leaned out and waved as Kinan flicked the reins and propelled the horses into motion. Ainsworth grabbed the rim of his hat and dipped his head to her. The edge of the wagon cover soon blocked him from view, allowing Deirdre to breathe a touch easier. To think, she had nearly gone to that man's house to confront him alone… A powerful shudder shook her from head to toe. Gaze on the frozen dirt road before them, Kinan reached back into the wagon and grabbed a blanket. He handed it to Deirdre and Sadie.

"Here you are, for the chill." His soft voice comforted and beckoned her. She wanted nothing more than to snuggle up to his warmth and feel safe—even if for a brief moment. But, of course, she couldn't.

She accepted the blanket and spread it over both hers and

Sadie's laps. Sadie scooted closer to her, drawing both strength and warmth from her.

"Thank you," Deirdre told Kinan softly.

It wasn't merely the blanket she was grateful for. If she hadn't come across Kinan that day after leaving the woods, she feared she would have gone to Ainsworth's. Seeing Kinan then had calmed her, allowed her to think rationally, and had changed her mind. Now that she had met Ainsworth, she realized, coming across Kinan that day might have also saved her life. Something dark clung to Ainsworth. It didn't feel supernatural, but that made it no less terrifying. Some humans held darkness within them that could rival the darkest of creatures.

Sadie shuddered. "That man leaves a foul taste in one's mouth, a powerfully foul taste," she said.

"Yes, and a chill in one's bones. I have a desire to gargle with whiskey to rid myself of the taste and sit by a fire for days," Deirdre agreed.

Kinan flicked the reins again, urging the horses faster. "As soon as we reach the inn, I'll have baths drawn and whiskey brought up to your rooms. In fact, I think I'll do the same for myself," he said.

Only one thing sounded better to Deirdre, and that was Kinan in the bath with her. She needed to rid herself of the seedy feel of Ainsworth's gaze on her. And what better way to do that than to experience a more memorable sensation, one sure to set her afire. Sadly, Kinan was far too proper for such things. This was one chill Deirdre would have to banish on her own.

16

Deirdre

Mid-September

The morning rays spilled over the distant hills to bathe the massive pile of lodgepole pine logs in a soft glow. It was quite possibly the most horrible and beautiful thing Deirdre had ever seen. This pile was smaller than the piles at her and Sadie's home sites. Cat intended to live with Rick, but a home needed to be built here to ensure they didn't lose the land. The barn for the horses and winery itself was not enough, according to the county official.

"There are so many of them," she said in a choked voice.

At her insistence, they had asked for trees cut to thin the forest for its own health, ensuring it would better survive a wildfire. Their supplier had assured them that was the case. Still, she felt each of their deaths like a blow to her heart. It seemed a horrible sacrifice to put a roof over their heads. But she was not naïve. Such deaths occurred all the time for the sake of civilization. That didn't mean she had to like it. She had also asked for seeds so they could plant one for each log it took to build their homes, to honor what the trees had given to them. It did not make up for taking their lives, but she vowed to remember and replenish each of them.

Frost crunched beneath her boots as she stepped up to stroke the rough bark of a log half as big around as she was tall. The pile of them was almost as tall as a single-story house. Their sweet pine scent filled her nose.

Sadie took her hand and squeezed tight. "They are indeed," she agreed, her face aglow with happiness, but her eyes tinged with sympathy.

Cat joined them on Deirdre's right. "Aye, but not to worry, Deirdre. Cofield is escorting several of Rick's ranch hands with the last load as we speak. And Rick has a bag of pinecones for us so we can plant in the trees honor," she said.

Eyes tearing up, Deirdre sniffled. Cat rubbed her back and leaned her head on her shoulder.

"Ranch hands?" Sadie asked, her tone filled with concern.

"No worries, they're old friends of his, freemen he met during the war."

Sadie's eyes widened. "Do they really think it's necessary to guard the logs, on our own land?"

The hard look Cat gave her surprised Deirdre. "Aye. We wouldn't put anything past Ainsworth. Rick thought it best for each of our home sites to have at least one guard from here on out, just to be safe," she said.

"Just one?" Deirdre asked.

"More when possible, but they'll also use brush as a signal fire should trouble come."

Chills traveled through Deirdre. Now that she had met Ainsworth, she wouldn't put it past him to send men out to spy on them. She was infinitely glad Rick had thought of guarding the home sites.

Male voices engaged in conversation came from their left, growing louder as they approached. A few moments later, Rick and Dylan emerged from around the pile of logs. The sight of Dylan made Deirdre tug at her breeches self-consciously. Men's clothes were something she had never worn, and while they fit quite comfortably, she was insecure about how she looked in them. But Cat had insisted they would be more comfortable for the work that had to be done.

Sadie batted Deirdre's hands away. "Oh, do stop, or you'll get me to fussing, too. These things cling in unspeakable places," she whispered. She did a bit of a twist and wiggle, trying to adjust her own breeches.

It would have made her smile if not for the oppressive feel of the trees' deaths so thick in the air. But Deirdre knew exactly how she felt. The urge to grab the seat of her breeches and pull them from her behind was almost overwhelming. That was something she wouldn't do in present company, no matter how uncomfortable it was.

Cat laughed. "You'll get used to it."

Dylan drew up at the sight of them. He blinked rapidly several times as if unsure what he beheld. The confusion on his face mingled with the desire in his eyes in a most conflicting manner. The reaction only made Deirdre tug at her clothes all the more. Not that she cared if Dylan found the outfit displeasing. If anything, it only infuriated her that he would be so traditional. Rather, it was the fact that being self-conscious was not a thing she was used to and she didn't like it.

"Good morning, ladies. I didn't realize you'd be working alongside us today," he said. She liked his displeased tone even less than the fact that he made her feel self-conscious.

"Yes, well, we may not be as strong as men, but you'll be surprised at how hard we can work," she said.

Mouth gaping, Dylan's flexed his fingers around the big hook in his hand, knuckles turning white. "I'm just sorry you ladies have to. 'Tisn't right what Ainsworth's doing to you all," he said.

Rick clapped the man on the shoulder. "No worries, he isn't going to succeed, and that's what matters. When me lads return, we'll have all the workers and materials we need to put up these cabins in no time at all."

He strode around the man, eyes only for Cat. One of his big hands cupped her cheek. The emotional look they shared made Deirdre look down out of a desire not to intrude. In his other hand, he held a curved metal device, not unlike a hoe, though with a much shorter handle.

"Don't be overworking yourself now, you hear?" Rick told Cat in a gentle tone. He pressed the metal tool into her hands.

"I won't, I promise," she said.

The crunching of frosty grass made Deirdre look up. Dylan stood before her, two more of the metal tools and leather gloves in hand. He hesitantly gave her and Sadie each a pair of gloves and one of the tools. She looked at the thing, the logs, and then Dylan. "I'm afraid I have no idea how to use this," she admitted.

He hid a grin, poorly. "No worries, I'll show you."

Already, Cat was trying out the tool on a log with Rick's guidance. Sadie slid on the pair of gloves, took up the tool, and nodded to Dylan. "Thank you. I've seen one used before," she said.

She strode off to the end of the log pile where Cat and Rick worked. Normally, Deirdre would have been thrilled to be left alone with a handsome young man who fancied her. But she couldn't stop thinking of how he had disapproved of her riding along to free Cofield. More than that, she couldn't get Kinan out of her head. Silly, she knew. The man was entirely wrong for her; far too proper, a businessman, a member of society. If only he didn't have so many other redeeming qualities. Like how he had stayed behind at the inn today to plan for next month's engagement party, sending all his help to town to maintain the ruse that she and her friends were engrossed in their party planning.

Distracted, she followed in a bit of a daze as Dylan led her to the opposite end of the log pile from Cat and the others. "The work will feel as if it goes faster if you work on the opposite end and move in toward the other worker. You'll want to put the gloves on so you don't get blisters," Dylan said.

Tucking the cold metal tool beneath an arm, she tugged the overly large gloves on as best she could. Dylan stepped closer to help with her gloves. His warm hands eased her pinky fingers into the proper places. "They'll also keep you warmer," he said in a tone soft enough to almost be intimate.

Still warm from her irritation with the man, she took a step back. "I plan to work hard enough to stay warm, thank you," she said a bit curtly.

Looking from the logs to the device, she turned it over in her hands, trying to figure it out.

"Like this," he said as he pushed the metal tool beneath the bark and lifted it away.

Heart lurching in her throat, she swallowed hard. Of course the tree didn't feel any pain. It had died and its energy moved on—most of it. Some of a tree's essence remained in the wood forever, fading only if it rotted away and returned to the earth. It was part of why wood felt warm to the touch.

She removed a glove and placed her hand on the tree laying before her. "Thank you for your ultimate sacrifice. I will plant a seed from your cone in your honor so you may return," she whispered.

One brow raised, face scrunched, Dylan asked, "What was that?"

"It was between me and the tree, thank you," she replied curtly.

That done, she did her best to duplicate the movement, but couldn't get the tool jammed all the way into the bark like he had. It slipped, sending her sprawling over the log. Dylan slid an arm under her elbow and helped her to her feet.

"Are you all right?" he asked, breath hot on her cheek.

Flustered and near tears, she brought her elbow back and turned, forcing him to take a step back. "Quite."

She glanced Cat and Sadie's direction, but they were out of sight. Close as Dylan stood, it occurred to Deirdre that he had chosen to come down here because it was secluded. She moved around the end of the logs, putting a little more distance between them. If the man had romantic intentions now was certainly not the time nor the place and she was in no mood for it.

"You get under the edge, like this, then push up," Dylan said, demonstrating how to push the piece of metal under the bark.

The bark popped away from the trunk. Deirdre imitated his technique. If she was going to use the proverbial bones of this beautiful thing to build her home, she was determined to do as much of the work she could herself and infuse every bit of the process with respect and honor.

"'Tis easier to start on the end of the log, where you can get under the bark, then work your way down," he said.

Grateful as she was to him for his help, his presence irritated her to no end for more than one reason. Like so many unsensitive to the magic in the world around them, he seemed oblivious to the sacrifice of the tree. Though he was bold and daring when it came to pushing the limits of physical propriety where a lady was concerned, he was old-fashioned in his beliefs on how that lady should act. Not that she wanted him to be more forward with her, not right now at least. The man was too conflicted in what he wanted.

Ignoring him, Deirdre placed the tool between the bark and trunk. She closed her eyes and reached out to the tree's remaining energy.

If you release your bark my friends and I shall craft you into a beautiful home and preserve you. I will plant your seeds all around this home so you may feel your children and be renewed through them, she told it.

Energy pulsed faintly from the tree and the bark suddenly popped free.

"Well done! Just like that," Dylan said.

She had to force a grin in reply. It wasn't his fault he couldn't feel the tree's energy, that he didn't possess any magical power or sensitivity to it. But it was his fault he was ignorant of the resources he took part in consuming and what doing so did to the land.

Deirdre worked her way down the tree until it lay naked before her. Together she and Dylan rolled it over so they could do the other side. The labor began to feel good, productive. Dylan worked alongside her, chatting about the quality of the logs and the chilly weather. All the while he came closer and closer, working down the logs toward her. She couldn't exactly move away, not without seeming rude. They were only working, after all. When his conversation shifted to how lovely her hair looked pulled up off her neck and how nice she smelled, she fixed him with a hard look. Words of discouragement stilled on her tongue at the approach of footsteps.

"You getting the hang of it there, Deirdre?" came Rick's voice.

Another chunk of bark popped off. "I believe I am," she said.

"She's a natural. Its as if the bark wants to do her bidding," Dylan said.

The side glance Rick gave her expressed concern. She wrinkled her nose up and gave a brief shake of her head to let him know Dylan didn't actually mean what he said that he was clueless to her abilities.

"All right, then." Rick leaned her direction as he walked past. "Keep an eye on Cat for me, will ya? Don't let her overdo it," he whispered.

Relief poured through her. She gave him her best salute—which was a far cry from proper military standards. "You can count on me."

He winked in a way that managed to look charming instead of inappropriate. "I knew I could. Let's leave the ladies to it and start hauling these stripped logs, shall we?" he said, turning to Dylan.

It was all she could do to keep her smile neutral. But she

had a feeling Rick knew he had just rescued her from an unwanted conversation.

"Aye, let's," Dylan said in a bright tone.

The two men sauntered off and began preparing the team of draft horses. They worked together quickly and efficiently with little conversation. Deirdre took the lack of either voices raised in anger or hushed as a good sign that Rick hadn't seen how forward Dylan had been with her. She let out a breath. Getting the man in trouble with his employer was the last thing she wanted, even if she was still irritated with him. He didn't know what she was, or that she shared a deep connection with plants, and that this was therefore torture for her.

A deep *woof* alerted her to the approach of Rick's massive hound a moment before he licked her cheek. One swipe of that tongue soaked the entire side of her face. Even though the energy of a *failinis*—a fae warhound—emanated from him, he exuded a sweet, caring air.

"Ew! Ugh, hello, Linc," she said as she gave his head a good scratch.

Apparently satisfied with the greeting, Lincoln trotted off toward Cat and Sadie. A startled cry told her Sadie received the same greeting. Laughing, Deirdre set to work with a vigor born of determination to ensure that she and her friends had many moments such as this right here on this land. Besides, she wanted to get the dirty work over and get to planting those pine nuts.

Half the stack of logs and several hours later, they finally laid their tools down and took a break to view their progress. The frame of the quaint cabin was up, more or less. Two of Rick's freemen friends had arrived less than an hour into the work to help. The four men had hauled the logs away as fast as she, Cat, and Sadie could strip them. Despite the cabin being little bigger than Kinan's family cottage, the progress impressed Deirdre. And she felt every chunk of bark chipped away, each placed log, and every nail pound of it. She rubbed at her sore palms, careful of the blisters on both. Even the men, who had been working nonstop, finally put down the massive saw they'd been using to saw the smaller logs in half for the walls.

Deirdre tried to keep her mind on the house instead of tree deaths, she really did. The only thing that seemed able to distract her was thoughts of Kinan. She kept thinking about how he had looked when they left the inn this morning. The way he had rolled his sleeves up, exposing his biceps, along with how his sweaty shirt clung to his defined chest as he mucked out the stalls, were just too much to resist. She didn't even mind the scent of sweat and horses that had wafted from him. It wasn't an entirely unpleasant mixture, not at all. In fact, it brought to mind other activities that made one sweat.

No! Bloody hell. She wasn't even sure he was right for her. What if he used her secrets against her, or at the very least didn't accept her because of one or both of them? She couldn't allow herself to be attracted to him. Not until she knew for sure. But how to know without telling him and risking everything?

A delicate fan of wood and silk appeared beneath Deirdre's nose. "You look like you could use this," Sadie said in a pointed tone. Her eyes narrowed in disapproval as she looked at Dylan. But Deirdre didn't miss the little detour Sadie's gaze took, going swiftly to the two freemen lounging in the grass next to Dylan.

"Aye, but not for the reason you think. I wasn't looking at him, but at the river," Deirdre said. Sadie made an unconvinced affirmative noise.

Deirdre hadn't even realized she'd been looking in Dylan's direction. *Oh Danu...* She hoped he didn't get the same impression Sadie had. Accepting the fan, Deirdre hid her smile behind it. She couldn't remember the last time she'd seen Sadie admire a man. It was encouraging, considering the extended mourning period her friend had taken when her husband died in the war.

Unlike her and Cat, Sadie had loved her husband—though Deirdre had certainly tried. But it was good to see Sadie realize she was not only still alive, but a woman with needs. She tried not to watch her watch him overly much from behind her fan, which she waved furiously to try and dispel some of the heat rolling off her skin. The day was far from warm, but she had been working so hard it may as well have been midsummer. She began to seriously contemplate a dip in the creek.

"Seems a shame to build a home no one will live in," Dylan said.

Rick took the stalk of wheat he'd been chewing on out of his mouth. "Oh, it'll be lived in. This'll be a home for the groundskeeper of the stables and winery," he said.

At a bark from the hound, he tossed a large branch off into the bushes. Linc bounded after it, huge tail swinging. Deirdre could practically feel the ground shake with each step he took.

Eyes going wide, Dylan sat up from where he'd reclined against a log. "You'd let the help live in such a fine home?"

Shock evident on her face, Cat paused in her rounds of refilling everyone's glasses of tea. "O' course we would. I won't need it as I'll be living at Rick's after we're wed. No sense in it going to waste," she said.

Puzzlement showed in the way Dylan scratched his chin

and scrunched up his eyes. "Such generosity is a rare thing in this world. You lot inspire a lad to believe in the good of folks." He looked at Deirdre as he said the last. She looked swiftly away, avoiding eye contact.

A line of sweat trickled down her back, no doubt wetting the laces of her corset. Being in men's clothing and all, she probably shouldn't have bothered wearing it. But, she had felt the need for something familiar. Now she was regretting that decision. The damnable thing would be hell to get off if she didn't cool down and stop sweating. Not to mention, the sweat would make her cold later. Rising, she clicked the fan closed and handed it back to Sadie. The moment she gained her feet, Lincoln bounded up to her, branch sticking out the side of his mouth. Everyone started to rise as well, eventually making their way back to their tasks.

Deirdre turned to Cat and Sadie. "I'll be back shortly. I'm going to walk down to the creek to refresh myself," she said.

"Would you like company?" Cat asked.

With a grimace, Deirdre tugged the branch from Lincoln's mouth. "I'll take the monster here with me," she said.

Cat laughed. "He'll keep you safer than I could, for sure."

Eyes narrowed, Sadie tapped Deirdre's arm with the fan. "Just don't take long enough to make me fret over you." Something knowing in her eyes made Deirdre wonder. Whenever she got that look it meant she'd 'seen' something. But apparently, whatever it was didn't concern her enough to elicit an argument about Deirdre not going.

Bending, Deirdre pecked the shorter woman on the cheek. "Impossible. You've already begun."

Happy grumblings came from behind her as she strode

down the hill toward the creek. Lincoln bounded along beside her like a pup despite being the height of a black bear. Little puppy noises of excitement issued from him. By breed trait, he was more slender than a bear, but far more dangerous. His behavior reminded her that he was barely a year old. To avoid getting inadvertently stepped on, she tossed the branch down the hill a ways. With a grimace, she wiped slobber from her hand onto her breeches. Tall, yellow leafed birch trees choked the bottom of the hill, hiding the creek from view. The pure, clean scent of water drew her down into their welcoming energy. The yellow leaves had begun to turn and many of them carpeted the ground. Not much longer and the trees would be bare.

Branch held up like a trophy, Lincoln bounded back to her side. She patted his gray-and-brown head. Something struck her softly across the rear. Eyes shooting wide, she turned, only to almost take Lincoln's tail in the stomach.

"You truly have no idea how big you are, do you, you dolt?" she asked the hound.

The gleam in his eyes told her maybe he did. He lifted his head, presenting the branch to her.

"Oh, no. I'm not touching that slobbery thing again."

As she started walking again, his tail thumped at her back. Leaves cushioned her step, crackling from frost more than being dried out. The frost meant she should be chilled, she knew, but between the day's hard work and her tolerance of New York winters, she barely noticed it. The meandering silver swath of the creek beckoned to her. Picking the easiest looking way, she started down the slight embankment to the water. The soft trickling of it tumbling over the rounded rocks nearly made her mouth water. At last, she reached the edge and picked her way along a few big rocks to get close enough. She could hardly wait to splash some on the back of her neck and between her breasts.

Out of a habit lectured into her by her mother, she checked the riverbank and did her best to peer into the depths of the crystal-clear water. Back on the land she'd grown up on one had to be wary of water sprites in and around the river. They were mischievous to the point of being dangerous. And there were worse creatures that hid on the rocky bottoms. But for the most part this new land wasn't like Ireland. It had entirely different creatures, and like Ireland, many of those of otherness were slowly being killed off and driven out. The expansive estate she had grown up on in New York was home to many of the endangered creatures because they had followed her grandmother's people over on the ships. She couldn't help but wonder how many had died or fled to Tir na nÓg after her late husband had sold the property. It saddened her somewhat when she didn't see the iridescent gleam of wings or hear the chitter of tiny voices.

Drawn by the cold wafting off the water, she crouched down and dipped her hands in. Cool water ran over her fingers, draining away the day's heat. Sighing in relief, she splashed some on her face and chest. The heat that had worked her into a very unladylike sweat slowly started to drain away. Big paws splashed into the river close enough to make droplets plop onto her right forearm. She opened her mouth to warn Lincoln away when the hound's tail smacked her in the back again with a soft, but very solid, thump. The impact was just enough to throw her off balance. Her right hand shot out to a boulder, stopping her from plunging into the water. Lincoln, on the other hand, walked right into it, the long hairs of his tail skimming the surface and sending droplets flying out to splatter her with each swipe.

Shaking her head at him, Deirdre stood. "You daft hound, get out of the water before you catch a chill." She'd never heard of a *failinis* falling ill, but one never knew.

His tail wagged all the harder. Nose pointing to where she had laid his branch on a rock, he let out a woof.

"Ah, is that what I have to do to get you out of the water?"

She eased her way into a crouch, picked up the branch, and slowly rose. Lincoln woofed again and wagged his tail faster. Holding up one hand to fend off the spray of water, she threw the branch back to the bank. As she stepped down on the follow-through of the throw, she slipped on a spot of moss. Her foot plunged toward the water and she started to fall backward. Rather than collide with hard rocks and icy water, she fell into warm arms. Those arms quickly righted her, but didn't withdraw. Deirdre knew those defined muscles exposed by rolled-up sleeves.

"Mr. O'Toole, you are becoming quite adept at catching me," she said.

This close, she could make out the blond stubble that covered his strong, square jaw. She tried to straighten and step away, but her foot slid on a rock again.

Dylan's arms slid down to her waist and pulled her a touch closer, making her gasp. "Then you should keep me close," he said. "And please, call me Dylan. Mr. O'Toole makes me sound like me grandda." His Irish accent gave her a thrill she couldn't deny. Too many people worked to hide theirs, herself included.

The thrill that went through her at his touch was eclipsed by her memories of him oppressing her independence. "Thank you, Dylan. But this is quite…inappropriate."

He bent down, but rather than kiss her like she feared, he hooked an arm beneath her legs and picked her up. Only when they were back on the solid ground of the shore did he finally set her on her feet. He let go and stepped back. Motioning to a large boulder in invitation, he sat down. She sat only when she realized one of the laces of her boots had come untied. Even then, she sat as far from him as the boulder would allow.

"You're a fine lady with a wild and free spirit, Deirdre," he said in a low voice filled with admiration. "What makes such a lass want to put down roots?"

"I got my fill of adventure on the journey here. You sound like you aren't sure if putting down roots is a good thing, or a bad thing," she said.

"Honestly, I'm not entirely sure. But don't you miss the thrill of danger at every turn, predators, savages, the excitement of not knowing what the day might bring?"

If he was so excited by the idea of her enjoying the danger of the unknown, why was he so overprotective? It was as though he couldn't decide if he wanted his women to be adventurous, or proper ladies. Deirdre liked a man who knew what he wanted, and Dylan most certainly did not.

"Not at all. I look forward to having a home, a family. You sound like a man who enjoys adventure. What keeps you here?"

Subtle as it was, it was hard to tell, but she thought he stiffened a little.

"I take care of the mum of a dear friend of mine. Ainsworth is her landlord and I can't in good conscience leave her to face his wrath. Without me here, he'd no doubt throw her out into the cold," he said, voice void of the passion it had contained only a moment before.

"That's very noble of you. She's lucky to have you by her side. What do you miss about the open trail?" she asked in an attempt to lighten his mood again. Though she was still a touch angry at him, she didn't want him to suffer.

"Can a man miss what he never had?" he asked in a wistful tone.

"Certainly. What is it you wish you had?"

His gaze cut out over the creek. "Aside from a free Ireland, I wish I had a woman to share the thrill of the open trail with." His hand slid closer to hers on the boulder. "Someone to share the heart-pounding excitement," he said in a low voice, emphasizing the word "pounding" so it sounded improper. "The thrill of discovering new things," he whispered.

Before he could touch her, she pulled her hand away. On one hand, he made it sound like he wanted a strong woman. On the other, when faced with one, he suppressed her independence. Dylan suddenly sat up straight. It took a moment for Deirdre's heart to slow and her vision to focus. Dylan, on the other hand, looked about, wide eyes alert. Leaves rustled and crackled as if beneath footfalls. Deirdre's heart started pounding again. Dylan reached for the pistol belted to his waist. Brows furrowing together, Deirdre put her hand over his so he couldn't draw the weapon.

Who on Earth does he think it could be that he would draw a pistol?

She leaned close to him. "'Tis likely Sadie or Cat," she whispered.

The noises sounded again, closer this time. Dylan's hand tensed beneath hers. Glaring, she gripped him tighter. One foolish move could endanger her friends. She wouldn't allow that. And why, because he was afraid of being caught?

"It could be Ainsworth's man," he whispered.

Fear pricked away at her anger, leaving her very aware of how chilly the day was. She longed for a return of the heat of passion, the flush of hard work, anything to banish the thought of that spindly man spying on her.

"He wouldn't dare," she whispered, the words more of a question than she had intended.

The hard look on Dylan's face was answer enough. A shape lunged from the trees. Dylan tore free of her grasp and drew his pistol so fast his movements were a blur. Nearly as fast, Deirdre threw herself between him and the shape that approached. Eyes wide and white, Dylan froze with the pistol pointed at her chest. A big gray-and-brown head poked itself beneath Deirdre's arm. Lincoln's joy-filled eyes began to glow red when they turned to Dylan. His lips curled back from sharp teeth growing longer by the heartbeat and a low growl rumbled from him.

Dylan let out a long breath and lowered the pistol. Lincoln's growl lost a bit of its menace but didn't stop. The fact that Dylan relaxed so quickly meant he hadn't seen the hound's partial transformation, which meant he wasn't sensitive to otherness. Part of her was disappointed at that.

"Bloody hell, Deirdre, I could have shot you," he said.

Anger seethed through her. "Or Lincoln, or Danu forbid, Sadie or Cat. Are you really that worried that Ainsworth would spy on us?" she demanded. *Dammit*. She shouldn't have let that invocation of Danu's name slip.

She rested her hand on Lincoln's head and the hound's growl reduced to a low grumble. Gaze on the hound, Dylan took a step to the right, placing the boulder between him and Lincoln.

"I am. That's why I came out here, to make sure you were safe."
A wistful look came over him. "And invoking the old gods, that's
something you don't hear every day." His tone was light as if he
were trying to deflect her from his actions.

Every muscle in her body tensed with fury, which brought
another growl from Lincoln. *Will this man never learn?* "As I
have told you, I can take care of myself," she said in a tone as
cold as the winter air. She'd learned when something slipped that
shouldn't have, it was best to ignore any mention of it and deflect
the conversation.

Hand held out, beseeching, Dylan took a step closer. "No,
'twas not the only reason. You can't fault a man for wanting to
protect a lass he fancies," he said.

At his approach, Lincoln gnashed his teeth. "Easy there,
pup. I was trying to protect her, same as you are."

The tension Deirdre felt in Lincoln made it clear the hound
wasn't convinced of Dylan's good intentions. She stroked his
back and murmured soothing words. After a moment, he sat
down at her side. The glow left his eyes and his fangs returned
to their normal length. Even with him and Dylan present, Deirdre
felt exposed, vulnerable. She couldn't stop picturing
Ainsworth's dark, calculating eyes. Would he only spy on them,
or would he try to harm them? She was afraid she knew the
answer to that. Gaze darting about the thick copse of trees, she
turned back toward the home site.

"We'd best get back. A lady shouldn't put herself in this
kind of danger," she said, throwing Dylan's words back at him
with a vehemence born mostly from fear.

Part of her was angry he was right. Right in a way, at least.
Despite what she had said, she couldn't shoot a pistol with

anything that resembled accuracy. On the journey over she'd had hired men to do that for her. They had taught her how to use a firearm to the point where she was comfortable with one. But the kick of the damnable things got her every time. She was an archer, not a pistoleer. Up until now she'd been able to ask the plants help any time she felt threatened. But now with winter just around the corner most of them were going dormant, or getting ready to. Waking them could mean killing them and she wasn't about to do that, not even to save her own life.

Fingers curling into fists, she stormed up the hill. She hated that she couldn't feel safe on her own land, or that of her friends, and, irrational as it was, she was mad at Dylan for pointing it out. The problem was, Ainsworth knew this land better than she did. It gave him an advantage that she could not tolerate. First thing in the morning, she planned to take steps to remedy that.

17

Deirdre

Mid-September

The shadows of dawn hid every manner of threat—at least in Deirdre's imagination. Every bush and leafless tree dotting the landscape could hide assailants lying in wait. Normally she'd be able to reach out to the plants and feel through their leaves, branches, and roots. But not only would that exhaust her power, the plants were almost all in hibernation. So she had to do this the human way.

Heart pounding and grip tightening on the bow in her hand, she kept constant pressure on Ciaren's side to keep the mare moving forward. No doubt sensing her rider's unease, Ciaren pranced and snorted at every bough that moved in the breeze. Deirdre held her other hand near her chest where she could swiftly reach back for an arrow if need be.

Up ahead lay a gathering of oak and aspen trees shrouded in fog. Dread pulled at her the closer she drew to it. The cloud-covered sky offered little help in seeing through the white, soupy mess that came up to Ciaren's nose. Good sense told her to steer clear of the place, but as was so often the case for her, she couldn't listen to it. This was the last bit of her property she had yet to explore. She needed to know every tree and bush, and the layout and terrain of every single acre. Only then could she know every potential hiding place, advantage, or disadvantage, the land might hold. Too much time had already passed for her to not know such things. After all, she had rows of grapes to plant in the spring, and a garden to plan.

At least, those were the reasons she told herself as she rode into the dense fog. Ainsworth could send spies—or worse, killers—after her at any time. It was possible they would know every rock, tree, and hollow better than she. Her arrow knocked loudly against the cradle of her bow. She hadn't even realized she'd drawn it. That instinct made her think maybe she wouldn't have as hard a time shooting a man as she feared. The realization both comforted and disturbed her.

The fog began to break up and settle a little more with each step she took into the trees. Though her gaze scanned the thick growing aspen and birch, it still caught her by surprise when Ciaren stepped around one and a man stood not twenty feet away. The muscles of that tanned, bare back looked familiar. The silky black hair hanging down just past his shoulder blades did not. Or did it? *No, it couldn't be.* Muscles in the man's back and shoulders flexed. Ciaren walked closer without any urging. Then Deirdre saw why. A beautiful, white, bareback stallion stood grazing not far from the man.

The twang of a bowstring snapped her gaze back to the man. An arrow sank into something solid several yards away, from the sound of it. Lowering his bow, the man turned just enough that she could see his profile. The tanned skin, slightly high cheekbones, full lips, and strong brow were unmistakable.

She lowered her own bow. "Kinan?" The encounter seemed dreamlike, a fantasy really, what with him looking all wild. To find him not only half-naked in the woods, but shooting a bow as well, felt surreal. That, and stimulating. Fantasy or not, she was eager to see where this encounter led. She shouldn't indulge in such thoughts about a man she wasn't sure was right for her. But when he looked like something out of an old tale, it was difficult not to.

"Deirdre, what are you doing out here? Is everything all right?" Kinan asked. He propped his bow against a tree and retrieved a burgundy shirt hanging on a nearby branch.

Ignoring propriety, which dictated she should turn her back, she rode straight for him. "All is well enough. I should ask the same of you. This is my land, after all."

She caught a grin before he turned slightly away and slid his arms into his shirt. "Actually, it's the border of your land and mine. I do hope you'll pardon me treading the line between the two. This is the most secluded place for miles that I can practice my archery." As he talked, his fingers worked at the buttons of his shirt, slowly taking away the alluring view of his hard chest. He turned back to her as he closed the button beneath his pectoral muscles. "And I apologize for my state of undress, which you have a knack for seeing me in." At that he raised a brow. "My morning exercises have me overheated despite the cold." He nodded his head in the direction of the bow in her hand. "Enjoying a bit of archery yourself?"

Clearing her throat, she looked down at the bow. "While I do have a passion for the pastime, I actually brought this along for protection."

Head turning this way and that, Kinan's gaze scanned

around her. "Ah, you've come out alone. In that case, the bow was a wise decision."

Eyes widening, Deirdre reined Ciaren to a stop. "You're not going to reprimand me for going out on my own?"

He shrugged. "You brought a weapon. You are a capable woman. And besides, I have a feeling it wouldn't do any good if I did."

"You're right, it wouldn't." She kept her tone clipped to hide her admiration for his attitude.

One tanned hand swept toward the target. "Would you like to join me for a bit of practice?"

The target he pointed to was a round bull's-eye mounted to a dead tree a good distance away. Three arrows stuck in the red center, crowded tightly together. The thrill of anticipation shot through her at the sight. "I would enjoy that very much, but I don't want to intrude."

Kinan waved a hand. "Nonsense. 'Tis no intrusion at all. Balder here isn't exactly good company for such things. I would enjoy it if you joined me."

"In that case, I would be delighted to."

A little archery practice with a handsome man would be harmless—or not. She certainly wouldn't protest at things getting a bit more physical.

By the time she moved her skirts and readied to jump down, Kinan stood at Ciaren's side, hands outstretched to her. She nodded and he took hold of her waist and lifted her down. Both the warmth of his big hands and the strength in them felt so good it left her light-headed. The way they lingered after he set her on her feet heated her to her core. No, no, she couldn't allow herself to feel that way, not before knowing if she could trust him with that which she shouldn't have trusted even her late husband.

"I'm capable of dismounting on my own, you know," she said, smiling to soften the words.

Nodding, he let go and took a step back. That had certainly not been the intention of her words. But then, it did go a step in the direction of proving her theory of him being too proper to endure. She adjusted the quiver of arrows on her back and draped her bow over her right shoulder.

"I know, but what kind of a gentleman would I be if I didn't offer?" he asked with a coy look. The look brought heat to her cheeks.

She nodded, using the movement as an excuse to look down and break the hypnotic effect of his gaze. "A remiss one, for sure," she teased, hoping it was enough to make him realize it wasn't his conduct that she disapproved of.

He surprised her with a laugh.

"What?" she asked.

"So much worse has been said of me."

"Of you? Certainly not! You're above reproach," she said in all earnestness.

"Hardly. There is much you don't know about me."

She indicated the target with a thrust of her head. "Like your proficiency in archery?"

The fact that he enjoyed archery was quite appealing. She led her horse over near his and secured the reins around a low branch. The two nickered at one another and tried to press their noses closer. Knowing her mare's affinity for the white stallion, Deirdre had tied her just far enough away. Kinan offered her his arm. *Above reproach, indeed.* She accepted it and enjoyed his closeness as he led her to the target.

"Well, 'tis one of the few pastimes accepted in polite society that actually builds a practical and interesting skill," he said.

She brightened. "That's precisely part of why I enjoy it so much. That, and I can't tolerate needlepoint."

The deep, easy laughter that came from Kinan rumbled across her in a way that made her skin tighten and tingle. Her body was deprived indeed to betray her with such a reaction for a man she wasn't sure she could have.

"I must admit," Kinan began. "I can't see you sitting around with a group of ladies doing needlepoint."

Deirdre put a hand to her chest. "Why ever not?" she asked, eyes wide in mock surprise.

"I fear such things would bore a lady of your intellect and spirit," he said.

A flush spread through her chest. But, she had to remind herself, men would say all kinds of things to pique a lady's interest in them. Her late husband had been quite good at such tactics, then turned out to be the type to expect her to do and be all the things she loathed. Not to mention his reaction to her secret.

"You would be right in that regard," she admitted, with an edge to her voice.

As Kinan plucked his arrows from the target, she regaled him with tales of her mother's attempts—and failures—to get her to enjoy ladylike pursuits. She wanted it to be very clear that she was not a typical lady, and never would be. Rather than chastise or disbelieve her, he laughed and praised her for her cleverness. Kinan in turn told her of his own mother's strict teachings and tales of how she tried to civilize him as a young man. Laughing, they walked back to the shooting area arm in arm. She found herself in no rush at all to be free of his touch. No matter how hard she looked, he didn't display any of the signs of a gentleman who expected a traditional lady. Yet, an arm around hers, or a hand on her waist to help her dismount, seemed to be the extent of his willingness to be physical. That in itself was a sign, or so she kept telling herself.

They lingered arm in arm, talking of bow design, arrow materials, and choice of fletching. Finally, unable to put it off any longer, Kinan slid free of her arm and picked up her bow. He handed it to her and stepped aside as she nocked an arrow. Like a good observer, he went still and quiet. She leveled the bow onto her target, let out a slow breath, then let the arrow fly. It settled into the wood a hand's width below the red bull's-eye. The blue fletching vibrated on impact. Glaring at it as if it was to blame, she stepped aside so Kinan could shoot.

He shook his head. "Please, take as many shots as you like. I've already had several."

She smiled and inclined her head. "Thank you."

Several shots later she still hadn't hit within three fingers of the bull's-eye. Clearly it had been far too long since she'd shot. The squeaky cry of frustration that escaped her only incensed her more. She could call to the residual energy in the wood and help it hit the bullseye, but that felt too much like cheating in the moment.

"I take it you normally shoot better than this," Kinan said.

She wanted somewhere to direct her ire, but his words hadn't given her an opening. She found that both refreshing and a touch annoying. Most men would have seized the opportunity to gloat, or point out how their own method and skills were superior. Why couldn't this man be more difficult?

"Normally, yes. I fear I haven't had much practice since leaving New York."

"We'll just have to remedy that," he said.

Thrills raced through her. Her late husband had insisted archery wasn't a ladylike pursuit. It had always driven her half-mad, considering how much she loved it. She and Kinan walked together to retrieve the arrows. When she couldn't find any reason to take his arm, she grew annoyed at herself for her lack of inventive thinking. His encouragement touched her so deeply that it left her flustered, a state she was not at all used to. Kinan talked about the decorations for the party next month and they discussed seating arrangements for the guests.

"Practically the entire town will be in attendance. That's quite impressive. I haven't seen them all come together since Thomas Brady's funeral."

The name wasn't one she recalled hearing, but the tender note in Kinan's voice piqued her curiosity. "Who was this Thomas Brady that could bring an entire town together?"

Clouds darkened Kinan's eyes. "A good lad who helped everyone he came across and never expected a thing in return."

"He was your friend," Deirdre observed in a gentle voice.

Kinan swallowed hard and nodded. She wrapped an arm through his and leaned her head against his biceps. "My deepest condolences."

She led him back to where she had hung her cloak on a branch. Chilly though the day was, the dress she wore had quickly overheated her during shooting. Finding a suitable spot of soft leaves, she spread the cloak out and sat down. At her pat on the space beside her, Kinan surprised her by sitting down. Not so much as one protest came from him. Any other time she might have commented on that, but now wasn't the time to tease the man.

"What happened to him?" she asked. She knew from experience that sometimes it helped to talk about such things.

Long, silky strands of his dark hair fell about him as he lowered his head. The impulse to run her hands through those locks, to wrap them around her fingers, almost made her reach for him. A long moment passed before he said, "He was killed escaping Canada."

Shock made Deirdre lift her head. "Escaping Canada?" So much about that didn't make sense that she didn't know what else to say.

Moisture glistened in his eyes but anger tightened the skin around them. "He was charmed into joining the Fenian Brotherhood, and became convinced it was his duty to do whatever he could to help free Ireland from England's rule."

Understanding settled heavy on Deirdre's heart. "He was among the Fenian Army that attacked the English outposts in Canada," she said. Even in New York they'd heard about the attacks. The Fenian Army had taken advantage of everyone being distracted by the war. Part of her couldn't blame them. Ireland had been fighting for independence from England for hundreds of years. It was part of why her family and so many others had emigrated to America. Not that they disagreed with Ireland freeing themselves from England's rule, just that they had grown weary of the tension and fighting.

The pain etched into the lines between his brows made her want to change the subject, but if he could endure the pain, she could endure it for him. "Had he recently emigrated from

Ireland?"

"No. He was born and raised here in California," he said, voice catching.

Not wanting to offend his sense of propriety, but unwilling to see him in such pain and do nothing, she took hold of his hand. His fingers wove through hers and squeezed tight. The palm-to-palm contact sent a thrill straight to her core. If Kinan were in his right mind, he likely wouldn't allow the contact, which was truly only acceptable for those courting. If only he didn't hold to such traditional beliefs. No, she couldn't think that way. Not right now.

His thumb started to make little circles on the back of her hand. The sensation it caused drove all thought away. Warmth spread from her hand, up her arm, and down through her breasts.

He gave her a sad smile. "It hardly seems right for me to accept your kindness and condolences when you've suffered such a great loss of your own. As a Californian, I didn't serve alongside the 69th, but I heard great things about the bravery of your husband's infantry unit," he said.

Deirdre cleared her throat. "Yes, they were a fine unit."

Thumb halting its circles, he leaned a touch closer and looked deep into her eyes. "Forgive me, but—you weren't close to your husband, were you?"

A shiver ran through her. She managed a tight smile and shook her head. "No. He wasn't a bad man, just a very…traditional man." She tried not to put too much bite into that second part and failed. "My parents arranged the marriage to secure my future, and as a lady in a man's world, I could hardly argue." He had been wealthy, but more importantly to her parents, fae. Such a match wasn't easy to find.

Letting go of her hand, Kinan grabbed his cloak and swung it around her shoulders. She snuggled into it with a smile of thanks, not wanting to tell him her body's reaction hadn't been to the cold. His wonderful spicy scent lingering in the cloak made her not want to let it go.

He leaned back on an elbow and looked up at her. "I hope he wasn't terrible to you, else I'll have a difficult time not holding it against his memory."

Almost of its own accord, one of her fingers traced circles on the back of his hand. She hadn't even realized she'd reached for him again. "Oh no, not at all. He was kind in the beginning, gentle even in the end, and tediously boring," she said with a laugh.

Kinan's shoulders relaxed. "That's good, because I'm not really sure how one would challenge a ghost to a duel."

Easy laughter bubbled from Deirdre. She gave his biceps a playful slap. Her hand bounced off the hard muscles, which compelled her to reach for him again. Bottom lip tugged between her teeth, she couldn't stop herself from wondering what kind of lover he'd be. If only she could find out. Maybe she could. At the cabin, he had seemed so close to giving in. If there was even the slightest chance he wasn't the stuffy high-society man she feared him to be, then she was determined to take that chance.

Licking his lips, he leaned toward her. Her heart swelled so big it felt like it blocked her breath. Her gaze slid down to his chest, admiring how his defined pectorals pressed against the fine cotton of his shirt. How would those muscles feel beneath her fingers? And was that movement the rapid beating of his heart? Unable to stop herself, she put a hand against his chest, needing to feel it. The soft thudding beneath the muscles confirmed it. Her fingers began to explore, working their way down his chest. His breathing sped up, matching hers. One of his hands reached up to cup her cheek.

Just as she managed to drag her gaze back to his face, he froze. The predatory look in his eyes surprised her.

"Do you feel that?" he asked as he straightened and looked over his shoulder.

She felt something all right, but it clearly wasn't the same thing he was referring to. The tension in his body sent a thrill of fear through her that doused her arousal. Suddenly, she wished she hadn't set her bow down out of reach. Then she felt it; the weight of eyes heavy upon them. The skin along her back tingled with the pressure of those eyes. That she hadn't noticed it before spoke of the level of her distraction. As a high-society woman, she was usually acutely aware of eyes on her. She turned slowly to look in the direction of the pressure.

At first, she only saw naked trees and bushes. Almost an arrowshot away sat a shape so large it looked like a tall, thin boulder at first, one with a few yellow and brown leaves on it. Part of it moved. A floppy ear rose.

"Lincoln? What are you...?" Her voice trailed off as the sound of hoofbeats reached her.

Rising swiftly, she straightened her skirts. Kinan's cloak settled around her. Well, that could look quite bad. If only they'd had a bit longer, it might have been all it appeared. Reluctantly, she unbuttoned the cloak, swung it from her shoulders, and handed it to Kinan. He nodded and accepted it with a smile. Cold settled around her in its absence. He picked hers up, shook it out, and wrapped it around her. Hands lingering on the clasp, he leaned down until their foreheads touched. For a brief moment, he stayed like that, touching in a subtle yet wonderfully intimate way that left her wanting so much more.

Then, in a flash of woolen material, he walked briskly off toward his horse. Swift steps carried her to where she had set down her bow and quiver.

Lincoln turned his head, let out a bark, then trotted toward them. Two horses crested the hill leading into their little copse of trees. Even though she knew it had to be her friends, due to Lincoln's behavior, her grip on her bow tightened. Anger flared, not for her friends' interruption, but over being afraid on her own land. Next month at the party, she would have to make a point to spend some time with Ainsworth. Torturous as that sounded, she needed to see if the man had a shred of decency in him, or more importantly, a chink in his armor. A glance back in Kinan's direction, at his fine backside, made her promise herself she wouldn't spend *all* her time with Ainsworth.

By the time Cat's tall painted horse and Sadie's little mare reached them, Deirdre had her things secured to Ciaren's saddle and was leading her toward them. Cat's cold-flushed cheeks dimpled with a smile as her gaze went from Deirdre to Kinan.

"There you are," she said with a raise of her eyebrows. One hand went to her stomach as she came to a stop.

Deirdre made a face in return. "Here I am. You found my letter, did you not?"

Sadie put one hand on her hip. "We did. That was very responsible of you, which is suspicious."

"I like to keep you guessing."

This made Sadie snort-laugh. It was a running joke between the three of them. As a seer it was nearly impossible to keep Sadie guessing. Though, as she so often told them, her visions didn't operate like a well-oiled machine on command.

The clip-clop of shod hooves preceded Kinan's arrival at her side. With a gesture, he offered to help her into her saddle. She smiled and nodded. The anticipation of his touch, no matter how slight, thrilled her to her core.

"Thank you." As she settled in, enduring the curious weight of her friends' gazes, Kinan swung up into his own saddle.

"You are worried about Ainsworth sending men out this way," Cat observed, sharp as ever—*damn it all*. Deirdre had hoped to spare her that worry.

Sadie gasped and mumbled something about the Powers That Be. "Is that true? Is that why you left us a letter letting us know where you'd be?" she asked, making it sound more like an accusation than a question.

"Yes, it's true. I fear he may send spies to watch us. And he has us at a great disadvantage since he knows our land better than we do," Deirdre said.

Groaning, Sadie squeezed her eyes shut tight. "Oh, Deirdre, what if you came across someone and he intended to do more than spy?"

Deirdre patted her quiver of arrows. "Then he would get an unpleasant surprise."

At that Cat shook her head. "'Tis one thing to be a champion archer in competition, but another altogether to shoot a man."

One of Sadie's dark hands thrust into the air in triumph. "Finally, we agree! It's too dangerous to go out alone."

Lincoln barked as if in agreement. Deirdre shot the hound a glare. He whined and cocked his head.

"I agree," Kinan said, surprising them all.

Deirdre turned her glare on him. "Do you now?"

He didn't wilt beneath her gaze, which only filled her with more fire.

"I do. I agree with you all."

The three women exchanged confused looks.

"Go on," Deirdre prompted him.

"It's too dangerous to go out alone. Ainsworth does know this land better. But he cannot be given free rein to spy and plot against you all. I recommend daily patrols of the land, in pairs," he said.

Sadie's shoulders sagged. "I don't think Rick has enough men for the task, not between that, building our homes, and guarding the home sites. The men have to sleep at some point."

"True," Cat agreed.

A slight smile turned up his lips as Kinan looked to Deirdre. "'Tis already my habit to take a morning ride. I could accompany Mrs. Quinn on morning patrols."

Deirdre sat up straighter in the saddle. "That's a brilliant idea. I can get in a bit more bow practice that way as well."

"I don't like it," Sadie said.

Cat touched her arm. "I don't like any of this, but..." she paused and looked to Deirdre. "Deirdre is going to go anyway, you know that. At least this way she won't be alone."

Sadie shook her head so hard, bits of tight black curls freed themselves from the bun that bound them. But she sighed. "I suppose you're right. Thank you, Mr. O'Leary. We would appreciate your assistance."

The smirk Kinan gave Deirdre could have charmed a nurse out of her pantaloons. But then, that could just be Deirdre's lingering desire. Regardless, she soaked in that handsome look, storing it away in her memory for later. She wondered what might have transpired between the two of them had her friends not shown up. Could it be that Kinan would have relaxed his sense of propriety and maybe kissed her? Even if he had, would it only have been because she put him in a vulnerable state by bringing up his deceased friend?

With the promise of many more morning rides came the opportunity to find out. She let her gratitude—and a touch of her desire—show in her eyes as she met his gaze and nodded.

Someone cleared their throat, Sadie, from the reprimanding tone of it. "Shall we get back to work then? We have houses to build," she said.

"We shall. Lead the way," Deirdre agreed.

She and Kinan fell into step behind Cat's and Sadie's horses. The secret smile he gave her warmed her and lit the fires of hope.

18

Deirdre

Late September, Mabon

Legs stretched out before her in an almost prone position, Deirdre floated in the tub. The thing was a decadent work of art. Formed of copper, it was twice the length of most tubs and had a wooden headrest carved to perfectly cradle the back of one's head. Upon seeing it, she'd decided on the spot to talk to the craftsman and commission one. Unfortunately, she'd been lounging in it so long the water was growing cold.

The day had been a hard one spent leveling Sadie's home site. Worse yet, it had followed a very long night of work. Deirdre had used her power to connect with the bushes and small trees and ask their permission to move them. They'd been happy to draw up their roots and allow themselves to be transplanted away from the site of the home. The problem hadn't been their cooperation, but how many of them there had been. Deirdre, Sadie, Cat, Rick, and Sean had spent hours digging holes and moving plants. But it was better than cutting them down or tearing them up.

As much as Deirdre wanted to crawl into a soft bed after

the bath, today was a special day, a sabbat. It was Mabon, the final harvest festival, and the time of year when day and night were of equal length. Normally they wouldn't have spent it working. But not even a day could be spared when it came to making progress on their homes. Just thinking about the night's plans renewed her energy. A ray of sunlight drew her gaze over to the window. The top of the massive sequoia was visible poking up over the distant hilltop. The need to go visit it almost made her stir. But she needed to take it an offering, especially today. Fading energy of flowers near the end of their life cycle drew her gaze. A vase of lovely yellow sunflowers sat on the windowsill.

She sat up out of the tub so abruptly water sloshed over the edge. "Those are perfect!" Delighted with her find, she quickly toweled off and slipped on a simple purple dress of silk from Japan edged with Irish lace. According to the rigid rules of society, it wasn't a dress at all, but little more than a night shirt not meant to be worn out among others. No bloomers, chemise, corset, corset cover, petticoat, hoop skirt, or over petticoat for her today. And she was most certainly going out. She stroked the front of her silky dress. It felt delicious and naughty and she loved it.

Eight times a year she and her friends shed all the constraints and expectations of society and celebrated their sabbats they way their ancestors had—in privacy and usually under the cover of darkness, of course. Today was one of those days and it was extra special because they would get to do it on their own property.

While humming an old Irish tune, she pulled a comb through her long, black hair. As she did, she thought about the joy she'd found in this new place already, about how the wildness of it freed her spirit. She decided she would leave her hair unbound.

Rubbing at a callous on her palm, she stared at the sunflowers a moment and contemplated. At last, she picked the two most bedraggled looking ones and extricated them from the vase carefully without pulling out the others. One was nearly the size of a dinner plate while the other was scarcely bigger than a tea saucer. Yellow petals had begun to wilt on the small one and the larger was missing a few here and there. She cradled them against her chest as she slipped into the leather moccasins she'd traded a string of pearls for on the trip over. Their escorts had scoffed and tried to convince her it was an unfair trade, but she loved the moccasins and had no use for the pearls.

Resuming the tune she'd been humming, she made her way from the room and down the lesser used servants' staircase. The stairs emptied into the kitchen. The golden light of dusk filtered through the thick glass window overlooking the garden. Beams cut warm swaths along the oak table dominating the room. Upon the air hung the nutty sweet scent of warm wood. Deirdre smiled as she imagined Kinan standing at this very table chopping vegetables. It was exactly the kind of thing he would do— prepare his own meal. In fact, she could envision it so well that it sparked a fire within her to get moving before he showed up.

Not that she didn't want to see him. She very much did— too much. But if he saw her now, dressed like this, he might be scandalized. It would be her great pleasure to scandalize him. But she didn't have time for it today.

The moccasins made no sound against the wood floor as she crept out. A creaky hinge on the door, however, made her cringe. Air far warmer for late September than she was used to swirled around her as she stepped outside. The sweet scent of cut wheat from Kinan's south field came on the wind. Muted golden light drew her gaze to the hilly horizon where the sun was quickly sinking in a pink sky.

"Better hurry," she murmured as she closed the door behind her and set out.

All but skipping along, she made her way across the landscaped grounds of sleeping evergreen bushes and down the hill. The feathery boughs of the sequoia beckoned her to its expansive red trunk. More than that, its energy called to her like a great heartbeat deep down in the earth. It resonated with her own energy, leaving her feeling like she could build her house in a day on her own. In a few more steps she came across the gazebo that stood close to the tree. Contrary to the popular trend, it wasn't painted white. Instead it was treated with something that darkened it and brought out the grain in a lovely way. Octagonal in shape, it sat dwarfed beneath a massive branch boasting bright green needles.

This entire place had such a harmonious feel to it that she could spend hours out here. She could imagine leaning up against the tree trunk and reading a book. And the gazebo would be a wonderful support structure for grapevines. Someday she hoped to get the chance to spend more time out here. For now, she needed to hurry, though.

The air grew thick with the sequoia's energy. It felt like breathing during a thunderstorm and walking through molasses. Undaunted, for it also resonated with contentment and connection, she walked up to the tree and placed a hand on its red trunk. Beneath the rough, fibrous bark, she felt an energy unlike any other plant or tree she'd ever connected with. This tree thrummed with a power that pulsed like a heartbeat. Though it stood on this hill alone, she felt its roots reaching wide and deep, connecting it to other sequoias in the forest down in the valley. The power of it brought tears to her eyes and made her knees tremble.

"Hello," she whispered in a voice choked with happy tears.

Hello. The greeting came as more of a feeling than a word as it wrapped her in its seemingly endless power, but the intent was clear.

After several moments of just basking in that amazing energy, she held one of the sunflowers up. "I've brought you a gift," she said as she reached for the lowest branch. Her fingertips just brushed it. Energy surged overhead. The branch reached down toward her until it was nearly at eye level. She tucked the stem of the sunflower into the crook of the large branch and a smaller offshoot.

This will attract birds to you for you to visit with, and so they may carry not just the sunflower seeds, but your seeds as well, helping to spread your children across the valley, she told it.

Feelings of gratitude surged from the tree to her.

Slowly, the branch rose back up until it had returned to its original position. The tree lowered another branch within her reach. After she tucked the second sunflower into it, needles tickled her face before the branch lifted back up. Giggling, she rubbed at her cheek.

"Deirdre? Is that you?" came a familiar, deep voice that made scintillating bumps rise along her skin.

She spun toward him. *What had he seen?*

Fear blew away as if on a stiff breeze as her gaze settled on him. Much like her, he wasn't dressed for a social call. His shoulder-length black hair blew freely about a face covered in two days or more of rugged looking stubble. A sleeveless, grey tunic with a deep neck that revealed the hint of a muscular chest took the place of his usual shirt, vest, and coat. The lack of sleeves gave her an enticing view of his toned arms. And his pants appeared to be cut off at the knees and hemmed. Everything about his outfit was inappropriate and stimulating. A thrill tightened muscles low in her body.

Eyes going wide, mouth working wordlessly, he stared at her. The shameless way his gaze raked up and down her body made her take a step toward him. It made her deliciously aware of the friction of her silken dress against her hard nipples. Without any underclothes, she realized her state of arousal would be obvious. As if her state of dress—or undress, rather—wasn't shocking enough to the man.

"Kinan…" For possibly the first time in her life, she had no idea what to say. Perhaps if he was so focused on her appearance, he hadn't seen her interaction with the tree.

Head whipping to the side, gaze casting away, he muttered, "I…uh…heard voices." The huskiness of desire filled his tone.

"Yes, well, I came to visit this magnificent tree and brought some wilted sunflowers for the birds," she said, deciding to go with part of the truth.

"Ah, yes. Um…well I see you didn't expect company. My apologies," he said. Though he wouldn't look back in her direction, he didn't leave either. Nor did he chastise her on venturing outside wearing scandalously little. It emboldened her.

"Do not be, please. You look rather fetching in your casual

attire," she said, letting her appreciation for his form show in her voice.

"As do you," he said breathlessly. The words erupted from his lips as if he couldn't hold them back. "I mean… Bloody hell I am being terribly inappropriate. I do apologize. I have a cloak back in the gazebo, should you so desire." The way the word 'desire' came out, whispered, dark, and needy, made her breath catch. But the intent incensed her. She no more needed to cover up than he did.

"According to proper etiquette, no doubt I should so desire. But I do not," she said in a clipped voice.

His gaze shot back to her, and their eyes locked in a battle of want and will. The interest hiding in the brown and gold depths made her wonder if a chance existed that he might not be as proper as he let on. But he looked swiftly away again, and the moment was broken, along with her hopes. Head craning back, he looked up at the sunflowers in the tree limbs.

"You like to climb trees?" he asked.

It took her a few moments of awkward silence to realize what he meant. "Oh, yes. I do."

The corners of his lips tugged into a smile. "You are a wonder."

One of her brows quirked up. "Well thank you."

Lengthening shadows reached out to touch Kinan's shoulder and mingle with his dark hair. She longed to do the same, to run it through her fingers and see if it felt as silky as it looked. Drawn in by the power of her desire, she took a step toward him.

"Deirdre?" came the distant sound of Sadie's voice on a breeze.

Disappointment at being interrupted warred with excitement over their plans for the night. "Coming!" she called.

"May I walk you back?" Kinan asked.

Hiding a smile, Deirdre nodded. "You may."

"Wonderful. Give me but a moment." He dashed off toward the gazebo, running backward for a moment and looking at her. A laugh drew from her at his uncharacteristic playfulness. Maybe, just maybe she had misjudged him. But when he returned with his cloak and wrapped it around her shoulders, her hopes dashed once again.

As much as she wanted to refuse it out of principal, it smelled amazing—like cedar and wet stone, like him. She could no more cast aside those delicious scents than she could refuse the arm he offered.

"Wouldn't want you to catch a chill," he said.

Looping her arm through his, she lifted her chin as she walked alongside him. "And your arms and knees aren't chilly?" she asked, voice haughty.

"Oh, well…uh…"

She laughed. "Let's not decline into senseless mutterings again." Leaning in close, she whispered the next part to him. "I rather like your bare arms and knees."

Dark lashes shot open, and she both saw and heard him swallow hard.

As they approached the inn, Deirdre steered him toward the barn. The door gaped open and inside stood two draft horses hitched to Cat's wagon. Nestled into the seat, wrapped in a cloak with a blanket over her lap, sat Cat. Sadie was just climbing in next to her.

Kinan let go of Deirdre's arm. "You're going out? At this

hour?" Though he didn't say it, she knew he was also wondering about her attire.

"Yes. We'll be staying at our property tonight," she said.

His face fell into a look of disappointment. "Would you like an escort?"

Compelled by that look, she touched his arm with her bare hand, delighting in the bumps it made rise along his skin. "Thank you, but we will be all right." She looked at her friends. "Won't we ladies?"

"Oh aye," Cat said. "Rick is waiting at the gate to see us safely there."

Still arm in arm with her, Kinan escorted Deirdre to the wagon. He offered his hand as she lifted her foot toward the step. Just to see him blush, she accepted it. The moment the warm skin of their palms touched, a rush of energy shot through her that reached deep down inside, touching her very power. Her hand convulsed around his on instinct. They stood staring into one another's startled eyes. There was no mistaking that he had felt it too.

Mabon was a special time, when such things were heightened.

A horse snorted, shattering the moment. She climbed into the wagon and sat next to Cat. Eyeing the silky dress covering her knee that poked out of the cloak Kinan had lent her, Cat draped part of her blanket over Deirdre.

"Thank you for the escort, Kinan," Deirdre said.

He dipped his head. "You are quite welcome. Will I see you tomorrow for archery practice?" he asked.

"I wouldn't miss it," she answered. Her quick response made her cringe inwardly. Being too eager wasn't only unseemly, but she knew too well that some men lost interest when they thought the chase was over. And right now she was rather enjoying Kinan's interest.

To salvage the situation some, she looked away as Cat clucked to the horses. The wagon lurched forward and they left the barn at a slow trot. A powerful urge tugged at her to look back at Kinan. It took all her self-control to resist. Her friends exchanged grins with one another before turning them onto her. No one spoke until they were halfway down the drive.

"My apologies for interrupting," Sadie said, the last word going up in pitch along with her eyebrows.

Laughing and humming suggestively, Cat bumped her shoulder into Deirdre's. "Is there something there to interrupt?"

Deirdre waved a dismissive hand. "Of course not. The man is far too proper for me." But the words rang hollow and untrue even in her own ears.

That there was something between them was becoming harder and harder to deny.

By the time they reached the gate the sun was no more than a sliver of gold on the horizon. Above it the sky had darkened to fuchsia that bled into sapphire. The first star sparkled in the north. Deirdre didn't see Rick anywhere, and the gate was still closed. Figuring he must be running late, she climbed down and started to open the gate.

"Don't be alarmed, D," Cat called from the wagon.

"Alarmed? Whyever would I be—" Then she saw it—the eyes of a predator staring at her from within the bushes beside the gate. The fact they were at her shoulder level closed her throat against a scream. The creature crept out of the shadows. The long snout and ears of a wolf became frightfully clear. But it stood taller than any wolf she had ever seen or heard of, including the timber wolves of the cold north.

Finally, it struck her. "Rick?" she whispered.

His nose dipped. Wonder filled her to bursting with questions. Out of respect for his privacy and because they'd been so busy, she hadn't asked to see his wolf form. Now that he finally stood before her, she regretted they hadn't made the time. One question in particular drew her gaze to the moon. The half full orb had just started to climb over the horizon. That was one question answered. It didn't control his ability to shift, at least, not completely. So he'd chosen to be a wolf tonight. Of all nights, it made perfect sense.

"Well hello there. By Danu, you are magnificent," she whispered.

Faolach were rare even back in Ireland, so her mum had told her. Knowing her dear friend was engaged to one was one thing, seeing it firsthand was nothing short of magical.

The Rick-wolf sneezed, which seemed more like a statement than an involuntary act. As Deirdre opened the gate he slipped back toward the bushes and melted into the shadows. Cat drove the wagon through, and she shut the gate behind them. When she climbed back into the seat beside Cat and scanned the darkening fields, Rick had disappeared—or at least, seemed to.

"You didn't tell us he was so big!" Deirdre said to Cat.

Sadie snort-laughed, which made Deirdre gape at her. "Sadie MacMurphy, did you just interpret my words how I think you did?"

Giggling, she shrugged and tucked her chin to hide inside

the hood of her cloak.

A delighted squeal came from Cat as she clapped a hand on Sadie's arm. "You did! Good for you."

Caught up in the spirit of the sabbat, they chatted about all manner of inappropriate things that made Sadie giggle and groan and hide. By the time they reached their property, their cheeks ached, and darkness had almost completely claimed the land. The golden glow of a lamp sitting on a rock illuminated a pile of firewood around which a ring of large stones had been stacked. Nearby sat three oak trees no taller than four feet with their roots wrapped in burlap sacks. Their energy hummed quietly. In their center sat a large watering can.

As they climbed from the wagon, Deirdre thought she saw the gleam of eyes in the distance—Rick watching over them.

"Cat, Sadie, you did this?" Deirdre asked, beckoning toward the firepit.

Head shaking, Cat held up a hand. "Before you reprimand me for carrying too much, Rick did the heavy lifting. Sadie and I only helped with the light things."

Deirdre's throat tightened. "And the trees?"

"You like them?" Sadie asked. "Since we're at the three corners of our property, we thought it would be appropriate to plant one near each corner and create our circle within them."

The next breath Deirdre drew in was ragged. She put an arm around each of her friend's shoulders. "I love them. They're perfect, just like you two."

Apparently, they were going to ignore the face that Ainsworth's land also touched the corner of theirs. That was more than fine with Deirdre. She didn't want to ruin this sabbat with thoughts of that man.

After hugs and sniffles, they walked the horses over to one of the many corrals they'd erected around their properties. Dark hadn't fallen fully yet, so it was easy enough to see. The branches that made it up were small and held together by rope and the few nails they could scrounge together. But with Cat to talk to their horses and calm them if the need arose, it worked well enough. Together the three of them made quick work of unhitching the horses, putting them inside the corral, and tossing them some hay from the back of the wagon. Excitement buzzed about them as they made their way back to the intersection of their properties.

Cat plucked three crowns formed of vines and flowers from the ground near the lamp and handed one to Sadie and one to Deirdre. They were made up of delicate blue, pink, and white asters, violet autumn crocus, bright red trumpet shaped fuchsia, and goldenrod. Silk ribbons wrapped around the vines and tied the crowns into loops. The fading energy of the flowers was adorned with the positive, loving energy that had gone into making the arrangement. The warmth of that energy seeped into Deirdre when she placed it on her head.

Without having to check the location, they stepped on the corner of their land, faced each other, and grasped hands. Energy built within each of them. Deirdre could feel it as surely as she felt the cool breeze that caressed her face. As her own power flowed down her arms to join that of her friends, she felt theirs do the same. When the fronts touched, sparks ignited that lit up the night to those sensitive enough to magic to see it. Their energy became a circle, then expanded into a globe that surrounded them.

As was their custom, Deirdre took up the first chant. "We cast this circle to protect us from any who would do us harm or interfere." The globe pulsed and strengthened.

Sadie took up the next chant. "We cast this circle to raise and heighten positive power for our purpose here." Again it pulsed.

Cat said the final circle chant. "We cast this circle to set our intentions and make our desires clear." One final pulse traveled through the globe, this one so powerful that for a moment Deirdre could see it around them like a giant, glowing bubble. Though the sight faded, the power did not.

Together they chanted, "To protect, strengthen, and focus, the circle is cast. As we will it, so shall it manifest."

Slowly, Deirdre let go of Sadie's and Cat's hands. The energy between them stretched like dough. At last, it let go with an almost cognizant reluctance. Eyes closing, Deirdre concentrated on her own energy. She imagined roots growing from her feet and toes, reaching deep into the earth. Those roots connected her to the planet, helped her feel how she was part of it and the circle of life. Through them she felt every living thing not only around them, but for miles. Life, reproduction, death, peace, and the rebirth of all things coursed through her. She reached up with her power, to the stars and the infinite energy of the Powers that Be that lay within them and beyond. Their power reached back, poured into her, purified her. But it was too much. Opening herself back up, she released it into the earth and universe until she could contain what was left. She then pulled her proverbial roots and branches back into herself and envisioned her energy drawing into the center of her being. Grounded and centered, she opened her eyes.

A mixture of white and emerald power with gold and purple sparks pulsed from Sadie. Green energy flecked through with gold and red surrounded Cat. From her belly emanated an entirely different energy, this one a lovely turquoise and aqua. Both Sadie and Deirdre gravitated toward Cat and touched her belly.

"It's a girl," the three of them said in unison.

Joyful laughter from all of them filled the night. After more hugs, they separated and turned toward their trees.

"Watch your step. Rick dug the holes for us already. They are just behind the trees," Cat warned.

For Deirdre that was easy despite the dark. Reaching out with her power, she felt the energy of the grass, using it to give her an idea of where the void was. She walked directly to the tree without issue.

The rope around the little trunk came lose with a tug and Deirdre freed the root ball from the burlap sack. She massaged the roots carefully until they let go of the dirt some. Cradling the ball, she lowered the tree into the hole, righted it, and began to pack the loose dirt piled nearby around it.

So as not to disturb the others, because she knew they were doing something similar, Deirdre chanted in her head.

Revered Dagda, God of the land and seasons, I thank you.

She fed power to the tree, encouraging the roots to explore deeper into the dirt, spread out, and secure the tree.

By planting this tree, I restore balance to the land so it may renew.

The dirt around it soon felt solid. She took up the watering can and poured a third of the water around the trunk.

May its roots grow deep and wide, and its limbs reach into the blue.

The tree buzzed with life, its small branches swaying

toward her, leaves brushing her arm. *Root then rest, little one. Winter is coming,* she told it. The energy coursing through it began to calm almost immediately. Soon it was no more than a slight hum.

Taking up the water can, she walked over to where Sadie was tamping down the dirt around her tree. With a smile, Sadie took the can from her and poured until her tree was watered in. As she did, Deirdre fed the tree some of her energy, encouraging it to spread it roots and drink deep. When finished, they went to Cat and repeated the process.

Finished with their planting, they came back together around the firepit. Deirdre chose a thin piece of kindling from within the stacked wood, removed the cover from the lantern, and held the wood to the flame until it caught. Sadie and Cat placed hands over hers.

Together the three of them chanted words they had long ago memorized from years of celebrating the holiday. "Dagda, God of nature and earth, we honor you this Mabon and thank you for the bounty we have enjoyed."

Hands still clutched around the end of the burning stick, they turned and placed it at the bottom of the stack. The small yellow flame crackled against the bark and dried moss, catching and spreading.

Again, they chanted together. "We have partaken of the earth's bounty, but we also plant. We have eaten of the animals, but we also raise and nurture them. We have worked hard, but we also play."

The fire grew, spreading to the small branches.

"We honor the earth, animals, and Powers That Be, and seek balance with all, this and every day."

Already the fire worked at the bigger pieces of wood. Warmth emanated from it. The three of them encircled the fire and clasped hands. Deirdre said, "Blessed be our new home."

"Blessed be our friends, old and new," Cat said.

"Blessed be our future here," Sadie said.

They raised their joined hands toward the sky and looked to the stars as they chanted, "As we will it, so shall it be!"

Hoots, cheers, and laughter rose into the darkness along with sparks and smoke from the fire, raising their intentions and joy into the night. Energy flowed between and through them. Throwing their cloaks and shoes off, they began to dance and sing. All the while, a wolf watched over them from the shadows.

19

Deirdre

October

Patrols and bow practice did not go as Deirdre hoped. Kinan remained the perfect gentleman. Well, perhaps not perfect, with the long looks and lingering touches, but close enough to drive her half mad. Why did he have to be so interesting, and worse, be so interested *in* her? Weeks passed and still she hadn't gotten him to do more than hold her hand. If only he weren't so fun and charming. That made it increasingly difficult to give up on him. His love of exotic cultures fascinated her as well. Perhaps it meant he might be open-minded after all. Still, she hadn't been able to bring herself to tell him her secrets.

But she grew closer every day, or so she told herself. Each day she got to know and trust him a little more. Perhaps soon she would tell him. The right time would present itself. And if it didn't, then she wasn't meant to tell him.

After Mabon, Kinan joined the workers in building and guarding their home sites. He remained ever at her side. From the glaring and muttered curses Dylan shot their way, the time she spent with him clearly frustrated him to no end. Unlike in the past with other would-be suitors, she didn't find the rivalry they'd struck up over her scintillating. Rather, it made her feel bad for Dylan. Bad because of the exasperation it caused him, or bad because she might fancy Kinan more? She hadn't decided.

As October arrived and the leaves began to fall in earnest, they had completed the framework and roofing for her and Sadie's homes and the barn. Deirdre's own house was starting to look like something close to a home, or the frame of one at least. When complete, it would be a sprawling blend of Victorian elegance with a wraparound porch, and rustic American with log siding. It pained her that so many trees had been sacrificed so they could survive the elements. But having their pinecones, and with them their seeds, meant they would have new life. And she'd already begun planting them all around the edges of each of their properties. In the spring, she would share her energy with them and help them sprout.

Already both stories of her home were framed, and log siding was up on the walls of the first story. It would easily be complete enough to be considered a dwelling by spring. With no sign of Ainsworth or his spies anywhere near their lands, her confidence that they could actually do this grew by the day. It didn't hurt that each home site always crawled with Rick's men, who not only worked tirelessly, but kept sharp eyes out for any unwanted company.

Looking at her home in the soft afternoon light, a swelling of pride filled her near to bursting. Behind her, someone cleared their throat. But it wasn't who she expected. Dylan stood with his hat in his hands, slowly turning it, his fingers massaging the rim. "'Tis going to be beautiful," he said, gaze fixed on her instead of the house.

Not wanting to endure the weight of it—or feel its pull—she looked back at the house. "'Tis, thank you." Kind as he was, she couldn't get over him treating her like a princess who needed saving. "Are you attending the engagement party this evening?"

"'Tis me night to guard the home sites."

Relief coursed through her, quickly followed by guilt. To counteract it, she asked, "Couldn't you get one of the workers to take your turn? I know Rick and Cat would like you to be there."

"Would *you* like me to be there?"

She both heard and felt him come closer. He stopped at her side. Knowing she didn't have the answer he wanted to hear, she allowed silence to stretch between them.

"I'm sorry if me forwardness offended you. Me intention was not to dishonor or compromise you." The shameful way he hunched over tugged at her.

"Dylan, that wasn't my impression at all, and that certainly isn't why I'm displeased with you," she said softly. Her gaze darted about to make sure no one else was near enough to hear them. This wasn't something she wanted Kinan to hear.

Shoulders squaring up, Dylan reached toward her. A step up the porch allowed her to avoid his grasp. Several more took her around the first support log where she could lean on the railing, keeping it between the two of them.

"Yet you're avoiding me," he pointed out.

She sighed and resigned herself to the conversation. It was best to get it out of the way, she supposed. "Your actions have shown me that you hold some rather traditional views of how a lady should act. I'm not interested in a relationship with a man who won't be pleased with my independent spirit."

Dylan ran a hand through his sweat-darkened hair. "Your

wild spirit is part of what draws me to you, but you being a fine lady is part of that as well." Moving forward, he placed a hand on hers, trapping it against the juniper railing. "Please, give me the chance to prove I can compromise. I feel something for you, and I think maybe you feel something for me, too. I think we owe it to ourselves to explore what it might be," he said.

In her experience, to compromise with a woman wasn't the way of the nineteenth-century man of this world. On the other hand, he wasn't a high-society man. The likelihood of him judging her based on her secret was far lower. She cast her gaze out over his head, looking at the fields that would one day be rows of grapevines. Would he be able to accept a woman who came with her own lands and money and not simply take it for his own if they wed? Would he even want to wed? Once a woman married, anything she owned belonged to her husband. She realized she knew very little about him. He wasn't one to talk about himself, even when prompted.

Dylan's hand squeezed hers gently. "Deirdre, please, all I'm asking for is a chance. I'll be the perfect gentleman, if that's what you want, you have me word."

She pulled her hand from beneath his. "I don't want a gentleman. I want someone adventurous, bold, loyal, and kind. Someone who accepts me for who I am, respects me and allows me to be myself."

He vaulted over the railing, landed beside her, and took her hand back in his. "I can be that man."

Without missing a beat, despite his impressive show of dexterity that got her heart pumping, she said, "I want a partner, not a husband to lord over me. I need someone who won't feel threatened by me and try to hold me back."

"I'm all right if you don't want to remarry. I can be whatever you need."

Shaking her head, she pulled her hand from his yet again and stepped back. Her words just weren't getting through to him. "That's not what I meant. I do want to remarry. I want children, a family, eventually. But I want that all with a man who accepts and respects me."

At the mention of remarrying and children, Dylan's eyes widened, and fear flashed in them. Deirdre refused to give in. She could not compromise on this.

"Just because I like that you're a proper lady and want to protect you, doesn't mean I don't respect your spirit. 'Tis a man's nature to protect, is all."

Her chin lifted. "True enough, but women are strong and capable, and the time for men to recognize that is long overdue."

"Perhaps not."

Deirdre's fists clenched. "Excuse me?"

"Maybe the time has come again. Our ancestors, the Celts, used to allow their women to fight alongside them. Maybe that time has come again."

Teeth clenched, Deirdre blew out a sharp breath through her nose. "Allow?"

The hopeful look on his face fell away into one of such disappointment that it shot a pang of guilt through her. *No.* She would not feel guilty for taking a stand on this.

Someone approaching from the side of the house caught her attention. Long strands of Kinan's hair flew about him in the afternoon breeze. The knot of hair at the base of his neck looked messy, no doubt from the day's work. Sleeves rolled up, top two buttons of his shirt undone, he possessed a casual air that Deirdre very much enjoyed. He was far enough away that she didn't think he had heard them. She felt guilty for the relief that washed over her at that, and wasn't sure which man made her feel that way.

She took another step away from Dylan just as Kinan turned their way.

"Deirdre, there you are. Hello, Dylan," Kinan said, voice darkening at Dylan's name. Though his posture tensed, he smiled as he looked back at Deirdre. "Cat asked me to fetch you to begin the preparations for the party tonight."

The very mention of the engagement party caused excitement to course through her. Returning his smile, she nodded. But as she turned to Dylan, she was unable to hold that smile. "Perhaps we'll see you at the party," she said.

"You may at that. I hope you'll think about what I said."

The encouraged look on his face almost made her regret her words. It didn't help that Kinan stood so close by. Acutely aware of both their gazes on her, she strode around Dylan and down the steps. Before marrying, she had often enjoyed the attention of multiple men. It had been fun. Now that she was actually interested in two men at once, she found it frustrating. She left Dylan standing on her half-built front porch and accepted Kinan's offered arm, allowing him to lead her away.

Several strides later, Kinan leaned in and asked her, "That man always seems to be telling you to think about his words." Oddly, he was right, and ironically, she really wasn't sure what to think about that. Halfway to the horses' enclosure, Kinan spoke again. "I'm very much looking forward to you ladies charming everyone tonight."

Doubt tried to worm its way into her. "Do you really think they'll be charmed by us? It would mean so much to me if they embraced Cat and Sadie."

Kinan surprised her with a hearty laugh. "The townsfolk of Goldenvale don't stand a chance. You could charm a bear awakening from hibernation," he said.

"Hardly! But that's not to say I wouldn't try."

Kinan erupted into further laughter and didn't stop. The carefree sound soon had her joining in. Worries forgotten, they laughed until they cried, neither one feeling the eyes watching them from the shadows.

20

Deirdre

October, Engagement Party

Hand touching down between the loops of dried leaves garland
that ran the length of the railing, Deirdre made her way slowly
down the stairs. The modern—and slightly scandalous—high-
heel boots she wore didn't hinder her steps at all. She walked
slowly so she could survey the grand room and foyer from above.
The sight made her breath catch so completely that one black-
lace-gloved hand flew to her breast.

Garland decorated with acorns led into a room filled with
gold, red, orange, and yellow decorations. Gold ribbon hung in
great coils from the ceiling, and orange and gold velvet runners
adorned the tables along the wall that held refreshments. The
scents of pumpkin and spice filled the entire inn with a delicious,
decadent aroma that made her mouth water. The dance floor
sparkled with scattered sugar, an indulgence of hers that Kinan
had been excited to try. The result was nothing short of
spectacular. True, it would require a lot of mopping tomorrow,
but she was all too happy to lend her hands to the task. It
reminded her of pixie dust. But unlike that aphrodisiac

substance, non-magic sensitive people could see the sugar.

The pulse of energy drew her gaze to the bottom of the stairs. On small tables to each side of the stairs stood orange pumpkins surrounded by a variety of gourdes and the bright green leaves of potted apothos cleverly placed behind them. A stomach-turning mixture of anxiety and delight washed through her as she beheld it all.

"Gods help me, but I fear you will outshine the bride-to-be tonight," Kinan's rich voice drifted up to her.

Had she heard him correctly? In her distracted state, she wasn't sure, but it had sounded like he'd made the reference to god plural. Surely not. She doused the thrill of hope that shot through her at the notion.

He stood just to the left of the bottom of the stairs in the open door to the kitchen. The gorgeous room paled beside him. In a fine black suit tailored perfectly to fit his body, he was the very portrait of an elegant gentleman. He had smoothed back his overly long black hair and tucked it into such a perfect knot that few could guess at its length. A purple vest close to the same color of her gown peeked out from beneath his jacket. The bold choice sent a thrill through Deirdre that started at her navel and ended in her cheeks.

The guarded look that came over him before he looked down stirred disappointment in her. But then he gestured to one of the pumpkins. "I hope it's all right that I added these. I've been coddling them since September as a surprise, turning them each day so they'd be the perfect shape. But, from your expression, now I'm not so sure they were a good idea."

Anxiety gave way to wonder. "You did all that for us?" she

asked softly.

Cracks formed in the shell hiding his emotions. Hope shone through. "I did."

There was no holding back the smile that came over her. "They are beautiful." She had to clear her throat before she could go on. "You look quite fetching yourself." Fetching didn't begin to describe him, but it would do. She wanted to strip him naked, roll all over the sugar-sprinkled floor with him, then lick every inch of him clean. But she couldn't exactly say that. Could she? The hungry look on his face as his gaze drank her in made her wonder. All that fretting over which dress to wear was suddenly worth every nail-biting moment. Taking up her purple skirts in one hand, she started to descend again. Kinan dashed up the stairs before she could even get down two steps, and offered her his arm.

"Thank you," she said, accepting with a gracious smile.

At the bottom of the landing she paused to survey the room again. Really, she paused because she didn't want to let go of his arm just yet, but it was as good an excuse as any.

Kinan gently cleared his throat. "I do hope you don't think it too forward of me to ask, but might I be the first to add my name to your dance card?"

She lifted the purple, velvety clutch dangling from her wrist, opened the booklet within, and handed Kinan the pencil tucked along the binding. "Please, be forward. I'd be delighted to have your name be the first added to my card."

She watched closely as he ran his finger over each dance planned for the evening, her chest filling with anticipation. Heat spread throughout her as he wrote his name beneath the slow waltz. Of all the dances he might have chosen, she had suspected that would be the last among them. But she was pleased it wasn't. Sadly, it was literally the last dance of the night.

He looked up in time to catch her smile. "My choice pleases you?"

She accepted the pencil from him and tucked it back into the booklet. "Very much so. I look forward to it. But only one dance?" she asked, brows rising with a suggestive look. With eleven other dances planned for the evening, she feared she might be stuck dancing with every eligible, stuffy, high-society man in town before the night's end. She could be in for a long, boring night.

Not only would Kinan's touch be welcome, but she knew he'd provide entertaining conversation about astronomy, strange cultures, and foreign lands. She feared the other men might be the opposite. In her few encounters with men of Goldenvale, she had found them to be either dedicated to and focused on their crafts, or tediously traditional in their beliefs and treatment of women. Tonight might prove to be different, but she held little hope of that.

"I wouldn't want to monopolize you and keep you from socializing," Kinan said.

Much as she wanted to, she couldn't argue with that. She needed to talk to the townsfolk to establish working relationships with those from whom the stable and winery would need goods.

"However." His hopeful tone drew her attention. "I would very much like to check your dance card again after you've greeted all our guests, and take advantage of anyone's oversight."

She smiled. "I would like that."

From the open door of an adjoining room off the ballroom, Cat and Sadie walked in, their dancing boots clicking softly on the wood floors. In a red velvet dress trimmed with white lace, and her tight black curls bound up with pearl-adorned pins, Sadie looked the very spirit of Samhain, which lay only a week away. The red set off her mahogany skin and black hair beautifully. Cat wore a forest-green gown of satin and lace, cleverly designed with a frilly sash that hid her slight belly bump perfectly. Most of her fiery red hair was tamed up into an elaborate bun with acorns woven into it. Small ringlets dangled around her face and neck.

Deirdre rushed toward them and grabbed their hands. "You both look positively splendid! Oh, Sadie, you outdid yourself on each of these dresses," she said.

Cat bathed Sadie in an adoring look. "She did indeed."

They spent several moments fawning over one another's dresses, making each other twirl, and laughing as if they didn't have a care in the world. Deirdre encouraged it with compliments and questions, wanting to keep her friends lighthearted and happy as long as possible. This night should be a highlight of Cat's life, but Deirdre knew it would take a stressful turn soon enough. Not only was this their first opportunity to truly mingle with the people of Goldenvale, but they would also have to deal with Ainsworth. Assuming he showed up. Deirdre had no idea how that was going to go, only that it likely wouldn't be good. Her goal for the evening was to keep the man away from Rick and Cat as long as possible.

"Mr. O'Leary," came Maria, the cook's, voice.

The older woman carried a fine silver tray with her as she emerged from the kitchen. Three delicate wineglasses balanced on it with the effortless ease that only a long-time server could pull off. The feat always impressed Deirdre, even more so in Maria's case, considering the woman had to be in her sixties.

Maria's eyes widened and positively lit up as she looked Deirdre's way. She strode straight for them, Kinan all but forgotten. Head inclining toward the tray, she said, "A little something to calm your nerves and smooth your social graces, ladies?"

Deirdre picked up a glass and lifted it to her nose. The scent stopped her. It smelled like grape juice, not the wine she'd been hoping for.

"Ah my pardon, Mrs. Quinn, but that one is for Miss Cat, her special drink for the night." With that, the woman winked at Cat. Sharing in the ladies' secret smile, Deirdre handed the glass over and chose another.

Maria perused their dresses with an approving eye. "You ladies are all visions of beauty, and those dresses! Miss Sadie, your skill is unmatched."

Looking down, Sadie blinked rapidly several times. "You're far too kind."

Bootheels clicked behind them, sounding deliberately crisp so as not to approach unannounced. "Quite true, your skills are unequaled, Sadie. You ladies look positively lovely," Kinan said before turning to Maria. "Maria, did you have word for me?"

The woman waved her free hand. "Oh, yes, yes." She cleared her throat and straightened so abruptly that her starched white apron snapped. "Mr. Fergusson has arrived and says he spotted many guests coming down the road behind him."

Eyes widening, Cat's her lips drew into a taut line. Even before her late husband had damaged her confidence so greatly, Cat had never been good around large groups of people. The woman could literally talk to animals. It made her infinitely more comfortable with them than with people. Deirdre laid her hand on her shoulder. "Don't you worry yourself at all. Sadie and I will charm the guests, you just enjoy the company of that handsome man who will be your husband in less than two months' time."

Sadie nodded as she accepted the last glass from the tray. "That's right. We'll take care of everything."

Slowly, Cat's lips relaxed into a smile. "You two are the best friends a lady could ever hope for. I am so grateful that you're here with me," she said in a voice choked with emotion. She raised her glass and Sadie and Deirdre followed suit. "To the best of friends, my chosen family."

They each echoed the sentiment before taking a long drink from their glasses. The strong oak finish of the vintage left a lot to be desired, in Deirdre's opinion, but it went down smooth. Four years from now they would hopefully be sipping wine of their own making. Until then, this would do well enough. As Kinan moved toward the door—no doubt to help Rick in the stables—Deirdre stole another glance at him. She hoped it wouldn't be the last time she saw him this evening before their dance. As he reached the door he glanced over his shoulder and caught her looking. The crooked smile he gave her lit a fire inside so powerful it felt as though it had been started by the Goddess Brigid herself. If the man didn't relax his proper ways soon, she was going to positively burn up.

By the time the flow of guests stopped, Deirdre's feet ached from standing in one place long enough to greet them all personally. But it was worth it. Gracious compliments fell from the lips of all in regards to everything from their dresses to the décor of the inn. Both Cat and Sadie had been pulled away by guests some time ago, leaving Deirdre to the greeting. She didn't mind at all. It gave her a chance to analyze the actions and reactions of each person who came in. For the most part, the people of Goldenvale were kind and genuine. Whether that was merely the spirit of the upcoming holiday, the chance to enjoy a party, or their true natures, remained to be seen.

Still, the first impression she got from most was positive, particularly in comparison to how she and her friends had been treated by the Widows of the 69th organization back in New York. But then, those women had been jealous of Cat's marriage to her late husband. Fools that they were. And Deirdre was relatively sure they had begun to think her and her friends were witches. Their true nature wouldn't have mattered one iota to them. As far as those women would have been concerned, that was precisely what they were. They needed to be careful and make sure no one here began to suspect anything untoward about their nature. This was the wild west. People weren't ostracized from society or run out of town here. They were hanged.

The sight of Cat's smiling face across the room as she chatted with Sadie pulled Deirdre from her foreboding thoughts. It was nearly winter. Her emotions wouldn't betray her connection to plants. For the here and now, they were safe. They could convincingly pretend to be normal human women. And once they were done charming the elite of this town's high society and they had the connections they needed to obtain supplies, they could fade into obscurity and become recluses.

Which meant for now, she needed to mingle. Both fortunately, and unfortunately, the eligible bachelors were plentiful and none too shy about asking to sign her dance card. Only one dance remained in her booklet when the flow of guests finally stopped. Across the room of chatting people, she caught Kinan's gaze. Had he been thinking the same thing she had all this time? They started toward one another. Somehow, over the din of people talking, she heard Maria's announcement.

"Mr. Bartholomew Ainsworth."

Though she cringed inwardly, Deirdre forced a smile and turned back toward the door. A hush slowly worked its way over the room. The man wore a cleverly cut gray suit that managed to make him look broader and more imposing than she knew his spindly frame to be. Silver cufflinks shone at his wrists, silver conches on his boots, and a silver-and-gold buckle poked out beneath his vest. Set deep in his clean-shaven chin was a cleft that probably had looked dashing in his prime, but only made him look sunken and shrewd now. Then again, that could just be her opinion of him tempering her impression. The man couldn't be much past his prime. Not a single gray hair marred the chin-length brown locks he had tied back with a silver ribbon. Many ladies who couldn't sense or see a person's energy might actually find him attractive.

The manner in which he surveyed the room, like a predator,

unnerved Deirdre so much she had to suppress a shudder. Regardless, she set her shoulders back and fixed her mind on making the most of the situation.

"Mr. Ainsworth, I'm glad you made it," she said. She didn't have to feign sincerity, she truly was glad. Now she would have the opportunity to speak to the man.

His eyes widened as they took her in, sliding along her form in an appreciative manner that turned her stomach. The spark in those eyes when they finally met hers was anything but encouraging. "As am I. Thank you, Mrs. Quinn."

She smiled and inclined her head like the good, demure lady she wasn't. "Do come in away from the cold, and I shall get the help to fetch you a drink," she invited.

His lips curled in distaste, but slowly relaxed as he looked around. People pretended to be engaged in conversation or busy sipping their drinks, but every one of them had an ear or eye on her and Ainsworth.

"You've managed to make this place look quite festive," he said in a shocked voice.

He offered her his arm. Unable to see any way out of it without being rude, she accepted and led him into the room. People nodded and offered greetings to him as if he were the community pillar he pretended to be. When he looked away or passed, Deirdre noticed their guarded expressions, animosity, and even fear in their rigid postures. What surprised her, though, were the sympathetic looks many of them gave her. To those she gave a wilted smile that conveyed how uncomfortable she felt on the arm of such a man. She needed them to know she was not joining forces with him. Their sympathy and support were things she and her friends would undoubtedly need later. The day would come when she would need them to rally together, and if she laid the groundwork properly tonight, they just might do it.

With each step they took into the crowd, the conversation around them picked up. Halfway into the room, one of the help offered a tray of various drinks to Ainsworth. No surprise to Deirdre, the man chose a glass of whiskey. It seemed a strong spirit to start the night with. Nor did it surprise her when he ignored the server altogether. Over the talk, Deirdre just barely made out the tone of a violin bow being drawn against strings. Her gaze scanned the crowd. Off to their right stood a young man with his hands behind his back, gaze fixed upon them—her first dance partner if she recalled correctly.

She looked to Ainsworth. "I do beg your pardon, Mr. Ainsworth, but it seems the musicians are about to begin, and I see the first name on my dance card waiting. But I do hope it's all right if I seek you out later so we may talk," she said.

The smile he gave her looked as though it exercised muscles he wasn't used to employing. "I would like that," he said, gaze on her cleavage.

Taking a pencil from his jacket, he lifted her wrist. "I trust there's room left for me on your dance card." He opened the booklet without waiting for her reply and wrote his name on the last dance available.

"But of course. Until then, I hope you enjoy yourself," she said, giving him a slight curtsy so she could look down and hide the contempt in her eyes.

That slippery gaze slid down to her chest again. "I'll do my best. But I can promise I'll enjoy the view."

She hoped the tight-lipped smile she gave him helped make the fury that flushed her cheeks look like a blush instead. Angering the man was the last thing she wanted to do. For now, at least.

Another long, pure note from a violin sang through the air, the acoustics of the high ceiling carrying it through the room with dramatic effect. People shifted about, finding their first dance partners with excited murmurs. Ainsworth melted into the crowd, tipping his head to her. The moment he was out of sight, the young man waiting stepped up. His fine clothes and stylish haircut marked him as a high-society man, likely one born to money, considering his young age. Despite how tedious such men could be, the smile Deirdre gave him was one of genuine relief.

"Mrs. Quinn, I do believe I am first on your card. Might I have this dance?" he asked with a bow as he extended his hand to her.

Since he had already written his name on her dance card, asking was a formal redundancy, but she decided not to fault him for it. She accepted his hand just as the violin pealed into a lively tune, soon joined by the piano. He swept her into the steps so abruptly that her boots left the floor entirely for the space of a heartbeat. Thankfully, he was skilled enough to right her with the next step. It turned out redundancy was something she should fault him for after all, for during their dance conversation he had a habit of repeating himself. Still, he was kind enough and generous with compliments. If only they weren't all about her appearance and the same ones over and over again.

Just when she thought she might burst if she had to hear

how like sapphires her eyes were for at least the third time, the dance mercifully ended. She moved to her next partner with an eagerness the distinguished gentleman misunderstood. She had to spend the entire dance convincing him she wasn't ready to remarry just yet. Dance after dance, partner after partner, she worked her charm on the gentlemen of Goldenvale, not as potential suitors, but as merchants, ranchers, and the people she might be able to do business with. All were pliable beneath her talents, but openly cautious. It didn't help that Ainsworth lurked in the corners, eyeing every man she danced with. Only rarely did he dance. The two ladies he did dance with were wide-eyed and rigid with fear the entire time.

Much to Deirdre's relief, Cat seemed oblivious to the tension around Ainsworth. She danced and laughed with abandon. Nearly every other dance she enjoyed with Rick, which was all well and good, considering the couple only had eyes for each other. Seeing them together made Deirdre think of Kinan.

Every now and then, she caught sight of him across the dance floor in the hands of another woman. Jealousy burned within her, despite the fact that he was looking her way nearly every time she was looking his.

Every dance that ended brought Deirdre closer to the one she had to share with Ainsworth. Dread began to make her feet heavy and her conversation skills lacking. It was a good thing her final partner before Ainsworth talked nonstop about his flour mill. The man barely noticed her nods or small words of affirmation. The opportunity to go over in her mind what she wanted to say to Ainsworth was well worth enduring all the talk about bleaching methods and grinding levels. By the time the dance ended, she felt confident she knew what to say and how to say it. She thanked the flour merchant for an informative dance—to which he grinned as if quite pleased with himself—and turned to find Ainsworth waiting.

She'd been half-worried and half-hopeful that she'd have to track him down. The bright green leaves of the apothos beside the bottom of the stairs perked up and reached leaves toward her. Panic made her heart strike a frantic rhythm. For a moment, she closed her eyes and imagined an impenetrable brick house around her power. It effectively closed it off and hid it. The plant went quiet and still. She glanced about in hopes no one had seen—only to find Ainsworth looking directly at her, eyes narrowed, head cocked. Surely, he hadn't seen. If so, maybe it had only looked like the skirt of her gown had caught it. She was standing close enough. Most people would dismiss it as such.

The musicians didn't pause for more than a few beats of her anxious heart. Without a word, Ainsworth extended a hand to her as the first clear piano notes echoed through the room. Deirdre accepted it with a nod. Despite the warm room, his hand was cool almost to the point of being cold. The man felt so much like a dullahan—a dark fae creature of death and destruction—that it made her shudder. But no, those creatures had fled this world long ago when the Tuatha had. He was just a man, and men could as dark and horrible as any monster. The first turn of the dance he drew her in closer than was socially acceptable. His left hand put enough pressure on her back that she couldn't pull away without making a scene. Each step forward he took with his right foot pressed his bony thigh against her. She covered her disgust with a look of mild shock at his impropriety. It wasn't how she wanted to start, but it was the best she could manage. They made several more turns to the beat of the music and still he didn't give an inch. Clearly, he intended to take control of the situation and possibly embarrass her at the same time.

The man did not know whom he was squaring off against.

"Pardon me, Mr. Ainsworth, but where I am from, 'tis not appropriate to dance this close," she said.

Ainsworth grinned. "Welcome to California."

If he thought she'd lower herself to allowing him to grope her just to win his favor and sway his intentions, he was daft. She returned his grin, pouring all of her irritation into the look. "Yes, well, you know what they say; you can take the lass out of New York, but you can't take New York out of the lass." At the next turn of the dance she stepped purposefully on his foot, then took a huge step back and attempted to lock her arm.

His hand clamped tighter on hers and with a yank, he spun her back into his embrace. After their chests collided, he slid his arm around her, but took a step back to a proper distance. He barely missed a beat of the dance steps. Over his shoulder, Deirdre saw Kinan set his drink on a side table and start in her direction. She shook her head at him. He stopped, but looked poised to leap. The idea of a knight in shining armor wasn't something she was opposed to, but if he stepped in, this encounter with Ainsworth would be unsalvageable.

Ainsworth sighed, a heavy, frustrated sound. "My apologies," he said with absolutely no sincerity. "We seem to have gotten off on the wrong foot. It has merely been too long since I've danced with a beautiful woman." The way he cringed when he said "foot" made her suppress a smile.

Eyes widening, she feigned shock. "Really? But, Mr. Ainsworth, surely a wealthy, powerful man such as yourself would be the most sought-after bachelor in all of Goldenvale."

He shrugged as his eyes roamed the room. "True. But the women here aren't exactly to my taste. No one has turned my head since my Catherine died." The genuine sound of pain in his voice surprised her. She was about to offer her condolences when he went on. "Until now." Lust turned the words into something dark and foreboding.

Deirdre blinked several times and cleared her throat before she could answer. "Yes, well, losing one's spouse is a traumatic thing that takes time to recover from." She hoped that would be sufficient to lay the groundwork for a response to what she feared might come out of his mouth next.

"Yes, but eventually we must. In that recovery may lie the answer to both of our problems," he said.

"I'm afraid I don't follow you," she said in an effort to delay him.

His eyes pinched together. "Don't be coy, Mrs. Quinn, you are far too intelligent for that. It demeans you."

Refusing to justify that with a response, she merely returned his glare. He tried to pull her close again, but this time she was ready and kept her elbow locked. The strength in his cold hands made it clear he could overpower her, but if he did he would make a scene. She held both her breath and her ground in hopes that he wasn't willing to do so. Instead of overpowering her, he leaned in close.

She could smell the sickly sweet whiskey on his breath as he demanded, "Marry me."

The proposal made her stomach heave. When she didn't respond for several steps, he went on. "Such an arrangement would benefit us both. I am wealthy and powerful, as you pointed out, a good match for a woman trying to find her place in a strange town."

Deirdre had to unclench her jaw to answer. "Mutually beneficial, you say. How, precisely, do you see yourself benefiting from this…arrangement?"

His grin turned smug. "As your husband, I will have the access to the creek that I seek, via the land I obtain through you. To show my benevolence, I will give up my efforts to…convince your friends to relinquish their claim to their land." Something sinister sparked in his eyes as he leaned closer. "And I will keep your secrets," he whispered.

Fury and fear burned through her, turning the snappy response she had in mind to ash—which was all well and good, considering how many unladylike curses had been included in it. *Secrets? Which secrets has he become privy to? And how?* No one in California outside of those she trusted with her life knew her secrets.

Ainsworth nodded as if her silence pleased him. "No need to answer now. In fact, I think it's best you think on it, it being a decision that could change your life, and the lives of your friends."

She nodded, not because she would consider it, but because she wanted to buy time. No easy feat, with how much anger roared through her at the moment. The time to throw another card on the table had come.

"Another option may be for you to purchase my land," she

said. She wouldn't sell, but she wanted him to think she might. Either would take time, time in which they could secretly finish building.

Ainsworth's wickedly joyful laughter startled her so much she jumped and nearly missed a step in the dance. Taking advantage of that surprise, he pulled her against him again. "Why would I buy what I can take? By summer of next year, your lands will be mine, one way or another," he whispered in her ear.

Frightening as the man—and his threats—could be, Deirdre saw the last part for the bluff it was. If he had been capable of taking her land, he would have done it already. Each attempt had ended in failure. By proposing to her, he merely showed his hand, revealing how desperate he was becoming. And perhaps, considering his threats, somewhat fearful. But fearful men could be more dangerous than greedy ones.

The music stopped and she stepped away so abruptly she nearly rolled an ankle. She turned the stumble into a low curtsy in which she dipped her head to hide the flash of fear that shot through her. Once she had her emotions under control, she looked up at him with a carefully placed smile. "Thank you for the dance, and the proposition, Mr. Ainsworth. I will give your words extensive thought," she said in the most formal tone she could muster. Her voice sounded strained to her ears, but she was glad it didn't quiver.

He raised the hand of hers he still clutched and bent over it, using the motion to pull her close again. "See that you do, for both your sake, and that of your friends," he whispered.

He kissed the back of her hand, staring hard at her all the while. Even through her satin gloves his lips felt cold. Never had she been so happy that propriety and fashion required a lady to wear gloves for such an event. She slid her hand free and stepped back. The music started up again and couples began to dance around them. Inclining his head to her, Ainsworth took several steps back and melted into the crowd. A quick glance around revealed many sympathetic eyes on her. Off to her right, Cat and Rick danced, drowning in each other's gazes. They hadn't witnessed any part of her interaction with Ainsworth.

Deirdre let out a relieved breath and started to make her way toward the kitchen door. She took a slight detour toward the fireplace. There she paused, peeled her gloves from her hands, and tossed them into the crackling orange flames.

Thank Danu he hadn't actually touched my skin.

She felt the gazes of many of the ladies in the room on her. But their expressions weren't shocked or appalled like she feared. They were sympathetic.

Near the kitchen door, she encountered Sadie chatting with a group of ladies. She caught enough of the conversation to know they were praising her for her dress designs. By the time Sadie looked her way, Deirdre had fixed a delighted look on her face.

Wise to her, Sadie asked, "Is everything all right?"

"Of course, don't let me interrupt. I'm merely going to check and see if the kitchen has any more of those delicious wraps Cat is asking for. 'Tis wonderful to see you ladies, do enjoy the party," she said.

They offered kind words of praise for the decorations, spirits, and food before she was able to slip away. Once inside the kitchen, she closed the door behind her, leaned against it, and closed her eyes. Tears started to sting behind her lids. She pushed away from the door and stood tall. A few of the kitchen help labored nearby over the cutting board, giving her questioning looks. Maria stepped forward and handed her a wineglass. Relief coursed through her the moment her fingers wrapped around the stem.

"Thank you," she told her.

She scarcely heard her reply as she went for the back door. If she didn't get some air, she was going to need a fainting couch, and that was not how she wanted to end this evening. Cool air rushed around her as she opened the door and stepped outside. It drained away the flush of anxiety and allowed her to breathe again. The air soothed her body and calmed her mind.

Once her eyes adjusted to the dark, she stepped out onto the cobblestone patio. Moonlight shone through the slats of the pergola overhead. She followed the stripes of light out to a support beam and leaned against it. Frost reflected the light of the moon, revealing the English-style garden of evergreen bushes and bare planting beds stretched out before her. Here and there the trunks and branches of bare trees stretched up and out. They had been so busy building their homes, she had yet to make it out here. The frosty, sleeping garden tugged at her heart. She hoped to have one very much like it one day. If Ainsworth had his way, that would never happen. Would the heartless bastard actually spare her friends' lands if she married him? *Unlikely.*

The fragrant needles of a juniper bush near her side brushed her elbow.

Thank you, dear one. But sleep. I am well, she lied to it. It went still and dormant once again, its energy slumbering.

The sound of leather soles on cobbles stirred dread in her

and made her turn. The moon revealed a tall, gray-haired man approaching from within the garden. He held a cloak in his hands. "Frightfully cold this night, senorita, please accept this," he said in a thick Hispanic accent.

Smiling, she nodded and allowed him to drape the cloak around her shoulders. She sighed as she settled into its warmth. "Thank you."

"You are welcome."

While fine, his clothing wasn't quite formal enough for a party, and she didn't recall seeing him among the guests. "I apologize, but I don't recall meeting you when you arrived. I'm Deirdre Quinn," she said, extending her hand.

Instead of kissing it, he took it and shook it as if she were a man. "I am Felipe."

Shock and delight stole her words for a moment. She quickly recovered. "Just Felipe?"

His cheeks dimpled with a big grin. "The rest most Americans find too difficult to say."

"Well, 'tis a pleasure to meet you, Felipe. I didn't mean to interrupt your evening. Are you staying at the inn?"

"Tonight only." He gestured to a small table with chairs at it. "Sit with me, if you like."

"Thank you, I would like that very much."

He offered her his arm. Without a second thought, she accepted and allowed him to lead her to the table despite it being in the shadows. She couldn't put her finger on it, but something about the man relaxed her. Then again, after her encounter with Ainsworth, the company of nearly any other man would seem relaxing.

Felipe pulled out a chair for her.

"Where are you from, Felipe?"

"Ensenada."

Intrigue began to push away the tendrils of fear Ainsworth's encounter had wrapped around her. "You've traveled so far! Surely you must stay longer than one night. If it's a matter of room, my friends and I could share a room so one is available for you. We wouldn't mind at all," she said.

Hands up, he shook his head. "No, no, not necessary. I am staying at the original, how do you say…homestead?"

That made her set her wineglass down. "You mean the original house the O'Learys built on this property?"

Pride filled his eyes. "Yes, I helped build it."

That explained why Kinan would let him stay there. But, that had to mean he was either a worker who had helped in the construction, or Kinan's grandfather. "And you're here to visit Kinan?" She kept her tone light, casual. Or at least, she hoped that was how it sounded.

The man's chest puffed out. "Yes, for the holiday. Usually more come, but the cold was too much for them. But young, I am not. How many winters I have left, who knows? So I come visit."

Certainly the help wouldn't come back so far to visit, not even a long-time family servant. They wouldn't have the coin to pay for passage on a ship, not even such a short journey. Which meant Kinan had some rather big news he had yet to tell her. A Hispanic grandfather. It would explain so much, his travels, his interest in Mayan culture. But was she imagining intrigue where it might not exist? Hoping to make the man more mysterious? Every fiber of her wanted to press Felipe about it.

She took a long drink of wine to still her tongue and hold back the urge. Pressing this foreign gentleman who was likely still weary from his travels wouldn't be right. No. If Kinan had a secret, he was the one who needed to tell her. And she understood why he would hesitate to divulge such information. High society looked down on certain mixings of blood, and this would definitely qualify as one of them. Foolish and antiquated notions, in her opinion. None of that meant she couldn't divulge her curiosity in other matters.

"The cottage is a very unique build. The earthen walls are so beautiful, like flowing brick," she said.

"Adobe, we call it."

"Adobe. How do you make it?"

Elbows on the table, fingers steepled together, Felipe delved into an in-depth description of the process. Deirdre hung on each word. She prompted him to go on in places and asked many questions. Not only did the process fascinate her, but Felipe was funny and kind. A way to make a home and kill far less trees in the process seemed brilliant and groundbreaking to her. *Why doesn't everyone do it?*

Light and music suddenly poured out of the door to the kitchen as it opened. Irritation—and an unhealthy dose of fear— surged back up in Deirdre.

Ainsworth wouldn't dare follow me out here, would he?

But the tall, handsomely cut figure silhouetted by the light of the kitchen certainly wasn't Ainsworth. The wooden legs of Deirdre's chair scraped against cobblestones as she stood swiftly. Felipe rose as well. "Kinan," she said, feeling a bit as if she'd been caught at something.

From this distance, she couldn't make out his expression due to the shadows, but his rigid posture told her much.

"Deirdre, there you are. I became worried when I heard you left after dancing with Ainsworth. Are you all right?" he asked in a guarded tone.

"Quite, thank you. I needed some air after dealing with that man. Felipe here has lifted my spirits considerably with interesting conversation." She couldn't help but tease him by making him wonder what that conversation might be.

Kinan cleared his throat and finally managed to get out, "Um, well, I'm glad to hear it. Thank you, Felipe." He took a few steps out onto the cobbled patio. "The last dance is approaching and I thought you might like to show a strong front by returning to dance again. But," he paused. "I understand if you don't feel up to it, and I can make up a tale of why you can't return, if needed." The fear and lack of confidence in his tone was so unlike him, and so deep, that it made her sick with guilt.

She smoothed her skirts and hid a smile. "I feel hale and hearty, and I wouldn't want to miss our dance together."

Kinan's shoulders pulled back and she thought she saw him smile, though it was hard to tell in the shadows.

Turning to Felipe, she found him regarding her with wide eyes, the hint of a grin pulling at his lips. "It was a pleasure meeting you, Felipe," she said.

He bowed deeply to her. "The pleasure was all mine."

"I look forward to speaking with you again," she said.

"And I with you."

When she turned back around, Kinan waited with an elbow extended. She walked to his side and looped her arm through his.

His eyes shot open wide for a brief moment before he covered the startled look with a few rapid blinks. Part of her delighted in the fact that she had surprised him, and part became saddened by it. What kind of judgment and rejection had he been subjected to that would cause such a reaction? But then, perhaps she read too much into his reaction and assumed things that were not, in fact, so. Time would tell, and hopefully, so would he.

They entered the ballroom just as the music for the slow waltz started. No one stared openly, but Deirdre felt the weight of everyone's gaze no matter how indirect. At least the conversation with Felipe had renewed her spirit and Kinan's presence at her side fed her strength. She managed an easy smile.

Her breath caught as Kinan took her bare hand in his and swept her out on the dance floor. His lack of concern over everyone seeing them touch bare hands stimulated her as much as the contact. So gentle and supportive was his touch that she felt like she was floating. They swayed and spun in slow patterns. While his movements were light and graceful, his pinched expression and guarded eyes made it clear he couldn't relax. Perhaps he wasn't as unconcerned about the impropriety of no gloves as she first thought. Deirdre could take his discomfort no longer. Deciding to stir a fire in him one way or another, she broke the rigid frame that held them apart and moved in closer.

"Intimacy," she whispered.

Wide eyes blinking, he said, "Pardon?"

"'Tis what has held me back from you." A half-truth, but as good a place as any to start.

Using the next turn of the dance, she stayed close. "My next husband must be a nontraditional man who allows me to be who

I am, and part of that is being an adventurous lover," she whispered.

The pinched looked between his brows and around his eyes smoothed out. "Ah." The sound was filled with understanding, and intense interest.

"And I must be sure before I wed him," she said.

His brows rose high. "Oh." His voice was equally high.

Arms relaxing, he allowed her to move even closer, but he smiled mutely.

"Your turn," she prompted.

Clouds of confusion paled the excitement in his eyes. "Pardon?"

She laughed. "To tell me what has held you back, because I fear something has."

Four steps more of the dance passed before he answered. "Felipe is my grandfather. My mother is Mayan. I didn't want to pursue a courtship with you until I told you, but I couldn't bring myself to." He looked hard at her for a moment. "You figured that out when you met him, didn't you?"

"I did."

"And still you danced with me." His mouth remained open, but before he could say more, the music came to an end. Stepping back, he bowed to her and said, "You're a wonderful dancer, it was a pleasure. I would like to continue our conversation at a later time—if you're open to doing so, that is."

During her curtsy, she kept her eyes locked on his, letting him feel the heat of her gaze. "Very much so. Tonight perhaps, after the guests have left?" she suggested.

Even through his chestnut skin tone his blush shone. He

lifted her hand, seemed to remember at the last moment she wasn't wearing gloves, then slowly released it. The brush of his fingers against her palm made her pelvic muscles clench. The indecency of such a sensation experienced in the midst of so many people added an extra thrill to it. Instinct, desire, she wasn't sure which, made her take a step toward him. He moved toward her as well, but couples began to disperse all around them and suddenly Deirdre found herself in the middle of a group of excited women. A tide of well-wishers and tipsy revelers swept Kinan away.

The next hour was spent taking compliments, accepting cards of those who wished to call or hoped to be invited to the wedding, and seeing them off to their carriages. Sometime during the wind-down, Cat and Sadie made their way to Deirdre's side. They bade people farewell together, presenting a united front to those who seemed to want to be their allies, good neighbors, and maybe even friends. If it hadn't been for the horrible encounter with Ainsworth, she would have considered the night a complete success.

Yet it could turn out to be even more successful if she and Kinan picked up where they left off. She could hardly wait for everyone to leave so she could find out what other delights the night might hold.

21

Deirdre

Soon after the last guests departed, Rick and Cat said a long farewell and the ladies retired to their rooms. Unlike Cat and Sadie, Deirdre couldn't sleep. She kept going over Ainsworth's outrageous proposal. Her friends had been giddy from how well the festivities had gone. Unwilling to steal that happiness from them, she hadn't told them about the dance with Ainsworth. It would hold until morning. But she couldn't convince her own mind to let it go. All the while she waited for Kinan to knock on her door, but he didn't.

Her thoughts spun. What made Ainsworth think a lady of her standing could be pressured into such a proposal? Did he truly know her secrets? Surely not or he would attempt to expose them and use the scandal to steal their land. And if he had truly fallen for their ruse of being too busy with the party and wedding, why would he have proposed? Could it be possible he wanted a peaceful solution, one that would win him a wife? But if he wanted peace, why threaten her with exposure? If it were a genuine proposal, should she consider it?

Hands so like spiders, eyes so similar to a rattlesnake's. She couldn't imagine how horrible lying with him, having him in her body, would be. A wave of revulsion washed her from the fainting couch where she rested by the window. The room was suddenly too stuffy, too confining. *Air.* She needed air. She grabbed her cloak from the hook on the wall and slipped her feet into a pair of fur-lined house shoes. Beyond her door stretched a dark hall through which crept warm air from the fireplace below. She paused and listened for a moment. If she came across one of her friends, she'd have to tell them why she was up. No sense in sharing a sleepless night with them.

Only the occasional creak of the house settling for the night disturbed the quiet. She stepped out and closed the door softly behind her. The scents of pumpkins from the decorations and roasted chicken from the party wafted up from downstairs. Normally such things would comfort her, put her in mind of the coming holiday, but tonight it seemed nothing could comfort her.

She crept down the stairs and paused once again at the bottom to listen. The foyer and ballroom sat silent and dark, without a soul in them. The contrast to earlier this evening when both had been filled with light and laughter was so great, it gave Deirdre a chill. Granules of sugar sparkled on the floor here and there in the light that seeped through the large front windows of the house. The sight reminded her of her dance with Kinan. Smiling, she stole out the front door.

Cool air made her grasp her cloak closed as she stepped out onto the porch. The earthy scent of approaching rain hung heavy in the air. A strong desire to look out over the hills of her own property drew her around the side of the house. Once she rounded the corner, she found a figure leaning against the railing. Her heart tried to flee and take her breath with it. Tense and ready to run, she gripped the support log closest to her. The figure the moonlight revealed was too tall, too muscular to be Ainsworth. And that knot of hair at the base of his neck…

"Kinan?" she whispered.

"Good evening, Deirdre." His rich, deep voice rolled over her, warmed her. The sound of it made her want to think of anything but Ainsworth. It had been silly to think it might have been him in the shadows. The man just had a way of seeping into her thoughts and playing on her fears.

"A good evening to you as well, Kinan."

"You're welcome to join me," he invited. "I apologize for not seeking you out, but there are things I need to tell you, and I was contemplating how best to do so."

Not caring about propriety, she leaned on the railing right next to him. Warmth radiated off him, drawing her closer until their arms touched. He didn't pull away. In an attempt to be subtle, she perused him out of the corner of her eye. Both his coat and necktie lay draped over the railing near his arm. Even more appealing was that he had opened the first several buttons of his gray shirt. It inspired her to remove her lace gloves and drape them beside his articles of clothing.

As if feeling her gaze on him, he reached for the buttons of his shirt. "My apologies for my state of undress. It was so warm inside and the evening air felt good against my neck."

If only he knew she wore no more than a night shift beneath her cloak. *Would it send him running?* She grabbed his hand and stopped him from doing up any buttons. The skin to skin contact almost made her gasp. He felt so warm, so vibrant. It was almost as if something hot waited just beneath the surface. Perhaps it was just her desire for the man. "Don't you dare. Propriety be damned." When his fingers continued to fiddle with the button, she leaned closer and said, "I don't mind one bit. In fact, I rather like it."

Eyes opening wide and filling with interest, he dipped his head to her and returned his hand to the railing. Reluctantly, and slowly, she withdrew her own.

Kinan drew in a deep, shuddering breath. "My father met and fell in love with my mother while traveling to Mexico on business. She came back with him and they settled here. When my father died, she returned to Mexico, but by then I didn't want to leave, this was my home. The people of Goldenvale know of my lineage. While most are tolerant of my mixed blood, certainly not all are," he said in a long rush.

She had suspected as much, but to hear it aloud came as a bit of a surprise. An entirely new kind of excitement started to rise in her, but she stopped it. This didn't necessarily mean he would accept her once he knew her secrets.

She must have taken too long to respond because he went on.

"I'm not shunned by high society, as you saw tonight, but nor am I embraced by it. And there is more."

"More?" she prompted quietly.

All manner of mundane possibilities ran through her busy mind. He took a step away. The look on his face held such sadness that her breath caught.

"If you haven't heard the tales of my people, you will. Proper society considers us savages and like to think we were killed off. You will read tales about how we worshipped many gods, saw prophecies in the stars, sacrificed humans and told the future in their entrails, and played dangerous games in which many participants died. It is all true," he began. Turning toward her with beseeching eyes, he went on. "But what you won't read was how we built great cities to protect our people from enemies who wanted to erase us from existence. You won't hear how we lived in huge family groups, supporting and helping one another. Or of how we cultivated the land and lived in harmony with it and the animals around us."

When he paused for a long time, she smiled gently and said softly, "History is written by the conquerors, and your people were conquered."

Hope smoothed out the lines around his pinched eyes. They widened and his gaze traveled across her as if seeing her anew. "None of that bothers you?"

"Absolutely not. Why would it? Have you, or do you plan to sacrifice your enemies and read the future in their entrails?" she asked.

He smiled. "No." The mirth in his eyes washed away. "But there is more I must tell you. Or show you, actually."

Pulse quickening, her gaze traveled over his fine shirt to where it gaped, giving her a view of his hard chest. "I am intrigued," she said somewhat breathlessly.

He offered her his elbow. "Are you up for a brief walk in the garden?"

Though the garden contained many evergreen bushes that might respond to her, she replied without hesitation. "Absolutely." Since he was being so honest with her, she would return the favor, and the garden would be the best place to do it.

They walked arm in arm along the cobblestone path that wound through evergreen boxwoods and juniper bushes. The path opened up into the garden proper. Raised vegetable beds now barren of plants and covered in hay flanked them. Deirdre could feel dormant roots in some, snuggling down to wait out the winter. A raindrop plopped onto the wood of the raised bed to her right, darkening it. Another landed on her arm.

Kinan chewed at his lip for a few steps, then finally said, "It looks as though the rain might drive us back in. Perhaps we can pick this up at another time." The disappointment in his tone bolstered her courage.

"Only if we let it. Let's go to the gazebo out by the redwood tree," she said, tone leaving little room for argument.

But from the brilliant smile that spread across Kinan's face, he clearly wasn't going to argue. "Let's."

Soon the light glowing from the windows of the house faded. But it was far from dark. The nearly full October moon floated overhead, peeking out between clouds to cast its soft light across the landscape like spilled silver. It was so beautiful it elicited a content sigh from Deirdre.

"You enjoy the moonlight?" Kenan asked.

Deirdre pulled her gaze from it to look at him. "Very much so. Her pull is powerful."

A humming noise of interest came from him, and he cocked his head thoughtfully. "It is indeed." The way his voice dropped an octave deeper sent tingles dancing over her skin and made her wonder if he meant the moon or her. "As are the stars. See that one poking out there?" he asked.

An affirmative hum was her answer.

"That one is part of the handle of the Big Dipper."

As they walked, he went on about the constellations, pointing them out when the clouds allowed the occasional glimpse and making a game of each of them naming and finding them first. Laughter filled the night. She became so caught up in their conversation that she barely noticed when they left the garden far behind and more raindrops began to fall. Then she felt the thrumming energy of something massive and ancient. She knew instantly what it was. The sequoia. Though it slept like all the plants, such a great energy never truly went dormant, not even this closer to winter.

Raindrops began to patter onto her hair and dress in earnest. Their coolness drew a gasp from her.

Kinan grasped her hand and fixed her with a boyish grin. "Shall we run?"

Gathering up her long cloak in her free hand, she exclaimed, "Yes!"

They took off. As if sensing prey getting away, the rain came down even harder. Deirdre squealed and laughed. She tried to run faster, but her healed shoes sank into the softening ground and her damp shift clung to her legs. The material snagged at her and tripped her. Before she could tumble to the ground, Kinan scooped her up into his arms. He kept running without missing a stride. When they reached the cover of the gazebo, they were both laughing. Gaze locking onto hers, he set her down slowly. As he straightened, his hands trailed up her hips in a forward manner very unlike the Kinan she thought she knew.

And she loved it.

But as his hands reached her waist, he pulled away. He turned and reached into a cubby beneath the railing. Bright spots sparkled out of the corner of her eye, distracting her. Quiet, tinkling laughter echoed on the breeze like chimes, and a mischievous energy danced just out of reach. She turned her head quickly. The barest flash of a tiny wing, iridescent like that of a dragonfly, flitted away. But it was no insect. That had been a pixie. She would have bet her power on it. But pixies were attracted to magical workings. She and her friends hadn't had time to do enough here to warrant their attention. In fact, they hadn't done enough in New York to interest them much. Which meant something else was drawing them here. Turning in a circle to look for it, she found only Kinan holding a strange carving.

Gaze fixed on it, he tugged at his lower lip with his teeth. The wood had a reddish hue and emitted the same energy—though much reduced—as the sequoia. It was fashioned into the perfect likeness of a plump, little bird with holes in its back presumably made for fingers to cover.

"I carved it from a branch of the sequoia that fell during a windstorm. It felt like an offering from the tree, so I felt compelled to create something special from it," Kinan said.

Drawn to it, Deirdre reached out slowly in case he wanted to pull it away. He didn't. It buzzed slightly, not just with the tree's energy, but with something else as well, something not unlike magic. This night was shaping up to be more interesting by the moment.

"I am a *silbador*," Kinan said in a rush of words so fast she barely understood.

"*Silbador*?" she asked when her mind wrapped around the foreign word.

He explained. "It translates as 'whistler' and, well, it's just better if I show you."

Closing his eyes and taking a deep breath, he lifted the carved bird and placed the beak in his lips. The notes that came out sounded so close to birdsong that she felt the urge to look around and make sure one hadn't perched under the gazebo with them. But she didn't have to. The feeling of power drifting from

Kinan in the form of the musical notes was unmistakable. She could also see it as a warm, golden glow starting at his mouth and flowing out through the whistle. Something to his left just outside the gazebo caught her gaze. It floated four feet off the ground, moving through the misty air toward them. As it came closer, she realized it was a stone as big as her fist.

Levitation! She covered her mouth to stifle a gasp.

The stone floated in a circle around Kinan. Another joined in, then another, and another. They floated all around him, weaving and bobbing impossibly in the air.

Having grown up around people descended from the fae, having a friend who had occasional visions of the future, Deirdre had experienced many miraculous things. But never had she seen anything like this.

The tune he whistled picked up tempo. So did the movement of the floating stones. They swirled about him in a cone-like shape, working their way up around his head and spreading out into a spinning ring. The complete and perfect control he exhibited over them astounded her. One broke off from the ring and led the others in a line back out into the rain. Slowly, they settled to the ground outside the gazebo in a neat pile. The whistling stopped, drawing her gaze back to Kinan. Energy still glowed around his lips. It made them look as though they were covered in liquid gold.

No words would come to her. For the first time in her life, Deirdre was completely and utterly speechless with astonishment.

Kinan lowered the unique whistle. "If you don't want to pursue anything further with me because of this, I understand."

Laughter escaped her, catching even her completely by

surprise. Kinan dropped his head and took a step back. She grabbed his hands before he could get too far away. She could avoid it no longer. Her heart thudded so hard she feared he wouldn't be able to hear her over it. Fear tried to steal her voice away. She let out several shuddering breaths. In that moment, she realized just how badly she wanted Kinan to accept her, and how much it would crush her if he didn't.

The words spilled out in a rush. "No, no, you misunderstand. It strikes me as funny because I am of mixed blood as well."

His eyes narrowed and filled with confusion. She let go of his hands and stepped back, determined to give him the same courtesy he had offered her. The secrets she had to share with him were ones that could ruin her completely, cost her not only her social standing, but her land, her wealth, everything. To share them with him would be taking the ultimate leap of faith. Something deep down told her it was a leap she needed to make, one worth making.

The words didn't want to come, but she forced them. "My grandmother was a slave."

She gave him time to absorb the information. Ever so slowly, his gaze worked its way back up to her face. In his expression she saw fascination, excitement even. Surely not, it had to be a trick of the moonlight. She held very still as he touched her face, coiled one of her black locks around a finger.

"That's where you get this beautiful skin color, and ebony hair," he said.

"You aren't horrified?" she asked in a voice that quavered.

Her late husband had found out a year into their marriage, after he'd done some extensive digging into her father's history.

He had refused to touch her after that. Not that he had touched her much before. Thankfully, he'd been too concerned about anyone finding out to say or do anything. It gave him an excuse not to be intimate with her, and part of her believed that had made him happy. But the way he'd ostracized her family, refused to speak to them again, broke her heart.

It took her completely by surprise when Kinan smiled. "Not in the slightest. You aren't horrified by my news?"

"Not in the slightest. How could I possibly be, considering how scandalous my news is?" she asked.

Shoulders relaxing, Kinan took a step closer. "Only to fools who care about all the wrong things."

"Fools like my late husband. When he found out, he sold my ancestral home and refused to speak to any of my remaining relatives." After what he'd just shown her, she knew she shouldn't be afraid to say the last secret, but she was. She swallowed the fear and said it anyway. "Part of that is because I am fae."

His eyes widened and a look of wonder overcame him. "Like the Tuatha Dé Dannon?"

"We are descended from them, yes."

Brow furrowing, he shook his head. "Your husband was angry you weren't full fae. Does that mean he was fae as well?"

Such astuteness impressed her. Most would be too awestruck to process much more than her lineage. "Yes."

Slowly, as if giving her the chance to draw away, he reached out and caressed her arm. "Then he is a bastard who didn't deserve you."

She felt the urge to show him, as he'd shown her. Grinning, she grabbed his hand. "Come, let me show you my power."

A nod and bright-eyed smile was all the answer she needed. She dashed from the gazebo, tugging him after her. Rain fell in merciless curtains upon them. Giggling, she ran faster. In moments they reached the enormous trunk of the sequoia. Not even its far-reaching branches could block out much of the deluge. Not yet at least.

Concentrating, Deirdre dropped the walls around her ability and touched the energy of the tree. The strength of its power drew a gasp from her and made her entire body hum. She didn't even have to ask. From their connection it felt her shiver from the cold, it knew what she needed. The massive branches began to move. Though it was subtle, it was undeniably not the way a tree moved in a breeze. Several branches together over their heads. Both the tree's energy and that which she lent it made the needles multiply and thicken, creating a canopy the rain couldn't get through.

Head craned back, mouth gaping, Kinan watched. Once the canopy stopped forming, he gave her a wide-eyed look of astonishment. Giggling, she tugged him closer to the trunk of the tree. She reached out and touched it and motioned with her head for him to do the same. When he did, she opened the connection between her and the tree, and shared it with him through their joined hands. It was something she could only do with those who possessed magic to some degree. And even then, it didn't always work. Sometimes the tree or plant didn't want to connect with the person, and she didn't push it. But in this case, the energy of the tree surged through her and into Kinan.

A gasp followed by what sounded like it might be a curse in a language she didn't know came from him. But if it was a curse, it was a joyful one for he followed it with a laugh. And the smile he turned on her was nothing short of euphoric.

Twice his mouth opened and closed before he could get the words out, "From the first moment we met I knew there was something wonderous about you."

He lifted their joined hands to his lips and kissed her knuckles. "Well then, we have my condition out of the way. Shall we work on yours?"

Condition? It took her a moment to remember what he meant. *Oh yes, intimacy.*

Letting go of the tree, he drew her to him. His arms slid beneath her cloak and around her waist. To have only her thin cotton night shift between her skin and his was so scintillating it drew a moan from her parted lips. He drew her slowly against his chest, giving her time to stop him. Drinking in the look of desire in his eyes, she put her arms around his neck, weaving her fingers together behind it. The anticipation of what he would do, what he might be willing to do, made her pelvic muscles clench and roll in a dizzying way.

They shared a breath as his parted lips found hers. His tongue slid into her mouth. She pulled her own back, drawing his in farther. Her lips closed over the soft appendage and sucked. A moan vibrated from his mouth into hers and suddenly his hard body pressed up against her. Solid pectoral muscles rubbed against her unrestrained breasts, making her nipples hard. His groin drew away from her in what she could only imagine was a final attempt at gentlemanly manners. Through with such things, she pressed her hips against him, gasping at the feel of his hard erection against her stomach. It felt quite substantial. The desire to find out just how substantial made her pull her hips back and reach for him. Her fingers had barely brushed his erection when distant cries of alarm made them move away from one another.

A frustrated sound slid from Deirdre. Smiling with promise, Kinan drew her cloak closed, one hand brushing across her right breast slowly.

"We'd better get back and see what that's all about," Kinan said.

Reluctantly, she nodded. Hand in hand, they took off for the house at a brisk pace. The deluge of rain seemed to have spent itself. Now it barely drizzled on them. Moments later they stepped onto the deck. Before they let go of each other's hands, the front door flew open. A wide-eyed Sadie stood pulling her boots on. "Fire!" she yelled. The haunted look in her eyes told Deirdre she'd 'seen' it.

Deirdre grabbed her by the shoulders. "What do you mean? Where?"

"Our homes," Sadie said through a whimper.

A hand flew to her gaping mouth. She stumbled back, right into Kinan's arms. Before she could regain her composure and press Sadie for details, a horse came to a skidding stop in front of the porch. Dylan. A windblown, tangled mess of blond hair stuck up from his head in every direction. His wide, wild eyes grew wider as they beheld her and Kinan. Anger flashed in them, narrowed them.

"Fire! Get everyone you can. Come quick," he said.

"The widows' property?" Kinan asked.

"Yes," Dylan said.

Bumps rose all along Deirdre's skin. "Which one?" she asked.

It was Sadie who answered. "All of them."

22

Deirdre

Dirt clods flew as Dylan cantered off into the night, taking up the cry of, "Fire! Fire!"

Tears stung Deirdre's eyes. "No, no, no." She tried to tell herself to move, but shock rooted her to the deck.

Kinan took her hand, snapping her out of her daze. "Deirdre, can you and Sadie rouse Cat and the household and tell them?" he asked.

Slowly, she turned her head and focused on his face. He gripped her hand tighter. "Can you do that for me?" he pressed.

She nodded. He brushed a tear from her cheek, then cupped her face. "I'm going to go saddle the horses," he said,

At her nod, he took off like a bolt, leaping clear down the stairs, and hit the ground running. The sound of him sliding the barn door open launched her into action. She rubbed Sadie's arm and fixed her with a hard look.

"Did you see anything that might help us?" she asked.

"Silhouettes on horseback with torches, one at each of our homesites. Something spooked the one at the barn. They didn't get to light it on fire," she said, her voice distant as she lost herself in the vision again. "I should have seen it sooner."

"Hey, no. This is not your fault. Like you always say, the visions do not work that. I have to get some clothes on. Can you rouse the household and tell them?" she asked.

Swallowing hard, Sadie lifted her chin and nodded.

Deirdre plunged into the house and up the stairs. Not bothering to light a lamp, she threw on a tunic, breeches, and boots that she kept on hand for working on the property. On her way back out of the room, she grabbed a dry cloak and gloves. In the hallway, she encountered Sadie helping Cat put on a cloak.

"Cat, you should stay here, it's too dangerous," Sadie said as she fussed with the clasp.

Somehow, Deirdre found Cat's eyes amidst the wild nest of her red curls and held them in a steely gaze. "I have to agree with Sadie on this one, Cat. We don't know what we'll be running into," Deirdre said.

Cat drew aside her cloak, exposing the pistol belted at her waist. "I'm aware of that. And you know I have far more than this at my disposal."

As Deirdre turned and dashed back into her room for her own pistol, it struck her how profoundly Cat had changed. She was so strong now. Deirdre drew on that strength, allowing it to feed her. Buckling on the holster, she jogged back into the hallway and found her friends on their way down the stairs. Nothing was worth risking Cat's pregnancy, not even their homes. Deirdre really wished she would stay at the inn, but knew it was fruitless to press the issue.

"Dylan rode in like he was fleeing a horde of dullahan to tell us," Deirdre explained. It dawned on her that he hadn't been at the party, despite his assurances that he would come to make things up to her. What could have kept him away?

"Did he say any more?" Cat asked.

Brows pinched together as she thought, Deirdre shook her head. "Not really. Just that all our homes were on fire. Then he rode back out."

One hand went to her stomach when they reached the bottom of the stairs.

"Easy, don't want to overdo it in your condition. Slow breaths," Sadie reminded her.

She released her belly and started to wind her hair up into a bun as she walked. "Aye, I know, I'm just worried."

Sadie opened the door and they marched out into the dark toward the barn. Lamplight spilled from the open doorway, guiding them. She wanted to run, but she didn't dare leave Cat's side. It would be too easy for her to trip in the dark. Inside the barn, they found Ciaren and Balder saddled and standing in the aisle, tethered to a hitching post. Kinan stood in the aisle, hitching up the second draft horse of the team to a small wagon. Buckets of many sizes filled the back.

He looked up when they entered.

"Sadie, Cat, do you mind driving the wagon? We're going to need all the buckets we can get," he said.

Sadie grasped Cat's arm and marched her toward the wagon. "Of course," she said as she helped Cat aboard.

Ciaren neighed as Deirdre approached, the sound filled with nervous energy. Deirdre scratched the mare's forehead when Ciaren pushed it at her. A Spanish-style saddle perched on her back instead of Deirdre's English saddle. She was grateful for it, knowing how much more securely it held a rider. On a wave of agitated voices came Kinan's three staff members, Henry and Maria among them. The white-haired man carried a shotgun in one hand and a bag in the other. With a nod to Kinan, he climbed into the back of the wagon with the buckets.

The clang and bang of metal and wood made both Ciaren and Balder jump and snort. Cat's forehead began to glow a lovely golden hue that emanated from a knotwork symbol of the Tree of Life. The symbol was only visible when she used her power, and only to those sensitive to magic. It happened to all fae, but they used their power around others so infrequently that it surprised Deirdre. That energy flowed out from her and surrounded the horses. They calmed instantly. The slack jawed look of surprise on Kinan's face made Deirdre realize he could see Cat's power. He tore his gaze away and looked to her, a question in his eyes. She nodded in silent answer. Slowly his jaw closed.

Oblivious to their exchange, Henry said, "Don't worry, Kinan. The ladies here will keep me safe." He winked. Little did he know the truth of his words.

The bag he set down rattled with the metallic sound of bullets. Again, Deirdre had to fight the desire to ask Cat to stay behind. Instead, she contented herself with giving Sadie a pointed look. The poof of hair pinned atop Sadie's head bobbed once. She patted a pistol that rested in her lap. While her power lay in divination, she knew how to use a firearm if necessary. The men who had escorted them across America had made sure of it. And Deirdre had no doubt her friend would use it if she had to. She prayed she wouldn't have to. She looked long into the determined, fear-filled eyes of each of them. Both nodded to her, and she to them.

Words were unnecessary and Deirdre wouldn't waste time on any more of them. If she did, she feared her voice would crack and cause a fissure in her resolve. Facing danger on her own was one thing, but the thought of her friends facing it terrified her. At least the wagon traveled slower, which would give her and Kinan time to reach the fire first and make sure the arsonists were no longer there.

Breath held, she hurried back to her horse where Kinan waited to help her mount. Once she was settled, he doused the lamp hanging on the wall and plunged them into darkness. By the time her eyes adjust to the moonlight, Kinan had mounted and was leading them out. Maria and the other staff member called out their good wishes and warnings to be careful. Clouds passing before the moon made the ground hard to see. Kinan urged his horse into a canter, and she held her breath as she let Ciaren take off after him. Instead of relying on her sight, she reached out with her power, feeling each bush, grass, and tree along their path. It helped give her an idea of the layout of the ground so she could avoid holes.

Legs clenching tight to Ciaren's sides, she leaned into the wind and raced alongside Kinan. The cold wind soon drew moisture from her eyes, due to both their reckless speed, and her fearful heart. But she couldn't slow down. All those precious trees that had been cut down for their homes were burning. It was an affront to their sacrifice. Perhaps it wasn't only the wind drawing moisture from her eyes.

Orange soon lit up the horizon so brightly she could see great clouds of smoke wafting across the ominous color. The sweet, acrid scent of burning pine filled the air. They crested the hill they'd been riding up. Below them the valley—her valley—glowed from the orange-and-yellow light of the flames that were devouring her house. Ciaren tossed her head at the sight but stayed the course. Three figures moved in the light of the fire. From this distance she couldn't tell much, save that each time one got close to the fire a cloud of new smoke went up. It had to be Dylan and maybe Rick and a freeman throwing water on the flames. Fire engulfed the walls, crawling steadily higher toward the roof.

The sight was a blow to Deirdre's heart. "No!" she cried out.

The slightest squeeze of her legs plunged Ciaren down the hill with all the power and speed of a horse bred and born to run. Instead of riding her straight to the house, Deirdre took her to the creek where they had built a corral for the horses. It would be a good hike up the hill to the house, but at least here Ciaren would be safe from the blaze. Right now she needed fewer things to worry about. Even this far down the hill where the house wasn't visible, she saw flames licking up toward the sky. She jumped down and tethered Ciaren to the fence in case anyone left the gate open. This night would be bad enough without losing her horse on top of everything else.

Leaving Kinan to secure his own horse, she ran for the house. Halfway up the hill he caught up to her and passed her. They exchanged a brief look, one that gave her the strength to push her tired legs faster.

The sight she beheld as she crested the hill stopped her in her tracks. Fire had devoured the front door and half the wall to its right, leaving nothing but a gaping hole through which black smoke billowed. Snaps and crackles punctuated the roar that was the very life's breath of the fire. The living mass moved over her house like a predator determined to devour it. Fury launched her into a run around the left side where the wellhead was. There she found Cofield working the handle of the pump and Dylan holding a bucket beneath the flow of water. Her mind couldn't wrap around Cofield helping when he didn't have to, but she accepted it.

Knowing she couldn't handle the buckets as fast or full as the men, she ran to the pump. "I'll take over, you can carry water," she said over the roar of the fire.

To her surprise, he nodded, grabbed a bucket, and took Dylan's place beneath the spigot. She grabbed the handle and started pumping as fast as she could, using all her weight to push it down. Though only a few pumps filled the bucket, it felt like an agonizingly long time. He took off running toward the fire. Outlined by the orange glow that made the hillside bright as day, Rick rushed back toward her, bucket in hand. Deirdre started pumping again before he even reached her. He nodded and scanned the night as he held his bucket beneath the silver stream.

"She and Sadie are coming with the wagon and more buckets. Henry is with them," she said, knowing what he was looking for.

He nodded again and ran back to the fire. Kinan took his place.

How long they worked like that, she couldn't say. She knew only the flames crackling across her home not more than twenty feet away, the waves of heat that made sweat drip into her eyes, the burn of muscles from pumping, and the men she cared about rushing to the blaze. Dark, feminine hands came to rest atop hers. Wonderful cold seeped from those hands into her. A sigh of relief eased from her as Sadie pulled her aside and took over. That one sigh was all she allowed herself.

As she drew her next breath, she straightened. The clang of

several buckets landing at her feet had her reaching for one automatically. She grabbed hold of the same one Cat did. Looking up into her friend's eyes, she found the strength she needed to keep going. If only one of them had a connection with weather and could call down rain. But that was a rare gift among the fae. Once Sadie filled her bucket, Deirdre carried it toward the fire as fast as her legs would go. Kinan stopped her halfway there. He reached for her bucket, grabbed it in one hand, and passed his empty to her with the other.

"Let's start a brigade. It will go faster that way," he said.

She nodded and moved close enough to hand off the empty bucket to Cat and grab another full one. When she turned back with the next bucket, Dylan stood a few paces down from Kinan. Rick stood a few paces down from Dylan, and Cofield another few down from him. They passed the bucket from one to the other, pouring an endless stream of water onto the fire once they got a good rhythm going. She, Cat, and Sadie fed the men buckets as fast as they could. Thankfully, the building site she'd chosen for her home was far enough away from any trees that they were safe from the flames. For now.

Henry stood in the shadows nearby, firelight glinting off the barrel of his rifle now and then. He looked everywhere but at the fire. After a while, Deirdre realized he was watching over them in case anyone lurked in the shadows who shouldn't be there. It made her wonder who had started the fire. *Fires*, she had to remind herself. The other homesites were burning as well. Dread danced a jig along her neck and sorrow tried to grip her heart.

"What about your homes?" Deirdre yelled to Cat and Sadie.

"Rick's cattlehands are working on getting them out," Cat said.

The thought of their homes burning while they labored to save hers made Deirdre quite literally sick to her stomach.

"Let's worry about the here and now, because that is all we have power over," Sadie said.

She couldn't argue with that.

Working together with her friends, she found a rhythm that helped quiet her mind. Though water sloshed all over her, the proximity of the fire kept the cold at bay. Slowly, ever so slowly, they began to get the upper hand. The flames stopped advancing toward the roof. The light faded as the fire started to die. Despair gripped Deirdre as she realized the lack of flames was due in part to the walls having been all but consumed. Only the beams and roof remained. The men continued to douse the blackened framework, cooling what embers they could find. Their efforts slowed to a pace born of exhaustion. The need to rush had passed. They had done all they could.

The logs that Rick, Dylan, and the freemen had worked so hard to saw in half for her wall planks were all but gone. Taking the last bucket from her, Kinan's hand lingered on hers. The hot touch brought tears to her eyes, both over how hard he and the others had fought to save her home, and over the fact that they had all but failed. Covered in soot and smelling of sweat and wood, Kinan had never looked finer to her. He had fought to save her home, risked his life.… She wanted to fall into his arms and weep until no more tears would come. The sympathy and regret in his eyes only strengthened the desire. Swallowing hard, she took a step toward him.

A horrible crack rent the quiet that had fallen, followed by a crash and a cry of pain. Flames erupted anew from the half-burned porch. Whoever had cried out was nowhere in sight.

"Dylan!" Rick yelled. Bucket in hand, he ran for the porch.

Kinan tore away at an all-out run. Both he and Rick threw their buckets of water on the flames, but it wasn't enough.

Deirdre grabbed a bucket and ran after them. "No, no, no," she cried.

The small flare of flames had already begun to recede when she arrived, but she threw the water anyway. Kinan reached the smoking hole in the porch and jumped right in. A wordless scream of protest ripped from Deirdre. She lunged toward the charred steps. Strong, feminine hands grabbed her from both sides. Everything in her wanted to fight, kick, and claw her way free. But she didn't dare because two of those hands belonged to Cat. She couldn't risk hurting her friend's baby—not even to get to Kinan and Dylan. Falling to her knees, she screamed their names until she lost her voice, which wasn't long considering how hoarse she was from the smoke.

Moments that felt like an eternity later, Kinan stood up in the hole, Dylan slung over his shoulders. Most of Dylan's clothes were burned away, exposing red, blistering skin on his arms and side. His blond hair was singed in places and the left side of his face was bright red. He hung limp, eyes closed.

A small tug and Cat and Sadie let her go. "Dylan," she said as she rushed toward them.

Rick reached them first and helped carry Dylan down. They took him over near the well pump and lay him on the damp grass. Deirdre touched Kinan's soot-covered arm as she stood. He covered her hand with his.

"I'm fine, and he's breathing," he said softly.

She looked at him for a long moment before kneeling at Dylan's side. Rick leaned over him, putting an ear against his chest. For a long, torturous moment, he said nothing. During that time, Sadie knelt down next to Deirdre, a knife in her hand.

"His heart is beating," Rick finally said.

The stench of burned flesh wafted off Dylan's red skin. Thankfully, the only bad blisters were on the left side of his neck and his left arm.

Tears spilled down Deirdre's cheeks. "What do we do?" she asked. *If only Ashlinn was here.* Her healing magic could have fixed him right up. Deirdre wanted to comfort him, touch him, but she was afraid she'd hurt him. It hurt *her* to look at him. This was her fault. He'd been trying to save her home.

Sadie leaned down, reaching with the knife. Deirdre grabbed her arm.

"We have to cut his clothes off before he wakes up," she said.

"Why?"

With a gentle tug, Sadie freed her arm from Deirdre's grasp and cut open the front of Dylan's tunic. "In case the cloth has burned into his skin and peels off the skin when we remove his clothes," she explained.

"Oh Danu," Deirdre murmured, wishing she hadn't asked. Her mind began to go over all the plants she knew that would help burns. Aloe. They needed aloe vera. *Does any grow nearby? Would it still be alive this late in the year in this climate?*

Cat suddenly rose. Footsteps retreated rapidly before a retching sound reached them. A pang of sympathy for Cat pinched at Deirdre, but she couldn't leave Dylan. Cat would be all right. It would probably be best for her to be away for this part. Deirdre didn't much want to be here for it herself, but she had to. Together she and Sadie lifted Dylan's shirt away.

Thankfully, it only stuck in a few places, and those were not terribly bad. Bile tried to work its way up Deirdre's throat when part of his sleeve pulled away several layers of skin. Her throat had closed enough that she didn't think she'd be able to throw up anyway. She swallowed hard, forcing the bile down. It wouldn't be fair to Dylan if she had to run off to retch.

Someone set a bucket of water down beside them—Henry, judging by the wrinkled, age-spotted hands. "Thank you, Henry," Rick said.

A ripping sound preceded Sadie handing Deirdre a piece of cloth. Her friend dipped another bit of cloth into the bucket, wrung it out over the ground, and started to gently wipe the soot from Dylan's chest.

"Easy. Don't rub at the parts that look burned, just squeeze water on them like this," Sadie said.

Deirdre followed the instructions, being as gentle as she could. Once they had cleaned away as much soot as possible, most of Dylan's skin didn't look too bad aside from being so red the color could be seen even in the moonlight. Large blisters already turning white with pus rose here and there on his left side, but they were few and far between. A groan slid from his parted lips when Sadie dripped water onto one of the worst blisters. His eyes fluttered open.

"Bloody hell, that hurts," he said in a dazed voice.

Rick let out a whoop and leaned in. "He speaks! Ha, looks like you'll live, lad."

The weak smile Dylan managed was only slightly encouraging. "O' course," he said, as if surprised it was ever in question. But his eyes revealed the truth of his pain. His head rolled in Deirdre's direction. "Sorry..." He swallowed several times as if speaking were hard. "About your porch."

Deirdre accepted a canteen from someone who passed it her way. Together she and Sadie helped him sit up and she held the canteen to his lips. "You daft fool, my porch doesn't matter," she chastised.

He took several deep drinks before she pulled the canteen away. "Easy now, not too fast."

As Sadie eased him back onto the ground, a powerful shiver traveled through him that ended with him wincing in pain. Sadie looked up at Rick and Kinan. "We need to get him back to the inn. We have to keep him warm and get these burns cleaned better," she said.

A grunting noise of dissent came from Rick. "'Tis too far. Me home is closer," he said.

Sadie took Deirdre's hand and pulled her back as the men moved in to pick Dylan up. He started to protest but a scream cut off his words. The sound died as his head lolled back.

Deirdre rushed back in. "Stop! You're hurting him," she cried as she grabbed Rick's arm. But it was like grabbing an iron rod. She couldn't stop him.

Rick got under Dylan's arms and lifted him the rest of the way while Kinan lifted his legs. "'Tis all right, lass, he's passed out now," Rick said.

Sniffling, she allowed Sadie to pull her out of the way. They carried him to the wagon where Cat and Henry were preparing a nest of blankets in the back. Canteen clutched to her chest, she followed them, feeling horribly useless. Gently as they could, they laid him down on the blankets. As soon as the two men jumped out of the wagon, Sadie crawled in. Rick left, heading in Cat's direction, while Kinan stepped to Deirdre's side. He took her face in his hands, wiping tears away she hadn't realized had escaped.

"This is not your fault," he insisted.

His earnest brown eyes failed to convince her. Fighting the instinct to collapse into his arms and weep, she shook her head instead. If Dylan didn't fancy her, if she hadn't encouraged his attention, maybe he wouldn't have gone back up on that porch.

"But 'tis," she whispered.

"No. We are responsible for the choices we make. Don't blame yourself, please," he said.

For one restful moment, she allowed herself to lay the weight of her head in his hands. Moans sounded from the wagon behind her. She pulled away and turned to climb in. One last look at her burned out cabin nearly undid her control. Someone had done this. Ainsworth, she was sure of it.

Inside, she sat down opposite Sadie so she could be close to Dylan. When he looked her way, she lifted the canteen to his lips. The men had propped him up just enough that Sadie thankfully didn't have to move him so he could drink. Gaze glued to her, he drank slow and long. She gave him the best smile she could muster. A gasp came from him as the wagon jostled when Cat and Henry climbed in the driver's seat. Dylan grabbed hold of her hand and closed his eyes as the wagon started to move.

Trying to breathe through her mouth to avoid the smell of burned flesh, Deirdre looked back toward Kinan. The idea of him staying behind sent prickles of dread shooting all through her. What if whoever had done this was still here? She mouthed the words "be careful" to him. He nodded. In only a few turns of the wheels, the shadows hid his expression. Her gaze remained fixed on his silhouette, outlined by the gray smoke that continued to rise from the charred remnants of her house.

23

Dylan

Late October

A soft knock on the door roused Dylan from a restless sleep. Restless, but blessedly free of the pain that seared through his left arm and side the moment he moved. He wanted to yell at whoever it was to go away, but he didn't. It was likely Victoria come to dote on him again and she didn't deserve his ill temper. Or it could be Deirdre if he were lucky. Her attention and ministrations were all that made him want to wake up. The woman had a way with herbal poultices that was nothing short of magical.

"Dylan dear, you have a visitor," came Victoria's voice.

"Who is it?"

"It be Mr. O'Leary," she said.

"Shite," he mumbled. *Must that bastard bother me? Isn't my physical pain enough for the man?* His presence dredged up all kinds of horrible feelings regarding Thomas's death. Not to mention the fact that O'Leary had clearly won Deirdre's affections. Not that Dylan didn't have every intention of winning them away. "Give me a moment," he called out.

"'Course, dear."

Gritting his teeth against the pain he knew would come, he reached for the nightstand and pulled the drawer open. The brush of the cotton sheets felt like someone held a torch to his skin. He had to stretch to reach inside the drawer, which pulled the worst of the burns on his left side. Gasps and quiet curses passed his lips, but he managed to pull out the two sheets of paper he had in the drawer. He folded them carefully, wincing as burnt bits of the edges flaked away. The writing on the parchment didn't suffer any more than it already had, that was all that mattered. He carefully tucked them beneath his pillow, turning enough to make sure they were completely hidden.

Liquid warmth spread beneath the bandage around his left forearm as he propped himself up into a sitting position. With it came a searing pain that took his breath away. But it was worth it. He didn't know if Kinan would dig into his nightstand, but he wouldn't put it past the man, and he couldn't take that chance.

Another knock sounded on the door, this one hard and impatient.

"Come in," Dylan called in a clipped tone.

The door opened and in strode Kinan. He closed it behind him. In his pristine breeches, pressed blue linen shirt, and black vest, he looked the perfect high-society gentleman. Anger drew deep lines between his dark brows, and his suspicion-filled eyes were as hard as flecks of brown jasper. Dylan sat up straighter. The movement hurt, a lot, but he didn't let it show. In fact, he grinned.

"Me being the hero has your knickers in a bloody big knot, don't it now?" he asked.

Gaze narrowing further, Kinan sneered at him. "You fancy yourself a hero because you fell through a half-burned porch your daft arse shouldn't have been on in the first place?"

Dylan's grin widened to expose more teeth. "'Tis always amusing to hear you use Irish slang, knowing your mum is Mexican." He covered his mouth, eyes widening. "Oh, me apologies. Did I say that out loud?"

The smug look that settled on Kinan's face was the last reaction he expected. "Say what you want. I have no secrets from Deirdre, unlike you. Tell me, does she know you ran my best friend's sister out of town after disgracing her, then dragged him off to fight a war that wasn't his own?"

Dylan tried to rise from the bed, but the pain it caused made him so nauseous that he collapsed back into the pillows. "You're just sore that she chose my poke instead of yours," he snarled.

Taking a step closer, Kinan's hands curled into fists. "You bastard, if you're pursuing Deirdre just to try and rile me, stop now. She deserves better than that. She isn't a conquest, she's a woman with feelings."

"Me reasons are none of your concern."

Another step and Kinan's hands gripped the footboard of the bed. "They are if you hurt her. If you do, that fire of yours will seem like a mercy compared to my wrath."

Dylan gripped the blankets. A thousand needles of pain shot deep into the muscles of his arm from the movement. He turned it to anger and poured all that pain into his words. "*My* fire? Out with it, O'Leary, what are you accusing me of?"

"Did you set those fires, Dylan?" he asked in a steady, quiet tone that sent a chill through Dylan. It was the tone of a man who had killed and would do so again if he felt justified. Dylan wouldn't give him that justification.

"O' course not. Where would you get a daft idea like that?" Dylan demanded.

He suspected he knew exactly where the idea had come from, but he wouldn't help the man by volunteering information.

"Cat's house was saved because you woke the freemen here at Rick's ranch and told them it was on fire. But if you had been coming from your home and saw the fires, Deirdre's house would have been the first you saw, and my inn would have been miles closer. If you were protecting Deirdre's property, like you should have been, it wouldn't have burned at all. What were you doing all the way over by Cat's property if not setting the fires?" Kinan asked.

Dread held his tongue as much as a need to formulate his story. He'd known someone might eventually ask this very question, but he'd been too tired and in too much pain to think about it until now. "Not that 'tis any of your business what I do, but one of Rick's milk cows got out and I was taking her back to the barn."

"You expect me to believe you abandoned your post to save a cow? You sure you weren't coming from Ainsworth's place? 'Tisn't far from there," Kinan said.

Dylan bristled, not out of anger, but because of how spot-on Kinan's instincts were. He managed to turn it to anger that he knew would show in his expression. "And why do you think I'd be coming from that blaggard's property?"

"Because you're working for him," Kinan snapped right back.

Fury gave Dylan the strength to lean forward. While Kinan was right about that, he couldn't be more wrong about the reason. He had no right to know. "I have reason to hate him more than anyone in this bloody town."

Waving a dismissive hand, Kinan turned to the door.

"And I would never do anything to harm Deirdre. Never," Dylan called after him.

"Right, you and Thomas's mom just rent this house from him, counting on his goodwill to keep a roof over your heads," Kinan said, voice thick with sarcasm.

A feral sound tore from Dylan's dry throat. "You're lucky I can't get out of this bed, you blaggard!"

Hand on the door, Kinan turned back with a smile. "About that you're right, because while you're lying here, I'll be out proving to Deirdre that I'm the better man for her."

Dylan let out a humorless laugh. "Keep telling yourself that, while her hands are rubbing ointment into my bare skin."

The scoffing look of amusement Kinan gave him sent another chill through him. Could the man actually have enticed Deirdre to let him touch her? The look said as much. Dylan grabbed an extra pillow from the bed and pitched it at Kinan. The feather-stuffed missile only hit the door as it closed behind him. The colorful expletives that passed Dylan's lips helped him push back the excruciating pain his movement had caused, if only for a few moments. The sight of blood seeping through his bandages made him relax back into the pillows after a while. Parchment crinkled near his ear. The blaggard was right. He would get his time with Deirdre, but not because Dylan was too hurt to get back out to the home sites. Because the locked floor safe he had pulled those sheets of paper from held the entire journal, and he had to get it back.

24

Deirdre

A soft knock sounded on the door as Deirdre packed the last of her underthings into her suitcase. She sighed and brushed an errant curl from her eyes. *Could Dylan be asking for me again already?* The very thought made her weary. She'd hardly slept since the accident because whenever she left, he woke and called for her. Bad as she felt for him, the constant need for her attention was wearing on her. The bone-deep exhaustion made her forget for a moment that he couldn't possibly be asking for her, considering she was back at the inn.

"Deirdre?" Kinan's voice drifted through the solid oak. The very sound of it comforted her.

He didn't ask anything of her, just offered continuous support. It was wrong to compare the two that way right now, she knew. But she couldn't help it. Exhaustion and heartbreak over the loss of all the trees that had gone into building her home were also wearing her down. She hadn't had time to process it all, to take care of herself.

"Selfish, selfish, Deirdre. Stop being so selfish," she mumbled.

She closed her suitcase, smoothed her hair as best she

could, and fixed what she hoped was a strong look onto her face. "Come in," she said, forcing some of that strength into her voice.

The door opened. After a long look at her, Kinan's gaze moved to her suitcase. His shoulders sagged. "You're leaving," he all but whispered.

She shook her head, realized he couldn't see it because he was looking down, and said, "No, not for long, at least. I'm only getting a few things for my short stay at Victoria's and Dylan's residence."

Kinan didn't look up. "To take care of Dylan." Though he tried to hide it, she heard the jealousy in his tone, and worse, the defeat.

Recalling that night on the porch, thinking of how it might have ended, it pained her to hear him sound this way. More so that it was because of Dylan. While she was attracted to Dylan, it certainly wasn't the same as what she felt for Kinan. Kinan respected her, encouraged her, and even inspired her. The connection to him made her feel as though she had known him her entire life, as though they were old friends reuniting. That it had taken her this long to figure that out tormented her no end. Particularly now, when she couldn't turn her back on Dylan. The man needed her and she owed it to him to be there.

"Yes, he needs me," she said.

Without making a sound, Kinan crossed the floor and took her hands in his. "Just promise me one thing," he said. The urgency in his tone made her look up. The soft brown hue of his eyes was like the color of earth, the color of home. More than anything, she wanted to stay there, trapped in his gaze.

"What is it?" she asked, ready to promise him nearly anything.

"That in the end, you'll choose what *you* need."

She moved closer, about to melt against him, when a ruckus from outside stopped her. Voices raised in alarm carried up to her second-story window—that of Henry, and... *No, it couldn't be.* Letting go of her, Kinan spun and dashed from the room. She caught the barest glimpse of fury contorting his face. She ran to the window, needing to be sure. A man in a fine blue suit stood on the turnabout of the inn's drive arguing with Henry, who kept him at bay with a walking stick. The man looked ready to shove Henry to the side. Sunlight shone on the black hat of polished leather that sat atop the man's head. Though its brim hid his face, Deirdre knew who it was from his arrogant stance and sinewy build.

Cursing beneath her breath, she marched over to her armoire and grabbed her bow and quiver of arrows. The angry voices grew louder as she dashed from the room. Kinan's joined them. Fury fueling her steps and clouding her judgment, she stormed down the stairs and dashed across the foyer. By the time she stepped out onto the porch, she had an arrow nocked and the bowstring drawn back. Clearing her mind, she connected to the lingering energy of the tree from which the arrow had been made.

Kinan stepped close to Ainsworth, a finger thrusting into his chest. Ainsworth struck Kinan's hand away.

"I'm not leaving until I speak with her," Ainsworth said in a voice that radiated danger.

Fingers curling into a fist, Kinan slid one foot back into a fighting stance. As he moved, Deirdre let her arrow fly. It sank deep into the ground right between the two men, feathered shaft vibrating from the impact. Both men stepped back from it and turned to her. She stared at Ainsworth down the length of another arrow. His hands flew up.

"Whoa now, little lady, I've only come to offer my condolences on the fire, and to make sure you're all right," he said.

Keeping the arrow trained on him, she said, "I'm hale and hearty, as you can well see. Now, I believe Kinan told you to get off his land."

Hands lowering slowly, Ainsworth nodded. "And I will. But first, I want you to know you still have somewhere to go. You still have options."

"You're right about that, Ainsworth, I have many options. Not even my home burning to the ground will make me consider you one of them," she snapped.

Her finger itched to let go of the bowstring. With the arrow pointed at his chest, that would be a terrible idea. The man wasn't wearing a pistol. Hell, he wasn't wearing so much as a hunting knife, which meant he'd come here expecting hostility and intent on not giving them any cause to shoot him. At the moment, though, Deirdre needed cause *not* to shoot.

"The West is a rough place for a woman alone, Mrs. Quinn. All the more reason for you to seriously consider my proposal," he said.

Angling the bow just so, she let the arrow fly. It sank into the ground right between his legs, fletching barely flicking his inner thigh. A little high-pitched noise tore from him as he leaped back. His surprise melted away, turning into a calculating smile. "I don't mind a feisty woman, not at all. You think about it, for your well-being."

From the corner of her eye she saw Kinan grin and cross his arms. "I think you better worry about your own well-being,

Ainsworth," he said.

Deirdre nodded and nocked another arrow, this time pointing it a touch higher. The smug look on Ainsworth's face slid a little. He walked backward, tipping his hat to her. His heel collided with the raised circle in the center of the drive. With a jolt, he turned and strode back to the gate where his horse was tied. He climbed over the gate and onto his horse. Heavy gaze fixing on her again, he tipped his hat. A hard kick of his large spurs launched his horse into a reluctant canter.

Laughter erupted from both Kinan and Henry. The old Irishman guffawed until tears ran down his cheeks and Kinan held him up by the arm. Back rigid, Deirdre fetched her arrows. She wanted to join in their laughter, but she couldn't bring herself to. The last arrow she'd shot so deep into the ground, she couldn't pull it free. Kinan's hand closed around hers and helped. Looking up at him, she realized Henry's hiccupping laughter was receding as he walked back to the barn. The look of pride on Kinan's face made her forget all about the elderly man.

"You amaze me every day, Deirdre," he said.

He took the arrow from her, leaned in close, and slid it into the quiver on her shoulder. As he lowered his arm, he brushed his fingers slowly across her cheek. She leaned into the touch, not caring if anyone was looking.

"Did he mean a proposal of the business kind, or personal kind?"

A growling noise came from her throat that surprised her. "Everything is business with that bastard. I think he burned our homes down so I would feel like I had no other choice."

"Than to marry him?" Kinan's question held a deadly calm to it.

"Yes. The night of the party he proposed to marry me in exchange for giving up his pursuit of Cat's and Sadie's lands."

"That son of a bitch. I will hang him from the uprights of the entrance to his own ranch," Kinan growled.

Imagining vines or roots wrapping around Ainsworth's scrawny neck, Deirdre lay a hand on his arm. "No need. I'll come up with a way to make him hang himself, never fear." She could do it, too. Convincing the plants would be easy.

Brows lifting, Kinan laughed again.

"What?" Deirdre asked, remembering that he now knew her secret, and with it, her capabilities.

Fearing condemnation, she looked into his eyes and was surprised to find a spark of desire. He put an arm through hers and started to lead her back to the inn. Leaning close enough she could feel his breath on her neck, he said, "There you go, amazing me again."

25

Deirdre

Early November

A week after the fire, Deirdre finally broke down and rode out to her property. Dylan had improved more each day, his strength clearly returning faster than he let on. But Deirdre saw through his attempts to keep her close. The first two days they'd kept him at Rick's place and she and Sadie had changed cold compresses on the worst of his burns every few hours. The third day they'd taken him by wagon to his house. She'd been surprised to find that he shared it with an older woman, the mother of a close friend who had died in the war, he said. Deirdre found it sweet that he helped take care of her. By the fourth day, the woman— Victoria—was helping her wrap the worse of his burns with ointment-soaked bandages. Kinan had aloe vera that he grew around his inn, and he had been kind enough to bring some to them. It was speeding the healing process along nicely. Now, he was up and about and helping Victoria with small chores around the house.

Though Dylan had remained kind and gracious to the ladies throughout it, he only wanted Deirdre. All that time to think about what she should be doing at the home site drove her half mad. On the fifth day, she'd had enough.

The warm afternoon air made her open her cloak after less than a mile. It was as though the fires had warmed all of California, despite it being November now. She passed a group of aspen trees that she had come to think of as the marker between her land and Sadie's. Their energy swelled and reached out in greeting. After sending them positive feelings, her gaze cast out beyond them. Even though she knew she couldn't see Sadie's home because of the hill, she couldn't help but look. From what Rick said, Sadie's home had sadly fared about the same as hers, though it retained more of its walls. Rick's freeman friends had fought that fire and the one that threatened the small cabin on Cat's property.

It pained Deirdre deeply to think of Sadie losing another home. When her husband died in the war, the state had repossessed her home. Being not only a woman, but of African descent on top of that, meant she couldn't own property. Deirdre hated the situation with a ferocity that had gotten her thrown out of more than one state office as she tried to fight the decision. Things were supposed to be different here. Sadie was supposed to have a home, a fresh start where she might be happy again. They all were.

The scent of charred wood reached her before she crested the hill. She blinked back tears and dug deep for her strength. The silhouette of a man standing at one of the support logs of her home halted her tears. Waves of fury and fear made her fingers fumble as she lifted her skirts and drew the pistol holstered to her thigh. Her hands shook so bad she couldn't pull the hammer back. Grass, suddenly several inches taller and bright green, tickled her ankles beneath her skirt. Sage brush reached out toward her.

When she was finally able to see through her rage, she was glad she had been unable to cock the pistol. Kinan stood there in only a pair of breeches, scraping the charred bits of wood carefully away from the support log. He looked amazing, like an ancient god from one of his tapestries. And that was due only in part to the fact he was working on what remained of her house. He saw her and froze.

Slow, so as not to drop it, she lowered the pistol. "I'm sorry. You surprised me. I didn't know anyone would be here," she said.

Though it meant lifting her skirts, she holstered the pistol. For one, she didn't want to drop the blasted thing and have it go off. For two, she'd been ready to show Kinan all that lay beneath her skirts a week ago. Seeing him bare-chested, sweating, and laboring over what remained of her home, she realized she was still willing, very willing. But right now was not the time to indulge in her desires.

"I have good news," Kinan said.

His gaze fixed on her legs as she holstered her pistol, longing shining in his eyes. The joy she felt over his attention faded when her gaze moved back to the skeletal remains of her house.

"Good news?" she asked in a doubtful tone.

She walked up to what remained of her porch. It wasn't much, especially considering the pile of burned wood someone—presumably Kinan—had cleared away. Now that she truly looked, she realized a large amount of cleanup had occurred while she'd been taking care of Dylan.

To her utter surprise, the more she looked at the skeletal wooden frame, the more she realized energy remained in the wood.

"The support logs are viable and intact. The fire only scorched them," he said, confirming what she saw and felt.

While this was good news, Deirdre couldn't bring herself to be happy. The skeleton of a house would not satisfy the government as a dwelling. Ainsworth would make sure of it. And she couldn't very well encourage that energy to send out roots and branches to form walls and a roof. Even in this day and age, such a thing would likely see her hanged, with Ainsworth kicking the stool out from beneath her himself.

"You don't look happy. What's wrong?"

Her gaze moved to the snow-covered hills, a sight that depressed her as much as her shell of a house. "Cofield says the snow means our wagon won't make it over the hills with any more timber. He said it could be as long as April before we can get more. We're going to lose our lands. All those trees were sacrificed for nothing." The words made her want to break down and weep, yet she didn't—she wouldn't.

But her body had other ideas. Her legs gave out and she sank to her knees. Screaming in frustration, she slapped her palms against the sooty earth. Pain from the impact reverberated up her arms. The heat of the fire must have baked the ground. The smooth, hard surface felt like ceramic, or adobe. Kinan knelt beside her, a hand on her back. He murmured comforting, encouraging words, but she didn't hear. Her fingers splayed across the ground, feeling the contours hardened by the fire. An idea began to form. She sat up straight and blinked her misty eyes.

"It has grown unseasonably warm," she said.

"Not really. Actually, this is typical for this area. This valley stays much warmer than the hills above it," Kinan said.

"How long does it usually stay this warm?"

Shaking his head, Kinan resumed rubbing her back. "All winter. But Deirdre, the hills are much colder. Cofield is right about the snow up there, I'm sorry."

Gaze fixed on the hillside directly behind her home site, Deirdre rose to her feet. "Is your grandfather still visiting?"

He moved between her and the hill. The planes of his defined chest brought her back to herself. "Yes," he said, drawing the word out and making it into a question.

Grinning, she took hold of his hands. "Do you think he can show me how to make adobe?"

Kinan's eyes widened and a smile crept slowly across his face. Whooping like a savage, he lifted her by the waist and spun her in a circle. Laughter tumbled from her lips. He soon set her back on her feet, took her face in his hands, and pressed a kiss to her lips.

All too quickly, he drew back. "Yes, I think he can, you brilliant woman!"

They both burst out laughing as he picked her up and spun her around again. When he set her down this time, he took hold of her hand. "Let's go get him right now!"

Hand in hand, they dashed down the hill.

26

Deirdre

Mid-November

As Deirdre had hoped, the hill behind her home site turned out to be excellent soil for making adobe. The main support structure helped, but they still needed more framework. Under the cover of night, she coaxed the remaining energy in the wood, encouraging it to send out branches that would serve as trusses. It didn't resurrect the tree so much as utilize the energy that was still there. Morbid as it sounded, Ashlinn had once equated it to how human hair still grew after death. Also utilizing the dark nights, Kinan whistled in large boulders and stones from the river that would have otherwise taken draft horses and several men days to move.

With Felipe's guidance, work marched on at a good pace during the dry days—which were blessedly plentiful. They used Kinan's boulders, stones, bricks they made themselves, and mud that hardened quickly into clay. The fireplace was the first thing they built. It was up in a day with Kinan whistling the stones into place while Felipe and Rick laid the grout. They kept a roaring fire going in it at all times to help warm the house so it cured faster.

Rick's spy kept tabs on Ainsworth, who had left to move his cows out of the hills for the season. The arrogant bastard assumed they were doomed, since he had burned down their homes and the hills were impassable to wagons. In two weeks, the roof and outer walls were rebuilt.

Trowel in hand, Deirdre surveyed the first of the inner walls to go up—a dividing wall containing an arched opening that lay between the foyer and the main hall. The design of the home was unlike anything she'd ever seen, but she loved it. It would end up being an open floor plan with minimal interior walls once they finished. Big as the house was, the interior would take months more. But that was fine by her. Already it would satisfy the government as a proper dwelling. Next week, they would start on Sadie's home, and if the beautiful weather held, they'd have the roof and outer walls finished before the end of December.

The sound of Cat and Sadie talking drifted to her moments before they entered the room.

"There you are. Are you still working? Honestly, Deirdre, you need to take a break," Cat chastised.

One hand rubbing the very slight bump of her belly, Cat walked over and sat in the chair by Deirdre as if taking her own advice. Deirdre set down the trowel on the archway.

"Looks to me like you're the one who needs a rest," she teased. She looked to Sadie. "You're not letting her overdo it now, are you?"

Sadie shot a glare at Cat. "Like I have much of a choice. The woman's getting near as impossible as you," she said with a touch of pride in her voice.

Drawing a deep breath, Cat leaned against the wall. "You and Rick don't let me do much more than spread mud, and very little of that. I'm fine, truly. 'Tis you I'm worried about, Deirdre." She gave her a hard look. "Are you sure you want to stay the night here?"

She thought she saw a twinkle of mischief in her friend's eyes, but Cat was so good at hiding her emotions, it was hard to tell. With a lift of her chin, Deirdre indicated the large wooden table on which her bow and quiver sat. The table and four chairs were the only pieces of furniture in the entire house so far, other than the bed in the guest room. Those only existed because Kinan had insisted on bringing her some of the basic comforts this morning when she said she wouldn't be leaving.

"I have my bow. We'll be watching for Ainsworth's men, and if they show up, I won't hesitate to shoot them."

Worrying her fingers around a loose curl, Sadie said, "I don't like it."

Deirdre patted her shoulder with a muddy hand. "I know. But I'm not willing to leave my home unguarded any more than you are."

Big brown eyes narrowed at her. Sadie almost smiled as she brushed flecks of dried mud from her shoulders. "Yes, but Cat and I will have a half score of Rick's workers guarding our homes with us. You'll have only Kinan, Felipe, Henry, and Maria," she said.

"That's all we need. Henry was a sharpshooter in the war, Felipe can bring down a deer at fifty paces, Maria can swing a rolling pin like you wouldn't believe, and you know what Kinan can do. I will be fine," Deirdre said. With Kinan's blessing, she'd told them about his ability the day she'd thought of building their homes out of adobe. They'd had to know so he could use it to help them rebuild. To her surprise, he'd been more than happy to reveal his power to them.

Cat sighed as she pushed away from the wall. "Come, Sadie. You know you're wasting your breath. Besides, she's right, and we both know our Deirdre can handle herself."

She patted Deirdre's arm. That was when Deirdre became convinced. There was definitely a sparkle in her eye. Perhaps Cat and Rick had a rendezvous planned for the evening.

"One of Rick's best men will be checking the perimeter of each property all night. He'll be on my painted horse. Don't shoot him," Cat added.

The three of them started to walk toward the front door together.

Sadie lagged behind with reluctant steps. "But what if one of Ainsworth's men attacks him and steals his horse? And I don't see it until after it happens, or without time to get word to you, or if I don't see it at all," she asked.

Groaning, Cat rolled her eyes upward before fixing them on Deirdre. "If 'tisn't a freeman, 'tisn't Rick's man. Then you can shoot him, but don't shoot my horse. Is that satisfactory, Sadie?"

Lips pursing, Sadie asked, "What if Ainsworth employs freemen?"

Deirdre took her hand and all but pulled her across the huge, open foyer. "Trust me, he wouldn't. The rumor around town is that the man fought for the South."

Cat opened the door and stepped out into the golden twilight onto the new porch—which was covered and now had a hard-baked dirt floor that would one day be flagstone. Sadie hesitated at the threshold. She wouldn't let go of Deirdre's hand. Her big eyes beseeched Deirdre. "We've made your bed up with plenty of blankets, filled the woodbox on the side porch, and," she leaned in close and whispered, "there's a loaded pistol under your bed, just in case."

Deirdre led her by the hand off the porch and out into the fading sunlight to stand beside Cat. "Stop fretting. I'll be fine." She felt bad for her. Ever since the fires Sadie had been beating herself up mentally for not 'seeing' the fires until the moment they happened. It was making her second guess everything.

Grumbling to herself, Sadie made her way to the little cart she and Cat had taken to using as their main transportation.

"Sadie," Deirdre said.

"Yes?"

"A good friend once told me we aren't meant to see everything. There would be little challenge in life if we did," Deirdre said.

Sadie harrumphed. "Well, she does sound wise. And possibly beautiful."

Deirdre kissed her friend's dark forehead. "You are indeed."

The horse hitched to the wagon nickered softly to Cat, reaching its nose toward her. Cat took hold of Deirdre's hand and squeezed tight. "Truly, Deirdre, stay safe, no matter what. I'm going to need you throughout this pregnancy."

Deirdre drew her in and hugged her as tight as she dared. "I'll be there every step of the way, never fear. Keep an eye on Dylan for me, will you?" she asked.

A twinge of guilt over not returning to check on him this evening bit at her. It would be the first time she hadn't since work had begun anew on their homes. Over the last week, he had become distant and distracted during her visits. Whenever she brought up progress on her house, he turned the conversation to travel, speaking of natives, wild animals, and the thrill of the open trail. Perhaps an evening alone was what he needed.

As Cat climbed into the buckboard seat of the cart, Deirdre hovered close just in case.

"O' course. I won't let him overdo it," Cat promised.

In her peripheral vision, Deirdre saw Kinan coming around the corner of the house, a load of wood in his arms.

Cat thrust her head in the direction of the oak tree on the hill where a mounted man waited. "Come along, Sadie. Rick's waiting."

Sadie wiggled the reins across the back of the single, dun-colored draft horse hitched to their cart and clucked her tongue at him. A huge smile spread across Cat's face as they rode away. Whether it was for Rick, or another reason entirely, Deirdre couldn't be sure. It could be the joy of rebuilding their homes, or the pregnancy. Regardless, Deirdre was glad to see her so happy. Both ladies waved as they pulled away.

Soft steps started on the hard-packed earth of the front porch. Deirdre rushed to open the door for Kinan. He stepped aside and smiled at her as she passed. The bulge of his arms and taut muscles in his back stirred the burgeoning fire in her abdomen. For two weeks she had planned, worked, and laughed alongside him, all the while suppressing her desire. The work demanded she do so. Every day she awoke at the crack of dawn and labored until she rode back to Dylan's residence at night to check on him.

Though Ainsworth seemed oblivious of their progress, she didn't dare leave her home unguarded. And while she trusted her friends to watch over it for her, they had their own homes to work on and protect. Tonight, she would stay in her newly built home and relax. The problem with that was, everything she'd been suppressing caught up with her. Dylan's constant need for her presence had quickly become stifling. And, she had started to suspect much of it was an attempt on his part to keep her away from Kinan. She felt bad for what happened to him, but it had become increasingly clear that he was more worried about her spending time at his bedside than rebuilding her home. Despite knowing what not getting it completed would cost her. She was glad to be free of worrying over him for one night.

Beyond the foyer, in the main entertaining room, Kinan bent beneath the stone mantel to feed the fireplace. Deirdre took great pleasure in the view of his backside. Having him in her house, doing something so domestic, felt intimate and nice. It didn't hurt that he filled out his yellow cotton shirt so perfectly, or that it picked up the goldish flecks in his eyes. When he stood and turned to her, his gaze found hers in an instant, as if drawn to her. The look in his eyes pulled at something deep down inside, something tied to muscles in her most intimate parts. He crossed the room to stand before her. She'd been staring the entire time, but so had he.

"I regret that I don't have a proper kitchen yet in which I can cook you a warm meal in return for guarding my home with me," she said.

The desire in his gaze turned to delight as he smiled. "I don't, because if you did, it would complicate my surprise," he said.

She perked up with excitement. "A surprise?"

He fetched their cloaks from where they hung on the wall. "If you're up for a short walk outside, that is," he said.

At her nod, he draped her cloak around her shoulders, donned his own, and offered her his arm. A pleasant breeze swept around her as they stepped out into the long shadows of dusk. She snugged her arm tighter around his, pulling him in against her side. Though it was warmer than it had been a few weeks ago by far, the weather felt brisk in comparison to the cozy interior of her home. Any reason to snuggle up to Kinan was a good one.

"Never fear, you'll be warm soon," he said in a low voice that moved over her in a tantalizing way.

Did she dare hope he meant to pick up where they'd left off at the engagement party? It felt like so long ago. He led her around the side of the house. The framework of what would be a wraparound covered patio stretched overhead. Peekaboo views of the orange and indigo sky flashed between the remaining support logs of the overhang. Such a lovely sight made her feel incredibly lucky that this was her home. While not a single part of this venture had turned out to be easy, moments like this made it worth it.

In the short time it took them to walk around to the back of the house, the sun slipped below the horizon. The crackling of a fire and yellow flames licking at the shadows of what would become a garden in the spring, made her throat tighten with panic for a moment. Slowly, the moment passed as her eyes adjusted and she realized what lay before her. At the end of a meandering flagstone path was a fire pit of stacked stones with a bench and a small table beside it. Fear turned to delight as Kinan led her there. The last time she'd been out here, the garden had been nothing but a muddy mess. The closer they got, the more the light of the fire revealed to her. Stacked stones and boulders here and there looked to be raised planting beds. But they turned out to be something else entirely.

Turning to take in all the stones, she realized they were a recreation of the Mayan observatory from the tapestry at the O'Leary homestead.

"Oh, Kinan," she whispered.

At her insistent tugging, he led her to the first stone. Some were stacked stones, but most were boulders so large he had to have whistled them into place. Many rose up taller than she stood. The flagstone path wove through it all with purpose.

Kinan pointed up. "Just like in the tapestry, these stones lay out the pathway of the stars. Over the top of this one you see Orion," he explained, voice filled with boyish excitement. Hands on her shoulders, he turned her. "And through the gap between these two you can see Ursa Major."

He walked her around to each one, pointing out the different constellations that could be seen. Awestruck, she hung on his arm and his every word. The place felt nothing short of magical. She couldn't believe he had done all this for her. For days she had been busy working on the interior walls with Cat and Sadie. All that time she thought he'd been working on the exterior of the house.

She must have gone quiet for a long time, because he

withdrew his arm from hers and dipped his head.

"It's a Yule gift, but if it's too much for your back garden, I can move it, or remove it completely. I apologize. I should have—"

Unable to resist any longer, she rose up on her toes and stopped his words with a kiss. His full, soft lips moved against hers with an eagerness born of suppressed desire. As much as she wanted to keep kissing him, she had something she needed to say. Before she lost her resolve, she drew away. "You will do no such thing, Kinan O'Leary. It's the most amazing gift anyone has ever given me. I love it exactly how 'tis."

Laughing with delight, she took another stroll around, taking in the view of the stars from every vantage point. At the boulder pointing to Orion, the one as tall as she, Kinan rejoined her. The heat of his body as he leaned close felt decadent—and made her want more. He extended a wineglass with a delicate stem to her. She accepted it and raised it to her nose. The heady scent of red grapes mingled with undertones of cherries and cedar. Over the top of the glass, she saw Kinan's gaze travel the length of her body with slow appreciation.

Brows rising, she smiled. "Aged in cedar? What a refreshing idea. Is this Italian?"

It tasted even more delicious than it smelled, having a nice, smooth finish that left the lingering taste of grapes instead of oak like so many did.

"No, this is Henry's concoction. His Italian grandparents left him with a love of the art of wine-making, and knowing how much I enjoy a particularly good wine, he does a barrel a year for the inn."

She took another drink, rolling it around on her tongue. "Henry and I shall have to talk."

Kinan extended an elbow, which she took readily. "Henry would like that. But for tonight, you're all mine." Possessive as the words themselves were, Kinan made them sound alluring with the hopeful tone he used.

They walked back to the bench and sat down together. The scents of meat and various cheeses wafted up from the plates on the small table.

Hope stirred to life inside her. "Does that mean Henry, Felipe, and Maria won't be along tonight?"

The wineglass only half hid his smile as he lifted it. "Oh, they're here, but they are camping in the aspens, keeping watch over the property. No one will disturb us tonight, if that's still your wish."

Heat far greater than that of the nearby fire raged within her. The intense look he gave her made her desperate for his touch. She set her wineglass down amid the plates of food. The slick folds between her legs rubbed enticingly against one another as she turned to face him. Slowly, she slid her hand into his, trailing her fingers across his palm as she did so. A powerful shiver ran through him. He closed his eyes for a moment.

"I would love nothing more than to pick up where we left off," she said.

One of his hands slid to her waist, but it stopped there and went still. The look in his eyes turned serious. "I love your spontaneity and wild spirit, Deirdre. They are things we have in common, but things you bear so much more elegantly than I," he said. His slightly open mouth and contemplative look told her he had more to say, so she held her tongue. He soon went on. "I also love that you are daring, independent, determined, and loyal to your friends." Each word sent a warm pulse through her that only made her want him more.

This time he paused so long she started to run her hand down his chest, letting her fingers catch on every button of his shirt. He sighed deeply, but didn't go on.

"Whatever are you getting at, Kinan?" she asked in a sultry tone, hand stopping at his belt.

Desire deep enough to drown in filled his eyes once again as he looked at her.

"My interest in you is far more than carnal. Should our coupling prove to be stimulating for you, what is it you seek?"

Deirdre laughed. "Your mother must have been relentless in her pursuit of making you a gentleman."

Brow raised, Kinan shrugged one shoulder. "She was. I was terribly wild as a lad. She wanted society to accept me despite my mixed blood."

Chewing at her lip, she started to work his belt out of its buckle. "Should you prove able to reclaim the spirit of that wild lad and put your gentlemanly manners aside when necessary, you'll have a hard time getting rid of me."

Growling, he grabbed her hand and pulled her into his lap. Laughing and squirming, she worked her way around until she straddled him, dress bunched up around her legs. A wonderful hardness pressed against her apex. Deep in his eyes lay something more than desire, something no man had possessed when he looked at her.

"Why would I ever want to do that?" he teased.

Head tilting to the side, she pretended to think long and hard, but truly it was impossible to do so, feeling his erection against her opening. "Well, I'm opinionated, strong-willed, and always sticking my nose in things considered men's business."

He made a humming noise. "You can stick your nose in my business any time you like," he said in a low, sultry voice.

Suddenly she wanted to do just that, to taste him, to hold him in her mouth. She wanted it so bad her core ached. So she ground it against him. The friction was delicious.

His arms slid around her. "What do you envision your future holding, aside from stimulating carnal encounters?" he asked.

Her answer came fast and easy, for it wasn't one she had to think about. "Vast gardens, trees covering the property, and a winery that produces barrels each year to supply the elite of California and New York, and maybe eventually enough to ship overseas, a husband who allows me to be who I am, and enough children to fill that house one day."

With each word, Kinan's smile grew bigger. She was about to ask him what he found so amusing when he covered her lips with his. Their tongues engaged in a frantic dance that needed no words. The warm, wet sensation of his mouth drew a little sigh from her. She explored the inside of his mouth, enjoying the flavor of wine that lingered there. Hard pressure pushed between her legs as his erection challenged the confines of his breeches. It made her wonder how big he was. From the feel of it, he was certainly larger than her late husband—though that would be an easy feat. Not that the size of his cock would matter to her, so long as he knew how to use it to its best advantage.

Large hands slid down over her buttocks, cupping them and giving them a gentle squeeze. The fervency of their kiss intensified, both of them working as if to devour each other. After several moments, Deirdre drew back to breathe. But Kinan didn't seem to need air. He kissed his way down her chin and to her cleavage, lips touching every bit of flesh her dress didn't cover. All the while his fingers worked at the laces on the back of her dress. Once they loosened enough, he gathered it in his hands and slid it over her head.

Aside from changing in camp on the trail, she had never been outside in only her corset and undergarments, and certainly never in the arms of a man in such a state. Then there was the arcane observatory surrounding them. The impropriety of it all invigorated her, even though it was really only her arms and shoulders that were truly bare. Kinan's fingers got to work on her corset while his tongue licked at her cleavage.

"Should we go inside? Someone might see us," she asked in a breathy voice.

Drawing back, Kinan looked at her. The fire crackling behind them gave off just enough light to reveal his heavy-lidded expression. "That is a possibility." He lay a hand on her chest. "One that seems to make your heart beat faster." That hand slid over to squeeze her left breast. He found her pebbled nipple and caressed it without mercy.

A little moan slid from her as she pushed into his grasp.

"But we can go in if you would like," he said.

Mischief sparkled in his eyes, and Brigid help her, but she loved it. Kisses worked back up her neck, over to her ear. Against it, he whispered, "What would you like, Deirdre?" The question thrilled her as much as his breath on her ear. Her late husband had not been one to ask or care about what she wanted when it came to carnal pleasures. It felt as though Kinan's hot breath reached all the way to her navel.

Reaching down between her legs, she finished unbuckling his belt. She leaned down and whispered in his ear. "I want you to take me here, now."

Her reward was a shiver that traveled through his body. His erection pushed so hard against his breeches, she had trouble getting the buttons undone. Suddenly, she could breathe easier as the laces of her corset gave way beneath his fingers. She gave up her efforts on his breeches to lift her arms so he could pull her loose corset up over her head. The chilly evening air caressed her bare torso and breasts a moment before Kinan's hands did. The heat from those hands was more than enough to warm her. His fingers worked back and forth over her hard nipples as his lips descended to hers again. She gasped into his mouth, unable to kiss him back and completely at his mercy.

Just when she thought she might die of need if his mouth didn't replace his hands, he withdrew from her. But his mouth didn't descend to her breasts as she had hoped. Instead, he rose with her in his arms, a mischievous look in his eyes. Or was it the fire? She couldn't be sure, but it excited her nonetheless. He stood her on the slightly raised base that supported the huge upright boulder whose oddly shaped top framed the North Star.

"This should do nicely," he said.

Laughing deep and throaty, she stopped him before his arms could slide around her again. One brow rose in question, but he waited. Feeling perfectly naughty in only her pantaloons outdoors, she took a moment to enjoy the night air on her skin. Darkness cloaked them, but the fire silhouetted them to any who might be close enough to see. Though she knew no one was around, the very fact that she stood mostly naked outside was surprisingly arousing.

As was the weight of Kinan's gaze on her. She released her hair from the pins that held it and swept the long curtain of it back over her shoulders. The sound of approval Kinan made emboldened her further. Ever so slowly, she let her hands trail down her neck and over her breasts. She squeezed and rolled her nipples between her fingers. The animalistic sound that came from him was as arousing as her own ministrations.

He started to reach for her, but she wagged her finger at him and shook her head. The groan of disappointment he let out contrasted with the huge grin that turned his lips up. Encouraged by his reaction, she hooked her thumbs beneath her waistband and slid her pantaloons off. In only her stockings and boots, she knew she should have felt exposed, scandalous. But she felt liberated and powerful, a power that came partially from the look of absolute need on Kinan's face. That look said he wanted to do all manner of naughty things to her. And she wanted him to. *Oh, do I ever*. But first…

She unbuttoned his breeches and slid them down over his hips. The impressive erection that sprung free drew her hands to it. His eyes flew open wide as she gripped him. Slightly elevated on the flagstone as she was, his cock was at just the right level.

"You're amazing," he said as he bent down to her.

While they kissed, she traced her fingers up the length of his cock and over his tip. His tongue withdrew from her mouth all too soon. He brushed a lock of hair back from her brow. "Yes, I believe this rock puts you at just the right height," he said.

"The right height?" she asked.

Arms wrapping around her, he pulled her close and suddenly she understood. With her standing on the rock, they were face-to-face, and his erection pressed at her opening.

"For that position I found in the book on your nightstand," he said.

Eyes flying wide open, she swallowed hard. He went on before she could respond. "I didn't pry, I promise. When I came in to talk to you I saw it, and recognized it."

"Recognized it?"

An absolutely devilish look that made her tingle deep down came over him. "I have the very same book. You can imagine my surprise. I thought you might have picked it up off the shelves at the O'Leary homestead." He laughed. "I rode out at once to check, and when I found it nestled in its spot on the bottom shelf behind a piece of artwork, I knew there was far more to you than met the eye."

The idea of him reading the same scandalous book, and knowing she was reading it, made her even wetter. She shifted her hips, letting his cock slide between her legs, not inside, but close enough to make her ache.

"Would this be the position you want to try?" she whispered.

"Oh, yes, but first…" He drew away, leaving the night to embrace her in his stead. But he made up for it when he bent down and kissed the mound of hair at her groin. The kiss deepened, his tongue probing, exploring. She cried out, her knees weakening. His tongue worked at the delicate folds of skin that had only ever received her own ministrations. A finger slid inside her, making her muscles clench in a wonderful way. The sensations that shot through her body made her weak in the knees. But she wouldn't let them give out. She didn't dare for that might mean and end to this amazing pleasure. Kinan's moist, warm, textured tongue slipping over and around the folds between her legs was so intense it made her eyes slam shut. At last his attention settled on the nub of wonderful nerves at the top of her opening. His tongue rubbed, flicked, and massaged it as his fingers worked in and out of her.

Breath quickening, she pressed against him. He sucked the nub into his mouth, drawing a cry of ecstasy from her that echoed into the night. Panting, she gripped his long hair as he licked her fervently and pumped his finger in her. The pressure inside her reached a crescendo that broke over her in a pleasure that made every muscle between her legs clench again and again in wonderful waves.

Something cool brushed her fingertips. She looked down to see green grass had sprung up all around the boulder and grew high enough to reach her. Giggling, she looked to Kinan. Licking his lips as if he relished the taste of her, he rose and embraced her again. He pressed his lips to hers. Their gentle pressure moved hers apart. His tongue slid inside and explored. On it she could taste her own wetness. At first, she wasn't sure if she liked it. But then she thrilled at the erotic idea of it, in the fact that he had taken pleasure in giving her pleasure, and now wanted to share it with her.

A subtle move of his body and his erection slid between her

slick folds. As they kissed, he rubbed it against her, drawing a tortured moan of need from deep within. Chuckling, he lifted his hips and moved inside her. That one little move started up the delicious spasms again, making her muscles literally pull him in deeper until he filled her. Hands clutching at his back, her nails raked along his skin. He groaned and nuzzled her neck. His arms supporting her, he started to move in and out, in long, slow movements of his hips that drove her wild. It went on and on— far longer than she had ever experienced—and still he remained hard as iron. She clung to him, gasping for breath, never wanting it to end.

After a while, his hands slid down to cup her buttocks and lift her. He carried her back a few steps, pressed her against the boulder, and started to thrust into her with abandon. She cried out for him to go faster, thrust harder, and he obeyed. Lost in the ecstasy of him moving in and out of her, she let her head rest back against the rock. When the head of his cock swelled, she knew he was close.

With a groan, he withdrew from her and worked his cock twice with his own hand. The sight sent her vaginal muscles into another mind-numbing set of wonderful spasms. As he screamed her name, he emptied himself onto her stomach. The warmth of his cum branding her felt euphoric. Trailing one hand through it, she threw her head back and moaned. Brilliant stars flashed above, some of them most certainly not on any astronomer's charts. But the one that shone the brightest, the North Star, told her she was exactly where she was meant to be.

27

Deirdre

The next day, Deirdre couldn't stop stealing looks at Kinan. From across the breakfast table back at the inn, around the horses as they prepared the wagon to go Yule-tree hunting. Each chance they got, they sneaked around corners and ducked behind doors to steal a kiss. Deirdre found the presence of her friends a challenge to her to improve her skills at slinking around. Kinan's warm brown eyes, euphoric smile, and the grace with which his muscular body moved, all captivated her. It didn't help that she couldn't stop thinking about just how talented that body was. But more importantly, his lovemaking had been thoughtful, passionate, and exciting—things she hadn't experienced with her late husband even before he knew about her mixed blood.

As he returned to the house to fetch a blanket, she searched for a reason to follow. But she had duties in the barn. A hand slapped her shoulder. She jumped and nearly dropped the brush in her hand. The horse that she'd been pretending to brush snorted as if to tell her he saw it coming.

"Deirdre Quinn, have you got something to tell us?" Sadie asked through pursed lips.

Though she wanted to play it coy, a grin started to tug at her lips and she couldn't stop it. Soft steps alerted her to Cat approaching her other side. "Aye, do tell us why you're staring at Kinan like he is a meal you've devoured and are eager for another taste of."

Deirdre looked from one to the other, grin growing so large it made her cheeks ache. "Because I think I may be in love," she admitted to herself as well as them. Euphoria fading a bit, she turned wide eyes to Sadie. "How much did you see?" The thought of Sadie having a vision of her and Kinan having sex sent a spark of panic through her.

"Not enough to scandalize me, don't worry," she said with a wave of her hand. Letting out a *squee* sound, Sadie hugged her. "Thank the Powers that Be for guiding you to a smart choice for once. But whatever changed your mind? You were so determined he was wrong for you."

A devious laugh came from Cat. "He *stood up* to your standards, did he?" she whispered.

Her face burned so hot she knew she didn't have to answer—it gave it all away.

The groan that came from Sadie made the horse snort again. "Oh Deirdre, you'll be a ruined woman if he decides not to marry you."

Pained by the desperate look in her friend's eyes, Deirdre took hold of her hands. "I'm a widow, therefore, I'm already considered tainted by most. Besides, if I decide to marry the man, it will only be because he is right for me. And if I don't, I have the means to take care of myself."

One brow rose in that look Sadie got when she wasn't satisfied. "The world is just now allowing women to start owning property. That right could be challenged or taken away at any time," Sadie argued.

"You worry too much," Deirdre said.

"I worry because you do not. I only want you safe and happy."

Deirdre's smile returned. "Well, I'm happier than I've ever been."

Eyes sparkling, Cat gripped both her and Sadie's arms. "Enough fretting. Tell us how he was!"

A flush traveled through Deirdre's entire body. The power of the memory made her eyes close. "Like a locomotive. Powerful, exciting, and very…modern."

Cat let out another squeal while Sadie groaned something about being scandalized. But a smile began to work at breaking through Sadie's stoic expression.

"Did you try one of the positions from the book?" Cat asked, ignoring the slap Sadie directed at her forearm.

Deirdre leaned closer to them. "One of the standing ones, the first time."

Gasping, Cat covered her mouth. "You did it more than once?"

Eyes wide, Deirdre nodded.

"At least you can't get pregnant in an upright position," Sadie said.

Cat's hand rubbed her belly. "That actually isn't true."

"You didn't!" Sadie exclaimed.

"I most certainly did," Cat said with a touch of pride.

Both she and Deirdre erupted into laughter that drew Sadie in as well. Beneath their laughter, Deirdre heard masculine voices arguing. She fell silent when she recognized them both.

"What's wrong?" Cat asked.

The answer arrived before she could speak. Dylan stormed into the barn fast enough to make the sleepy draft horses jump in their hitches. Kinan strode in right on his heels. He gave Deirdre an apologetic look that she dared not guess the meaning of.

Cat put on a cheerful mask so good only Deirdre or Sadie would know it was false. "Dylan, you're looking quite well. 'Tis good to see you up and about," she said.

Some of the tension relaxed out of his shoulders as his gaze shifted to her. "Thank you. I've healed up well, thanks to you and Deirdre's care. I don't mean to interrupt, but I've news about the wedding preparations that Deirdre needs to hear."

The mask fell away from her dear friend, revealing the anxiety beneath. Cat started to wring her hands. "Is it the flower arrangements Victoria is making?" The concern in her voice made Deirdre put aside her own problems for the moment. She couldn't let Cat get worked up, and any complication with the wedding would do exactly that.

"Aye, the cold has changed what she had available, but no worries, she has several options for Deirdre to choose from," Dylan said.

"Perhaps I should come, too," Cat said, voice high-pitched with anxiety.

The edge in her tone made Deirdre want to slap Dylan. This had nothing to do with flowers and everything to do with him and her. Such an excuse to talk to her was selfish—and reckless—where Cat's well-being was concerned. Too much stress could cause complications with the baby, especially considering the condition her last pregnancy had left her in. The doctor hadn't thought she'd even be able to get pregnant again. Shooting Dylan a hard look, she looped an arm through Cat's and led her to the wagon. "Not at all. You need to pick out the perfect tree for the foyer since it will be the focal point of the wedding this Saturday."

"But—"

Deirdre shook her head as she passed Cat's hand to Sadie. "I'll hear no protests from you. That tree is the most important decoration. Flowers are merely garnish. Trust me, I know what you like, and I will choose the perfect arrangements." She gave her a wink, one that said she'd grow them herself if necessary.

Sadie pulled Cat into the wagon before she could resist, but that didn't stop her from protesting. "But you have to help pick out the tree. We can wait for you." The choosing of the tree was of the utmost importance since it meant taking a life in the eyes of the fae.

One glance at Dylan's tense profile and Deirdre knew it would be a long conversation. She smiled at Cat. "No need to worry. You all go on ahead and Dylan will escort me to you once we've chosen the new arrangements. The wagon takes longer than Ciaren anyway, so I'll easily catch up," Deirdre said.

Cat eased back into the seat. "I suppose that will work."

Forcing her smile to stay in place, Deirdre turned it on Dylan, showing a bit more teeth. "Dylan, if you would be so kind as to saddle Ciaren while I settle Cat and Sadie, I would greatly appreciate it," she said.

His gaze darted to Kinan and back to her. "O' course," he said with false cheer.

He dipped his head to her, spun on a heel, and marched off toward Ciaren's stall. Ignoring him, Kinan moved between her and the wagon, putting his back to it and blocking Cat and Sadie's view. He took her hand. Tension sang through his fingers, despite his gentle grip.

"Are you sure?" The concern and vulnerability in his tone tugged at her.

Even though she feared he may have just told Dylan about their night together, it didn't change how she felt about him. On one hand, she didn't want anyone trying to claim her as their property. On the other, it felt good to know he cared enough to be jealous. She took his hand in hers. He almost smiled, but his lips couldn't quite turn up enough to be convincing.

"I'll be fine. I'll probably catch up with you before you even reach the forest," she said.

A nod of his head and the tension drained from his body. "You have your pistol in case of...wolves?" he asked.

She had to resist the urge to lower his hand to her thigh where it was holstered. "I do."

"In that case, I shall leave you to your arrangement choice, and hope to see you shortly." The double meaning of his words sank in deep.

He was stepping back and allowing her to choose. Breath shuddering, she struggled to speak and couldn't. All her life men had tried to tell her what to do. Kinan allowing her to make this choice without a single plea or demand meant the world to her. He lifted her hand to his lips and placed a long kiss on the back of it. Without another word, he climbed into the wagon and took up the reins. He watched her until the wagon pulled out of the barn. She thought she caught the edge of a wistful smile as he disappeared around the corner.

The sound of a throat clearing loudly made her spin toward Ciaren's stall. Arms crossed over his chest, Dylan propped himself against the stall. Eyes as sharp and pale as slivers of ice cut straight into her. "Looks like you've made your choice," he said.

"Dylan…"

"Have you lain with him?" he cut in. He pushed away from the stall with enough force to make it rattle and stormed over to her.

Chin going up, she stood her ground. "That is not your business." Relief let her breathe a little easier despite the man bearing down on her. Kinan hadn't told him.

Dylan's hand came toward her. She dodged to the side, but his palm only struck the wood beside where she had stood, as if it hadn't been his intention to hit her. Still…

"You did. That son of a bitch. I'll kill him," he growled.

Baring her teeth, Deirdre stepped up to him. "You will do no such thing, because you will have to go through me to do it."

All that fury melted right out of him. He ran a hand through his blond locks and sank back against the stall again. "It should have been me. It would have been me if I hadn't gotten hurt." The defeat in his voice stirred sympathy in her. But his words kept her anger burning.

"Do you really think I made such a decision that lightly, based solely on physical attraction? Don't be a fool. If we had lain together, Dylan, what then?"

Hope lit his eyes as if he had only heard half of what she'd said. It was the opposite of what she'd been going for. "I'd have taken you away from here, on a grand adventure, maybe even eventually to Ireland. I still would." He reached for her, but she took a step back.

She didn't try to soften the look she gave him. "You can't have both a proper lady who knows her place and one who wants to run off on adventures. At least not in me you can't. Besides, did you ever think of what I want?"

Expression softening, he took a step closer. "You want me, or at least, you did. If I'd made it to the party that night—"

She put a finger to his lips. "Stop. If you'd made it to the party, my house would have burned completely to the ground."

His head dropped as if he couldn't bear her gaze any longer.

"It wouldn't have changed anything. I want a home, a husband, children. You aren't ready for those things," she went on. Not to mention, instinct whispered to her that telling him her secrets would change everything, and not for the better.

In one swift movement, he stepped forward and took her in his arms. "What if I was?"

She shook her head and tried to pull back, but he held her fast. He begged and pleaded for another chance. Breath coming in panicked gasps, Deirdre's eyes darted every which way, looking for the best way out of this.

"Let go," she commanded.

But he didn't hear, or wouldn't. He just kept pleading. Seeing a rake laying across the aisle behind him, and Ciaren's head poking over her stall door, ears pinned and teeth bared, Deirdre decided. A pinch of concentration allowed her to call to the sleeping energy left in the wooden handle of the rake. It flew toward her and smacked Dylan in the back of the head hard enough to elicit a curse from him. One hand went up to rub his head. While he was distracted, she stepped into him, shoving him back. He stepped on the tines of the rake and fell against Ciaren's stall. The mare promptly bit down on his shoulder. With a yelp, Dylan's arms fell from her. She leaped away.

"Let go, lass!" Deirdre commanded, knowing the damage a

horse's bite could do.

Ciaren let go of him. Dylan dashed several steps away from both the stall and Deirdre. Squealing, Ciaren struck the stall door with her hooves several times before dashing out into the attached paddock.

Misty eyes on Deirdre, Dylan rubbed at his shoulder. "I'm sorry, I'm so bloody sorry. I didn't mean to scare you. I would never hurt you," he said.

Guilt tried to worm its way into her. The man was recovering from bad burns, after all. And she believed that he didn't mean to scare her. But he had.

"Yes, well, pull your shite together, man. Did she hurt you badly?" she asked.

"No, no more than I deserved. I don't think she even broke the skin."

Something crackled beneath her boot.

Dylan went on in a desperate tone. "I'm leaving for Oregon, and I was hoping you'd come with me. Think of what a grand adventure it would be, the two of us, out in the wild." He went on but she stopped listening.

A leather journal with several loose sheets of paper spilling from it lay at her feet. She bent to pick it up. Names and addresses occupied the loose sheets of paper, which were charred around the edges. Embossed on the front of the journal were the letters "F" and "B" surrounded by a circle of Celtic knots. She knew that symbol. Some of the men her father had done business with had used it.

"Oh no! I'm sorry, I must have dropped that," he said, an edge of panic in his voice as he reached for it.

Holding it tighter, she stepped back. "This is yours?"

"Aye, and 'tis very dear to me," he said, hand held out.

She let him take it.

A horrible thought knitted her brows together. "Sadie said you had two sheets of paper on you when she first dressed your wounds. It was those, or some of them, wasn't it?" she asked, pointing to the loose sheets poking out from the journal.

He caressed the charred edges. "Aye. That's why I didn't make it to the party that night. I was trying to get this back from Ainsworth."

"His men were able to set those fires because you left your post guarding my home."

His head dropped. "Aye, and for that, I will be eternally sorry. I knew Ainsworth would be attending. It was the only chance I had to get into his house—"

An upheld hand halted his words. The excuses, the justification, it was too much to bear. She pointed to the front of the journal he clutched so closely to his chest. "That's the mark of the Fenian Brotherhood. You're one of them, aren't you?" she demanded.

He lifted his chin. "I am. We're patriots in America who continue to fight to free Ireland. You know I love our motherland, I told you as much."

Not so much as a hint of remorse showed on his face. She had to swallow several times before she could speak through her fury. "Were you part of the group that attacked the British outposts in Canada last year?"

His fingers started to turn white where they clutched the journal. "We were fighting to draw the British navy to defend Canada. With them busy there, our Irish Republican Brotherhood in Ireland could have driven out the English ground forces at last."

The glare she fixed on him felt harsh, but she couldn't suppress her anger. "The newspapers said it didn't work. They said innocents were killed, Canadians who had no stake in the conflict. Worse, you ignored the call to fight a war here on the soil that nourishes you now, ignoring the plight of another people who deserve to be free as well."

He flinched repeatedly as if every word stung like a vengeful bee. Moisture filled his eyes and he shook his head. "You haven't been there, you don't understand. I was born there. I watched me friends starve to death, me grandparents get evicted from the farm that had been in our family for generations so an English lord could have it, and me mum work her hands bloody to feed us. The English treat us like vermin in need of exterminating—which they do at any given opportunity." He paused to suck in a shuddering breath. His eyes closed tight and a tear ran down his cheek.

A pang of sympathy coursed through her.

"I can't explain it to someone who hasn't seen it, hasn't lived it." Carefully, he tucked the loose pages back into the journal and placed it in his jacket.

Those his words prickled at her. The defeated way he hung his head made her feel bad. He was wrong, though. She did know. Long before the English had turned on the Irish, their ancestors had fought her ancestors. The only difference was, the fae had been so utterly defeated that the majority of them fled this world. Those left behind had to go into hiding. Still, she had no right to judge him. His pain was no less than hers. "Do not assume you know what a person has been through. I am not unsympathetic to what you've endured."

He shook his head with a vehemence that surprised her. The look of guilt in his eyes when he looked at her chilled her. "Don't give me your sympathy. I don't deserve it. But I do hope you'll try to understand that if I hadn't gotten this book back from Ainsworth, hundreds, maybe thousands, of my countrymen would have died."

Gaze darting away, he stopped talking. A terrible feeling settled in Deirdre. When he didn't go on, or look back at her after a while, she took a step closer to him. "Dylan? What did you do to get that book back?" He held his silence and continued to stare at the ground. Desperation spreading through her chest, she grabbed his arm. "What did you do?" she demanded.

"I had to get Ainsworth out of the house so I could sneak in and get the journal back. The night of the party I was only able to grab the loose pages that were poking out of the safe door." He swallowed hard as if the rest of the words stuck and wouldn't come out.

Today. He meant today. She slapped a palm against his chest so hard he flinched. "How exactly did you get him out of the house?"

Another long stretch of silence made her contemplate drawing her pistol. Lucky for him it was winter, otherwise he'd be wrapped in the wisteria vines that grew on the side of the barn. But she wouldn't awaken them, nor would she use her pistol on him. Part of that was due to the fact she didn't want to put herself in the vulnerable position of raising her skirts. Not that she thought Dylan would hurt her. Run, now *that* she feared he might do.

"I told him I saw Kinan at the edge of his property with a wagon."

Shock stole her breath, but she reclaimed it fast enough. "He'll think we're after timber. He'll come gunning for Kinan— and anyone with him," Deirdre whispered.

Her mind tried to get her body to move, to run, but it froze in place. "Cat, Sadie…" The thought of Ainsworth hurting them or Kinan launched her into action.

Screaming in frustration, she shoved Dylan aside and flung open Ciaren's stall door.

Dylan called after her. "Once he sees the wagon is too small for timber, and that Cat and Sadie are with him, he'll realize they're only after a holiday tree. He won't have any recourse to take action."

The horse wasn't in her stall. The back paddock door stood wide open. Despite her constricting throat, Deirdre managed to whistle loud and shrill. She waited, listening for hoofbeats, but Ciaren didn't come. There could be only one possible reason for that. Someone had opened her paddock gate, which would allow her to run into Balder's paddock.

"You've nothing to worry about. They'll be fine. Please, come with me. We'll have an adventure traveling, then we can settle down and have some wee ones after," Dylan pleaded.

Ignoring him, Deirdre grabbed the lead rope and halter from where it hung on the front of the stall. She marched through the stall and out into the paddock. Low fog swirled with each step, tendrils of it curling up around the edges of her fine blue satin skirts. She had dressed for a wagon ride with her lover and friends, not a hack on horseback. But she had no time to worry about that. Each time her foot touched the ground the grass turned green—not from melting frost, but because it grew up to meet the furious power flowing from her.

Neither Ciaren nor Balder were in or around their paddocks. Balder's gate also stood wide open. A wordless scream tore from Deirdre's throat. Though she knew it would do no good, she whistled again. Far out in the field that bordered the paddocks, two equine figures frolicked in the fog, one black, one white. She stormed back into the barn, threw the halter and lead rope at Dylan, and kept marching toward the sliding door. Dylan snagged her arm as she passed him, pulling her to a stop. Spinning around, she slapped him as hard as she could across the face, putting all her weight into it.

"Ainsworth won't care that they aren't getting timber. It's an excuse he'll use to justify killing them all!" she roared. He swallowed hard and shook his head. "Deep down, you know that. It's why you're trying to delay me, because if I'm there, he'll kill me too," she hissed.

The fact he stood between her and the door only drove that realization home all the harder.

He grabbed both of her arms, his touch gentle, but firm. "No, I delayed you so I'd have time to convince you to come with me. I love you, Deirdre."

For a moment, pity broke through her anger. "No, Dylan. You love the idea of me, an idea that keeps changing. And I am not going to change for you. Now let me go."

"I can't do that, just in case you're right about Ainsworth."

Swallowing her fury, Deirdre smiled and nodded. Dylan let out a breath and nodded in return, starting to smile as he rubbed her arms. She stepped swiftly to the side and slammed her knee into his groin. A terrible wheeze of pain rushed from his lips as he doubled over. Hands going to cradle his bruised bullocks, his wide eyes fixed on her. With a calm born of need, she lifted her skirts and drew her hidden pistol. What he didn't see was the wisteria vines slipping under the barn door behind him, snaking closer.

A new kind of pain entered Dylan's eyes.

"I am going. If you try to stop me, I will stop you. People I love are in danger. The man I love is in danger. There is nothing in this universe that can keep me from getting to them, not even you."

Her shaking thumb tried twice to cock the hammer and failed. Instead, she had to use her left hand. The entire pistol shook so badly she knew her shot would come nowhere near her target if it came down to it. She prayed it wouldn't come down to it for more reasons than that.

She had to get him moving. "Get on your horse and get the hell out of here. I don't ever want to see you again," she said.

"You love him, truly?" Dylan gasped.

She realized with a wonderful and frightening clarity that she did. "Yes."

Tears shone in Dylan's eyes, but whether they were from her confession, or the kick to his bollocks was hard to tell. Without another word, he stumbled toward the barn door. A few moments later pained curses preceded him hollering his horse into action. The thunder of receding hooves followed.

Pointing the pistol at the floor, just in case, Deirdre eased the hammer down. She ran for the tack room. There she replaced the pistol with the extra bow that Kinan kept on the wall for varmints. A pistol did her no good if she wasn't comfortable enough with the damn thing to hit anything with accuracy. Just holding the bow eased enough of her anxiety that she stopped shaking. Fear gave way to determination. She would make it there in time. She had to. Grabbing the biggest bridle off the wall, Deirdre dashed to the only horse left in the barn—Kinan's old plow horse.

28

Deirdre

Huge, feathered feet arching into animated steps, the draft horse loped across the snow-dusted grasslands. The pace was barely more than a jog, really. No matter how hard Deirdre urged or begged, the creature wouldn't break into a full gallop. Once the inn fell out of sight behind them, she gave up, realizing this was likely the fastest pace the old horse could do. It was probably for the best anyway. The low fog that clung to the ground obscured her view of the terrain. At this pace, she could guide him by feeling the dormant energy of the plant life, but it was so faint any faster and she wouldn't be able to 'see'. To go any faster would be reckless on this frozen ground. And were the horse willing, she wouldn't have cared how reckless it was.

After what felt like an eternity of torturous worry, she finally reached the tree-covered hillside that was the edge of Ainsworth's land. She slowed the horse to a walk as they entered the trees. Over the huffing and puffing of the tired creature, she couldn't hear much else. She pulled the bow slung from her back and nocked an arrow. Gaze scanning the ground, she did her best to travel along where she knew they would have entered the forest. The farther she rode up the hill, the thinner the fog became until it soon gave way to a dusting of snow. In the only gap through the trees wide enough to allow a wagon passage, she finally saw what she was looking for—wheel tracks cutting through the snow.

She put her bow in its riding sheath, the arrow back in the quiver, and dismounted. Normally she would just throw her leg over and slide off, weapon in hand. But the likelihood of slipping on the snow-covered ground was too risky. She lifted the horse's reins to a sturdy branch. But as she started to wrap the leather strap around it, a twig broke behind her as if beneath the heal of a boot. Breath catching, she spun toward the sound.

The sharp angles of a harshly handsome face made her breath catch—in a very bad way. Ainsworth. "What…where…" Considering her rambling mind, she snapped her mouth shut before she could say anything damning.

"What indeed," he pondered as he strode close enough she could smell his oily scent. "What brings you to my land in the frigid cold? Have you come to accept my proposal?"

Straightening her fur-lined cloak, she lifted her chin. "I have come to tell you that I am declining."

His eyes narrowed to slits. "You came all the way out here on the coldest day of the year so far to tell me? Why do I find that hard to believe?"

"I did not want to keep you waiting any longer, especially with Catriona and Rick's wedding just around the corner," she said. Though she'd been going for a haughty air of propriety, it fell to shambles when her voice shook with fear.

"So be it," he said, making her think for one delusional moment that she might walk away from this encounter.

A blur of movement made her raise her hands. An arm

collided with hers painfully hard. Inches from her face, a fist hovered, blocked by her quick thinking. It withdrew and another strike came at her. Arms up, she blocked another blow. But she didn't see the one coming toward her stomach. It hit her just below the ribcage and sent all the breath blowing from her lungs. Pain throbbed through her. She tried to suck in a breath and couldn't.

"This land is mine, bitch. And I will have it back if I have to bury you in it to get it," he snarled.

The need to reply allowed her to draw enough air. "Not...yours."

"Oh but it is. Or it was before my idiot siblings sold their portions off. And I will have it all back, one way or another," he said through a hiss that made him sound so snakelike she cringed away.

Gaze skittering toward the plow horse where her bow was, she desperately thought of ways to distract him. But the scuffle had scared the horse off. Movement snapped her attention back to Ainsworth, but not in time. The butt of a pistol struck the side of her head. Pain exploded across her temple. The ground rushed toward her. She didn't feel the impact, but suddenly she tasted dirt and found herself looking up at Ainsworth. Trails of heat worked their way down the side of her face. One ran over her cheek and dripped off her nose.

Ainsworth came at her again, pistol raised for another strike.

Desperation tore through her, causing her power to dive deep into the ground, searching. It found the roots of the pine tree sheltering her and called to them. One poked up out of the ground and caught Ainsworth's foot. The man tripped and fell to his knees only a few feet from her.

Too close, too close. Her breath came in short gasps. She tried not to panic and failed. She struggled to rise, but only managed to push up to a half-seated position. The movement made her head feel like thunder was echoing through it.

Sensing her fear and need, the tree sent up more roots—dozens of them. They wove through the air like snakes, wrapped around Ainsworth's legs, and yanked him away from her. Though he screamed and writhed, they relentlessly tightened and wove around him. First one, then others, wrapped around his neck. Mouth working as he struggled to draw air in, he stared at her, eyes wide with horror. His fingers clawed at the roots. Nails broke, blood seeping from where several tore off. She knew she should stop the tree, but fear got the better of her.

Black narrowed her vision until it felt like she was looking through the small opening of a cave. More heat poured down the side of her face. Dizziness swept over her. The ground rushed up to meet her once again.

Something tickled her nose. She swatted at it, but her arm was sluggish to answer her command. The world moved, tilted. Nausea moved over her in waves. The nicker of a horse sounded. Along with it came the memory of what had happened, and on its heals, fear. She opened her eyes, or tried to. One of them was stuck shut. She swiped at it. Her hand came away sticky with bright red blood. Gently probing, she realized the eye wasn't hurt, only covered in blood. She managed to pry it open. The pain that throbbed from her temple gave her a good idea of where the blood had come from. But she could see now, and that was something.

Roots lay beneath her hands, legs, everywhere. They supported her like a fainting couch, having lifted her up to a seated position. Stroking them, she looked to the huge fir tree they came from. It had saved her life.

Thank you, she told it. *I am safe now.* She poured as much of her own energy into the tree as she could spare, replenishing it. The roots retreated. She stood.

Reins dangled in the air a few feet from her face. Slowly, so as not to risk vomiting from the dizziness, she looked up. Attached to the reins was her draft horse. He nickered softly. She grabbed the reins and used them to haul herself to her feet. All the while, he stood still as could be and took it. Once up, she pressed a kiss to his wide, black forehead.

"Thank you, too," she whispered because to speak any louder hurt her head.

Movement came from behind her. She looked to see the roots of the tree sink back into the ground. Panic rose within as she realized Ainsworth was no longer across from her. The tree could have drawn him down into the ground. Her grandmum had told her of such things happening before. Letting her eyes drift closed, she felt along the roots of the tree. Ainsworth was nowhere to be found. The panic in her chest tried to spread. She wouldn't allow it.

He couldn't have gone far. But then, the wagon couldn't have gotten much farther either. Pulling her bow and quiver from the saddle, she dug deep and found her strength. Her friends needed her. Bow at the ready, she crept through the trees off to the side of the wagon tracks. Near the crest of what she knew preceded a hollow—for they had traveled this way before—she heard voices raised in anger. Crouching low, she moved to the top of the crest, careful to keep a tree between her and the direction the voices came from. Feathery spruce boughs hid her from sight—or so she hoped. Not thirty feet ahead lay the wagon. In front of the team of horses, Cat and Sadie huddled together, holding hands. Kinan stood between them and Ainsworth, his arms spread wide, his body shielding her friends from the barrel of the shotgun in the Englishman's hands. To their right stood Dylan, hands out as if pleading with Ainsworth, or Kinan, she couldn't tell.

The fool had beat her with ease on his fast horse. *Damn.* She should have thought to steal it from him instead of taking the old plow horse.

Deirdre resisted the urge to run into the fray and instead crept one tree closer, then another. The men were far too busy arguing to notice her. Red-faced, Ainsworth was yelling, "—witches, you're all witches! I'll see you burned for this."

Another man moved out of the trees on the other side of the wagon, coming up behind Cat and Sadie. No one seemed to notice him yet. Deirdre crept another tree closer, now less than twenty feet away. Sunlight danced along the blade of a large knife in the sneaking man's hands. The man and Ainsworth exchanged a look. Ainsworth nodded.

Breath held, Deirdre connected to the energy in the wood of her arrow and bow. She whispered her intent to it.

Fly true. For the love of Danu and all her children, fly true.

Just as the man lunged, she launched to her feet, took aim, and loosed her arrow. The crack of gunfire immediately followed the twang of her bowstring. The man with the knife halted in mid-lunge, the feathered shaft stuck in his armpit. He crumpled to the forest floor like a broken doll, his blood turning the snow crimson. Both Cat and Sadie screamed as they turned and saw him. A second arrow nocked, Deirdre spun toward Ainsworth, striding out into the open as she did so. But he lay on the ground too, blood welling up out of his chest. Dylan cocked the hammer back on his smoking pistol as he advanced on Ainsworth's twitching form.

Behind them, pine boughs rustled and men shouted and grunted. A moment later, Cofield and Rick emerged, dragging another man by the hair. Rick let go of him and ran to Cat's side. Sadie stepped back so the two could embrace, but he pulled her into the hug as well.

"Thank Danu, Brigid, and the entire Seely Court you're all right! I was coming to meet you when I heard the shot. Thank Danu," he said against Cat's hair. He let them go almost as quickly and bent to check on the man lying on the ground. Making a grunting noise of satisfaction, he rose and turned to stare straight at Deirdre. "Thank you, Deirdre."

Unable to answer, she nodded and turned her bow on the man Cofield was restraining.

Rick's nostrils flared as he scented her blood. "Are you all right?" he asked.

She started to shake her head and winced. Suddenly Kinan was at her side. His arm went around her back and supported her. "How bad are you hurt?" he asked, voice filled with concern.

"Not as bad as it looks. Head wounds bleed a lot," she managed to get out.

A pained sound came from low in his throat. He clutched her tighter.

"Should we kill this one, boss?" Cofield asked, looking to

Rick.

Shaking his head, Rick returned to Cat and drew her back into his arms. "O' course not. We didn't come here to cause any trouble. Let him go."

Cofield did as he was told, but his scowl said he wasn't happy about it. Dylan swaggered up to the man as he holstered his pistol. "That's true. I'm the one who came here to cause trouble," he said.

He removed the journal from his pocket and waved it in the man's face. The man's eyes widened. "Yeah, you recognize this. I took it back from Ainsworth because he stole it from me. Bloody fecking Englishman," Dylan said, spitting after the last word. Grinning, he motioned to Ainsworth's corpse. "I did this. And I'd have killed them, too, if they'd gotten in me way." He thrust his head in Rick's and Kinan's direction. Teeth bared, he grabbed the man by the shirt. "You can tell your lawman he's lucky no more died here by me hand today. Tell him to consider this a warning not to feck with the Fenian Brotherhood." With that, he shoved the man away from him.

He and Kinan exchanged a long look that ended with them both nodding. The hardness in Dylan's eyes softened as he strode straight for Deirdre. He stopped at her side. "Are you sure you won't come with me?" he asked.

She touched his arm and whispered, "I am sure. But thank you for what you just did."

He stared at her for a long moment. "No need to thank me. Just promise me you'll look after Victoria."

Deirdre smiled. "As if she were my own grandmother. You have my word."

Letting out a shuddering breath, Dylan nodded, then turned

and walked off into the forest. Part of Deirdre wanted to look back at him, but it was a very small part.

A cry came from Sadie who lifted her skirts and ran to Deirdre. Releasing her slowly, making sure she could stand on her own, Kinan stepped out of the way. Sadie all but collided with her, hugging her tighter than a corset. Deirdre dropped her bow and returned her friend's fierce hug. She'd barely caught her breath when Cat joined them and the squeezing began anew. When they finally let go, she looked them both over.

"Are either of you hurt?" she asked.

"Us? By the Powers that Be woman, you are insufferable!" Sadie exclaimed.

Though it sent shooting pain through her head, she smiled. "And yet, you suffer my presence still."

The three of them embraced again. Eventually, they drew away, Sadie to fetch a blanket from the wagon, and Cat to return to Rick's arms. Under the guise of picking up her bow, Deirdre took a look at the still body of the man she'd killed. At first, she felt nothing but relief. Because the man was dead, Cat, her baby, Sadie, Rick, and Kinan were alive. She started to wonder if the man had a wife, a mother, a family, anyone to mourn him. Had she to do it over again, she wouldn't have hesitated, but still...

"Deirdre, thank Itzamná you're all right," Kinan's soft voice broke through her thoughts.

Tears started hot trails down her cheeks at the wonderful sound of that voice. Part of her had feared she'd never hear it again. The way he had been standing between her friends and the barrel of a shotgun, she might not have if she hadn't arrived when she did. And if Dylan hadn't made the choice to come help. They reached for each other so fast they didn't embrace so much as collide. Once inside the warmth and security of his arms, with his heart beating against her ear, the tears stopped. Here she was safe, here she was home.

29

Deirdre

December

Part of the fun of being a fae was having two weddings. The first one felt somewhat pretentious to Deirdre, but it was fun to dress up and have a social gathering. The second was what she truly looked forward to, the handfasting. But for now, they had to get the one for show out of the way. The other would come tonight under the full moon. Watching Cat walk down the pine-bough-and-poinsettia–decked staircase in her white, satin gown made the last few months worth every heartache they'd endured. So full of life and love, her friend glowed with the promise of a beautiful future for them all. Rick basked in that light, looking so happy and in love that Deirdre had to dab tears from the corners of her eyes.

Throughout the ceremony beneath the huge Yule tree in the inn's foyer, Deirdre held Sadie's hand tight. But her gaze kept returning to Kinan, who stood opposite the aisle from her. He smiled the entire time, looking nearly as happy as Rick. It soon infected her. She smiled until her cheeks ached.

After the priest pronounced Rick and Cat husband and wife,

the attendees flooded in to wish the couple well and congratulate Deirdre on a perfectly planned wedding. Considering that was nearly the entire town, it took a while. No one mourned or mentioned Ainsworth. That made Deirdre a little sad. He must have had a terrible life to have treated so many others so badly. A gentle, white-gloved hand came to rest on her arm. Bright red curls spilled around a face that was positively euphoric. Many of those curls made it down to rest on Cat's shoulders, contrasting beautifully with her pristine white gown. The look of gratitude Cat gave Deirdre warmed her to her soul.

She took hold of one of Deirdre's hands, and one of Sadie's. "Look at you two, my emerald witches. I'm so blessed to have you both," Cat whispered in a choked voice.

Deirdre did a little half-turn that made the skirts of her emerald gown swirl out. "Sadie did a fabulous job," she said.

Cat nodded. "She did indeed, but the women within them are even more beautiful."

They cried and hugged, uncaring of the attentive audience all chatting about them.

"Just think, this time next year, we'll be looking out over our grapevines and horse pastures, our dreams realized," Cat said.

They both agreed. Notes of a piano and violin tuning to one another rose above the din. At the sound, Rick excused himself from a nearby conversation and stepped over to take Cat's hand.

"I believe 'tis time for my first dance with me wife," he said.

Tearing up even more, Cat became lost in his gaze as he led her away. The crowd parted, clearing space for the dance. He lifted a hand high above the crowd and the musicians started up at his cue. Rather than a slow waltz as Deirdre had expected, they struck up a lively tune with bagpipes joining in after the first few notes. Cat laughed with abandon as Rick spun her around into a sprightly dance. After the first few turns and dips, Rick encouraged an excited crowd to join in.

Hand in hand, Deirdre and Sadie practically skipped onto the dance floor. They twirled, dipped, and swayed beside Rick and Cat with abandon. Deirdre had no doubt the display would be the talk of the town for quite some time. Once the song ended and the music slowed, she and Sadie left the couple gaze-locked couple to their mooning and made their way over to the Yule tree. It towered over the party like a sentinel adorned in gold and white. From around the side of the tree stepped a tall, handsome freeman in a fine suit that hugged his muscular frame to perfection. Deirdre recognized him as Zeke, one of Rick's friends from the war who'd been helping them build their homes. After bowing deeply to them both, he extended his hand to Sadie. "May I have this dance, Miss Sadie?" he asked.

Eyes widening, Sadie looked to Deirdre. Beneath the panic in her friend's eyes, Deirdre saw a bright spark of interest. Frozen with indecision, Sadie wouldn't look back at the man. Deirdre took her hand and placed it in his. "She would love to dance with you."

Sadie's eyes pinched into slits that promised Deirdre would get an earful later. The slow smile that worked its way onto her lips as the tall man turned her onto the dance floor made it worth it.

A man's voice came from directly over Deirdre's shoulder. "You're an amazing friend. It's a thing of beauty to watch."

Pleasure shivered across her at the sound of that voice. She turned. "I was wondering where you'd gotten off to," she said.

He grinned like a man with a secret, as he so often did. She loved that about him, among many, many other things. Presenting his hand with a flourish, he bowed deeply. Lovely, dark eyes stared at her from beneath the locks of black hair that didn't reach his hair ribbon.

"May I have this dance?"

With a dip of her head, she placed her hand in his. "Mr. O'Leary, you may have every dance."

Only his eyes showed his surprise as he pulled her close and placed his other hand on her hip. A few deft turns and dodges of other dancers and they moved around the side of the tree. No one save for them danced in the hidden corner. Everyone else wanted to see and be seen. Deirdre was glad for it. That was fine by her. The seclusion gave her naughty ideas. Absorbed in one another's gaze and touch, they completed the dance and were well into another before either spoke.

Kinan leaned scandalously close. "Tonight, I'll strip you, lay you down beneath this tree, and give you your other present," he whispered.

She leaned close to the source of the warm breath that caressed her neck. "Other present?" she asked in a daze.

He laughed but didn't answer. When she got tired of waiting and prompted him, they both spoke at once. Deirdre laughed. "You go first," she said.

"No, ladies first."

"I'm no traditionalist, as you know," she insisted.

The slightest blush brightened his caramel skin. "I do indeed."

She waited patiently for several more steps. "I think I love you, Deirdre."

Though the words knocked the air from her lungs and sent her soaring over a cliff, she didn't miss a step. One corner of her lips rose in a crooked smile. "You think?" She let him stutter and search for words for all of a second before having a little mercy on him. "Well, Kinan O'Leary, I *know* I love you."

Laughing, he pulled her close with the next spin. "You delicious, devilish woman. I know I love you, too."

The remainder of the party she refused to tolerate dancing with anyone else. Thankfully, only a few asked, and only when Kinan left her for brief moments while they rested or ate. The evening passed quickly in his arms, and somehow not quickly enough. As soon as it was socially acceptable, Cat and Rick began saying their goodbyes to guests and escorting them to the door. The chilly December air helped motivate people with a desire to get home before dark and the deeper cold of night set in. Finally, only Cat, Rick, Deirdre, Kinan, Sadie, and the help remained.

Giggling like schoolgirls, Cat, Deirdre, and Sadie rushed up stairs to ready for the real party. Excitement quickened Deirdre's steps for she knew what awaited them in Cat's room. A vision had told Sadie a special surprise was coming, and as always, it had been right. She and Sadie shared a secret smile behind Cat's back as she threw the door open. Sitting on the chaise beneath the window, was a woman in a simple gold dress with a long braid of blond hair draped over her shoulder.

"Ashlinn?" Cat whispered, part in surprise, and part in horror. It wasn't difficult for Deirdre to guess why. Cat was the widow of Ashlinn's youngest brother. No doubt she feared Cat would judge her for remarrying so soon—let along being pregnant already.

Tears shone in her eyes as Ashlinn stood.

They collectively held their breath.

Ashlinn opened her arms and laughed. Cat bolted into her embrace.

"You aren't angry at me?" she asked against her shoulder.

After hugging her tight, Cat drew away enough to stroke a loose red curl back from her face. "Why in the name of Danu would I ever be angry with you? You have found happiness with a man who is going to treat you like a fae queen. All is as it should be," she said.

"How are you here, why?" Cat asked.

Taking her hand, Cat walked her over and sat her down on the chaise. Deirdre and Sadie followed.

"Shortly after Deirdre and Sadie left, Sean and I decided there was nothing more for us in New York. We sold my home and my father's medical office there and set out immediately. We would have been here sooner, but Sean had some business to attend to," Cat explained.

"Business?" Cat asked.

A twinkle sparked in Ashlinn's eyes as she looked at each of them before answering. "At first, we were trying to purchase building supplies in San Francisco and have them shipped up here. But Ainsworth's reach extended even to there. Then when the blockades stopped and we found out he had died, we purchased his land."

Gasps sounded all around. Sadie hadn't seen that in her vision. Or if she had, she hadn't mentioned it.

"You did?" This time Cat sounded hopeful.

Looking down, Ashlinn rubbed her belly. "The city is no

place for fae, or their children."

"You're pregnant?" Deirdre exclaimed.

Deep dimples formed in Ashlinn's cheeks as she smiled. "Aye."

Congratulations, gasps, laughter, and even weeping sounded all around. Deirdre went to her knees beside the chaise and touched both Ashlinn and Cat's bellies. "You are right where you should be."

Sadie's hands settled on her shoulders. "As are we all," she said.

They shared hugs and warm smiles. Finally, as Ashlinn and Cat wiped their tears away, Deirdre stood. "Let's go get this one properly handfasted then, shall we?" she said.

Taking Cat's hands in hers, Ashlinn rose and pulled her up with her. "We shall indeed."

Even the snow stopped as the world seemed to hold its breath in anticipation as the women walked up the cleared path to the gazebo. In a white, fur cloak and boots, with her flame-red hair loose down around her shoulders, Cat looked like a member of the Seely Court. And from the enamored look on Rick's face, clearly Deirdre wasn't the only one who thought so. She and Sadie walked together behind Cat, dropping flower seeds into the snow. Normally, Deirdre would have poured power into them and encouraged them to sprout, but considering it was December, that would have to wait for spring.

Torches stood all around the gazebo, casting a lovely golden-orange light that reflected off the snow and made the entire area glow. In the center of that glow stood Ashlinn, looking regal in her simple gold robes belted with a beautiful rope of woven knots. Of them all, she knew the rites best, so she would be the one to perform the handfasting. Their ceremony wasn't something that required an official like a typical wedding. For them a handfasting was more about intent and energy sharing.

The warmth drew them in as much as the sight of the men waiting within the gazebo. Rick looked delicious in nothing more than a loincloth—because apparently *faolach* barely felt the cold. But Deirdre only had eyes for Kinan. In a black, fur cloak with his shoulder-length, black hair loose about him, he looked wild and untamed. Their eyes caught and locked. Tongue darting out to moisten her lips, Deirdre fingered the collar of her own fur cloak. She wore nothing but boots under it. None of them did except Sadie. To bless the union, the night would end in amorous frolicking. The fact Kinan not only tolerated their tradition, but had agreed to embrace it wholeheartedly, filled her with anticipation.

A sniffle came from Cat as she ascended the steps into the gazebo. The sound worked like fishhooks that dug deep into Deirdre's heart and pulled hard. Knowing it was born of pure joy made it so special. Having watched her dear friend endure a horrible marriage to a man who abused her both emotionally and physically, had been horrible. But watching her now, so confident, strong, and in love with someone who cherished her, helped bring balance back to the world. It didn't matter that Rick wasn't fae. He would never harm Cat in any way, of that Deirdre was certain.

Holding each other's right hand, Cat and Rick faced one another. Deirdre and Sadie went to stand beside Kinan.

A golden glow surrounded Ashlinn as she began. "Welcome family of blood and of choosing, to this sacred place, on this sacred night where we witness and celebrate the handfasting of Patrick Fergusson and Catriona O'Cuolihan."

Hearing Cat's maiden name, the name of her fae bloodline, pushed a tear from Deirdre's right eye. It traced a hot line down her cheek. Kinan's gloved hand encompassed her own.

Hands out, palms up, Ashlinn looked to the sky. "As your children, great Goddess Danu, we asked that you witness and bless this handfasting so it may be fruitful and happy."

"Praise Danu," Cat whispered. Deirdre echoed the sentiment.

Ashlinn untied the rope from about her waist. It was actually three sisal ropes woven together in expert knots. Much like Ashlinn, the rope glowed varying shades of gold. She draped it over Cat and Rick's clutched hands and started to tie one end of it around Cat's wrist.

"Catriona, this knot is tied to bind your life to Patrick's. It is a symbol of your importance in the union throughout the stages of your life as a maiden, mother, and crone," she said in a smooth, lyrical tone that had the cadence of a chant.

Green power with gold and red flecks through it began to glow around Cat. The call of an owl sounded from somewhere outside. If they weren't quick about this, they'd awaken every forest creature within half a mile and soon be surrounded.

Taking up the other end of the rope, Ashlinn began to tie it around Rick's wrist. "Patrick, this knot is tied to bind your life to Catriona's. It is a symbol of your importance in the union throughout the stages of your life as a lad, father, and elder." When he nodded to her, she went on. "Make your vows to one another."

For several moments they stared at each other. At last, Cat spoke her vows. "I will stand by your side not only through the good times, but also all the trials of life. I will support, honor, and love you for who you are, now and always." The strength in her unwavering voice made more tears spill down Deirdre's cheeks.

It took a few swallows before Rick could speak his vows. "I will stand by your side through the good and bad times. I will treat you with respect, dignity, and gentleness. And I'll support, honor, and love you for who you are, now and always."

Picking up the ends of the rope that dangled from their individual knots, Ashlinn tied them together. "With this final knot you are bound by heart, power, and soul. May the ties of this handfasting grow with love and a light to outshine any darkness." With that, she stepped back.

For several heartbeats they stared at one another. Slowly, they moved in and pressed their lips together. Cheers filled the gazebo. The kiss deepened, mouths opening, hands beginning to grope. That was their cue. The rest of them turned and made their way out of the gazebo.

Kinan let go of Deirdre's hand and lifted a whistle hanging from a chord around his neck. As he put it to his lips and played a lovely tune, large rocks began to float up and stack all around the gazebo. Sounds of amazement came from Ashlinn and Sean. Having seen it before when rebuilding their homes, Sadie just watched with a smile. Deirdre beheld it through bright eyes. In moments the rocks rose to create walls all around the gazebo, leaving a door-sized opening at the front, and a gap between the top of the rocks and the roof that allowed the torches to breathe.

Cat and Rick would be toasty warm inside and wouldn't have to go rushing back to the inn. When Kinan lowered the whistle from his lips, Deirdre rose onto her toes and kissed his cheek.

After watching the placement of each stone with unabashed wonder, Ashlinn gave Deirdre a wink, looped her arm through Sean's, and led him off into the darkness.

Tugging her cloak tighter around her, Sadie waved a finger at Deirdre. "Don't be out here long enough to get frost bite. I'll have a fire going in the library and hot cocoa ready when you all get back," she said.

The very thought of a warm fire and cocoa almost made Deirdre want to follow her back to the inn. "Sadie, you are amazing, sweet, and above reproach!"

An adorable snort came from Sadie. "Hardly. I plan to spend some time with that handsome Zeke while you all are out here freezing your fae behinds off," she said with a laugh. Leaving Deirdre staring in open-mouthed shock after her, she set off for the inn at a brisk pace. The powdery snow swirled in the wake of her billowing cloak.

At a tug of Kinan's hand, they began to walk into the snowy landscape. But they didn't walk down the path toward the inn, or in the direction Ashlinn and Sean had gone. The direction Kinan led them was down a path that had the snow beaten down enough to make walking easy. The further from the light of the torches they grew, the darker it became.

"Alone at last," Kinan said. "I have something to show you."

Deirdre made a humming noise. "I do hope its something under that cloak."

"It most certainly is."

Warmth coursed through her, a lovely contrast to the frozen evening. She was about to pull him to a stop and open his cloak when a muted orange glow caught her gaze. The slow but steady pulse of a familiar power resonated through the ground. They were near the sequoia. In a few more steps she realized the glow was coming from within an animal hide tent that sat beneath the tree. Atop the tent was a smaller dome from which smoke puffed.

Kinan drew the flap of the tent open and revealed a cozy interior. A fire crackled in a pit in the center and a bed of furs and blankets was made up to one side of it. Warmth enveloped her as she stepped inside. A deep sigh of relief eased from her as her chilled cheeks began to thaw. Following her inside, Kinan closed the tent flap behind them.

"I hope the impropriety of my planned rendezvous doesn't offend you," he said.

Thrills raced through her. "Hardly. You know my fondness for impropriety." She started to step toward him but stopped when he removed something from within his cloak and knelt down.

Firelight danced along a ring.

"Deirdre Quinn, will you marry me? After an engagement length of your choosing, during which we explore our compatibility often and thoroughly."

She tried to speak and couldn't. A hand flew to her mouth to cover the squeal that tried to escape in the place of words. Blinking back tears, she straightened and gathered her wits. "Kinan O'Leary, I would marry you this very moment."

His eyes closed tight and his head dipped for a moment before he stood. She held her hand out to him, fingers splayed. Two strands of gold wove together in a Celtic knot, cradling an emerald in their center. It fit perfectly on the ring finger of her left hand. When she was able to finally tear her eyes from the ring, she found him biting his lip as he looked down at her.

"I hope you like it. This felt far more like it was right for you than a traditional band and diamond," he said, a nervous shake in his voice.

She grabbed his hand and pulled it in close to her heart. "It's perfect, as are you."

Drawing her bottom lip between her teeth, she threw her cloak open wide. A quick tug on the clasp of his own sent it tumbling to the ground behind him. He stood, lifting her in his arms as he did. Their bodies molded together in a most inappropriate—and perfect—way.

GLOSSARY

Brigid: Celtic Goddess of hearth and fire.

Culo: Ass in Yucatan.

Dagda: Celtic God of the Earth.

Danu: Celtic Goddess and mother of the Tuatha.

Faolach: Irish werewolf.

Itzamná: The Mayan God of the sky who was ruler of night and day.

Silbador: A person who can use whistling to move earthen object such as rocks, dirt, etc..

AUTHOR'S GRATITUDE & HUMBLE PLEA

Thank you with every bit of my heart for reading. If you enjoyed the read, I would be eternally grateful for a review on retail sites and any mentions on social media.

Wait, please don't go!

I know the words "please review" tend to make people run for the hills because we all have extremely busy lives, and many just don't know what to say in a review. But trust me, they truly make all the difference to an author because they affect the way the retail sites handle the book exponentially, which in turns greatly affects the book's sales—or lack thereof.

So what do you write? Short and sweet is great as long as it's from the heart. One to three things you loved about the book will do. A review can be as short as a sentence, or as long as you like.

ACKNOWLEDGEMENTS

Thank you to the outstanding members on my ARC team: Kimberly Dabbs, Jasmine of Jasmine E Reads, Heather Mylek, Taryn of Taryn's Book Confessions, and Katie Wastlund. And not to be forgotten are my new ARC members: Jessica Perrin, Jess of Oracle of Madness, and Tifany Ness. I also must thank all my Booktok besties who have inspired me to keep going, and have given me more support and encouragement than I could have ever imagined. Lucky doesn't even begin to describe how I feel to have met and become friends with all of you.

Thank you to Lizzy Gayle, fantastic author and out of this world friend, who cheers me on every step of the way and keeps me believing I can do this crazy thing.

To readers old and new, I cannot thank you enough for reading. You are the blood that keeps my creative heart pumping. Entertaining you brings me so much joy.

ABOUT THE AUTHOR

When she's not writing, Heather can be found on the slopes, the hiking trails, or paddleboarding. She enjoys the outdoors nearly as much as the worlds she creates, and strives to live as green a life as possible. No need to travel to the Great Northwest, though, you can find her on social media and her personal site.

www.heathermccorkle.com

www.ingramcontent.com/pod-product-compliance
Lightning Source LLC
Chambersburg PA
CBHW072109250626
47159CB00007B/2369